INHERITANCE

☩

The Trilogy
by
<u>Christine Sunderland</u>

Pilgrimage

Offerings

Inheritance

INHERITANCE

Christine Sunderland

OakTara

WATERFORD, VIRGINIA

Inheritance

Published in the U.S. by:
OakTara Publishers
P.O. Box 8
Waterford, VA 20197

Visit OakTara at
www.oaktara.com

Cover design by Trinka Plaskon, Muses9 Design
Cover image, From Glastonbury Tor, © Christine Sunderland
Author photo © 2007 by Brittany Sunderland

Copyright © 2009 by Christine Sunderland. All rights reserved.

All services are taken from *The Book of Common Prayer, 1928, for use in the Episcopal Church*. All hymns are from *The 1940 Church Hymnal* (New York: Church Pension Corporation). All scriptural references are from the King James Version, except for the Psalms, which are taken from *The Book of Common Prayer*.

ISBN: 978-1-60290-219-0

Inheritance is a work of fiction. References to real people, events, establishments, organizations, or locales are intended only to provide a sense of authenticity and are used fictitiously. All other characters, incidents, and dialogue are drawn from the author's imagination.

Acknowledgments

I wish to acknowledge with gratitude:

Friends and family, who patiently read my many drafts and gave me invaluable suggestions.

Clergy and laity who have, by their example and their instruction, showed me the sacramental nature of life and love.

Editor Susanna Brougham, who critiqued an early draft and gave me thoughtful and useful advice. Editors Margaret Lucke and Alfred J. Garrotto, who helped me craft *Inheritance* into a compelling story. Editor Mark Hugh Miller, who finetuned the manuscript with his many excellent suggestions.

Ramona Tucker and Jeff Nesbit of OakTara, who believed in my work and have walked me through the publishing process with patience and skill.

My dear husband, Harry, who continues to show me the amazing worlds of Italy, France, and England, and has been my rock of encouragement, humor, and love.

O Lord, save thy people, and bless thine inheritance...

Evening Prayer,
EPISCOPAL *BOOK OF COMMON PRAYER*, 1928

Preface

In my descriptions of historical persons and places I have tried to be accurate. Saint Anne's House and Abbey are fictional. All characters are fictional and are not intended to represent any persons living or dead.

I have also attempted to accurately describe (at least in their essence) the hotels and restaurants, abbeys, cathedrals, and churches visited by Jack, Madeleine, Victoria, and Cristoforo in their travels through England.

Prologue

Her great aunt had asked to be buried on a Sunday afternoon, "on resurrection day amidst the grapes," and now, in the July heat, Victoria Elizabeth Nguyen watched six pallbearers lower the silver-lined casket into the rich soil of the Napa Valley. The burnished mahogany lid gleamed, and Victoria thought how she too was in that coffin, at least part of her. Brushing a long strand of hair from her face, she squinted in the bright light, and her lip quivered. She had loved her Aunt Elizabeth, and her aunt had loved her. Why wasn't she here, now, when Victoria needed her most? Her body still ached.

Victoria touched the birthmark running over her nose, mourning the death of her aunt who had loved her the way she was. Elizabeth often proclaimed that her niece's almond eyes and burgundy-black hair were like an ancient image of the Virgin Mary. "There's no two ways about it," she would say, holding Victoria's face in her parched palms. "And as for the birthmark," she would add with a dry but joyous laugh, "that's the mark of God, so don't you complain to me about it, young lady. And I want to see that pretty smile of yours."

Now, before the grave, Victoria couldn't smile. Her father, Andrew, looked sad as well, a dark cloud settling over his face as he stood beside her in his Vietnamese calm, eyes closed as though praying, brows pinched. He held her hand firmly, with assurance, but her mother Candice, a tense presence on her other side, her platinum hair expertly coifed and her Scandinavian skin protected by a wide-brimmed hat, sent waves of anxiety through her.

"*Unto Almighty God,*" the young priest read from his missal, "*we commend the soul of our sister departed, and we commit her body to the ground; earth to earth, ashes to ashes, dust to dust...*"

Victoria followed her father to the open grave and released a handful of earth onto the coffin. She glanced back at her mother, who looked toward a TV news van coming up the drive, and returned to her place between her parents. The priest continued his smooth soothing words as others filed past the grave, dropping their soil onto the lid. The earth fell, tapping the wood, keeping time, but her aunt was beyond time now. Where *was* her Aunt Elizabeth? Was she anywhere at all? Although Victoria had not shared her aunt's beliefs, she refused to think that her aunt was really *gone*. How could she possibly think such a thing?

A warm breeze fluttered the parchment pages of the missal resting in the priest's palm, as he read, "*In sure and certain hope of the Resurrection unto eternal life, through our Lord Jesus Christ; at whose coming in glorious majesty...*"

Candice muttered under her breath, and Victoria hoped her mother wouldn't make a scene. She inched closer to her father, whose stocky form and placid face, even his double chin, gave her comfort. At seventeen, she *wanted* to be more self-confident, more grown-up, but in her mother's presence she felt like a child. She couldn't control it. Candice was *so* beautiful and *so* assured. Victoria slipped her arm through her father's.

"*...to judge the world, the earth and the sea shall give up their dead; and the corruptible bodies of those who sleep in him shall be changed...*"

Candice shook her head, as though amazed anyone could say those words in this year, 2001, and walked toward the news van. She never missed a chance, Victoria thought, and the press always liked interviewing Senator Crawford-Nguyen.

Victoria glanced at her father for a cue. He bowed his head, ignoring her mother. Victoria did the same.

"*...and made like unto his own glorious body; according to the mighty working whereby he is able to subdue all things unto himself...*"

The large funeral gathering slowly dispersed. Car doors clapped the silence, and a light chatter fractured the hot air. A reporter, having concluded his interview with the senator, approached the priest, who waved him away. The elderly Elizabeth Crawford made news in death as she had in life. Victoria had seen her great aunt on TV only last month, the oldest praying protester in front of the Berkeley Free Clinic. A magazine show had interviewed her, thinking her eccentric, and she had launched into a fervent speech about "angel babies."

Victoria's father squeezed her hand and led her toward their Mercedes, where her mother waited. She slipped into the back seat, anticipating the inevitable fight.

Candice turned the key in the ignition and shook her head in apparent relief. "She's finally gone, and at ninety-six. Simply because she was a Crawford from old San Francisco society, she thought she could do as she pleased. She was *such* an embarrassment."

Her father glanced at her mother. "Candice, please show some respect."

"Respect? Where was *her* respect?" She gunned the car onto the road. "Giving the estate to Victoria's firstborn, even bypassing my parents. What kind of a will is that? She was clearly senile. Our attorneys will have a field day."

"It was the abortion," her father said through his teeth. "She was really upset about Vicky's abortion."

Victoria swallowed hard, her throat dry.

Candice grunted. "As though a fourteen-year-old should have a child. A baby having a baby. The father was a child too—fifteen, I believe. At least *he* never found out. Elizabeth was out of her mind. She's always been one of those reactionary Christians. They have little compassion for the poor who can't afford children." She spoke as though Victoria wasn't there.

"She believed that life is sacred," her father whispered, "and we're not poor."

Her mother gripped the wheel. "Why do you always take the other side?"

Victoria stared out the window, thinking of Danny and his Ford Mustang and the overlook and his groping hands and her immense desire to please him. Then her mother and her fury and the hospital steel and the wrenching regret, the loss, the tears. What had she done? The act still weighed upon her, thrusting her deep into the earth.

And now, what would she do?

As they followed the highway through the dry hills, she gazed with a needy hope at her father's profile and wished the tense air could swallow them both. Still trembling from the last few days, she tried to quell the fear she could almost taste, the confusion, the unanswered question. That evening by the lake, nearly two weeks ago, replayed in her mind, over and over.

Victoria had run the lakeshore trail, her shoes tap-tapping the familiar path, as the late evening sun dropped toward the horizon. A Red-tailed Hawk soared above gnarled oaks and crickets chirped in the manzanita. *Only another mile or so...plenty of time before dark.*

The warm peace of the summer's evening soothed her, and the

rhythmic motion of her legs' muscle memory lifted and carried her, making her a creature of power and drive. Her mother's critical glances, the laughter beneath her words, and in the end, the sure conclusion that she, Victoria, was a grave disappointment—these parameters of her life— receded as she bounded along the trail.

She had tried to be like her mother, so beautiful, blond, competent. But she would never be beautiful, not with her birthmark and her slanted eyes peering out like an owl's in mottled plumage. She had even tried to be blond, but the dye job when she was twelve gave her a hard look, and she returned to her natural black soon enough. Hoping to absorb her mother's competence, Victoria stood by her side at party fundraisers. She distributed flyers for Candice's run for the Senate. She copied Candice's clothes and smile, her firm handshake and way of taking charge. But Victoria sensed she only appeared ludicrous, like a dark mouse peeping out of its hole and finding a room full of cats.

Her father consoled her when he was sober and when he wasn't watching his own back. Victoria hated what her mother did to him, twisting his words into insults so that *he* became the cause of the argument, and once again Candice became the victim.

The trail looped back toward the lake, the home stretch. As she ran, her thoughts turned to her great aunt Elizabeth who, in spite of her age, had been her real mother, opening her heart and her home to her niece. Soon Victoria would once again visit the ranch in the vineyards, with its cherry-paneled library and dusty volumes of Dickens, Austen, and Eliot. There, in Augusts past, sitting in the window seat, turning the pages of C.S. Lewis' *The Lion, the Witch and the Wardrobe*, she followed Lucy through the wardrobe of furs and into Narnia, a world of witches and talking animals, a frozen land of eternal winter without Christmas. In the window alcove, with the sun slanting through the shutters, the fountain raining a dance on her ears and the deer lapping from the pond, she had fallen into Tolkien's *Hobbit* and traveled with Gandalf and Bilbo through an ordered universe, where good was good, evil was evil, and, in the end, good won. Victoria's summers in her great aunt's rambling old house had shaped her into a creature so different from her mother. She wondered if, someday, she could find her true self in that house, could learn who she really was.

As she ran the lakeside trail, she dreamed. Suddenly she heard a rustle in the bushes and sensed a large man behind her. She had no time to scream as he covered her mouth with a strong-smelling cloth and pulled her down. Her leg scraped the pavement, and she struggled for the whistle in her pocket. The last thing she remembered was a powerful blow to the side of her head and her right ear ringing into darkness.

Victoria gazed out the window as the sedan took her farther and farther from her aunt's grave. She would know this week if a child had been conceived on that lakeside trail. She would face that then. "No use borrowing trouble," her aunt would have said. Victoria had not told her mother, who was in Washington. As usual, her father had mothered her through the days of pain and shock, filling out the sheriff's report and seeing to her doctor.

Her father would know what to do. When the time came, he would know.

Chapter One
San Francisco

In Rama was there a voice heard,
lamentation, and weeping, and great mourning,
Rachel weeping for her children, and would not be comforted,
because they are not.
Matthew 2:18

On a cold Sunday in San Francisco, Madeleine Seymour stood with her husband, Jack, as the organ sounded the recessional at Saint Thomas' Anglican Church. Father Michaels, robed in Advent purple, genuflected before the altar, turned, and followed the crucifer, acolytes, and deacon down the aisle to the double doors. As the December storm battered the skylights, Madeleine and Jack sang with the others, "O come, O come, Emmanuel…."

Once again, beneath the white Romanesque vaults, the Mass had been offered, the Body and Blood of Christ had nourished their own bodies, and Madeleine was thankful for this moment, when time became eternity, when her middle-aged flesh could fly with the angels. The last chorus of the hymn ending, she dropped to the soft leather kneeler for a final prayer as an acolyte returned to snuff the altar candles. She looked up to the comforting Madonna and Child and said a Hail Mary, then to the burning sanctuary lamp that continued to flame, signifying the Real Presence of Christ reserved in the stone tabernacle. This one light would not be put out, would be kept burning, as a sign.

Madeleine and Jack joined the line filing down the aisle toward Father Michaels who pumped hands, kissed cheeks, and hugged with his hefty arms.

Jack held Madeleine's raincoat open as she slipped her arms inside, then put on his own, glancing at the skylights. "Rain stopped. Don't need the umbrella."

He was a careful man, Madeleine thought, especially since his successful surgery two years earlier. He noticed weather, people, the things around him. Now he turned to the elderly woman in front of them, as though he sensed she was about to speak.

Mrs. Sanderson spun on her heel. "Love your short hairdo, Madeleine."

Madeleine touched the nape of her neck where her auburn hair feathered lightly. The layering and trim had added fullness, but the new style would take some getting used to. She raised the collar on her coat and smiled. "Thanks. I wasn't sure about it."

"It's *so* lovely. Now, will you be helping with the Christmas pageant this year?" Her lined face was full of hope. "You did such a fine job costuming the little ones last year."

"Sure," Madeleine said, grinning. "I'd love to." The triplets, age four, had made a spectacular heavenly host. She had even cut tag board wings glittered with gold.

"Do I get to be a king?" Jack asked, raising his brows with mock expectation.

"Of course, Jack," Mrs. Sanderson replied. "Which one? The one with the line?"

Madeleine loved that the pageant included all ages, although the children had first choice of roles. Her husband, at sixty-six, made a venerable and graying king, with his emerald green cape and foil crown.

Jack's blue eyes squinted with concentration. "That's the one. *Where is he who is born King of the Jews? For we have seen his star in the East and have come to worship him.* How's that?"

"Excellent. I'll sign you up." She pulled out a notepad and pencil.

A small face peered around Mrs. Sanderson's skirt. "Mrs. Seymour, I'm going to be the Starholder this year!" Madeleine recognized Cynthia, nearly five now. "When are you going to be my teacher again?"

Madeleine bent down to the child's eye level. "One of these days. But for now, we'll make that Starholder costume perfect for you." She had retired from teaching Sunday school to finish writing her book; at fifty-four, time passed too swiftly, and she needed to be published. Had she made the right choice? She had prayed about it, but she wasn't sure. Was *Holy Manifestations: God's Presence in Our World* to God's glory, or was teaching children to God's glory? She gave Cynthia a hug. "I sure miss you guys."

A deep voice came from behind. "Morning, Madeleine and Jack." It was elderly Joe McGinty, dapper in his three-piece suit, his thick silver hair neatly combed to the side. He was in good shape for his age, Madeleine thought, although he walked with a cane.

"Hello, Joe, good to see you." Jack touched his own tie as he shook Joe's hand.

Madeleine kissed Joe's cheek in greeting. "How are you? Any news from your brother in London?" She recalled that Joe McGinty had been keenly interested in establishing a children's home in London, along the lines of their Coronati House in Rome. As chairman of the board of the Coronati Foundation, he had been their chief financial backer. He had helped Jack organize fundraisers in San Francisco. Jack knew folks, as Joe liked to say, from his days in the wine importing business.

"I've been meaning to call you," Joe said, as the line moved slowly forward. "How would you two like to go to London, all expenses paid? Fine hotels, fine dining." He looked encouraged as he saw Jack's face light up. "My brother's made some contacts and says the political climate is ripe for our children's home project. Might help a good number of women with their choices. What do you think?" He slapped Jack on the back.

"Sounds good to me." Jack looked doubtfully at Madeleine. "But Madeleine's beginning a short sabbatical. She has a book deadline."

It would be her first published work. But even so, she could see Jack was thrilled with the prospect of a trip to London. Since he retired, he had been bitten by the travel bug but didn't have the means: champagne taste on a beer budget. Their income, even with her part-time teaching, hadn't stretched as far as they'd hoped. But London *now?* Her editor at University Press had given her a June deadline, and she was far behind. Maybe Jack could go to London on his own. "Could we get back to you?" she asked Joe.

"Sure, but could you let me know soon? I'd like to ask the Wilsons if you can't do it. But Jack, I'd prefer you handle a property search like this. You have the legal background in contracts, as well as experience with British solicitors."

Jack rubbed his chin. "What did you have in mind, exactly?"

"Something like our Rome orphanage with the clinic and adoption agency. But I was thinking of adding some of the services that Sandy Taylor offers here in the city—unplanned pregnancy counseling with ultrasound technologies, prenatal *and* postnatal support. Have you seen Sandy's clinic?"

Madeleine had been meaning to visit. Sandy Taylor was a member of the parish, and had invited them to the opening of their San Francisco clinic, but Madeleine's teaching schedule was full that day. Still, Sandy had mentioned it often, and Madeleine had felt guilty about never making the time. "We haven't, but we've always wanted to."

Jack nodded. "Their fundraiser last year was terrific. I've been meaning to ask her about it—the giant video screens, the live music, the testimonies of the children and mothers. Wow! We could learn a few things for our own events."

They turned toward Father Michaels in the doorway. He was a man who clearly enjoyed his food and wine. His wide face was flushed, and he stood as though planted on the porch, a fixture of permanence and satisfaction. Madeleine liked him. His sermons held wisdom beyond his thirty-five years: he understood the reverence required in worship, for he was a true believer, believing they worshiped a living God present among them. He wasn't Father Rinaldi, God rest his soul, but who could be? For a moment, Madeleine winced with loss. Grief hit her like that, sudden and unexpected, and right here on the porch stoop of their pretty chapel, just as the rain was drying up and the sun was coming out.

Father Rinaldi had been their priest and friend, a good pastor. He had taught her about the faith, had helped her raise Justin. (Could her son really be twenty-nine with a family of his own?) He had blessed her marriage to Jack nearly twenty years ago. His heart failure had been a shock to them all, but he had lived a good life, sacrificial and joyful, and Madeleine was sure that he stepped right into heaven. One day she would see her old priest and friend, on the other side.

Madeleine beamed into Father Michaels' face, so open and unguarded. "Great sermon. Thanks for letting me take notes."

"I'm flattered you do. But don't forget next Saturday. We're decorating the church for Christmas."

"We'll be there," Jack said. "Shall I bring some festive libations to accompany lunch?"

"That would be excellent. Do you still have connections in the wine business? But it's Advent, a penitential season. Oh, well, a little won't hurt. So close to Christmas."

Madeleine laughed. Father Michaels had a way of working in festive libations. "We have a pageant rehearsal, don't forget, in the morning."

"Now how could I forget that?" Father Michaels glanced at Mrs. Sanderson waving from the bottom of the steps, several children in tow, heading for the parish hall in back. "We're all looking forward to the pageant. Christmas wouldn't be the same without it!" He turned to Joe McGinty and grasped his thin hand in his thick one.

Monday morning was overcast with a cold wind as Madeleine and Jack emerged from the downtown parking garage. They soon found the vintage medical building.

She studied the elevator listings and stepped into the old-fashioned cubicle. "Sandy wanted easy access, but parking would be a problem here, or, at least, expensive."

"She also wanted to be close to other doctor's offices," Jack added. "And there's always public transit."

They found the clinic on the third floor. A scripted sign on the door read *Sandy's Prenatal Services.*

They entered a small waiting room, much like any other medical office. Pamphlets filled a wall rack, Christmas carols played through a sound system, and a fir tree decorated with blinking lights rotated in a corner.

A frosted glass panel slid open. "May I help you?" a receptionist asked.

They introduced themselves, and moments later Sandy Taylor appeared in the doorway. "So glad you folks could visit. Come on in."

They followed her down a narrow hallway. Sandy's honey-colored hair fell straight to her shoulders. Of medium height, she carried herself with a competent air as though she always knew exactly what she needed to do and did it. For a moment Madeleine envied the younger woman's energy, vision, and assurance, as she recalled her own race with time, her struggle with her book, her manuscript divvied into piles with thick clips and color-coded Post-It Notes covering her desk at home. Writing was such a fragmented business, with all the bits and pieces dangling in various cranial corners, with phrases jotted on notepads and odd scraps of paper captured under paperweights. How did one pull it all together? How did one impose order on chaos, make sense of life?

Sandy led them into a tiny parlor. A burgundy loveseat faced two teal armchairs, and white daisies in a clay vase sat on a low coffee table. "I've been wanting to show you our new facility here in the City," she said, speaking quickly. "Do you have a few minutes?"

"We do." Madeleine nodded, recalling Sandy had three other locations in the Bay Area.

"All the time you need," Jack said, "as long as you tell me your

5

fundraising secrets."

"Good, and I'll do that, Jack." She gestured to the couch. "Please, have a seat. This is our counseling room, where we hold our first interviews. Many women hear about us from our website, and this is where we all get acquainted. I wanted the room to have a homey feel."

"Good idea." Madeleine thought the space inviting, comfortable, like a family den.

Sandy sat in an armchair and leaned forward. "I understand Joe McGinty wants to do something like this in London?"

"That's right," Jack said.

"The London project sounds great. And Joe has the backing and the connections. What's your Rome orphanage like? I've been meaning to ask you."

Madeleine adjusted her glasses. "It's a small orphanage for the children we aren't able to place in homes, twenty beds, run by an order of nuns. The sisters teach the children and staff a free clinic. We've recently added a women's shelter." Father Rinaldi had founded the convent and later the orphanage at the Church of the Four Crowned Saints, *Santi dei Quattro Coronati*, and she and Jack had visited the church on their pilgrimage to Italy over four years ago. Had it really been four years? It seemed like yesterday.

The pilgrimage had changed her, healed her of haunting nightmares, and in thanksgiving, they had set up a foundation to continue the work Father Rinaldi had begun. Coronati House was thriving, and Jack soon discovered that volunteering his time enriched his retirement. Madeleine had also been blessed by her work with Coronati House—writing articles, brochures, sending care packages and toys at Christmas—for her healing had continued.

Sandy nodded. "We emphasize prenatal counseling for women who have unintended pregnancies, including married women with families."

Madeleine grew thoughtful. "Are there many women with that problem?" Madeleine had wanted more children but hadn't been able to conceive. Even so, she was grateful for her son, Justin, and then there were Jack's boys too. *And* seven grandchildren.

A shadow passed over Sandy's face. "Indeed there are. I've been surprised how many women who are frightened by unplanned pregnancies have husbands and children. They're worried about another mouth to feed. Once again they have to put off their careers, their plans."

"It makes sense," Madeleine said. "I can see that." She thought of her own job.

Sandy turned to Jack. "So Joe says you'd like to offer these services?"

"Exactly." Jack nodded.

Madeleine glanced at her husband, happy in his satisfaction. She could see he was mentally planning the trip. He saw himself as a transplanted Brit, with his aristocratic nose, fine bones, and freckled skin. She hoped, with her looming book deadline, she wouldn't disappoint him.

"Then let me show you where we do our prenatal exams."

They crossed the hall to a room where a nurse was setting up electronic equipment.

"Our sonogram unit." Sandy's brown eyes twinkled. "And this is Amanda, our very capable RN. She just joined us from school. She wanted to work with a nonprofit for a few years before moving on to a hospital."

Madeleine and Jack exchanged greetings with the young woman.

Amanda eyed them earnestly and smoothed her white smock. "It's so amazing when the women see their baby move on the screen. And hear the heartbeat." She turned to Sandy. "All set to go," she said and excused herself.

Sandy turned to Madeleine and Jack. "We don't argue for or against abortion. We simply provide information. The sonogram is part of that information. Some women choose to have their child, and we help them do that. We helped sixty-seven children come into this world last year."

As Madeleine listened to Sandy, memories of her own Mollie flooded her. The room shifted precariously, and she reached to steady herself. Her daughter had been less than eight months old when she drowned. *And it was my fault.* The old demons stabbed her again as she reached for Jack's arm and slid into a chair. "I'm sorry," she said to Sandy, "just felt a little faint. Okay now."

"You sure?" Sandy looked worried.

"It's a long story," Jack explained.

Sandy gazed at Madeleine, then gently touched her shoulder. "I have a story too." Sandy's face, so open and upbeat, clouded, and she grew quiet. "It's the reason I got into all of this." She sat on a stool.

Madeleine sensed a sister, one who had also suffered.

"You see, Madeleine, I had three young children, and when I found myself pregnant with my fourth I truly didn't want the baby. Being a Christian, abortion wasn't an option, but nevertheless I pretended the baby didn't exist." Sandy looked into the distance, and her eyes grew moist. "I can't believe that now, but it's true. When my daughter was born prematurely, she only lived a few hours. It was awful. It was as though I had caused her death by willing it."

Madeleine could feel the depth of Sandy's grief, the remorse, the guilt. Mollie flashed before her again, her large eyes entreating, as she had in so many nightmares.

"But God pulled good from the tragedy. He gave me a vision." She opened her palms. "And here it is."

"God does that," Madeleine said. "He takes our wrong turns and makes them right." She inhaled slowly. "My story goes back to 1975. Really, even earlier, as most stories do. In 1967 at the age of twenty I married Charlie, a high school sweetheart. We were pacifists then, romantic idealists. We immigrated to Canada and tried to make a life there. Justin and Mollie were born in Vancouver." She paused.

"You don't have to tell me," Sandy said quietly.

"No, it's okay. That summer of 1975 I left Mollie alone in a wading pool. She was less than eight months. She drowned. I was responsible. It's been over twenty-six years, and it still hits me." Her words sounded stilted, far away, as though she had re-entered a distant country.

"How terrible," Sandy said.

"I returned to San Francisco, my marriage dying, haunted by nightmares. When I married Jack they receded, but then they returned a few years ago. Father Rinaldi sent us to Italy on a pilgrimage of healing. One of the places we visited was the Quattro Coronati Convent in Rome, and you know the rest."

"I see the connection now. I wish I had known Father Rinaldi during my own tragedy."

"But God has used your suffering," Madeleine said.

Sandy leaned forward, hands clasped. "He has. And I understand these women. I remember what it was like to fear such a pregnancy, so unplanned, not part of my future, not the way I saw my future. I no longer had control. And I understand why some women choose abortion. They are under a lot of pressure from parents, boyfriends, our cultural assumptions. They have to give up all those plans they had, or at least postpone them. Then there's the financial impact."

Jack's brow pulled together. "I bet they have tremendous pressure."

"It must be so hard for those who make that choice," Madeleine said, some clarity of mind finally returning. *And through their own act, their own free will.*

"As a matter of fact, we do a good deal of post-abortion counseling.

Grief counseling, actually." She stood, and led them to the waiting room.

"What other services do you provide?" Jack asked, glancing at the brochure on the rack, as though wanting to shift the conversation to another level.

Sandy pulled out some pamphlets. "Whatever is needed. And for whoever needs our services. Nobody likes abortion, and everyone wants to make it rare. We can all agree on that. So we're trying to make that happen."

"Well said." Madeleine was at a loss for words, her own tears near. Ever since she read the words, *A child dies every twenty minutes from abortion*, she had heard the clock ticking, the silent screams of the unborn.

Sandy turned to Jack. "We offer help mostly, help with the choice that must be made, help with the pregnancy, help with the birth, help with the doctors. During the last months and after the birth we enroll the new family in our Godparents Program, where a local church adopts them. The church gives the mother-to-be a baby shower, finds housing if needed, daycare, that sort of thing. Follow up services. Community support." She spoke quickly and glanced at her watch. "I'm really sorry, but I have an appointment. Could I have our Marketing Manager call you, Jack?"

"Sure, that'd be fine."

"And check out our website. You might get some ideas there."

Madeleine cleared her throat. "Thanks so much, Sandy. We really appreciate it."

Sandy grinned, her good humor returning. "Good luck with London. Keep me posted, and contact me if you have any questions, okay?" She opened the door and they stepped into the hall. "So glad you folks could come by."

As they headed for the elevator, Jack turned to Madeleine. "What do you think?"

"Wow. I can see why Joe is so excited. This is a whole new approach." They had learned much of this at Sandy's fundraiser, but seeing the clinic made it real. "I love the ultrasound."

"Should I call for flight reservations?"

"Give me another day, Jack." There were the stacks of papers on her desk. The footnotes. The research that hadn't been worked in. And there were three calls from Lois Beecham, her editor, that she hadn't returned. "I'll call Lois this afternoon."

Chapter Two
Sea Cliff

The World is trying...
to form a civilized but non-Christian mentality.
The experiment will fail; but we must be very patient...
meanwhile redeeming the time:
so that the Faith may be preserved alive through the dark ages before us;
to renew and rebuild civilization and save the World from suicide.
T.S. Eliot

Madeleine climbed to her attic study. The walls of the stairwell were covered with icons and photos: saints gazed from gilded wood, family posed behind framed glass. They were a host of witnesses and they comforted her.

She entered her precious work space, where so many words had been placed on so many pages, giving life to her thoughts. Dormer windows on two sides allowed filtered light, and low shelves ran under the pitched roof, crammed with books on theology and philosophy, history and literature, poetry and memoir. There was T.S. Eliot, Evelyn Underhill, Russell Kirk, Raymond Raynes, Dom Gregory Dix, Dorothy Sayers, C.S. Lewis, G.K. Chesterton. Numerous Bible translations shared a shelf with the 1928 Episcopal *Book of Common Prayer*, the 1940 Hymnal, and the Anglican Missal. There were the apocalyptic novels of Michael D. O'Brien, the great Canadian novelist. There were dictionaries, thesauri, word menus, a hefty concordance alongside Butler's *Lives of the Saints*. Gertrude Himmelfarb, Paul Johnson, Barbara Tuchman, Walter McDougall, the journal of Alexander Schmeman, a biography of Charles de Foucauld, the saintly hermit of the Sahara. On her old oak desk two framed pictures kept her company: one of her wedding day with Jack, standing before Saint Thomas' altar, Madeleine in her cream dress, Jack in his dark suit; the other of Justin and Lisa Jane with little Luke on her lap. Madeleine's grandson must have been about one, the picture taken the previous August. Her son's smile held justified pride, and Madeleine ran her finger over his face. Lisa Jane grinned ingenuously into the camera, her natural beauty shining through. *Aspens in the background, the Rockies,* Madeleine thought.

A foghorn sounded and Madeleine crossed to a window. She unlatched it and looked out to the Golden Gate, breathing in the moist air. The afternoon fogbank, propelled by sea winds, was moving in rapidly, sliding over the bridge, heading for the East Bay.

Madeleine and Jack had bought their Sea Cliff house in 1982 when Madeleine proposed. Justin was nine, and she told Jack that she didn't have time to date anyone who wasn't interested in a serious relationship. She wanted a husband and Justin needed a father. So what, exactly, were his intentions? Time pressed upon her.

When she left Vancouver and came home to San Francisco with her young son she knew her marriage with Charlie was over. The divorce was a sad affair, an ashen thing, a gray death in itself, all those hopes and dreams, embers dying. She and Charlie had been so young, green with longings and desires, so sure of life, so full of passion. What went wrong? Was it Charlie's inability to hold a job? Was he too lazy or too proud? Did he really think he would be the next great American novelist, the Vietnam War expat living in Canada? Or was it her exhaustion, working full-time and keeping house so that he could write? Then came Justin, her great joy. And Mollie, her great sorrow. She often thought it was Mollie's death that separated her from Charlie as nothing else could, as though a rushing river rose up between them and left them standing on opposite shores. Charlie withdrew even more into his books. Abandoned, Madeleine fell into a deep depression, far from reality, as though she watched herself move about, another person. Finally, she and Justin flew home to San Francisco, with two deaths—her child and her marriage—weighing upon her soul.

She found a clerical job, and not long after that, she found Saint Thomas' Church on Sacramento Street. The white chapel with its booming organ invited them in and they stayed. A lapsed Presbyterian, she now learned a new way to believe, one of ritual and song, flames and incense, pageantry and purpose. She learned to dance the rhythms of the Church Year, from Christmas to Easter to Trinity and back to Christmas again. She learned about the sacramental life, how God worked through matter, that he was present in the Eucharist. At Saint Thomas' she made close friends. She helped with Sunday school. It was there, in the parish family, that Justin grew up, and it was there, before Saint Thomas' altar, that Madeleine married Jack.

Their Sea Cliff house was not large. A small living room, a smaller den, and an even smaller kitchen and dining area occupied the ground floor. Stairs descended to a cellar where Jack stored his wine finds, good years at great buys he had collected over the years. They had converted part of the cellar to a guest suite with its own street entrance. A grander set of stairs ascended from the main floor to two bedrooms, and further up, a narrower staircase rose to the attic.

Madeleine soon turned the attic into her reading room. She placed a wing chair and a lamp in an alcove and retreated there when Jack and Justin, and later Jack's golfing buddies, watched sports downstairs. She had never understood football and, after trying to understand, decided she never would. After earning her doctorate and beginning to teach history, she prepared lessons at her antique desk, and when she bought her first laptop, came here to jot down her musings that would metamorphose, she hoped, into *Holy Manifestations*. The musings were the offspring of her reading, her meditations on Sunday sermons, conversations with Father Rinaldi, and the travel journals she kept as she and Jack visited Italy, France, and England on wine buying trips for their stores. The musings had come too from her doctoral thesis, *Miracles: Fact or Fiction*, and from the ongoing research involved for her classes.

Indeed, teaching undergraduates was profoundly satisfying, for she taught the lessons of time, history's thrust upon our present, particularly in the Western world where culture shifted so precipitously. She enjoyed her students and their questions, the evolving discussions, the counterpoint of young minds making connections. But she was only part-time, and her job was never secure, for the university was cutting back and Madeleine was no longer young. They favored a more modern approach, what Madeleine saw as history revised to suit current tastes. But if she published, that would make a difference. She didn't want to lose her job. Not yet. It had become an important part of her.

A children's home in London. How could she not be involved in such an undertaking—especially when it landed in her lap like this? She sat at her desk, opened a drawer, and pulled out a faded snapshot, taken with a Brownie camera. Mollie first sitting up. She set it next to a photograph of Justin and his family.

Establishing the London home would continue her healing. *Is that your will, Lord?*

She looked at the phone, then at the three messages from her editor waiting under the stapler. If she went to London, could she finish this book on time? Maybe she could get an extension.

She dialed Lois. No answer. She left a message.

She turned back to her laptop and opened her manuscript to the British chapter. Perhaps a trip to London would help, not hinder, the book.

Holy Manifestations: the Early Church in England
A few years after the death and resurrection of Jesus of Nazareth in the Roman province of Palestine, the Emperor Claudius conquered eleven kings of the British Lowlands. As Claudius pushed the borders of his empire, Christ's apostles preached wherever they could, telling the astonishing good news of a living, loving God who sent his son to die for man's sins. They claimed that God's son—Jesus—rose from the dead, redeeming mankind from sin and death. As they spread the news that the Jewish Messiah had finally come, they were stoned, jailed, and martyred. Still they formed communities of believers, and these first churches told and retold Jesus' life and words until known by heart. They celebrated holy suppers, claiming the bread was his body, the wine his blood, and that eating him would save one's soul.

As these ragtag apostle-bishops, in all their poverty and travel dirt, wrote letters of witness and encouragement to beginning churches, and as these seeds of the church of *Christus*, the anointed one, took root throughout the Mediterranean basin, Romans built roads crisscrossing their new island province. In this first century AD, the Romans bridged the Thames at the forlorn outpost of the empire, Londinium.

The growth of young Londinium suffered with the revolt of the tribal Queen Boudicca[1] in 61 AD. Upon the death of her husband, the Romans had seized her property, flogged Boudicca, and raped her daughters. The outraged warrior queen rallied her kingdom and other disaffected tribes, sacked Camulodunum (Colchester), massacred the citizens of Londinium, and torched the town. Britain's Roman governor, the general Gaius Suetonius Paulinus, marched south from his victories in Wales, swiftly and brutally quelled the revolt, and Rome had little trouble with the Britons for the next several centuries. Queen Boudicca is thought to have taken poison, and today her sculpted image races an iron chariot below

Big Ben, Parliament's bell tower. Flanked by her daughters, this wild soldier queen screams from the past.

The image of the queen and the Roman rape had been branded on Madeleine's mind. Was every civilization born out of such tragedy? Or more to the point, how did Boudicca relate to Christianity in Britain? The answer flashed like a road sign...the queen was the voice of island independence. Her body *was* the island; her daughters *were* its people. She made a note—**tie in Boudicca, island queen of independence*—and read on.

> The first Christians witnessed to the world with a passion born of an interior fire, populating and converting centers from the eastern Mediterranean through Gaul (France) and as far as this island province of Britannia, finally subdued. It is believed that Joseph of Arimathea, the wealthy Jewish counselor who provided the tomb for Jesus' burial, carried the news of his Lord's resurrection to the Glastonbury marshes in the first century. But the earliest *written* records of Christianity in Britain come from third-century Tertullian and Origen. The Venerable Bede, an eighth-century monk and historian, records a certain Alban martyred in 304, having sheltered and defended a Christian priest. With the conversion of Emperor Constantine, the son of the British princess Helena, in 312, Christianity in the Roman Empire was legalized, and the Church grew in England, a bearer of God's living legacy to man.

But it wasn't called England then, Madeleine thought, *since the Angles hadn't arrived.* Did she need to worry about that? She starred *England* to check later.

> The legacy would be molded by the great minds of those years, those august Church Fathers. Varying in shape and substance, the words of this legacy, expressing the inexpressible, would be fired by councils and creeds in the forge of time and the power of the Holy Spirit, as questions of truth and heresy were sorted out.
> Of the many heresies, the peculiarly British temptation came from Pelagius, a Briton monk who left for Rome in 380, never to return. Educated and worldly, he argued the natural goodness of man. He denied Original Sin, the belief that men are morally tainted by the disobedience of Adam and Eve, and claimed man

could live a perfect life without the grace of God. Augustine of Hippo convinced the councils otherwise, arguing man's imperfection and need for a savior.

Pelagius' ideas took root in the island kingdom and shaped its history, bequeathing to its people a confidence in man and bolstering their separation from the continent.

This Pelagian question nagged her, for a reader whose advice she respected claimed she had overblown Pelagius' influence. "It's just a thread," Madeleine replied, but he had shrugged, as though every thread contributed to the weave and none were to be taken lightly.

Thus Boudicca's fury descended through the ages, a fierce and uncompromising sense of self and purpose. And what of Christianity? Would the Christian God, that all-powerful being demanding total worship and providing only one way to him through his son, a narrow road indeed—would such a Father Almighty put up with such a people? Perhaps not since his own chosen race, the sons and daughters of Israel, had such a headstrong nation wrestled with him.

Wrestling with God. Jacob wrestled with the Angel of God and was renamed Israel. Such wrestling was the inevitable result of free will, Madeleine supposed. The Psalms were full of such give and take, conversations with God, choosing to follow him, or not.

The English Church shaped itself over the years, molded by monarchs and preachers and time. All the while, the Church reflected a seriousness of purpose, a sense that belief mattered, that the practice of that belief mattered, and the language of that belief mattered as well. A foundation of catholicity going back to the early Roman church continued to support the building: man's imperfection and his need for God's saving grace. But the pillars and walls and bricks and mortar of the English Church were formed from the sand of island independence: man's abilities and wit would give him direct access to that God. It was this sense of action, this drive to solve problems, this ultimately Protestant work ethic, that formed Anglicanism and indeed, England...and eventually America.

The Church in Britain grew, preserving the creeds of those

Fathers of the Church, illustrating manuscripts by candlelight in windswept huts in the north, in Ireland and Scotland and England. Patrick, Ninian, Columba, Aidan, and Dunstan built monasteries and preached the love of God.

And to ensure that the wayward island didn't stray too far from papal reach, Augustine of Canterbury arrived from Rome in the late sixth century. He converted King Ethelbert of Kent and strengthened the ties between the Roman church and the Celtic bishops, ties that would not be broken until Henry VIII cast his eye on Anne Boleyn nearly one thousand years later.

But what of Pelagius and Augustine of Hippo, of the goodness of man versus the need for grace? Did Rome succeed when Pope Gregory sent Augustine of Canterbury to Britain? Pelagian ideas had blossomed in the north and were soon identified with Celtic Christianity in Wales, Ireland, and Scotland, in huts rather than cathedrals, organized from rural monasteries rather than city episcopates. Roman Christianity was preached in the southeast of England by missionary bishops from Italy.

Then came the Angles and the Saxons, fortifying the Celtic side.

As Rome withdrew from its British frontiers, Celtic communities hired Saxon tribes for protection. Eventually these fierce warriors turned and took that which they guarded, devouring the hand that fed them. They were heroic peoples—free, courageous, and ruthless. So, as Celtic monks converted the Angles and Saxons, a religious and fiercely independent people were born—the *English*, the people *of the Angles*.

The northern Pelagian party may have been free and independent and strong, but the southeastern Roman party was organized and articulate. At the Synod of Whitby in 664^2 the questions of Celtic versus Roman Christianity, of island isolation versus continental connection, and Pelagian self-salvation versus Augustinian grace were answered with the decision to observe the Roman date of Easter. With this decision, largely dictated by political expediency—the need for connection with the continent forcefully argued—England joined the Roman community which was, in that time, the world community in the West.

For the moment, Pelagian pride bent the knee.

The phone jangled. Madeleine started and reached for the old-fashioned black receiver.

"Madeleine, glad I finally got you."

"Sorry, Lois, been busy working on this book, you know."

"Good. That's what I wanted to talk to you about."

"Oh?"

"Listen, another publisher has shown some interest in the manuscript. They might buy it from us. It's a major publisher, Madeleine, a real feather in your cap. But it has to be on schedule. Can you do it?"

"June?"

"June."

"Would I have job security then?" *Lord, guide me.*

"Absolutely. No one could refuse you, at least after your book tour and talk shows."

"Book tour and talk shows?"

"Like I said, these are the big guys."

"Then of course," Madeleine said, "June it is. Count on it." What had she promised?

As she hung up the phone, Madeleine heard Jack's heavy step on the stairs. He lowered his long frame into the wing chair.

"Was that Lois?" he asked.

Madeleine's throat was dry. "It was."

"And? Can she give you an extension?"

"I'm afraid not." What should she do? "The deadline's still June. Jack, she said a big publisher is interested."

"Really? That's great!" He raised his brows, waiting. "I sense there is a catch here somewhere."

"The book could give me job security, even as a part-timer." *Job security.* She could hardly believe it.

"But you're coming to London with me, right? June is ages away."

Madeleine looked at her calendar. Six months. She looked at the piles on her desk. "I don't know, Jack." She glanced at Mollie's picture.

"You can write on the plane. And once we're there, we'll be in hotels. You don't have to cook or shop or clean. You'll actually have *more* time."

Madeleine recalled that Jack was a gifted negotiator; she didn't have a chance. She looked back at her screen, the words spilling over the white space so nicely. *What is thy will, Lord?*

"And you can polish the English part. The French and Italian portions are pretty much done, right?"

"True." Madeleine's mind raced. She looked at her husband's hopeful face. Maybe, to save time, she could hire a student to help her with the final draft. "Could we be back, say, by April?" That would give her two full months at home after the trip.

"Sure. And Madeleine, this project would help me in another way, one I hadn't thought of until now, as I walked past all your saints on the wall."

"Oh?" *Another way?*

"You recall the vow I made in Lourdes on our trip two years ago, when we went looking for Doctor DuPres?"

Madeleine had often thought of that trip. Like the Italian pilgrimage, it had been a trip of healing, only this time for Jack. They visited shrines of martyrs and saints, and washed in the waters of Lourdes where Bernadette saw the Virgin Mary. They lit candles in the many churches of Mary Magdalene. Indeed, Mary Magdalene became a sister, and the Virgin Mary a mother. And the French segment of her book had been completed that autumn of 1999.

Madeleine, happy with the memory, added, "And Doctor DuPres healed you of cancer with her miraculous hands."

Jack shook his head. "That's just it. I made that vow in Lourdes. It was God who healed me, Madeleine. Through the good doctor."

"Didn't you promise God you would build a church if you were healed? Is that what you're talking about?"

"Right."

"And you haven't done that, have you?"

"No, but this would be the chance. Naturally, the London project would have a church or chapel attached."

Madeleine nodded, stood, and moved toward her husband. She bent down and kissed him on the lips. "Yes, this would be the chance, my love." How Jack had changed since that trip. God had healed him, in so many ways, since his time in France. What was God's will for them in England?

"So I can make the calls, set up some flights?"

"Make the calls. London it is. But after Christmas." *Take not thy Holy Spirit from me, O Lord.*

Chapter Three
Danville

*To have a right to do a thing
is not at all the same as to be right in doing it.*
G.K. Chesterton

Victoria looked out at the December rain lashing the broad terrace and wind rattling the glass doors. She laid her hand on her tummy. The storm swirled beyond the spillover pool, a wall of gray obscuring Mount Diablo to the east. Her home crested a foothill in the suburban community of Danville, where custom houses commanded large lots. It was their fifth house, and the most spacious, for they had moved when something better turned up, or an architect talked her mother into a new design. Of the five, this house was Victoria's least favorite, a modern construction of stacked cubes and giant panes of glass peering like rectangular eyes. Even so, she loved the view. On a clear windswept day, and there were many at this elevation, you could see northwest to the Napa Valley, a misty glen between folding hills.

Her mother reigned behind the granite island in the center of the kitchen. She looked up from her espresso and glared at her daughter. "You are *what?*"

Victoria glanced at her father, who sat next to her at the nook table. She nervously smoothed her tight shirt over her expanding waist, then reached for a carton of soy milk. "I guess it happened last July."

"You *guess* it happened last July?" Candice repeated as though she had misheard. "What are you talking about? Exactly *what* happened last July?"

Victoria shifted her gaze to the storm outside, to the chilling gray whiteness.

Her father stood and rested his steady hand on Victoria's shoulder. "We didn't tell you, dear," he said. "We didn't want to upset you in the middle of a session, and then there was the funeral." He stared at Candice, whose fingers were splayed on the counter, her body rigid. "It was terrible," he continued, waving open palms through the tense air. "Our little girl...dear God...." He buried his face in his hands.

Her mother joined them at the table. "Okay, okay. Let's stay calm. Tell me about it."

Victoria locked her eyes on a dried cranberry bobbing in the granola, recalling the searing pain of the man's attack. She opened her mouth and willed the words. "I was raped...jogging on the lake trail." She had hurt for so long. She focused on the cranberry as though it were a life raft.

"It was two weeks before the funeral." Her father shifted his gaze to the storm.

The cranberry was sinking. "I woke up lying on the dry grass. A park ranger found me...took me to the clinic. Daddy made the report."

"I still don't understand why you didn't tell me." Candice paced, her anger surrounding her like a cloud. She turned to stare at Victoria, then Andrew. "Rape! Did they catch him? I'll have him castrated!" She strode to her daughter and Victoria rose to meet her, embracing her mother and feeling her bones. Candice stroked Victoria's long hair "My baby, my little Vicky. How could this happen to you?"

"Mother," Victoria said, her voice thin and muffled by the tweed collar, "I'm sorry."

"Baby, it's not your fault. You know that."

"I'm sorry for not telling you." She tried to lean back, thinking she wasn't really sorry, but her mother held her head firmly in the hollow of her shoulder.

"You *do* remember," her father said, "that you were in Washington?"

"That's right." Her mother released her and turned toward Andrew. "Still, I had a right to know. We could have taken care of it right away."

Victoria winced. She returned to the table and pulled the cranberry out of her cereal with a spoon, cradling it. How she had longed for her mother, as the female officer interviewed her and the young male doctor, coldly professional, with his gloves and his instruments, probed where he had no business probing. Even with her father waiting in the next room, she had retreated to a place of detached loneliness.

"And why," Candice said, "*haven't* you taken care of it? You must be five months along."

Victoria felt her father's gaze and forgave his silence as she stirred her granola, watching the seeds and grains float around the almonds, the flecks of wheat germ swirling in white eddies. Her spoon scraped the bottom of the bowl.

"*Well?*" Candice returned to the counter and gulped her coffee. She glanced at her watch. "This is not a good time for me, but it's not too late to do something."

"Mother...," Victoria began. She set down the spoon, then looked into her father's encouraging eyes. She had practiced the words, and now she would say them. "Mother, *I want...to have...this baby.*" She watched herself from far away, another person.

"*Have it?* This was an accident, a mistake, an act of violence we'll put behind us. You're only seventeen. I'll call Hoffman after my meeting this morning—he took care of the last one. We can trust him." She moved toward the door to the garage. "And you, Andrew," she said, pivoting on her heel, "how could you do this to me? How could you plot like this?" She cursed, grabbing her coat and keys. "We'll deal with this later." She turned to Victoria and kissed her on the forehead. "Sweetie, don't you worry. Everything will be fine." She closed the door behind her.

Her father looked resigned and inhaled deeply. "Rather what we expected."

"Yes."

"Plan B."

"Plan B."

"You need to get away, my dear. Your grandmother thinks so, too."

"Couldn't I stay with Grandma?"

Andrew shook his head. "She would love that, but she's too close by, as are my other family members. We need some distance here."

"Distance? But why?"

"Your mother will pressure you. She won't force you, but she will have her way subtly. You and I are too emotionally involved—she would use our love to talk you into an abortion. You know she would."

"She would, wouldn't she? I know you've explained this before. I just wanted to hear it again." Her father's hair was graying early; his eyes, red and watery, were crinkled in distress. Could she recall a time when his forehead wasn't pulled together in worry? "How's Grandma Nguyen?"

"She'll live another hundred years, not to worry."

"I have to see her before I go." Could she really leave Danville? How had she come to this moment in her life? She glanced at the familiar kitchen, her home.

"She will bless you and pray for you and the baby. And I'll call Frederick. It should be about four in the afternoon in London."

"Is Frederick nice?" She would be living with total strangers.

"Frederick had better be nice. He owes me his life."

"But that was a long time ago."

"It wasn't *that* long ago."

"It was before I was born."

"Yes, before you were born."

Andrew looked again at the rain splattering the flagstone. They sat in the silence of common misery, Andrew unable to speak of the war years, and Victoria not wanting to push him. She had pieced some of the story together over time, how her grandparents had sheltered the British journalist who was hiding from the Viet Cong. That was enough for her.

"I'm sure I'll be fine with Frederick and his wife. And London—what girl wouldn't want to go to London?"

Her future loomed large, but a seed was planted in Victoria's soul, a seed of determination, and this time she would nurture it. She would not kill another child. *This* baby would live. She didn't care how it was conceived or who the father was. He or she was beginning to kick.

The line of ticketed passengers wound outside the Oakland Airport, down the walkway to the back of the terminal, finally ending in a tented queue. Victoria and her father began the slow progress forward.

Andrew surveyed the crowd. "We haven't flown since nine-eleven. Look at all the security."

"Mother said the lines were bad, but I didn't expect this."

"The terrorists got what they wanted, and more, didn't they? They've stolen our freedom."

Victoria recalled the repeated news images—the planes flying into the towers, the plumes of smoke, the stunned reporters. "Maybe it will settle down after awhile."

Andrew shook his head as though he knew better. "Things won't ever be the same."

Victoria's heart clutched. Nor would they be the same with her. "What are you going to tell Mother when she finds I'm gone?"

"She'll storm as usual, and as usual I'll hide." Andrew pulled up his collar against the wind.

"I don't want her to find me, Daddy. Not yet."

"I know. It's hard to stand up to her once her mind is made up."

"It *is* hard. What did my school say?"

"They were concerned, then happy for you. I told them you were spending the spring semester in London, which is true. What did you tell Maria? Lying isn't good. You've been friends for a long time."

"I said it was a great opportunity, and I believe she was actually envious. She'll pass the word along. She loves to gossip. I'll miss her, but it won't be forever. If I keep the baby, she'll find out eventually, but not now, Daddy, not now. And I haven't really decided, have I?"

"No, there's time for that, and no one needs to know at this point. We'll protect your mother as long as possible."

"Daddy..."

"Yes, Vicky?"

"Why did you marry her?" It was a question she had often wanted to ask but hadn't found the right time. Perhaps there was no right time.

Her father sighed. He sighed often lately, Victoria thought. His eyes scanned the crowd, as though the answer lay hidden in the winding lines.

"She was beautiful, Vicky, really stunning. I was a deckhand. It was the summer of '85 on the QE2, the most luxurious ocean liner in the world. We were sailing Paris-New York, and she was returning to Smith after a summer at the Sorbonne."

"A deckhand? You never told me that."

He nodded, smiling. "I was a deckhand, not something your mother wants known. It was hard work, but it paid well, and it satisfied something in me, some yearning to see the world. I didn't want to work the fishing trade in Oakland like my brothers. Some days, though, I wish I'd joined them."

"She was beautiful? I can imagine—she's beautiful now."

"We're not exactly ancient, my dear. Your mother's only thirty-nine and I'm barely forty-six."

Victoria touched her father's arm. "Of course, Daddy, I'm sorry."

"So we fell in love. I thought it was a miracle she even noticed me! I was the luckiest guy in the world. I looked her up in Northampton the next month, and we picked up where we left off. I couldn't believe any of it was happening. She literally took my breath away...and my heart and mind, it seems." He looked pleased but a bit chagrined with the memory.

They emerged from the tents in front of Departures, where police officers shouted warnings to cars dropping off passengers, and passed through glass doors that slid open automatically.

"And the following year," Victoria said, "you were married and I was born."

"And Candice achieved her revenge on her parents."

"Revenge?"

"She hated them for never being home. She was raised by nannies and governesses. She attended the best grade school, then the best prep school, *came out* in the San Francisco Cotillion. A real debutante. Her parents, according to her never-ending complaint, were jetting here and sailing there. Her great-grandfather, you know, made a fortune in oil."

"So where is the revenge?"

"Marrying me, a poor Chink. Her folks nearly disowned her. They had other plans."

"Didn't Mother love you?"

"I suppose so, in her own way. Convenience and control probably translated to love." He shook his head sadly.

"She was an only child. Maybe she was used to getting her way." Victoria wondered if she was like that, being an only child.

"Maybe. She was certainly spoiled."

They stepped forward in silence. Once again, Victoria felt the baby move inside her, and her uncertain future touched her, awaking her fears. "What will become of me, Daddy?"

"We'll take one step at a time, okay? We'll get you to London, get that baby born, and then decide what to do. I'll be there for you, Vicky. Maybe not in person, but I'll never let you down. You made the right choice. This child should not be punished for the sins of his father. It's just not right, is it?"

"No."

"Keep telling yourself that."

"And the father's not around and isn't likely to show up, is he, Daddy?" They had avoided speaking of the father of her child, executing him in absentia.

"The police don't have many leads."

"I'm sure I couldn't identify him."

"He's a creature not worthy of your attention, Victoria. This child is no more related to that beast than a baby abandoned on a doorstep."

"Daddy, I'm scared."

He glanced at her with a strange boldness. "Maybe you should try praying."

Prayer had seemed so foreign to Victoria. Were they rote phrases that made a person feel good? And to whom would she pray? Was there truly a God who listened? "We prayed in Sunday school. You used to take me. Why did you stop?"

"It upset your mother. She said religion was 'a crutch for the weak and an opiate drugging our culture.' It wasn't a battle I wanted to fight."

"I've heard her say that. But Daddy, do you really believe in God...in Jesus?" None of Victoria's friends did.

Andrew looked at her tenderly. "I do, Vicky, and I've never stopped praying for you. In fact, it's prayer that's gotten me this far. I'm sure of it. Give it a try. Start with an *Our Father*. It will calm you, if nothing else. And be sure and keep your heart open to God."

"That's what Grandma Nguyen says."

Andrew laughed. "She likes that one."

"Daddy, have...have you *ever* been happy with Mother? I mean, besides the first year?"

"We were happy for some time. The lifestyle was all new to me, and it *was* exciting! We had the big house, the cars, the toys, all the distractions to entertain us. And we traveled, as you know, dragging you and your nanny along, and those were great trips for me, a poor country boy from 'Nam."

"That was before Mother taught at the university? Before she got involved in politics?"

He nodded. "Women's Studies led to women's rights and finally political fundraisers. She set up women's shelters in the Bay Area, and arranged transportation to voting booths. She's helped a lot of people, and on that score you can be proud of her, my dear."

Victoria embraced that side of her mother, the caring for the poor and less fortunate. "I am, Daddy. She *has* made a difference in peoples' lives." Victoria realized with a start how angry her mother must be over the rape—the very violence her shelters dealt with daily, handing out morning-after pills.

"All of this gave her a political base for her first run for office. She also had the connections with the country club set, with our tennis and golf, and the academic network through her career. Not to mention the family name and fortune, running as a Crawford-Nguyen. Her father's Washington ties came in handy. The Nguyen name probably didn't hurt the ethnic vote."

"And *you* raised me."

"I suppose I did, as best I could."

"Will you carve something for the baby?"

Her father had a workshop over the garage where he whittled animals and trains and fabulous scenes from fairy tales. They had enchanted her ever since she could remember.

"I'll do that. Victoria, I've been thinking about Aunt Elizabeth's will. This baby could inherit something." Her father seemed pleased with the idea, shaking his head in amazement. "That Elizabeth, what a lady. I admired her spunk, changing her will like that and defending that unborn baby, although a little late, but she didn't know about the child until after the abortion. I don't know how she figured it out."

Victoria's remorse, weighted by grief, surged again. If she could only do it all over again—undo it. If only she knew its gender, didn't have to call it an *it*. She patted her tummy tenderly. "But wouldn't he or she have had to be born before Aunt Elizabeth died in order to inherit?"

"It's a legal point worthy of a judge."

"Then does Mother want me to have an abortion so she will inherit?"

"It's possible, but more probably, your having the child would be an embarrassment. It would be seen at the very least as unwise to give birth to a child conceived by rape. Such a choice might discourage others. A poor example. After all, you are the daughter of a champion of women's rights. But it would need to appear to be *your choice*. Does that make sense?"

Victoria nodded. She knew how important image was, how everything they did had public consequences. She had known this from an early age. "Daddy?"

"Yes, Princess?"

Victoria's throat was tight. "Did Mother *ever* love me?"

She looked into his eyes as he traced his baby finger across her birthmark and down the side of her chin.

"Your mother, my dear, loved you very much, as much as she is capable of loving. She couldn't bear the thought of plastic surgery on your face, of using the knife. In her own way, she loves you still. She just loves herself more. And to be fair, she sees herself as the protector of women in this liberated age."

How ironic, Victoria thought, *the protector and persecutor, all rolled into one. How fine the line could become.*

They paused near the security X-ray machines.

"I'm afraid this is good-bye," her father said, embracing her. "I love you, Princess."

Victoria held onto him for a moment, memorizing his warm

softness, his lemony aftershave.

"Call when you arrive," he added as they drew apart.

"I will, Daddy. I love you too."

He turned, wiped his eyes, and walked briskly toward the parking garage.

She watched him leave, a tight-knit man of purpose and dignity, a good man. She, too, would be good.

Alone but feeling a little taller, Victoria and her unborn child moved forward in the line. She laid her London ticket in the fold of her passport, then, shifting the weight of her backpack to her other shoulder, stepped into her future.

Chapter Four
Farm Street Church, London

Glory be to God for dappled things–
For skies of couple-color as a brindled cow...
Whatever is fickle, freckled (who knows how?)
With swift, slow; sweet, sour; adazzle, dim;
He fathers-forth whose beauty is past change; Praise Him.
Gerald Manley Hopkins

Time was precious to Madeleine. Time past, time present, time future. Time hovered like seagulls flapping the air. Indeed, Madeleine woke each morning with the terrible sense of another day gone, of time lost. She went to sleep each night sure she had not done enough, not prayed enough, not loved enough. Yet this increased sensitivity to the movement of the hours increased their value. *Pay attention*, the birds cried. And Madeleine did. Or tried to.

Today, shortly before dawn on the first Saturday of February, 2002, Madeleine could feel the plane descend toward London, ten hours from San Francisco. As she closed her worn *Book of Common Prayer* with its frayed leather and wrinkled onionskin, a folded paper fell out, her grandson's finger-painting. At eighteen months, Luke had run his fingers happily across the sheet, and Madeleine touched the red and green smudges tenderly. Lisa Jane had printed neatly in the bottom corner *To Grandma Maddie, with love from Luke, Christmas 2001*. Madeleine would shop for a teddy bear for Luke. Or maybe a nice picture book from a London shop. She would find time. She carefully refolded the sheet and placed it between the pages to mark her place.

The prayer book had been a gift from good Father Rinaldi. "Madeleine," he would say, "make prayer a habit and you won't regret it." She hadn't exactly made it a habit, but worked on it in fits and starts, Advent and Lent, and times like these, times of great transition and portent, when the Office of Morning Prayer seemed appropriate. Saint Thomas' would never be the same without Father Rinaldi, but, in some ways, it would always be the same. Amused by the contradiction, she was glad that with Anglo-Catholic parishes one always knew what to expect, regardless of the priest.

Would *she* ever be the same without her old friend? She sensed he watched over her, sometimes through others. In Italy she had met the tall dark friar, Brother Cristoforo, who had been raised by Father Rinaldi in the Rome orphanage, long before the priest had become vicar of Saint Thomas' in San Francisco. Such links of grace, Madeleine thought, were often only seen from a distance as they formed a golden chain, a Godly communion. Today, in London, they would continue the work Father Rinaldi had begun in Rome, and Madeleine looked forward to seeing Cristoforo who was meeting them there to locate a property. Jack would fulfill the vow he made in Lourdes. And, with sufficient grace, Madeleine would finish her book.

Raising her window shade, she peered out to the gray dawn. Necklaces of diamond-lights sparkled over sleeping London. The Thames snaked past Parliament, winding around skyscrapers and under Tower Bridge. Green Park and Saint James Park snuggled back-to-back like Siamese twins; Hyde Park merged into Kensington, a long green swath of silence. London lay like a fairy tale world awaiting Peter Pan to fling open the shutters.

Tomorrow would be Sexagesima Sunday, the second Sunday in Pre-Lent. Where would they go to church?

She turned to Jack and nudged him awake.

The amber stone of Farm Street Church could be seen through their bedroom window and Madeleine gazed at the leafless trees guarding the eastern end. Arriving at the Connaught Hotel around noon the previous day, bleary eyed and travel weary, they unpacked, showered, and slipped into cool linen sheets for a two-hour nap. After a light supper at a nearby café, they slept the strange sleep of jet lag: deep dreamless oblivion broken by sudden wakefulness.

Madeleine returned to the breakfast table and poured Jack's tea, then stirred milk and sweetener into her coffee. Jack was reading the

Telegraph's business page, munching slowly, his glasses slipping down his nose, a proper Englishman in his castle. He did, after all, claim Lady Jane Seymour as an ancestor. He had the delicate English skin; his freckles had spread into age spots the sun had planted on his neck, giving him a dappled look. Madeleine wasn't sure where the curly red hair, turning silver, came from, an Irish streak perhaps.

Jack handed her a page of the paper. "There's an article about our hotel."

As she sipped her coffee, she skimmed the piece, glancing occasionally at her watch.

The Connaught had a fashionable history. Eighteenth-century London had expanded into the Mayfair fields to provide lodging for visiting squires. In 1803 Alexander Grillon opened two townhouses on Charles Street, which became Carlos Place, and named his new hotel The Coburg after Queen Victoria's Prince Consort, Prince Albert of Saxe-Coburg. It became the Connaught in 1917, honoring Arthur, the Duke of Connaught, Queen Victoria's third son. Charles De Gaulle made it his official residence during the Second World War, receiving General Eisenhower from the American Embassy nearby. While impressed with the lineage, Madeleine liked its homey décor, which made her feel as if she were visiting a wealthy and welcoming grandmother.

"Wow. De Gaulle. Eisenhower."

"Thought you'd enjoy that." Jack glanced up, then returned to his stock figures.

Madeleine reached for the honey. "How's Amazon?"

Jack placed his finger on a column of numbers to keep his place and looked at her over his glasses. "Down, at least at Friday's close. We'll see how it opens tomorrow."

"Oh dear."

"Oh dear is right. The market is still reeling from September 11. It was near recession already, and the terrorist attack didn't help."

"Are we in trouble?" An old anxiety tugged at Madeleine, her hungry days as a single parent not forgotten.

"Not *trouble*, but I'm watching things closely." He returned his gaze to the numbers.

Madeleine checked her watch. "We've got half an hour."

"That's lots of time. The church is right across the street. Stop worrying, Madeleine."

"That's a switch, *you* telling *me* to stop worrying." It was true; she seemed to worry more than Jack these days.

Her husband's surgery had changed his body; God had changed his soul. The cancerous tissue growing in Jack's esophagus had been removed. Acid no longer bathed his tender stomach, rising into his mouth. And as they journeyed through France, Jack had encountered God. He had learned to trust.

Today he even read the Bible regularly. "If Mother could only see me now," he would say, as he studied the Sermon on the Mount or Paul's letters. Madeleine read Scripture too, but her selections were part of her Prayer Book discipline, such as it was. Jack simply opened the Good Book and read. Or he would pick up a commentary from somewhere—she had seen several subscriptions in the mail—and follow the thoughts of an evangelical preacher. His mother's Methodist genes lived on.

"Ten minutes, Jack." She pulled her raincoat from the closet.

"Right."

Jack stacked the dishes neatly, leaving little for the waiter to do, as was his habit. "I love this place, Maddie. The Connaught makes me feel like a country squire. Joe McGinty was really generous to put us up here." He adjusted his tie in the foyer mirror, grabbed his jacket, and beamed at his wife. "And you, my dear, are stunning as always."

"Thanks." She still blushed at her husband's compliments after all these years.

She slipped into her coat and closed the door behind them. They walked down the hallway and waited for the elevator to creep its way to the top. She could hear in the distance a few dishes clinking in the kitchen down the hall, probably the butler making tea.

"Do you recall," Jack asked as they squeezed inside and punched the lobby button, "where Cristoforo is staying? He must have arrived from Rome by now. I'm looking forward to seeing these properties."

The paneled walls smelled of beeswax and lemon oil.

"I believe he's at the hostel at Westminster Cathedral. We should call over there."

"The descriptions he faxed look promising. It will be a relief, I must say, to find something. I'm counting on this project as a fulfillment of my vow."

"I know, and it will help me too." Helping continued the healing. While her nightmares about Mollie had not returned, her grief was distantly present, and Madeleine thought she might always need healing, at least in this world.

Madeleine prayed the friar would find something suitable. The June deadline for her book pressed upon her. In fact, the deadline was really April, for she needed at least a month to get feedback from other professionals and make last-minute changes. Time was a shrinking frame in which she lived. It was already February. Since Christmas, she had made significant progress on the manuscript, molding it into a unified piece she could now access as one document on her laptop. She had worked in the additional research; the task now was to read and edit, read and edit, read and edit.

The gleaming door slid open, one slow inch at a time. They stepped into the hushed lobby and walked toward a counter where keys hung neatly over mahogany cubicles. A dapper concierge was in deep conversation with a svelte blond in a black mink. Jack left the room key on the counter, turned, and slipped his hand under Madeleine's elbow. He guided her toward the revolving door, then stopped suddenly.

"Just a sec. Let me check our dinner reservations." He returned to the counter.

Madeleine crossed the foyer and peeked into a front salon, decorated in rich reds and deep greens—a room, she thought, where cocktails and tea were served to genteel guests conversing in subdued tones. She pulled aside a drapery panel and studied the sky: no rain yet, but that steely gray meant a cold, wintry day. She peered across the street to the iron gates leading to Farm Street Church and recalled the church's remarkable history.

For centuries after Henry VIII's break with Rome, Catholics had worshiped in secret, hiding their priests in hollow castle walls called "priest's holes." But in 1844, fifteen years after Catholicism was legalized, the Jesuits built this glorious Victorian Gothic church in an alley running through Hay Hill Farm in Mayfair field, home of the yearly May market. Surrounded by stables called *mews*, the church was dedicated to Our Lady of the Immaculate Conception, but was soon called Farm Street Church. How appropriate, Madeleine thought, that a church dedicated to Mary stood in former stables.

The Jesuit Fathers served the community and became known for their preaching. The neighborhood changed over time, as fields and farms gave way to mansions and parks, soon to be replaced by shops and townhouses, then hotels. Gerald Manley Hopkins wrote and preached at Farm Street; the church had been a spiritual home to the actor Alec Guinness, the novelist Evelyn Waugh, and the poet Edith Sitwell.

A grandfather clock chimed and Madeleine returned to the lobby, where Jack leaned on the counter, in conversation with the concierge.

"I understand, Mr. Walton, but we looked forward to dining here, and there's really no excuse...." Jack's complaint carried a new tone; his former panic had subsided. He spoke with authority, but kindness underlay his words.

Mr. Walton's face held a reserved satisfaction. "I'll take care of it, Mr. Seymour. Simply leave it to me. We'll see you at eight o'clock."

Jack looked relieved as he turned to Madeleine. "It's okay now, Maddie, but they lost our dinner reservation, wouldn't you know it."

"And now we *are* late."

They twirled through the revolving door, past a footman who bowed in greeting, then turned right toward Mount Street.

"We've got a few minutes, Maddie, not to worry."

"But I don't know how they'll begin Mass here. It's Pre-Lent, and they *are* Roman Catholic and sing Latin and all...."

They crossed the street, entered through the gate, and followed a path under bare trees through dormant flowerbeds. Slipping into the church through the back door, they tiptoed past the glittering chancel and down the north aisle to the narthex entrance. The service had not yet begun, but a procession was forming in the south aisle. Madeleine dipped her finger in the baptismal font, made the Sign of the Cross, and followed Jack to a pew halfway down the nave. She dropped onto the kneeler and gazed at the altar, its tabernacle a crèche in a golden stable of light and color.

Above the tabernacle, sculpted saints stood in shallow niches, and above the saints, crimson and teal mosaics portrayed *The Annunciation* and *The Coronation of the Virgin*. Higher still, above the mosaics, apsidal stained glass showed the Madonna and Child bright with glorious rays. Had these images been created three hundred years earlier, rioting dissenters would have smashed them.

From the loft over the narthex a choir sang ancient Latin motets of praise, *"O sacrum convivium, in quo Christus sumitur, recolitur memoria passionis eius, mens impletur gratia, et futurae gloriae nobis pignus datur."* The Mass danced its way through the minutes, a minuet of chants, punctuated by English Scriptures and an English sermon, as the packed congregation followed the Latin phrases in their leaflets and missals. Several robed nuns knelt in the front pew; old and young, working class and wealthy, formed a communion of believers in this act of worship, this Sexagesima Sunday, fifty-seven days before Easter.

Madeleine gazed at the lacy tabernacle with its alabaster doors, then up to the Christ on a white cross, and higher still to the jeweled mosaics of Mary. As she gazed, she thought of time, those rare, precious seconds of life, given from the moment of birth, seconds numbered with each breath, minutes more rare than diamonds, hours more costly than emeralds, days more dazzling than rubies. From her first breath, indeed, before her first breath as she grew in the watery womb, God showered her with these jewels. Yet only recently had she come to appreciate how precious they are. Only now, when her own jewels of time seemed to be fewer and fewer in her shortening span of life, did she understand their worth. *Here we are, nearly buried with this avalanche of love from heaven, and we see trickling sand, not precious stones.*

Madeleine understood there were times when time stood still, when one ruby minute meant only boredom, only waiting, only frustration, only pain. She thought of the eternity of waiting in line, waiting as voice mail played, her life on hold. She knew the seconds in the dentist's chair stretched into years only in her mind, not in real time, and the agony of migraines only *seemed* to swirl forever. She shuddered when she recalled her old nightmares: Mollie disappearing to nothing, those accusing eyes, and her fear of losing Jack to cancer, the reality of his pain. In those moments, imprisoned behind her own bars of blindness, she retreated into a vacuous evil, as the jewels of love turned into stones of suffering. Indeed, there were moments of near despair when she would rattle those bars, hoping to turn those stones back into jewels. For even in her deepest anguish, Madeleine knew Christ could enter her heart and transform each second, minute, hour, and day into diamond joy. He could wake her soul and flood it with light. She need only ask.

"*Missa est.*" The priest carved a cross of blessing in the air. "Mass is over. Go forth in peace."

The organ boomed, and they followed the crowd through open doors and into the heavy mist.

"Let's go to the Savoy for brunch," Jack said as they stepped quickly through the park toward their hotel, "after we freshen up."

Chapter Five
Westminster Abbey

*And what the dead had no speech for, when living,
They can tell you, being dead: the communication of the dead
is tongued with fire beyond the language of the living.*
T.S. Eliot

Sunday brunch at the Savoy River Restaurant was a traditional London affair. Peach draperies looped in Belle-Époque pleats from the ceiling, roses and lilies clustered on white linen tablecloths, and violins played. Through the windows, beyond leafless sycamores, rolled the Thames.

Madeleine wrapped a glistening strip of smoked salmon around a caper and dabbed it in sour cream. "The view *is* better here than our hotel. This is a real treat."

"Joe said to enjoy ourselves, and I'm taking him up on it."

"And the Savoy has such a history. It's like we're having lunch with famous Londoners from the past." Madeleine pulled a leaflet from her handbag.

Jack raised a brow. "Londoners from the past?" His tone carried years of patient acceptance. Jack loved the present far more than the past; Madeleine saw the past as texturing the present, giving it greater depth and meaning.

She read from the glossy page. "In 1243 Henry III gave this riverfront property to Peter of Savoy, his queen's uncle. In the fourteenth century, the palace passed to the Dukes of Lancaster and in 1356 King John of France was imprisoned here."

"Imprisoned?"

Madeleine nodded as she skimmed the text, knowing she was losing Jack's attention. "It was finally taken over by Henry IV. In 1881, D'Oyly Carte built the Savoy Theater for Gilbert and Sullivan."

"Gilbert and Sullivan!" Jack appreciated music. His tenor was smooth and resonant. He had once played the violin, but arthritis had recently stiffened his fingers.

"And eight years later a new hotel was built. Escoffier was chef and Cesar Ritz, manager. European royalty and American stars came. Whistler, Monet, Strauss, Caruso, and Pavlova. The Savoy claimed the first martini and produced the first Peach Melba, named after the singer Nellie Melba."

"I've a new appreciation for the place. Especially Escoffier. Very impressive. And the crowd here is pretty impressive too."

Madeleine scanned the room. Sunday brunch proceeded in a civilized manner. Girls in white tights and patent leather shoes sat properly alongside boys in neckties and navy blazers. Families filled the larger tables, and couples sat along the picture windows. Waiters in maroon jackets sautéed and flambéed and poured sparkling wine, and a light chatter seasoned the slow progress of this traditional Sunday meal.

Madeleine peered into Jack's blue eyes. A few more crow's feet had appeared around the edges. "Jack, I'm glad I married you."

His face lit up. "I'm glad you married me too. It was the best thing that ever happened to me, but to what do I owe this sudden burst of love?" He waved his fork in the air, reminding her of Bertie Wooster.

"I was watching that couple over there, so clearly in love and so young, maybe on their honeymoon. Remember those days?"

"I took you to Trader Vic's on our first date. I remember that." Jack dabbed a bit of pâté in a pool of Cumberland sauce.

Madeleine nodded. "And you included Justin on the second date. Very smart."

"He was eight, nine? We visited Golden Gate Park and Fort Point. Good choices, I thought."

Silently, the waiter removed their empty plates.

"And then I put you to the test." Madeleine recalled how time had pushed her even then. Was Jack the answer to her prayer?

Jack laughed with sudden recollection. "The potluck supper at Saint Thomas'."

"Right."

"We had scrambled eggs cooked by the vestry, an interesting dish, to say the least."

"It was Shrove Tuesday—they use up the last meat products before the Lenten fast."

"On Ash Wednesday."

Their entrees arrived, and Jack looked up from his steaming mixed grill. "I'll never forget the margarine. I guess I'm a bit of a food snob. I like my butter. But I passed the test, right?"

"I wanted to see how you felt about church." Her father, once a devout pastor, had left the faith and his calling when she was sixteen. She had never truly understood why. "Tillich, Russell, Rogers, and the Jesus Seminar," her mother explained with condescension, "proved Christianity a grand delusion, a hoax." Over the years, Madeleine had grown careful with her trust, at least in matters of faith.

"I was lucky you couldn't read my thoughts," Jack said.

"You were used to fancy business dinners. Do you miss that?"

He gazed out to the river. "Not a whit. I've no regrets. Sometimes I wish I'd retired sooner. It's nice to keep my own hours even if we do have to watch our pennies."

"Don't you miss the negotiating, the deals?" Madeleine sipped her water.

"There was a thrill, a high, but it wasn't worth the price, with my ulcers and esophagitis, not worth it at all." He grew thoughtful.

"I suppose not." Madeleine gazed at Jack. He had aged since his bout with cancer, but had returned to her a whole man. "We were worried. Justin was worried. *You* really raised him, Jack."

"Justin was a good kid, *is* a good kid. Although twenty-nine and married isn't exactly a kid, is it?"

"Remember when he ran into you in the church hall and spilled your coffee?"

"How could I forget that suit? I've kept the pants in honor of the occasion. There's a nice big stain that never came out, and in an awkward location."

Madeleine winced, recalling her embarrassment as she had frantically handed him paper towels. "But you were Justin's real father. You gave him your moral compass, your sense of responsibility and hard work. God answered my prayers."

"And you're as beautiful this minute as the day I married you." He raised his glass gallantly.

"Thanks, sweetie." Madeleine's life before Jack had been difficult, fraught with challenge, little sleep, and overwhelming loneliness. How poor they had been, she and Justin, living hand to mouth, paycheck to paycheck, not quite making ends meet. The times slapped her as if they were yesterday.

When their coffee and tea arrived, Jack asked for the check.

Madeleine couldn't shake her sudden sadness. "And Jack, sometimes I think about—"

"Yes, Miss Memory Lane?"

"I think about what would have happened if I hadn't found Saint Thomas', or if you hadn't, or if—"

"What-ifs go nowhere, Maddie."

"I suppose you're right."

"Anyway, any two people who loved good hymns and great organ music were bound to find each other in church, wouldn't you say?"

Madeleine latched onto the happy images, thinking of Farm Street's soaring chants. "Music *is* a kind of perfection, isn't it? It's rather holy, really." She sipped her cappuccino thoughtfully and eyed a creamy white chocolate truffle. "You could say music contains eternity. Maybe all forms of art hold a kind of timelessness or at least pull us out of the moment, into another dimension."

The waiter handed Jack a silver salver with a folded sheet of numbers. "Saint Thomas' certainly has good music and definitely great acoustics." Jack unfolded the sheet as if it held a bomb.

He was both right and wrong, thought Madeleine. The music may have been the means, but she was sure the angels or God himself had brought them together, and she would be forever thankful.

"So where to this afternoon?" Jack slipped his credit card into his wallet. "Westminster Abbey has their famous evensong."

Madeleine recalled young voices soaring into Gothic vaults, a gilded high altar and carved mahogany choir stalls. "Yes, the Abbey."

"The Abbey it is then. But first let's go back to the hotel and rest up a bit." Jack steered her toward the revolving doors.

As Jack napped, Madeleine opened her laptop. She would read and edit, and she would choose the parts of the past she could experience in the present. The wholeness of it appealed to her. And one aspect could feed, color, enhance the other. She found her file on Westminster Abbey, the heart of London's history.

Holy Manifestations: Saint Edward the Confessor and Westminster Abbey

By the eleventh century, midway between Augustine of

Canterbury's mission and Henry VIII's divorce, England had drifted away from Roman control. But the Normans along the French coast changed all that.

During the reign of Danish King Cnut, ten-year-old Prince Edward—next in line to the English throne—was sent to Normandy for his safety. Raised by French monks, he made a holy vow: If he could wear the crown of England, his by right, he would make a pilgrimage to Jerusalem. At the age of forty, he returned to England as king, but the long absence required for a pilgrimage would threaten England's delicate peace. The pope granted Edward a dispensation from his vow, if he would give his journey money to the poor and build a church dedicated to Saint Peter.

Pious Edward noticed a small abbey along the River Thames. On the marshy Isle of Thorns at the mouth of the River Tyburn, struggled twelve poor monks in a priory founded by Saint Dunstan. Edward replaced the priory with a large Romanesque monastery and built his own palace alongside. His abbey and palace (which became Parliament), unified Church and Crown.

The abbey was called *Westminster*—being west of Saint Paul's, *minster* meaning church. With its foundation, Rome, through the king's French Catholicism, renewed its hold on the English Church. Five hundred years before Luther's devout objections and Henry's political maneuvers, Edward, who was an ineffective king but a generous soul, had invited the "Scarlet Woman"—Rome—back to England. He appointed his French Norman friends to clerical livings[3] for which they were often unqualified. The reins of Rome tightened.

Edward died on January 5, 1066, six days after the dedication of his abbey. Harold of Denmark seized the throne but was defeated by Edward's great-nephew, William of Normandy, at the Battle of Hastings that same year. William wove Norman influence and papal order into the English Church, continuing what Edward had begun.

Edward was buried in his abbey in front of the high altar. Beloved by his people for his peaceful reign, his kindness, and his generosity—he gave his army tax to the poor—he was called the Confessor for his pious life and was canonized by Rome. A century later, when Thomas Becket moved Edward's body to a grander shrine in the abbey's choir, the body was found to be incorrupt—undecayed—a sure sign of sainthood. Today his remains rest behind the high altar, the only surviving saint's relics in England, too beloved to be destroyed even by the mobs of the Reformation. Edward's cult grew and his shrine became a pilgrim destination.

The abbey was a place of national mourning, Madeleine thought, and thus a reminder of death, our final earthly destination. Life was so precious, a visit here would be a healthy Pre-Lent ritual, a reminder of God's words to Adam, *Remember o man, that dust thou art, and unto dust shalt thou return.*

Madeleine and Jack arrived in the darkening afternoon in a trundling cab, the wet pavement reflecting light from the streetlamps. They found their way to the chancel and took a seat in the choir before the high altar. Madeleine checked her watch. Evensong would soon begin.

The carved wooden choir was relatively new, but here, through the centuries, monks had chanted the daily offices, those rounds of prayer that joined their own sacrificial lives to their Lord's on the cross. Somehow, this choir and its high altar were the crux, the cross, of England's history with God.

Behind the stalls a wall of gilded tracery rose above the dark wood of the choir to limestone vaults. Madeleine's soul, rooted in her flesh, was like this wood, trying to soar, to fly, to experience another part of her nature, both outside and inside, both eminent and imminent.

Twenty-two boys from the abbey school silently processed in, two by two, robed and serious, hands folded, eyes down, followed by twelve lay vicars and adult choristers, and took their places in the opposite choir, facing the small congregation. The younger ones self-consciously stared into their red folders.

Then they began to sing.

Their voices soared, a trilling stream of larks winging, diving, rising, now gliding smoothly through the vaults, circling the stained-glass saints in the western facade, returning home to the chancel. As the boys sang, Madeleine and Jack followed the 1662 rite in the old prayer books provided, and Madeleine looked up, searching for the famous organ, hidden in the loft over the choir screen. The lessons were read, a canon preached a short homily, and the boys sang the Psalms of Evensong, ending another day in their life, praying to be preserved through the night to wake safe and sound in the morning. They filed out as silently as they had entered, and Madeleine and Jack stepped down from the choir.

"I try to imagine," whispered Madeleine, as they walked down the north aisle to the narthex to view the magnificent Gothic nave from the entrance, "what the medieval pilgrim saw when he entered through these doors."

"You once mentioned something about lots of color."

Madeleine nodded. "There would have been paintings of saints and kings, and walls covered with blues and reds and golds."

"And the stained glass. Even *I* appreciate that sight, although I have a problem with the expense of the thing. This place could have fed more than a few families."

"Certainly the jewels on Edward's shrine could have. But they were stolen by the Reformers, so maybe they did feed a few families, after all."

"Here's Purcell's gravestone. A great composer." Jack paused and studied the script.

Here lies
HENRY PURCELL, Esq.
Who left this Life
And is gone to that Blessed Place
Where only his Harmony
can be exceeded
Obijt 2 J die Novembrs
Anno Etatis sua 37
Annoq Domini 1695

"Thirty-seven was so young," Madeleine said.

"You should appreciate his work. He wrote some of our Anglican prayer settings."

"I'd forgotten. But *you* are the musician in the family, or were. Did you ever play Purcell?"

"No, but I was a big fan of his organ music. Did you know he was organist for Charles II?"

Madeleine looked at her husband. His mind was like a steel trap. Nothing escaped. Where did he read that and how long had it been camping in his brain, waiting to be heard?

"I read it in the guide."

"Ah."

"And it says he probably died of pneumonia."

Tourists and pilgrims ambled up and down the long aisles, staring with wide eyes or studying their guidebooks in the dim light. Madeleine and Jack walked to the foot of the nave, turned, and gazed up at the high vaulted space.

Jack pointed to vast space. "It's immense, like those French cathedrals. The guidebook calls it the Perpendicular style. I can see why."

"But the vertical space is broken by the choir screen. Early on, the congregation was not allowed in the choir. That was monks' territory. The laity sat in the nave." Did they feel distanced from the liturgy, like spectators?

"Shall we do a quick tour and go back to the hotel? Jet lag is hitting me."

"Good idea." Madeleine could feel the time pulling on her too, a dizzying weight behind her eyes. "But I want to find T.S. Eliot's plaque in Poets' Corner."

They found Poets' Corner in the southern transept. Gravestones and plaques covered the floor and walls. Sculpted busts gazed from corners and pedestals. So many great minds and talents, thought Madeleine, forming our Western values, giving us the world we have today: T.S. Eliot, Geoffrey Chaucer, John Dryden, Samuel Johnson, Charles Dickens, Robert Browning, Alfred Lord Tennyson, Rudyard Kipling. Some were buried beneath their words, some only memorialized and buried in other sacred spaces.

"There's Handel," Jack said. "I'd forgotten he was here. Did you know that he wrote the *Messiah* while staying around the corner from our hotel? He was a German court composer for George I. And look at these others. Here's Laurence Olivier."

"And Darwin and Isaac Newton—"

"Hey, I found one whose work I played, Ralph Vaughan Williams. At the age of fourteen," Jack said, tapping his chest with his thumb, "I, poor, skinny Jack Seymour, with his little violin, performed *Fantasia on Greensleeves* at the Oakland Paramount. So what do you think of that?"

"Impressed, but not surprised. Let's peek into that chapel over there." She pointed to a sign that read *St. Faith Chapel.*

"You go ahead. I want to look at these other names."

Madeleine pulled opened a low heavy door in the southern wall, leaving the crowds milling in the abbey. She entered the dusty silence. The only light in the rustic chapel came from a glowing red sanctuary lamp suspended in front of the altar. A fresco of young Saint Faith, a third-century martyr, mysteriously soothing in reds and golds, rose above. Madeleine knelt in the back and focused on the stone tabernacle. As her eyes adjusted to the dark, she could see the form of a girl in the first pew, slumped, holding her head in her hands and moaning softly. What tragedy did she carry to God, what hopelessness possessed her? Her grief weighted the damp air.

From the outer tower far above, muted by thick stone, bells rang five. The girl rose, turned, and hurried out. She was heavy with child, and Madeleine sensed that she had been weeping. Her dark hair fell thick and straight down her back, and as she approached the door, their eyes met briefly. She was Asian and looked to be in her late teens.

"Good evening," Madeleine said, smiling, hoping to comfort her.

"Evening," she murmured.

The door creaked open, and Jack stepped inside.

The girl slipped out of the chapel and into the abbey.

"We'd better make a quick visit to Edward's shrine," Jack said wearily. "We might not have a chance to return."

Madeleine, thinking about the girl, followed him back into the abbey.

They found Edward the Confessor's tomb behind the high altar, and Jack opened his guidebook. "This is where the sick were laid, sometimes overnight, in hopes of healing."

Madeleine touched the bleak stone, a memorial to centuries of veneration and loathing. She tried to focus on the sarcophagus, bereft of decoration, having been dismantled and finally restored under Queen Mary. They stood in the silence, and Madeleine moved the girl to the back of her mind as a familiar bewilderment troubled her. Why did the Puritans destroy beauty? Why did they hate these visual signs of honor? Were they greedy for gold and jewels? She knew they believed images were idols and wanted to purify the Church of heresy. But she would never understand their thinking, no matter how often Jack tried to explain, for Jack, indeed, understood. The church of his boyhood had given him a love of plainness and instilled a fear of image and beauty. He had shaken off taboos on movies, dancing, and alcohol, but the legacies of Wesley and Calvin lingered.

Jack's arm fell on her shoulders, weighted with fatigue. "Come, my dear, let's move along."

They entered the ornate apsidal chapel of Henry VII, housing Henry's remains and those of other monarchs.

"It's overwhelming, Jack. There's so much history, and your

ancestor Jane Seymour isn't even here. She's in Windsor with Henry VIII, right? They say she was the favorite of Henry's queens, but she really didn't have a chance to be anything else, since she died in childbirth, and she *did* produce the wanted son and heir, even if he was sickly."

"Jane was one of the good Seymours. Not all our family were quite so meek and mild. And how can the history professor have too much history? "

"Easy, on our first full day in London. Let's head back."

As they taxied through the glistening streets, Madeleine pondered the young girl in Faith Chapel, so soon to have a child and in such grief. "Jack..."

Jack was scowling at the traffic and the meter's rising tab, and Madeleine saved her thought for another time.

The rain poured, and the taxi rolled around corners, skidding between cars three abreast. They passed Buckingham Palace, the Wellington Monument, Hyde Park, and turned into the lanes of Mayfair. Arriving at their hotel, they stepped into the shelter of the porter's giant umbrella.

They passed through the revolving doors and picked up their key, along with a message, neatly folded. The elevator creaked open. They entered and the tiny wood-paneled box rose slowly, creaking, one floor at a time.

Jack opened the note. "Cristoforo called. We meet him tomorrow at Claridges."

Chapter Six
Brook Street

For my reins are thine;
thou has covered me in my mother's womb.
I will give thanks unto thee, for I am fearfully and wonderfully made:
marvelous are thy works, and that my soul knoweth right well.
Psalm 139:12-14

Victoria Nguyen settled into the Mayfair townhouse of Frederick and Fanny Collingwood. She worked for her keep—cooking, washing, cleaning, and running errands. One morning in mid-December, she watched her hosts from the upstairs landing as they left for work.

"No reason," Fanny said to Frederick, "why the girl can't give us a hand." She studied her image in the foyer mirror and smoothed her short hair, worn combed to the side like her fellow barristers. "God knows she has little enough to occupy her, just watching her belly swell. *I* certainly worked during *my* pregnancy. Why, it was like having an alien in me, but I wasn't going to let it ruin *everything*." She admired her svelte reflection, a product of three-times-a-week aerobics.

"Fine," Frederick agreed, wrapping a wool scarf around his coat collar. His bloodshot eyes spotted Victoria on the stairs, and his gaze softened. He shoved a rain hat over his thinning hair and stroked his substantial nose. "Whatever you decide, my dear." The door slammed behind Frederick's hefty figure, and Fanny soon followed, her briefcase bulging.

Victoria felt only relief with their departure. She had been with the Collingwoods for ten days and she was forming a routine, for she found habit comforting. As they left, she knew the house was hers for the day. She didn't mind the chores Fanny had assigned. The work gave her something to do, something to fill the hours, and it seemed only fair. She had little experience with housekeeping, it was true, but she would learn.

That morning as sleet slanted against the windows, she polished antiques and dusted shelves in the library. Spotting a Jane Austen novel, she set it aside to take to her basement room. She loaded the washer and folded the clothes from the dryer. She nibbled on bits from the fridge for lunch—cheese, fruit, leftovers—and found chocolate ice cream in the back of the freezer. As dusk approached and lights appeared along Brook Street, she began dinner preparations. She heated ham slices and a package of vegetables from a local deli. She tossed a salad. Perhaps she would try real cooking one day, she thought.

She laid her hands on her womb, feeling the living, growing creature roaming within her.

As Frederick walked in the door promptly at six he handed her an envelope. The handwriting looked like her father's. "Seems to be from home," he said and winked.

Her heart pounding, Victoria sat on the stairs and slipped her thumbnail under the fold, the moment dangling before her.

December 10, 2001
Dear Vicky,
I am not good at writing but I will try. First your mother was angry. Then she cried. She says she's sorry. But it is best you stay in London. It is good you left the note explaining you were all right, and I told her I can reach you where you are.

She has so much work to keep her busy. Don't worry about me. I am okay too. I miss you. Remember the baby. Think about the baby. And it will be okay.

I hope Frederick has found you a good doctor. Write to Grandma Nguyen. Say your prayers. Grandma says open your heart. We both send our love and kisses and hugs. I pray for you, my dear Vicky. I think the baby will be a boy.
Love, Daddy

"Everything okay?" Frederick asked from the front salon, as he poured whisky from a crystal decanter.

Victoria stepped into the room and lowered herself onto a damask chair. She nodded and glanced up at him. "Daddy thinks the baby will be a boy."

"Andrew was always thinking things like that," Frederick said, walking to the window. "He predicted weather, good fortune, mail drops.

Too bad he wasn't always right." A flash of memory saddened his flushed face. "Here she comes." He turned toward the door.

Fanny entered and shook her umbrella in the foyer.

Her hair was wet. "It's awful out there."

Frederick set down his drink and helped her out of her coat.

"What a day," she said. "Gridlock. And the case is looking slim, at this point."

"Let me pour you a drink, my pet."

Victoria slipped the letter into her pocket with a secret smile and headed for the kitchen. *Daddy.*

That night Victoria crawled into bed with her letter, angled the light for reading, and felt her baby within her. She was lonely but not alone. The growing child made her feel important and necessary, and she embraced being needed with both physical and emotional gratitude. The child demanded safety and nourishment and love and life. Victoria could provide these things. As her skin stretched to include the other, she knew she nurtured this person with her own blood. The swelling asserted a life of its own and Victoria watched with delight. What would tomorrow teach her? What would the child grant her? What would he demand? Surely, she was a major player in a fantastic, fabulous drama, an ancient act known only to mothers, the creation of a human being.

She reread the letter and set it on the nightstand. She placed her patchwork doll next to her pillow. She opened the Austen and began the first chapter of *Emma*. Soon her lids grew heavy. As she turned out her light, she said an *Our Father*, the only prayer she remembered. She hoped it helped, hoped that God, if he existed, was listening. She patted her baby good night and thought about having a son. Was her father right? He usually was.

It was Christmas Eve, dry and cold. Victoria had finished the dinner cleanup and sat with her hosts in the front salon. A fire blazed in the hearth. Fanny worked at her computer on a desk in the corner. Frederick sipped a brandy, staring into the flames, his forehead pulled together in worry.

Fanny looked up from her screen. "Frederick, why don't you take Victoria to All Saints for the caroling service? It will take your mind off work."

"You come too, my pet." He massaged his brow, then the back of his neck.

"I'm exhausted. You know it's not my thing. I'm going to bed early." She glanced at her watch.

Frederick turned to Victoria. "What do you think, young lady? It's rather chilly outside."

"Only if you want to go." Victoria could see he was enjoying this moment in front of the fire. Was his job stressful? He seemed tired most of the time.

"It *is* Christmas Eve," he said, "and your father would like it, to be sure. We don't do Christmas very well here, I'm afraid. But I recall Andrew is Catholic, isn't he now?"

Victoria nodded with the pleasure of a fleeting memory. "His family is." *Grandma is.*

"Well, All Saints isn't Catholic, it's Anglican, but the verger is my brother Basil, and I could wish him Merry Christmas, or some such thing, I daresay."

"You could do that."

He ran his fingers over the bowl of his glass thoughtfully, then peered at the amber liquid. "Maybe take him a bottle of rum or something. Might be rather jolly."

"That would be nice."

Fanny climbed the stairs. "Have fun." She waved. "Say hello to Basil."

They walked the six blocks in the crisp air, crossing busy Oxford Street and entering a quiet neighborhood where the old church was surrounded by townhouses. A choir sang "Silent Night" in the dim, candlelit sanctuary, and Victoria sang along, sharing a leaflet with Frederick. As her eyes adjusted to the dim light, she saw a red lamp hanging before a stone altar, and to the side of the altar, nestled in a bed of red poinsettias, Mary and Joseph knelt before the baby Jesus.

Every pew was packed, and the smell of musty stone mingled with the pungency of sweet incense. A priest read from a missal about the sacred night, the journey to Bethlehem, the inn with no room. Victoria breathed deeply, seeing the scene—the cold, the strange town, the barnyard. Mary had given birth in a stable. Victoria would manage too, even without a Joseph. She laid her hands protectively over her child and glanced at Frederick. His wide face relaxed, the worry lines gone, as he sang in his deep bass. Others too seemed to have left their cares behind for this one evening and joined their voices in timeless praise and longing. Longing for what? "The First Noel." "Away in the Manger." "Hark the Herald Angels Sing." All familiar songs from another time, another era, songs that cradled her, held her. She clung to the music and the moment so she could relive them later.

As they left the church, Frederick handed the bottle of rum to his brother and introduced Victoria. Basil shook her hand warmly, his gaze resting only briefly on her face and her form, his face full of a quiet happiness. "A pleasure, I'm sure. Lovely service, what?"

"Indeed," Frederick replied. "First rate, old chum."

"Lovely," Victoria agreed, buttoning her jacket. "I'll never forget it."

"Duty calls," Basil said, glancing at the altar. "A merry Christmas to you all!" He spoke as though words could not convey his heart and headed up the aisle.

They stepped into the snowy street. White flakes floated through the night air, light as feathers. Victoria breathed in the cold, stepping through the silence with Frederick, back to Brook Street, the music filling her memory. It was a Christmas Eve like no other, Victoria thought, as she glanced up at the ruddy face of her host. What would Christmas Day bring?

Christmas at home was usually at her grandma's where the small apartment smelled of sage and apple pie, cinnamon potpourri and nutmeg candles, and fresh evergreens on the mantle. There were presents under the tree, ribbons and assorted decorations hanging from the branches. She would miss Christmas this year. Suddenly her heart ached. Grandma Nguyen said to keep her heart open. She would try.

On Christmas Day Fanny and Frederick presented Victoria with a cookbook. Victoria gave them local finds: lemon curd for her and Dunhill tobacco for him. The day was swallowed by the couple's holiday routine. Mr. Collingwood watched sports on the telly in his den, and

Mrs. Collingwood scanned the Internet for local sales, jotting times and places, then worked out on her fitness machines. They shared a goose from Harrods' Food Hall, the trimmings packed in neat foil wrappers, delivered promptly at six. The couple took two days off work, Christmas and the day after, a day they curiously called Boxing Day.

It was on Boxing Day that she met William Collingwood. Frederick and Fanny had mentioned their son, only in passing. They had said that William was "up at Oxford."

The fact that he came home the day *after* Christmas at first perplexed Victoria. Hearing piano music coming from the library, a Mozart piece she guessed, she peeked in. A small blond figure perched on the bench, elbows out, fingers flying. His wiry frame hovered over the keys like an Arthur Rackham faerie, conjuring emerald notes from the shiny baby grand. She stood in the doorway and listened for some time. She couldn't see his face, but the intensity of his presence filled the room.

He stopped abruptly and turned. "Well, now, you must be Miss Nguyen. Welcome to our cozy little home."

The sarcasm was not lost on Victoria. She smiled timidly and offered her hand. He stood, shoved the bench back with his leg, and crossed the room toward her. His handshake was gentle and firm.

"You must be William," she said. He was no taller than she, about five-foot-six.

He bowed from the waist. "At your service." He grinned. His teeth were white and straight, his mouth small. He stared at her facial birthmark and quickly looked away, his pale cheeks reddening. "When's the baby due?" he blurted in an apparent effort to change focus. He moved toward the window and gazed into the street.

"April tenth."

"Ah, my date of ordination, God willing."

"Are you becoming a priest?"

He turned to face her. "Deacon first. Please sit down—forgive my manners."

She lowered herself into a damask chair as he returned to the bench, his back to the piano. "Are you Roman Catholic?" she asked.

"Anglican. Anglo-Catholic Anglican, actually."

"Oh. Your parents must be proud."

"I'm afraid holy orders have not made my parents proud, not even happy."

"I'm sorry."

"But our fights were long ago, and they've grown used to the idea. Even so, my vocation has created a chasm none of us can bridge. I cannot bear Christmas here, especially." He steepled his fingers and looked at them for refuge.

Victoria was surprised at the easy pace of their conversation, as though their phrases were hooked together by an invisible thread. "That's sad. Did your father expect you to follow him in banking?"

"Something like that. Mums wanted me in the law." His voice was edged with sorrow. He glanced away.

"That's hard," Victoria said, speaking from experience.

William nodded. "And *your* family? Have you turned out like they expected?" William eyed her swelling body, shook his head with embarrassment, then walked to the window. He covered his face with his hands. "Sorry," he groaned.

"It's okay." A fire burned in the grate, and the walls of books were friendly. This was her favorite room. "Most people are startled by my face, then my body. I'm used to it." She often said those words to put others at ease, but each time she winced. She shrugged and gazed with understanding at his back, hoping to make him comfortable too.

"I'm such a fool, sometimes. I can never get things right. Maybe God will straighten me out. Do you believe in God, Victoria?"

They chatted quietly all afternoon, as the day fell into dusk and lights appeared in the street below, about God and music and Oxford and the Anglo-Catholics, and what William called the miracle of the Mass. He spoke earnestly and passionately, unlike anyone Victoria had ever known.

"You play the piano beautifully."

"Thank you. Some say so. By the way, I'm performing tomorrow at noon at Saint Martin's with some friends, a small chamber group. Care to come? It's the real reason I'm here."

"I'd love to."

In the month that followed, William returned to London for more recitals, and Victoria found in him a welcome friend. She looked forward to his sudden appearance in the library and a few hours of conversation with the intense young man.

She heard him play at other London churches: Saint James' Piccadilly and Saint Bride's Fleet Street. She wished she had paid more attention in her music appreciation class at Danville Academy for Girls.

The class had been small, an elective with limited enrolment. She chose Music Appreciation because she needed the units and had heard it was fun and easy. But at William's recitals she recalled little about the composers or their concertos, and the music of Bach, Beethoven, and Mozart, while familiar, here seemed somehow new and different, filling her with a surprised delight. The jeweled notes showered over her, and she left each performance feeling slightly changed. Was that the power of art: to create new visions, new ways of thinking? She and William often talked about it afterwards, as they sipped tea in an undercroft café, their words meandering like quiet rivulets intersecting and forming streams.

He listened to her with rapt attention as she spoke of her mother and her father and her life in Danville. "Sounds a bit like Mums," he once murmured, scratching his chin. Never did he push her to explain her current condition, and for that she was grateful. He assured her that she "had made the right choice about the baby and all."

She told him about her friends, Maria and Joanie and Beth, and tried to keep the longing out of her voice. Home was far away, and she missed her former life, a life she could not have. Tennis lessons at the Swensons' and swim parties at the Gallaghers'. Friday night socials with the boys from Town School and ski weekends at Tahoe. She could see that whenever her homesickness became apparent to William, he gently changed the subject, usually to matters of faith.

She tried to understand his world of Christianity, for he continually returned to the subject, often using the word *sacramental*. Her childhood Catholicism, a blend of sayings and loving rules encouraged by her Grandma Nguyen, had been arrested early by her mother's intervention. William spoke of another way, one making sense of the world about them. Man was a selfish, warring creature, a result of the Fall from Grace, when Adam and Eve disobeyed God in the Garden of Eden. He said that man was created by God and could be redeemed through the death and resurrection of his Son, Jesus; that God's spark was in each person. Fed by the Mass and prayer, sanctified by the Church through the sacraments, man could be healed. He could know joy. William spoke of a way that recognized man's wrong turns, yet put him back on the right path. Sin was simply selfishness. If admitted, confessed, sin could be washed away by Christ.

After his last concert in late January, as they sipped tea in Saint Martin's Café in the Crypt, he handed her a card with his name and address. "I won't be back to London for a bit. I've got to get serious about my studies. But if you're ever in Oxford, look me up. Promise?"

"Promise."

Victoria had Saturday off, sometimes Sundays. In other circumstances, she would have shopped for music or clothes, but with her future so uncertain, she saved her traveler's checks. She used her time to see London, walking within a two-mile radius of Brook Street, scanning guidebooks in the nearby Mayfair Library.

She found Dickens' Old Curiosity Shop and toured his home on Doughty Street. She located Dr. Johnson's pub and Sherlock Holmes' Baker Street. She visited the artistic Bloomsbury neighborhood, now medical offices and small publishers, recalling Dorothy Sayers' Harriet Vane, the mystery-writing heroine who lived there, and Lord Peter Wimsey, the aristocratic sleuth in *Strong Poison*. Victoria combed the dusty shelves of Cecil Court booksellers and perched for hours on stools and stepladders, exploring other worlds, occasionally glancing outside through foggy windows to see faces peering in. On these exploring trips, she packed her own lunch—a tuna sandwich, an orange, a carton of milk—and picnicked on a bench. Always aware of her baby, she rested often and shared her adventures as she walked. "Now here is where Handel lived and wrote," she would say, or, as she wound around Soho, "Just look at all these theaters. There must be twenty in three blocks."

She visited the more famous sites too. In Buckingham Palace she toured rooms of state and gaped at gilt ceilings and velvet thrones. She walked through Kensington Palace, the home of Princess Diana, as the guide chatted about royal habits and scandal. She wanted to visit Saint Paul's Cathedral where Diana married Charles. The wedding had occurred before Victoria's birth, but she had seen it replayed often on TV, the Cinderella carriage passing through throngs of waving admirers, the billowing antique satin floating down the crimson carpet, the demure eyes blinking from lowered lids, the powerful glances sealing Diana's marriage with her public.

Victoria hoped to visit Westminster Abbey, the scene of Diana's funeral. She had heard about Poets' Corner, where famous writers, artists, and musicians were honored.

Each day, with its unknown possibilities, offered new enchantments, and each evening she reread her father's letters.

December 23, 2001
Dear Vicky,
I do not believe it is Christmas already. And without you. London must be nice at Christmas. I remember going with you and your mother when you were little. They string lights on Regent Street.

I hope you are okay at Frederick's, and as happy as possible. It finally stopped raining, your mother is jogging, and I am making a surprise for the baby. A late Christmas present. Do not worry. It will be okay. Go to church on Christmas. We will make plans soon.

Love, Daddy

P.S. Your mother is especially sad this time of year. She doesn't understand you or me. She said to say she loves you anyway. She said you mustn't throw your life away on a criminal's child. I said she was wrong. It was still a child. She said that women needed to be strong and independent. I said not this way. She said she had spent her life working for women's rights, how could her own daughter hurt her like this?

I am telling you this, Vicky, so you will understand her better. She means well, but you must not let her find you.

January 5, 2002
Dear Vicky,
Your letter about Christmas was good. Did you like All Saints Church? And the caroling? I am glad you liked the jacket I sent. I am happy the doctor said all is well with you and the baby. Only a few more months, Victoria. We will decide soon. The Christmas present is almost finished. Our secret is still safe. I love you, Vicky. Pat my grandson.

Love, Daddy

The last letter, the one she had dreaded, was the most important.

January 13, 2002
Dear Vicky,
I am sorry but I have to tell you now, I did not want to worry you. Your mother hired a detective. He knows you are in London. The plane tickets gave us away! I will come soon. I will warn Frederick. Stay there for now, Vicky. London is big. She will not find you. Do not worry. It is okay.
    Love, Daddy

P.S. The present is done.

Chapter Seven
Westminster Cathedral

Ten thousand difficulties do not make one doubt.
John Henry Newman

On the first Friday of February, Brother Cristoforo Francesco stood in the narthex of Westminster Cathedral. As he listened to Sister Lucille, casually dressed in sweater and slacks, he ran his large hand over the rough brown cloth of his robe. He leaned down toward the young nun, hoping to shorten his six-foot-five height and put her at ease, and composed his face with what he hoped was an interested and friendly expression, his lips closed to cover his silver tooth. He knew his dark scarred face and fanning Afro were sometimes seen as threatening, yet she seemed undaunted, thoroughly absorbed by her words. But to Cristoforo's ears, her words sped too fast, up and down and gone; he studied her lips to follow the racing English lilt.

Cristoforo nodded as though understanding, then turned his eyes again to the glorious apse. He had been with the community for a week, helping at the hostel as he had been instructed to do, but he coveted his time in the sanctuary.

Lucille adjusted her thick glasses. "Now, Brother...Cristoforo, is it? Are you listening? You're visiting from Rome, and you must learn about the Catholics in England and our cathedral. The superior insisted."

"*Si*, Sister." He continued to gaze at the high altar's magnificent crucifix, a giant suspended Franciscan crucifix, the Christ painted in reds and golds.

"We will walk while I read. Mother Catherine wrote the text herself, and, you need to know, she's considered a poet in her own right, a kind of historian-poet. Mother Catherine says poetry can express reality better than facts."

The monk thought they made an odd pair—he so tall and she so short, he so dark and she so fair—as they began to tour the immense church. Sister Lucille held her leaflet close to her myopic eyes as Cristoforo stared at the marble pillars and side chapels. She read aloud in a high, reedy voice:

> "The Benedictine monks of Edward's Westminster Abbey drained the surrounding swamp called Bulinga Fen for a market ground. When Henry VIII dissolved the religious orders and their works, the land became a maze, then a garden, then a bull-baiting ring. A prison was erected in the seventeenth century, and, finally, the Roman Catholic Church purchased the land in 1884.

"Are you listening, Friar?"
"*Sì*, and thank you, Sister, for I do not read English well."
Lucille nodded and continued:

> "The Irish Potato Famine of 1845-49 flooded England with Catholic refugees, creating a need for Catholic churches. In 1850, the pope granted the English their first cardinal and archbishop in three centuries. But Protestant England cried 'no popery,' for they remembered Queen Mary's executions, just as Catholic England remembered Queen Elizabeth's. Cardinal Wiseman was burned in effigy on Bethnal Green, but his Appeal to the English People eased the threat. By 1884 Catholics searched for a site for their cathedral."

Lucille led him midway up the nave where they sat in a pew before the suspended crucifix. Cristoforo felt Lucille's gaze as he looked upon the Christ, the painted image a warm reminder of home.
Lucille returned to her leaflet:

> "The Cathedral Church of Westminster was dedicated to The Most Precious Blood of Our Lord Jesus Christ. Within eight years, it rose on the old marsh-turned-prison ground. The architect, John Francis Bentley, designed an Early Christian Byzantine cathedral with a three-domed nave leading to the altar. The red brick outer walls reflected Victorian London. The marbled inner walls spoke of Renaissance Rome."

Lucille breathed deeply and adjusted her glasses:

"A Franciscan crucifix hangs suspended before the altar. The baldachin is supported by four golden columns and the chancel's arch is covered in vivid blue-and-white mosaics."

They turned up the north transept to an ornate side chapel where several people knelt before a marble altar. A red sanctuary lamp burned. Lucille dropped her voice to a whisper:

"The Blessed Sacrament is reserved in a chapel off the north transept for adoration and thanksgiving. The entrance mosaic portrays Archangels Michael and Gabriel, and thus one must walk under their guardian gaze. The side wall mosaics prefigure Christ's Passion: Abraham offers Isaac; a lamb burns on an altar. Above the tented tabernacle a mosaic depicts a cathedral built on a rock. Four rivers pour into the floodwaters beneath, mirroring the incarnate God on the altar below who pours out his rivers of grace."

Lucille turned, and Cristoforo followed her down the north aisle, his leather sandals sliding over the stone floors. They paused before a side chapel and the nun continued:

"John Southworth's body lies in a chapel off the north aisle. Father Southworth was dedicated to the poor of Westminster. Vocal in his Catholic beliefs, he was hanged, drawn, and quartered at Tyburn in 1654, under Cromwell's Protectorate."

Cristoforo shuddered, and felt for the crucifix under his robe. *Such a death for such a life.*

"When civil war brought Puritan rule in 1641, laws restricting Catholics were sometimes enforced. Priests were sentenced a traitor's death. Secrecy became a way of life for many Catholics. They educated their children in secret and cared for their poor. They sent their young men to France under assumed names to be schooled and ordained. When these clergy returned, they hid in walled cavities. They said Mass in secret."

As Lucille read on, the friar found himself listening closely to the story of these terrible days and this dedicated priest:

"John Southworth returned from his seminary training in Douai, France. After working in Lancashire, he was arrested and sent to the Clink prison in London, then was paroled to work among the poor. For twenty years, through plague and famine, he fed and clothed them with funds collected from other Catholics. He nourished them with the Mass, heard confessions, and administered last rites. Finally, he faced execution."

Cristoforo did not think he would have such courage.

"The quarters of his body were retrieved by a Catholic family, sewn together and embalmed. The relics were taken to Douai and venerated. During the French Revolution they were secretly buried for safety. In 1927 workers uncovered the coffin, and the relics were returned to Westminster Cathedral.

Today his work continues in the Cardinal Hume Center. Food and lodging, education and guidance, daycare and medical services are offered to the young homeless."

"Ah, Sister, I would wish to be like him."

Lucille nodded, and they turned toward the narthex. As they walked, Cristoforo noticed a woman sitting in a back pew reading a guidebook. A boy knelt behind her. A small hand flashed forward and back, then the lad fled through the cathedral doors.

Cristoforo glanced at Lucille, who continued reading. "Please excuse me, Sister, I return soon."

Lucille looked up. "What? But, Brother—"

Running out to the porch, the friar saw the boy dart across the broad courtyard, toward the main road. "You there," he cried. "Stop!"

The monk wove through the crowd and down the wide sidewalk toward the Army and Navy Store. There, on the corner, his long arm found its target, a dirty neck scarf. The scarf tightened, the child fell, and Brother Cristoforo laid thick hands on thin shoulders. The shoulders rose with a jerk, twisting to escape.

A bobby sauntered over, scanning the heavy traffic and storefronts.

"My son," Cristoforo said with a firm kindness, "you must return what you borrowed."

"I didn't borrow nothing." Green eyes peered from under a frayed wool cap. One shoulder appeared lower than the other, and a jagged scar ran along the jaw line. Cristoforo traced his own jaw with his finger.

The policeman rested his palms on his hips. "Take your cap off in front of the Father. Show him respect now." He reached for the child's cap, and a nest of red hair, darkened with grime, tumbled out.

A girl. Cristoforo was surprised. She couldn't have been much older than ten years of age—or a small twelve, he thought.

"Now you've done it." The girl squirmed under Cristoforo's grip.

"Empty your pockets, please," the bobby said.

"*S*–" She turned out the pockets of her stained bomber jacket. A wallet fell out. "I suppose I'm going to jail now."

Cristoforo retrieved the wallet. "Not for borrowing. It is my friend's, Officer, and we shall return it. I—we—do not make charges, Officer."

The bobby looked him over. "You with the shelter?" he asked doubtfully.

"I am, sir."

The policeman eyed the girl, then the monk. "I *should* make a report." He patted his nightstick with one hand and searched for a pen with the other.

"As you wish, Officer." Cristoforo's hand still gently gripped the girl's thin arm.

The policeman's mobile phone rang, and he raised it to his ear. "Yes sir, right away, sir." He pulled his brows together with importance. "I've another call. You may go, but take responsibility for her." He glared at the girl and shook his finger in her face. "You'd better not be seen around here again, lassie. And I mean it. No second chances with me." He lumbered into the crowd.

Like a mother cat, Cristoforo shifted his hand to the back of the girl's neck and gently steered her toward the cathedral. He prayed that the wallet's owner was where he had left her, in the back pew, reading her guide and gazing toward the chancel.

He handed the woman her wallet. "I believe, madam, you misplaced this."

"What?" She turned a startled face toward him. "What have you done? Oh, thank you, Brother. I'm sorry, I didn't realize. Where did you find it?" Her eyes moved to the figure peering out behind the monk's robe.

"Be careful, madam. Hold onto your handbag, please. There are many pickpockets in London."

Cristoforo led his young charge up the north aisle and into the Holy Sacrament Chapel. "Kneel," he said.

"I don't have to."

With a careful tenderness, Cristoforo guided her to a kneeling position. "You see that?" He pointed to the altar.

"Yeah, I see that—a lot of rich stuff that don't do no good."

"Do you see the white tent?"

"Yeah, so?"

"God is in there."

The girl rolled her eyes. "Yeah, right."

"He is." Cristoforo leaned toward her earnestly.

"You believe that? You're cracked worse than my last pa."

"I *do* believe God is there." The monk looked back to the Sacrament, his heart beating hard.

"And I suppose you want me to apologize to God."

"I do."

The child's hands gripped the top of the pew-back. She opened her palms, as though to humor this madman. "Sure, if it makes you happy and being you saved me and all."

"Do it."

"Okay, I'm doing it. I'm sorry, God." She cocked her head, glancing at Cristoforo from beneath her lids.

"You have to say what you are sorry for."

"I'm sorry I took the wallet, God." She turned to the monk. "Is that good enough?"

"No, it is not good enough. You have to say you will not do it again."

"Okay, okay. I won't do it again, God."

"God has forgiven you, my child."

"Great. Now can I go?"

"No, come with me." He placed his hand on her thin shoulder, feeling the tiny bones, and led her through a door, down a long outer corridor and into another building. "Would you like some soup?"

"Now we're talking."

"What is your name?" Cristoforo asked, as Sister Lucille bustled toward them.

"Uh...I don't have to tell you."

"Yes you do."

"Uh, Nadia...Nadia. My name's Nadia."

"Nadia what?"

"Nadia...er...West."

"All right, Nadia West, may I present Sister Lucille. She will give you something to eat and maybe more. You do what the sister says. I am happy to meet you, *Signorina* West." Cristoforo held out his hand. Nadia ignored it and looked toward Lucille.

Cristoforo returned to the chapel. He fell on his knees before the Sacrament housed in the white tent on the golden altar. He knew this Presence of Christ was his only hope as his fingers touched the long scar under his beard. He barely sensed the huge nave of light and glittering chancel that stretched to his right or the walls of green and pink marble. They were only spaces, spaces of prayer and sacrament, territories of God's presence on earth. It was God himself that he needed now.

"Help me, Lord, for I am weak." He pulled out his rosary. As his big fingers caressed the small beads, he began the ordered round of prayers, visualizing scenes from Christ's life. The prayers usually steadied him, kept the demons at bay, but today the girl had opened a door long closed. He had seen others like her on the London streets and in Rome as well, but her scar, so like his own, wrenched him back forty years to his Alexandrian childhood.

He was seven. They had met him at the door, the men in their turbans, waving their scimitars, but he had jumped in time to miss the full thrust. He could taste the blood again, and the fear. He had run and hid, coward that he was, yes, he had run and hid, but had seen it all as the blood streamed down his face. The swords flashed quickly, slicing off his mother's head, then his father's, then his baby sister's—dear God, how could they do that to Sophia? And then, the red pools deepening, they had done the unthinkable: They had cut open his mother's belly and removed the baby growing there, and they had laughed, stabbing even this tiny life. He had heard horses and the cry, "What about the boy?"—then the pounding of hooves, vanishing into the distance.

Cristoforo was beginning the Glorious Mysteries when he raised his eyes to the tabernacle. Were flames shooting from the altar? Was a dove flying from the top of the white tent? He blinked his eyes, and the vision was gone. Still, a familiar peace filled him, and he rose to find the next Mass time, for he had a great hunger for his Lord, a great hunger indeed.

Saturday morning, sitting at a trestle table in the hostel dining room, Cristoforo poured canned milk on his porridge. The friar ate quickly, listening to the chatter and bustle of the young boarders. He would miss his work here when the Seymours no longer needed him in London.

Sister Lucille approached and handed him a worn envelope, postmarked Italy. "It came like that—I didn't open it."

Cristoforo unfolded a sheet of lavender-scented paper, neatly scripted. His superior had a flare for the artistic.

27th January, 2002
Order of Friars Minor, Rome
Dear Son,
You have not reported on your activities, and you have been in London over a week. I pray you are serving well the community at Westminster Cathedral. Please report by return mail.
Do not forget your rule and your vows, your vocational heritage. Please keep me informed of your progress with Coronati House Foundation. Signore McGinty, the Board Chairman, is in Rome and sends his best regards to you and the Signori Seymours.
+ Bernardo, O.F.M.

Cristoforo frowned into his porridge. He would try to meet with the Seymours on Monday, but he knew he had to return home soon.

Lucille picked up his empty bowl and, with a clattering of plates, woke him from his reverie.

"I am sorry, Sister, I am sorry. I will help." He slipped the letter into his pocket and received the stack of plates, then walked to the kitchen where he sunk the dishes into a deep basin of steaming sudsy water. Here, washing dishes, he had known his best meditations. He considered the example of Father Southworth, and he considered the many who needed to hear of his Lord.

He would return to Rome soon—soon, but not yet.

Chapter Eight
Oxfordshire

We can believe what we choose.
We are answerable for what we choose to believe.
John Henry Newman

Around noon on Sunday, Brother Cristoforo looked out the window as the train pulled out of Paddington Station, heading for Oxford. London's outskirts passed by: sooty warehouses and heavy machinery fenced with barbed wire, tenements with clothes drying on lines stretched over narrow balconies. It would be good, he thought, to get out of the city and preach in the country, just like the friars of old, and Nadia could help. Her jacket lay in a rumpled heap on the seat next to him and cast off a sour smell. He hoped she would return from the restroom soon. Sister Lucille sat opposite, reading.

Cristoforo eyed the nun's slacks and sweater. "I thank you for coming with us, Sister." Did all English nuns dress like this? How would people know she was a nun if she didn't wear a habit? Many Roman nuns wore black robes. Some wore pure white, some pale blue. He was proud of his coarse brown tunic. Father Rinaldi, who had been both father and priest in Rome, had given it to him when he made his vows over twenty years ago, and Cristoforo wore it with love and a deep satisfaction. Now patched in a few places, it served him well and would continue to serve him well. He ran his hand along a sleeve, feeling the rough fabric.

Sister Lucille laid her paperback on a foldout table and smiled tentatively. Cristoforo sounded out the title, moving his lips: *A History of the English Church.*

The nun leaned toward him, and he feared a lecture. "My superior didn't want Nadia to go alone with you."

"It was your idea, Sister Lucille, that Nadia come." He, for sure, had not welcomed this plan.

"Nadia begged me, and I thought it would be good for her to get out and into the country."

"*Si*. She will help, perhaps. And you will be our guide."

"More than guide, Brother Cristoforo, a chaperone. The world does not trust us. You know how the media loves these stories." She tapped her finger on the armrest.

Her protruding front teeth were crooked like the friar's own, her watery eyes framed by tortoise-shell glasses, her straight hair cut short with no bangs. Her hair was the color of wheat soaked by the rain, and Cristoforo had a sudden memory of late summer storms in Tuscany.

"*Si*, Sister. I understand. Thank you."

"What, exactly, *are* you doing? Please explain your plans."

"My plans, yes, my plans." Cristoforo gazed out to the vanishing red brick houses, the suburbs slipping away like smoke up a chimney.

The silence pushed him to speak. "Sister, my plans are to preach the love of God."

"Preach? But have you made arrangements in Oxford? Did you clear a church or hall with the bishop? Do you have permission, for that matter, to preach at all?"

He pulled out his mobile phone. "If you like, I will call ahead?"

"It's a bit late for that." She waved the phone away. "You can't simply walk in and commandeer a location. And where will we stay? You made no reservations? The sisters said it was all taken care of. Thank God I came with Nadia."

Cristoforo locked his dark eyes on her pale ones, hoping to win her trust. "We will stay, Sister, in the local youth hostel."

"And the bishop?"

"He will not mind that I preach. I shall direct my people to his priests for confession, absolution, the Eucharist, and all spiritual guidance."

"It is most unorthodox."

"Perhaps yes, perhaps no." Once again he saw the friars preaching in the hills; he saw Christ preaching on the mountain.

Lucille returned to her book, her features lined with worry.

"You like history, Sister?" Cristoforo said, hoping for peace. He understood that she worried, that she desired control, that fear shadowed her. He could see she had a good heart, if perhaps a small one.

Lucille set her book down and gazed at the monk. "It helps," she said, her tone wary.

"How does it help?"

"It helps me understand," she said, looking surprised by her own words. "And this book was recommended to me by my superior, so I trust it, although it *is* written by an Anglican."

She picked up the book, opened it, and thumbed the pages as though the answer lay hidden in the paper and ink. She turned toward him. "History helps me understand our world. I've never felt a part of it, you see, and it helps me...*connect*. I've had little schooling. My parents spent their savings on my brother. He's a barrister now. They're proud of *him*."

Cristoforo saw in a flash the depths of her loss, and his own chance—or command—to fill it. "Then, please, *per favore*, would you be so kind, while Nadia is finding the restroom, to read to me from your book?"

Lucille looked grateful. "I will, Brother. This bit's on Oxford, naturally, since we're traveling there. I've never been to Oxford myself."

"Nor have I been to Oxford."

Lucille adjusted her glasses and began:

"The Romans considered Oxford unhealthy, but the Saxons founded a community where oxen could ford the rivers Thames and Cherwell. Legend says the Saxon Princess Frideswide established a monastery along the shore in 727 in gratitude to God for delivering her from an unwanted marriage. Today, Christ Church College occupies the site of the monastery."

Lucille glanced up, and the monk bent forward eagerly, clasping his hands, offering his full attention.

"By the twelfth century, private teachers in various disciplines gathered small schools of pupils. After a dispute between pupils and townspeople in 1209, a papal charter restored order and created a university."

Cristoforo heard a sad longing when she said *university*.

"Friars following the rule of Saint Francis arrived in England in the 1220s to educate their brothers and recruit students. Barefoot and poor, they preached in town squares and fields. They believed many faithful did not understand the action of the Latin Mass and treated it lightly. The friars set out to explain the mystery, to preach the first-century gospel recalled in the Mass."

Lucille looked up. "Is that what you're doing?"
Cristoforo nodded. "I am, Sister, I am." While the friar could not read and write English well, he had heard many sermons preached by English priests visiting Rome. He could express himself with speaking if not with writing, of that he was sure.
Lucille appeared thoughtful as she read on.

> "These monastic teaching communities of Oxford—friars and students—evolved into today's colleges, making up the university. The school prepared students for Holy Orders, and, as the Church grew more at one with the Crown after Henry VIII's break with Rome, the priesthood became a requirement for government positions. Church and State were nearly indivisible.
>
> By the eighteenth century, the Church had grown corrupt: pluralism gave numerous clerical livings to a few aristocratic clergy. The absent clergy assigned vicars to work their parishes and turn over the stipends. The vicars, often uneducated, some not even ordained, produced an uneducated laity. They were soon performing mysterious rites for themselves, by themselves. The people came to watch, then ceased to come. There was little respect for the Church in England."

Lucille paused. "Do you follow all this, Brother?"
He nodded. "A few priests made the others work, then took home their offerings."
"Precisely." She looked at him with satisfaction, and turned back to the text.

> "But Oxford breathed new life into the Church through the student John Wesley. Wesley and his fellow scholars rededicated themselves to the rule of the Anglican *Book of Common Prayer*. They gathered to read Morning and Evening Prayer, attended weekly Mass, and observed a disciplined life in contrast to the worldly clergy in their disintegrating Church. They called themselves Methodists because of the rule they followed."

Lucille paused. "My parents are Methodists."

"Are they, Sister? The Methodists have done good things. Please, continue with your reading." It was another piece of Lucille, another part of her world. The pieces of a person fit together, he thought, but not always the way the person would like. God did the best job, of that the friar was certain. It was mankind who made a muddle of the pieces.

Lucille resumed her reading.

"In the 1730s, Wesley traveled the countryside and preached this renewed, disciplined dedication to God. In a way, the friars had returned, and the people responded to the fire and love of God channeled through this man and his followers. They appreciated anew the Church's sacraments made real in the Real Presence of Christ and in righteous living, the method of the Methodists.

But Wesley could not change the Church of England. Upon his death, his followers created their own sect and left the Anglicans to try again. In the nineteenth century, Oxford would again provide seeds of such renewal, as another group of devout men sought to bring back sacramental life.

These scholars called for a return to belief in the Real Presence and thus a renewed sense of worship. They demanded a greater separation between Church and State, mourning the politicization of the clergy. The university opened its doors to lay students. This Oxford Movement re-seeded the English Church with catholic belief and practice, seeds that continue to bear fruit to the present day."

"Now why," the friar said, "do you think they made such a fuss? Why not become Roman Catholics, members of the true Church?"

"I don't know. I became Roman Catholic, in spite of my parents."

Lucille looked out to the green countryside as though searching for something long lost. She breathed deeply, then returned to her book.

"The Oxford Movement spawned numerous Anglican monastic orders throughout England. These brothers and sisters led a life of prayer and work, and were most effective in city slums. The many women's orders included the Sisters of Mercy in Plymouth (1848), the Community of Saint Mary in Wantage (1848), and Saint Margaret in East Grinstead (1854). In 1865 Charles Grafton from America and R.M. Benson began the first men's order in Cowley—the Society of Saint John the Evangelist—and later, in 1892 Charles

Gore established the Community of the Resurrection, today located in Mirfield. Anglican Benedictines settled in Nashdom in 1926 and Anglican Franciscans at Alton Abbey five years later. Charles Grafton returned to America to establish the House of the Holy Nativity in Providence, Rhode Island, and later become Bishop of Fond-du-lac, Wisconsin."

Cristoforo tapped his thick fingers together. "They sound like men seeking God and worshiping him in the Mass. That is good." He glanced at the door at the far end of the car, worried about Nadia. He never should have let her out of his sight.

"Shall I finish?"

"Please do, Sister." Where had the girl gone?

"There's only a bit left.

"These religious houses represented traditional branches of Roman spirituality. They sought to return to pre-Reformation days and looked to the early Church. They desired union with Rome rather than division. Anglicans had abandoned the Eucharist, they argued, and therefore abandoned a vital conversation between Christ and his people, his Body on earth. To cut off the Body of Christ from the Body and Blood of the Mass was suicide. The early Christians clearly understood the Holy Supper to be spiritual food, necessary to the unfolding of God's great plan for the salvation of the world."

"Please forgive me, Sister, but I must find Nadia."

At that moment Nadia appeared in the doorway, balancing herself against the sway of the train. Her pockets bulged.

"And what have you there, young lady?" Lucille demanded.

"A kind man gave me some snacks. Please, ma'am, would you like some?"

Lucille eyed the pockets suspiciously. "I think not. He *gave* them to you?"

"Nadia," the friar said, "I would be most honored to share your snacks." He raised his brows and cocked his head hopefully. "Any chocolate?"

"Aye, Father." She moved the jacket and sat beside him, pushing a frizzy strand of hair from her eyes. Her hair, now clean, was ribboned with strands of burnished copper.

"*Allora*, let us see." He rapped the table with anticipation.

Nadia emptied her pockets and laid out her treasure. The friar bent his head close to hers, and they examined the candy bars and cookie packets. Lucille returned to her book. Cristoforo sensed that, at that moment, Nadia had the greater need.

He was not unlike Nadia, when, as a boy, a kindly friar had taken him in.

Cristoforo Francesco's nightmares of his childhood in Alexandria were nearly washed away by his memories of good Father Rinaldi of Rome. As a boy, Cristoforo had scrabbled for crumbs and shelter day to day. It was in the heat of summer that he spotted a short monk shuffling along a dusty lane near the bazaar. The monk was rubbing his beads, staring into the sky, and the boy figured him an easy target. But Cristoforo's fingers slipped as he pulled the wallet from the belted pouch. The monk turned abruptly, seized him by the shirt, and guided him to an attic room above a bookseller. When he learned the boy had no family, he took him home to his monastery in Rome. There he baptized him, renaming him Cristoforo, "after Our Lord," and Francesco, "after our founding saint."

Over the years, when Cristoforo remembered that trip, the old sense of salvation lifted him and carried him lightly away from the Alexandrian street-life of death and despair. He recalled the steady hand pulling him along the dirt road, the warm water of his first real bath, and the metal bowl of ewe's milk the monk produced. Each time he recalled these things a delirious relief returned and washed him anew. The pains in his stomach had receded, and his skin—ah, his skin—tingled with life, scrubbed clean. He floated.

He was seven when his new life began, his real life, his safe life. His earlier world still haunted him, phantoms in the dead of night, but with each passing year the horrors receded a little further. He helped the nuns of the neighboring convent, washing, cleaning, and repairing. He grew a garden, finding intense pleasure in plunging his fingers into the soil, working it, then dropping seeds carefully into deep beds. The tiny shoots that miraculously rose from the earth in some way raised him, too, and he knew a contentment rare in adolescence.

He had served Mass in the conventual chapel of Quattro Coronati, a medieval fortress-church guarding Rome from the top of the ancient Coelian Hill. Father Rinaldi taught him where to stand before the altar, how to hold the linen and the cruets of wine and water, what prayers to say and when to say them. Each action and each word possessed great meaning, and the boy absorbed the ritual, weaving it into his soul. The order pleased him; his job was clear, with a purpose, both here and in eternity. In a way, he often reflected, he assisted the Ultimate Calling, the calling of God into the created world, the pulling of the infinite into the finite. He understood this at an early age, and it was his idea to place the nativity crèche on the altar on Christmas Eve, uniting the Child in Bethlehem with the Christ in the tabernacle.

The God he called was Father Rinaldi's God, a God of eternal love, like Father Rinaldi. In his early years, Cristoforo merged the two—the priest and his God—and with each Mass his love for the man took on tones of worship. But as the boy matured, he grew in wisdom, and he knew there was more, that Father Rinaldi was a temple, a tabernacle, a channel for an even greater love. Cristoforo searched for the greater love and found it in each Mass, in the great sacrifice of Christ. He took Franciscan vows when he was eighteen, joyful and expectant.

Chapter Nine
Holloway

He uses material things
like bread and wine to put the new life into us.
We may think this rather crude and unspiritual.
God does not: He invented eating. He likes matter. He invented it.
C.S. Lewis

The train rolled into Oxford, and Cristoforo awaited the Holy Spirit's directions. A bus might take them even further into the countryside. Which bus? He chose the one going to Holloway, its destination lettered large over the driver's window, a town that sounded like it needed filling. Twenty minutes later, the friar disembarked with Lucille and Nadia. He paused on the sidewalk and gazed down the quiet main street with its neat houses and shops toward a steeple that rose over the rooftops. Lucille pointed and headed down a side lane toward the church. Nadia ran ahead.

The friar questioned where this would lead, but followed, sensing it was right. When he reached the end of the lane he saw Nadia and Lucille in conversation with an elderly woman on the church porch. A neatly lettered sign on the door read *Sacred Heart Catholic Church.*

"Mrs. O'Malley is going to help us," Lucille explained, turning to Cristoforo. "And we can stay in the guest rooms in back."

Nadia wandered to the side of the church where gravestones parted the grass.

A wide freckled face looked up at Cristoforo. "We'll do what we can, Brother...Cristoforo, is it? A pleasure I'm sure." She offered a stubby hand. "I'll call around to the ladies of the parish. Holloway could use a bit of a stirring up. Why, the sermon this morning was about that very idea." She wore a white lace chapel cap, fastened to thinning gray hair with a bobby pin.

"Thank you." Cristoforo looked at Lucille as the steeple bell rang two.

"They're going to help us with refreshment," the nun explained as she watched Nadia run among the graves.

"She's sprightly, now, isn't she?" Mrs. O'Malley grinned, showing long yellow teeth. "Reminds me of my granddaughter. Lots of energy, that one!"

"And you'll inform your priest?" Lucille implored as she moved toward Nadia.

"Yes, dearie, of course, now don't you worry about a thing." She placed a thick-veined hand on the friar's arm. "And I know the perfect place for your preaching, Brother. There's a hillside just beyond there." She pointed over the graves to a gentle slope with high grass. "But it might be a bit muddy with the recent rains. The neighbors use the land for grazing, but the cows won't pay you any mind. Haven't seen any today. Must be on the other side."

"*Grazie, Signora.*"

She clapped her hands. "Why, you're from Italy! I knew it! Maybe even *Rome?* A godsend indeed! Now you just think about what words you want to say and leave everything to me."

The friar nodded, his pride surging, and he steepled his fingers with gratification, bowing slightly from the waist. "I am indeed from Roma, *Signora.*"

The elderly woman rubbed her hands with pleasure. "Excellent. You have been sent by God. We had some troublemakers on that hill over the summer—screamed awful things at us down here in our little church. Lit a fire, they did. We had to put it out. We even cared for the young folks later...a few got burned, you see. Maybe you can make it a holy hill again, Brother."

Lucille returned with Nadia in tow.

"I will do that, *Signora.*" Cristoforo was pleased with this unfolding of events.

Mrs. O'Malley put her arm around Nadia. "We must make a sign for you to carry down the main street. And ring a bell. I'll find one. Can you do that, my dear?"

Nadia's face lit up. "Sure can, ma'am."

"And Sister Lucille, you help her, and I'll arrange my ladies."

His eye rested gratefully on the two women, Nadia huddled between them, and the friar offered a silent prayer of thanksgiving.

Within the hour, the monk stood on the muddy hillside in the high grass. The February wind caught his robe and wrapped it around his bare shins and sandals. The thick socks *Signore* Seymour had sent him now had holes, and an icy wetness seeped into his skin.

Once again, the joy and expectancy of his early years with Father Rinaldi returned. He would pass on the great gift he had received, this gift of God's love, just as his old priest, God rest his soul, had passed it on, and others would be lifted along the same wave of safety, certainty, and, above all, delight. He would preach like the Franciscans preached, seven hundred years ago, and like Saint Francis himself, urged by a force grand and compelling, an eternal star bursting in his soul.

The crowd was mixed. There were local villagers who must have seen Nadia's sign and heard her bell; some motorcyclists, their hair spiked, stopped by; a few hunters in their gear had wandered from the neighboring manor house. Around thirty souls, the friar thought. He scanned the crowd, desperately wanting them to understand, to understand how it all went, how it fit together.

"So what have you made of your life?" Cristoforo cried as he raised his arms, palms open, to the skies.

The crowd quieted.

"God gives us free will...to choose."

"Ha!" someone shouted from the back. "I've had little choice in my f— life."

Cristoforo winced at the language—the violence slapped him like a sudden blow—but he sought the man's eyes. "It seems so, many times. But I speak of a different choosing. And with this choosing, all choosing is easy." He clapped his hands together.

"Sure," the man shouted back, his voice edged with cynicism. He shook his head, waiting.

The friar continued. "We choose good or we choose evil. We choose God or we reject God."

The crowd moved about, but they were listening.

"Now, what happens with each choosing? A long time ago, David the shepherd boy said, *'To him that ordereth his way aright, will I show the salvation of God.'* This is true today. But what if we reject God?"

Cristoforo shoved his hands into the deep pockets of his robe and stared at the mud oozing through the new grass. He noticed a broken strap on one of his sandals. No one had told him how cold the winter would be in England, and how wet.

"If we reject God, we have no way of knowing right from wrong. God makes the rules, does he not? No God, no rules. So you say, *bene*, I drink more beer, come home late, do no work, pay no rent. My children go hungry. In the beginning no rules are *bene*, good. But soon comes sadness. Soon comes despair. And despair, my friends, is death. Death in life. This you know, I believe."

Some nodded, glancing at one another.

"And," Cristoforo said slowly, with some fear that he dared to say such a thing, "Saint Paul writes, *The Lord Jesus shall be revealed from heaven with his mighty angels, in flaming fire taking vengeance on them that know not God, and that obey not the gospel of our Lord Jesus Christ: who shall be punished with everlasting destruction from the presence of the Lord, and from the glory of his power.* That, my friends, is a good reason to choose God. But each of us must choose."

The crowd had grown quiet and the gunning motors of the nearby highway, muted by the creeping fog, had become a soft drone. Cristoforo spread out his arms as if to embrace the world, even this foggy marsh.

"Say we choose God. What does that mean?"

"It means," someone shouted with an American accent, "you're stuck in the f— church when you can be at the rugby game!"

It was the young man in the black jacket, the friar saw, one of the bikers. Was that Nadia holding her sign, beyond the bikers, at the foot of the hill near the road? He thought so, and he could see Lucille with her. Good.

Cristoforo breathed deeply, realizing he must speed this up. He was losing them. "Choosing God means choosing love. *Allora*, allow me to explain. Rules order our lives, make us happy. Choosing God means we live *forever*. Our lives matter for all eternity."

They were listening. Cristoforo moved down the hill, closer to his people. "God became man, Jesus Christ. Christians believe in this man. We know him, as you know me or I know you. We believe in a person, not ideas, but a person alive today, here and now! He is the *Word of God*. He comes from God as our words come from our mouths."

"So where is this Jesus?" a woman in a red coat asked. "I don't see him nowhere."

"Where *is* he?" The monk opened his palms to the skies, joy shooting through him. "His Holy Spirit comes when we call him. But

Jesus Christ is in the Mass."

"Far out, dude." It was the biker with the American accent. He had moved to the front.

Cristoforo raised his brows with appreciation. "You are correct, my son. Very *far out*. Here is a mystery: God has no beginning and no end. He is great and powerful. Then the *far out* comes *close in*. He becomes one of us. He becomes a human being, a tiny baby."

"Tiny so we can know him." The woman in red nodded.

"So we can know him."

"Kind of speakin' our lingo, eh?" the American added.

"Our lingo, *si*. We are one with Jesus. We know him in every Mass."

Nadia and Lucille had moved up the road, and Cristoforo could hear the shrill ring of her bell. They must be hoping for cars to stop by, he thought.

Another cry rose from the crowd. "Masses are for Catholics! We don't hold with all that mumbo jumbo!"

Cristoforo was ready for that objection. England was a Protestant country. And he wanted to speak of the Mass, the Real Presence of Christ in the Mass.

He accepted the challenge. "What we say to God is important. But we have to mean what we say. When we worship God, we use the best words. We make his house beautiful, and he is pleased. But sometimes, our words are *so* beautiful, we forget...what we are saying, and we forget...that *he* is the reason for our words. We forget that Almighty God is on the altar."

The crowd stirred, and the friar sensed their confusion. He wrung his hands, his powerful fingers laced in supplication. "We must speak from our hearts."

"So what about the Catholics? Down with popery, I say!" A hoarse voice shot from the far edge of Cristoforo's congregation.

"Yeah, no smells and bells, no idols!"

The friar shook his head and raised his hands to the skies, hoping for angelic or divine inspiration. "My friends, my friends, Catholics use beautiful words, no? They have beautiful churches, no? Do not fear beauty, my friends, but fear the *worship* of beauty. Catholics must mean their prayers. They must remember it is God's house. And Protestants too must remember this."

Cristoforo stepped carefully down the soggy hill, trying to avoid cattle droppings. Nadia had abandoned her sign and now held a basket, taking a collection. She was a good girl, he thought, very helpful. He would give the offerings to the hostel to feed and clothe more Nadias. Lucille was helping Mrs. O'Malley and her ladies set up tables for refreshments.

The friar sat on an outcrop of rock. "Please allow me to tell a story. Once there was a little boy." He beckoned to a lad, about four years old, to come forward. The child crawled onto his lap. The boy's mother leaned forward with concern, then waited.

"Once there was a boy," he repeated, "who loved his father. But he had nothing to give him for Christmas. The family was poor. The boy had no allowance, and no job. He wanted to make something beautiful, so he asked his priest to help. They made a book. They pasted leaves and flowers on the pages. The priest drew beautiful letters. The boy colored the letters. They glued gold foil around the edges and over the front and back. It was a fine book. The boy gave the book to his father."

The crowd listened quietly, seeming oblivious to the biting wind. They moved a bit closer.

"The father was happy. He knew the book held the boy's love."

Cristoforo set the boy on his feet and walked along the front of the crowd, his hands clasped behind his back in thought. The lad followed him and the friar lifted him into his arms, the mother standing close by.

"Now," he said, turning to his audience, "there was another boy in the same village. He also needed a present for his father. He had a good allowance. He had a job tending the neighbor's garden. He bought a plastic clock. It cost little. He could keep most of his money for himself. His father unwrapped the gift. He was sad. He wanted a gift from his son's heart."

Cristoforo lowered himself onto a flat rock as he gazed into the boy's eyes. "You, lad, would make something fine...from your heart." He handed the child to his mother. "So you see, God wants our best. He gives us *his* best. He wants *our* best back. It is for *us* to find the right gift for *him*."

With these words, Cristoforo raised his arms and scanned the crowd for Nadia. Her red hair, streaming down her back, would be easy to spot, but where was she?

"Choose God, my friends. Today! Ask him into your heart. He will live there. Worship him! Receive him in the Mass! Do not fear beauty. Enjoy him, my friends! Never know despair!"

Where had the child gone?

"There is refreshment for us." He pointed to the tables set with baskets of rolls, platters of cheese, and bowls of small green apples.

"Bless this food to thy use, O Lord," he cried as he signed a cross in the cold air. "Make us truly grateful and ever mindful of the needs of others. In Jesus' most holy name we pray. Amen."

The group moved toward the tables, and Cristoforo walked among them, his head down, looking from side to side, humming his favorite hymn, "Joyful, joyful we adore thee, God of mercy, God of love...."

Nadia and the basket had disappeared. The friar's heart beat hard. Had she run away again?

Cristoforo turned and strode toward the church, its stone steeple solid against the gray sky. Inside, he knelt in a back pew and covered his face with his hands. *Nadia.* Each child, each person, each soul, placed in his charge by God, became a part of him, and when he lost them he lost part of himself as well. He knew what he would do next. The next time he preached he would tackle the hard one. He would talk about suffering and, with suffering, forgiveness.

With tears streaming, he knelt before his Lord and wept.

Chapter Ten
London

The trivial round, the common task
Will furnish all we ought to ask;
Room to deny ourselves—a road
To bring us daily nearer God.
    John Keble

In the morning Jack set out for Harrods' food stalls and Madeleine headed for Hatchard's Books. She turned right on Carlos Place, left on Mount, crossed Berkeley Square to Bruton—where the present Queen Elizabeth was born, she recalled—and turned right on Bond with its fashionable shops.

She walked quickly, hoping to burn a few calories, weaving between shoppers and pausing at intersections where boxy black taxis lumbered suddenly around corners. As she walked, she glanced up, beyond the red brick townhouses and their chimney pots, to skies that had partially cleared; a brisk wind opened a small blue window, soon to be filled with more scuttling white clouds.

Madeleine passed a bronze sculpture of Roosevelt and Churchill sitting on a park bench, turned left at Ferragamo's, and entered the Burlington arcade. Here more shops, their windows displaying silver, cashmere, and fine china, bordered the walk running under wrought-iron arches. As she emerged onto busy Piccadilly the wind picked up, and raising her collar, she crossed the street, watching for red double-decker buses careening from the wrong direction in a country where drivers drove on the left, not on the right.

Fortnum & Mason's windows revealed tall, thin mannequins modeling slinky dresses clinging seductively to their plastic bodies. Did real women wear those dresses? Did real feet teeter in those heels? Not for the first time, she was sure men designed them.

As she turned toward the shop next door, her heart beat with anticipation.

She entered venerable Hatchard's, passing under a Queen's Royal Purveyor crest, stating that John Hatchard had founded the store in 1797. Today the wood floors creaked elegantly under thin oriental carpets, and Madeleine had the sense she was in the library of a great manor house. Shoppers whispered in groups of two or three, but most meandered alone. Book browsing, she often thought, was best a solitary affair, demanding total attention, an immersion of the soul into a well of reflection, a pool of fact and fiction. And if the fiction was *good*, it was factual too, reflecting, perhaps embodying, one could even say *incarnating* truth. She maneuvered around the bestsellers and latest releases, their tempting covers balanced artfully into a central pyramid. Far in the back, beyond a mahogany stairwell, she found the biographies.

Madeleine paused in front of a wall of paperbacks. She scanned the titles, watching for familiar names and intriguing subjects that reflected her interest in history and theology, her constant search for answers to the human condition. When she found such a book, she opened it to note the publisher. She jotted details and debated whether to buy here or search for it at home, then climbed the stairs to the Children's Department.

She had never outgrown picture books, and her grandson Luke gave her an excuse to look through them. On the fifth floor she found the tall colorful volumes and she began to check for Christian titles. After all, this *was* an Anglican country with a national Church, and they might have something special for Luke, or something to rest on a nightstand for a houseguest or loan to Saint Thomas' Sunday school at home. One could never have too many good picture books, ones with vivid illustrations catching the glory of life, and, yes, the glory of God.

As she squatted to view the bottom row, she sensed someone nearby, waiting. Looking up, she saw a young Asian girl with a shadowy patch across her nose, probably a birthmark. She was with child and quite far along.

"Anything I can pull out for you?" Madeleine asked with a smile.

"Thanks, but I'll just sit on this stool and browse a bit when you're finished."

"I recommend these." Madeleine handed her a board book, one in a series. "My grandchildren love them, and they are, well, you know, *good*."

The girl turned the thick pages. "I like the pictures."

She was very young, thought Madeleine, and seemed familiar, with an American accent. Madeleine pulled herself up. Was she the girl in Faith Chapel? "I believe I saw you yesterday," Madeleine said, standing up, "in Westminster Abbey."

The girl looked at her with guarded eyes. "Oh?"

"In the side chapel—off Poets' Corner."

"Yes, it was dark. You were the lady in the back?"

Madeleine nodded. "It's an ancient chapel."

She looked wary. "Sorry, have to go. Thanks for the tip," she said nervously and turned toward the stairs.

Madeleine watched her leave. There was an air of mystery about her, as though she held a secret close. There was fear too, she thought, that the secret might be discovered. Madeleine was curious. What was her story?

Returning to the lower bookshelf, she selected a title for Luke, *The Story of Easter*. The drawings were vivid, the text age-appropriate and accurate. Maybe one day she would read it to her grandson, cradling him in her lap, caressing each word and pausing with each picture, as he turned the pages. She had many warm memories of reading to Luke's father who would invariably demand, as they came to the end, "Again, again!" It was a sort of miracle, she thought, the way a book and a child and a lap could merge through the power of words and images, through a story that wove through the minds of teller and listener in the same moment. A true miracle of love, a union of matter and spirit.

As she pulled out a five-pound note from her bag and handed it to the cashier, she thought of all the books she could collect for the new children's home. Used-book stores would be a good place to start. She hoped she could visit the shops in Cecil Court before meeting Jack and Cristoforo at Claridge's for tea.

It was nearly three when Madeleine followed a suited young lady to a corner table in Claridge's Art Deco lobby. Red leather sofas and striped chairs clustered in groups under a crystal chandelier of swirling glass. A black baby grand stood next to a cello propped against a marble column. Jack rose as she approached.

"Is he here yet?" Madeleine asked as she took a seat.

Jack motioned toward the entry. "As a matter of fact he's coming in the door now. And I do believe he's wearing the new robe we sent him."

Cristoforo looked lost as he crossed the black-and-white tiled lobby. Jack met him, and Madeleine watched fondly as the monk lumbered toward her with his characteristic awkwardness. He stood in two worlds, intensely present yet far away, his chiseled face and fanning Afro reminding her of an age-darkened icon. His chestnut eyes sparkled in greeting.

"*Signora* Seymour!" He took Madeleine's hand and held it between this own large palms. "It is good to see you. You are well?"

Madeleine, as always, was surprised by his firm but gentle grip. "It is good to see *you*, and yes, we are well. And you?"

"I am well." He lowered himself into a silk chair and arranged his new robe, running his hands over the fabric. "You are missed in Rome." He spread his fingers on the table as though he could not find a better place for them and looked about the ornate room.

The waiter arrived with silver pots of Earl Grey tea and plates of sandwiches: salmon, ham, chicken, cucumber, and deviled egg, cut into neat white triangles. Jack said grace, and Madeleine offered a plate to the friar.

"Thank you. These are fine indeed, *molto bene.*" He popped a sandwich in his mouth and chewed rapidly.

They were going to disappear, Madeleine thought, before the tea was poured.

Jack leaned back and tapped his toe. "Now, Cristoforo, do we have any properties lined up? Did you check out the list I faxed you? Did you find an agent?"

Cristoforo wiped his mouth with a pink napkin. "*Si, Signore.* The factory in Chelsea, we see tomorrow morning, Tuesday, and the warehouse in Bloomsbury, in the afternoon. I have been working with an agent, Mr. Dick Barton."

"Good work," Jack said. "And the property out of town, near Oxford?"

"We have an appointment for Wednesday next week for the house in Aylesbury, an abandoned monastery. I am sorry, but the owner was difficult to reach. It was the best I could do."

As Madeleine listened to the plans, her heart filled with hope. She turned to Jack. "A week from Wednesday? That will give us a few more days in London. Do you think Joe will agree to it?"

"I'll call him tonight, but he's enthusiastic about the project, and we'd better check out all three properties. He'd probably like the monastery, but it will no doubt need some work."

Madeleine searched her memory. "Didn't we stay in Aylesbury once? The name sounds familiar."

"We stayed at Hartwell House in Aylesbury, one of those historic hotels."

"I recall a monastery next door surrounded by a stone wall and shade trees."

"London would be better." Jack sipped his tea thoughtfully.

"Even so, it's a monastery, so it should have a church." She watched Cristoforo finish the last sandwich.

The pianist and cellist began to play, and the friar looked up.

"*Molto bene!*" He grinned, revealing his silver tooth. "*Musico!*" He threw his hands in the air and brought them together with a loud clap. Other guests turned and stared. "*Festivo!* Music lifts the heart, no?" He patted his chest with his palm.

Jack wrinkled his brow. "But what are they asking for the properties?"

Cristoforo nodded as a waiter brought another platter. "Maybe too much? I do not know. We will see? I will call you with prices, okay? But now, I must go." He gulped the last of his tea. "The hostel has few to help today, and Nadia...maybe comes home to us."

"Nadia?" Madeleine stirred two sugar lumps into her tea. "Do we know Nadia?"

"A girl from the streets. She helped me in the countryside. But she ran away." He bowed his head and folded his hands.

Madeleine could feel his grief. "Oh dear."

"In the countryside?" Jack asked, as though the friar might provide even more interesting news.

"Preaching." He nodded, eyeing the sandwiches.

Jack reached for a smoked salmon triangle. "Preaching?"

"I am sorry, *Signori*, I must go now. *Molto grazie* for the sandwiches. They are good. Nadia would like them. I take more, maybe, please?" He pulled a plastic bag from his pocket and stuffed several inside.

Cristoforo disentangled himself from the chair legs and stood slowly. He said good-bye, bowing from the waist, padded through the lobby, and disappeared through the revolving doors.

"But you missed dessert," Madeleine said, partly to herself, as a three-tier silver tray arrived, filled with scones, clotted cream, strawberry jam, and petit fours.

Jack stared at the retreating brown robe dusting the marble foyer.

"Did you hear that?"

"About the preaching or Nadia?"

"The preaching."

"He said in the country. What's he talking about?"

Jack motioned for the check. "You don't suppose he's outdoors like John Wesley, converting the multitudes?"

"And like Christ. *That* I would love to see. Cristoforo on a hillside, preaching in the rain. He's full of surprises. I'd like to know what his superior says to that."

"I do too."

At seven-thirty that evening Madeleine and Jack emerged from the tiny elevator and stepped into the hotel lobby, then followed a narrow hallway to the bar. Madeleine fingered the enamel cross Jack gave her the previous Easter. What would she give up for Lent? And what would she take on?

"Two, Madame?" a young man asked, bowing slightly.

"Please."

They slipped into a velvet settee. The intimate room was paneled in dark wood; jewel-toned bottles glittered behind a mahogany bar. On the opposite wall was a large portrait of a woman in a red gown in a last dance from another world.

Madeleine ordered a martini straight up, dry, with a twist. Jack, careful since his surgery, ordered sparkling water.

"To the new children's home," Madeleine toasted as she tapped Jack's glass with her own, "and to Joe McGinty's generosity."

"To Saint Joe," Jack agreed.

The headwaiter from the dining room approached, silver-haired and serious. His face expressed a reserved familiarity and with fine-boned fingers handed them menus as though presenting awards, gratified with their presence and with his graceful gesture. "Madame? Monsieur? La carte? Thank you very much." He nodded and retired quietly.

Jack turned to Madeleine, placing his hand on hers. *"And know ye not that your body is the temple of the Holy Ghost which is in you, which ye have of God, and ye are not your own?"*

"What?" Madeleine asked, pleasantly surprised.

"First Corinthians 6:19. How about that?"

"I'm still not used to you quoting Scripture."

"It's taken me a long time to appreciate the benefit. Scripture is like food really. It feeds and nourishes. And I only learn the parts I like, so I can't claim too much credit."

"That's better than most people, better than me."

"I suppose." Jack sipped his water, studying it.

"And it's true that our bodies *are* temples of the Holy Spirit, a real mystery."

"It seems pretty straightforward—and a great excuse to go shopping."

Madeleine laughed, seeing the rationale. "And how did your shopping go today?" She gazed into his blue eyes with a new appreciation.

"I didn't buy a thing, but I enjoyed walking through Harrods' food aisles. The place is like an art museum. The displays are incredible. How did Hatchard's go?"

"I have a list of titles to order over the Internet and several British press books I couldn't resist, including a biography of Trevor Huddleston."

"Trevor *who*?"

"An Anglican monk who worked in South Africa, taking over the work of Raymond Raynes."

"Raymond Raynes?"

"They're both Anglo-Catholics, pioneers really, or perhaps custodians, of the traditional faith, the sacramental faith—the early Church faith, as a matter of fact."

"Really? Early Church? High Church is early Church? Come on now."

"*Really*. Elaborate liturgies came from the early Church's emphasis on the Eucharist, the Real Presence of Christ. When Anglo-Catholics reaffirmed Christ's presence in the bread and the wine, they wanted to worship with fanfare—with images, processions, music, candles—to create glimpses of heaven on earth."

"A little too much fanfare for me, but I do appreciate the hymns."

The waiter led them down the hall to the restaurant, and they sat in a corner banquette. Paneled walls, waxed to a high gloss, reflected light from the chandeliers. Windows were draped in peach-and-green damask looped over white sheers. The servers appeared silently, setting down and whisking away.

First came the salads, crab and langoustines, artichoke hearts with truffles and mushrooms. Then a leg of lamb, carved from a trolley. Courses were plated tableside, along with salvers of French beans and baby potatoes, and pitchers of mint vinaigrette and Cumberland sauce. The dessert cart rolled to their table loaded with apple crumble, bread pudding, sherry trifle, and fruit salad. They chose the crumble with vanilla sauce, lots of vanilla sauce.

Jack scooped up a last bit of apple and cream. "So did you get to the secondhand bookstores you researched? The ones near that church, Saint Martin-in-the-Fields? We have some of their CDs. I read they have free lunchtime concerts."

"Not Saint Martin's, but I did get to a bookstore in Cecil Court and found some out-of-print Evelyn Underhill in the back corner. Quite Dickensian, a hodgepodge of books in nooks and crannies, stacked on tables. The owner climbed a ladder for me."

"Good. So what shall we do the rest of the week, after seeing the properties in London? Let's have lunch at Fortnum & Mason's."

"I do recall a plate of tomatoes and goat cheese I had there." Madeleine smiled sleepily, warmed by the cocktail and wine, enjoying Jack's enthusiasm. "What's at the National Gallery?"

"You'd better read up. Museums are your responsibility."

"Maybe we could get half-price theater tickets in Leicester Square."

"I read an Oscar Wilde production is going on, *Lady Windemere's Fan*."

"Not until Saturday. I'm looking forward to tomorrow, to seeing the Chelsea property." What would it be like? Something child-friendly, Madeleine hoped. Room for twenty beds to start, a kitchen, a classroom. An office, a sitting/counseling room, an exam room with sonogram technology. They would encourage local churches and shelters to send them referrals. They would give women an *educated* choice.

The red brick factory had once manufactured shoe polish, reminding Madeleine of Charles Dickens and the "blacking" factory where the writer worked as a child. Not a pleasant association, but intriguing.

Nevertheless, she liked the location, near the Thames on the western edge of Chelsea. Thomas More lived in this neighborhood and, in 1528, remodeled the local chapel, today called Chelsea Old Church. Another local church, Holy Trinity, was the home of the Pre-Raphaelite artists William Morris, Dante Gabriel Rossetti, and Edward Burne-Jones. The poet T.S. Eliot attended Holy Trinity as well. Others who resided in Chelsea included the writers A.A. Milne, Mark Twain, Oscar Wilde, and Hilaire Belloc.

"What do you think?" Jack asked as they toured the enormous space.

Cristoforo gazed through the window to the river, clearly lost in his own thoughts.

"This was a shoe polish factory?" Madeleine asked the agent.

Dick Barton loosened the tie around his thick neck and hiked up his pants over his ample girth. He wore a corduroy jacket over a paisley shirt. "Most recently it was a gym. I used to come here myself when I worked down the street. That back wall was all mirrors."

Today, Madeleine thought, the spacious room could easily be used for a dance studio, a ballroom, perhaps a concert hall. The wood floors were polished to a high gloss, and the tall windows let in natural light, perfect for a children's classroom. She joined the friar and tried to unlatch a pane. It wouldn't budge.

"Been sealed, I'm afraid," Dick Barton said. He added under his breath, "Safety issues."

"Break-ins?" Jack seized the slip-of-the-tongue.

The agent groaned. "Afraid so."

Jack frowned. "High insurance?"

"Everything's high these days."

Madeleine found the place charming in a Dickensian sort of way, in spite of the sealed windows. Surely, they could open them. The river view was spectacular, the location historic and close to museums, churches, and public transportation.

"Can we see the other rooms?"

"Other rooms?" Barton replied. "I'm sorry, but this is it. There's storage in the basement. The other floors are all owned and occupied. The building was subdivided in the fifties."

"Oh." Madeleine looked at Jack. "That's too bad. We need more space, don't we?"

"We could get by," Jack said, rubbing his chin. "It would be a start, but I don't like the safety issues."

Cristoforo turned toward them, his face apologetic. "I did not know this was all the only space. I am sorry."

As they walked to the car, Jack asked, "Mr. Barton, exactly how large is the warehouse property we see this afternoon? Is it subdivided too? Don't you have any residential properties, say in Kensington?"

"A house would be so much more inviting," Madeleine said as she eased herself into the backseat. "And we wouldn't have to add a kitchen and baths."

"I'll get back to you," said Barton. "But you've got to know the market's tight right now."

The warehouse, on the eastern edge of Bloomsbury, was a new construction of steel and poured concrete. Madeleine was disappointed before she even entered the building.

"What did they store here?" Jack asked as the elevator rose to the second floor.

"Books. They stored books. Shipped them all over the world."

"And where's Brother Cristoforo?" Madeleine was sure he had agreed to meet them here.

"The monk called to say he couldn't make it." Dick Barton fumbled for a key on a heavy ring as they lurched to a stop. They crossed the hall to a steel door, and he inserted the key with his fleshy fingers.

"Security looks good," Jack said as they stepped inside. He pointed to cameras in the ceiling corners.

"Too good," Madeleine added. The place gave her the creeps, even if it *had* housed books. It was a much larger property, with access to the enclosed park across the street—a nice plus, thought Madeleine—a full kitchen (the publishers had hired live-in custodians and shippers), several baths, and three large rooms.

"The windows are so tiny, way up near the ceiling," Madeleine said.

Jack followed her gaze. "But it's a great location, and safer with small windows."

Dick Barton nodded. "Safe it is, sir. There's a children's hospital around the corner and a police station across the street. Good insurance rates on this one."

"It's central, close to everything." Jack looked at Madeleine, then to the high windows as though he could force more light through them. "And the park nearby. That's nice."

"We'll think about it," Madeleine said. The British Museum was only a few blocks away. That would be another plus.

"There's another offer coming in, I'm told." Once again, Dick Barton hiked his pants and loosened his tie. "Not many central properties this size on the market right now. Don't wait *too* long."

Jack looked thoughtful. "We'll let you know."

"Mr. Barton," Madeleine said, "aren't there any *houses* in a safe neighborhood we could look at?"

Dick Barton placed his thick hands on his hips. "There *is* an old place they're talking about tearing down on the other side of Marylebone, near Regent's Park. I was told it was condemned, but I'll look into it."

Jack looked worried. "Condemned?"

"You're a church group, right? You don't have a lot of money to spend. The monk said no more than five hundred thousand. This one is, or was, going for seven."

Jack raised his brows. "I suppose we could call Joe. Could you find out if it's still on the market and check back with us?"

"Righto."

Dick Barton called and said that the property was still available but had some disclosure problems. They could see it Thursday. He wouldn't go into details and Madeleine and Jack were left with two days to imagine what the problems might be. Brother Cristoforo agreed to meet them at the house, and apologized for missing the Bloomsbury property, explaining that he was needed at the hostel.

On Wednesday, Madeleine and Jack explored London, Madeleine promising herself she would work on her manuscript that evening. After all, they were here in London, the ancient capital of the Western world. What would God show her here? She listened for his "still, small voice" as the minutes passed into hours, and the hours disappeared into the day. She tried to keep her heart and mind open.

At Saint Paul's Cathedral they studied golden apsidal mosaics and Holmon Hunt's *The Light of the World*. So profound, thought Madeleine, the Christ waiting outside the door in the dark, holding the lamp. Would the door open? Some would and some would remain closed. In the meantime, the light of the world would light the dark. She recalled William Holman Hunt was a founder of the Pre-Raphaelites, an artistic movement who sought to return to styles prevalent before Raphael and the Renaissance. Their classical forms were pleasing to Madeleine, drawing her into the paintings, so full of vivid color and detail. Pre-Raphaelite paintings captured something ethereal, she thought, something of the divine in man.

They meandered under soaring arches and down polished aisles, and peered up to Christopher Wren's glimmering dome. Madeleine recalled John Donne had preached at Saint Paul's from an outdoor pulpit before the church was destroyed by the Great Fire of London in 1666. She tried to picture the war years of the twentieth century, the bomb-damaged Cathedral rising from the ashes, surrounded by London's charred ruins. But Saint Paul's was also a place of celebration, of royal weddings, of rippling silks and military regalia.

They lunched at Fortnum's on avocadoes stuffed with crab. They toured the Duke of Wellington's Apsley House, a memorial to his victory over Napoleon at Waterloo. They visited the Royal Portrait Gallery in Trafalgar Square, where they paused in the Tudor room. Madeleine gazed at the remarkable painting of the young Princess Elizabeth in her red dress, holding her prayer book and Bible to her side, the two halves of her great compromise between Catholics and Protestants.

Jack pointed to *The Allegory of Power*, a family portrait of Henry VIII and his children. "There's our Jane Seymour and young Edward." The future king, Protestant Edward VI posed alongside the future queens, Catholic Mary and Protestant Elizabeth.

"And so the fate of England and her Church rested on three children," Madeleine said, in awe of the power of the individual to influence history. That reminder alone made the hours worthwhile. Still she wondered, for not the first time that day, about the mysterious townhouse near Regent's Park.

Chapter Eleven
Saint Mary's

And these are the garments which they shall make;
a breastplate, and an Ephod, and a robe, and a broidered coat, a mitre,
and a girdle: and they shall make holy garments....
And they shall take gold, and blue,
and purple, and scarlet, and fine linen.
Exodus 28:4

On Thursday morning Madeleine picked up her pace to keep up with Jack and Cristoforo, her spirits rising as they headed for the Edwardian mansion near Regent's Park. A cold damp seeped through their jackets as the sun emerged sporadically between rolling clouds. They crossed busy Oxford Street, where shoppers strode five abreast down wide walkways past huge department stores and red double-decker buses inched their way through traffic. Soon they entered a quiet neighborhood of large residences with neoclassic facades, white pillared porches, and neat green doors. Madeleine scanned the house numbers as they approached, imagining each as their next children's home.

They found Dick Barton in front of one of the more dilapidated structures. Three stories supported a pitched roof stippled with chimney pots. The house stood detached from its neighbor row houses, as though it were the original occupant in a large tract of land.

Madeleine was enchanted. The residence, she thought, had *character*, the windows beaming an ageless wisdom. Dick Barton unlocked the front door, its paint peeling, and they stepped into a substantial foyer leading to a circular staircase, roped off, presumably for safety reasons. Madeleine looked up to the high ceilings, decorated with intricate carvings of leaves and roses. Such plasterwork was a true craft, she recalled, peaking around the turn of the nineteenth century. She imagined the walls with a coat of paint, the wainscoting a shade darker, the chandelier repaired. But the floors sagged and portions of the interior walls were rotting, revealing rusting pipes.

"It was a grand place in the old days," Dick Barton said, as though he were a frequent visitor to social salons. "Six bedrooms upstairs. Ballroom in the back. Maids' quarters in the attic and cook's quarters in the basement. Big back yard, at least by London standards. It just hasn't been kept up."

"I'll say," Jack said as he wiped a cobweb from his brow. "How many square feet?"

Dick Barton checked his papers. "Nearly ten thousand."

Brother Cristoforo was wandering from room to room. "A garden!" he shouted from the rear of the house.

Madeleine found him peering through a smudged kitchen window. The yard was overgrown with bushes and weeds, but traces of a garden bed could be seen.

"It is good," the friar said, "for children to grow things."

"It is." Madeleine recalled Cristoforo's rows of vegetables in Rome. "Who's caring for your garden while you're gone?"

"It is winter, and less to do, but Elena is looking after it."

Madeleine happily recalled her friend, Elena Coronati, nearly twenty-one now. They had met at Quattro Coronati and had traveled together through France two years ago. "How is she? I haven't heard from her since Christmas."

"She is well. She is busy now with the accounts. She is very smart."

"And does Pierre still visit? She hasn't mentioned him lately." In Paris the young man took a keen interest in Elena, and Madeleine wasn't sure where their relationship might lead. Elena had been smitten with Pierre's good looks and charm, but there had been heartbreak too. It seemed they were taking their courtship slowly, probably wise at their young age.

"We see him often," Cristoforo replied, "but he has spent the winter months helping his family in France. He wants to study medicine in Rome." Cristoforo could not take his eyes off the overgrown tangle of bushes, vines, and weeds. "Maybe we plant roses close to the house, and vegetables in the back. But I fear the growing season is short."

Madeleine nodded. "It's certainly shorter than Italy. Beans and root vegetables do well. Maybe a hothouse?"

Voices drifted in from the front rooms, but Madeleine couldn't catch what Jack and the agent were saying. She joined them in the entry.

Jack was shaking his head. "You're kidding."

"What?" Madeleine looked from face to face. Jack looked worried. Mr. Barton seemed to be enjoying a bit of gossip.

Jack glanced up the stairs. "The disclosure, Maddie. Are you ready for this?"

"I'd forgotten about that. What *is* the disclosure? What's wrong with the house? Did something happen here?"

"A murder," Jack said.

Mr. Barton looked from face to face, his hands planted in his pockets. "The police found the culprit soon enough. It was the old woman's nephew with a grudge. He gave her an overdose of meds. Figured he would inherit. Not a very bright boy."

"But there's more," Jack added.

"More?"

Cristoforo joined them, and Dick Barton stared at his rapt audience. The agent's eyes, the whites mapped red, grew wide. "She visits," he whispered, as if *she* were listening.

"Who visits?" Cristoforo asked in a calm voice.

"Mrs. Beetleston, she that's been murdered, the ghost of Mrs. Beetleston. That's why the sellers are having a hard time of it. Of course you could use that to your advantage, now, couldn't you, in your offer?"

Jack studied the agent thoughtfully. "True. We could."

"I don't know," Madeleine said. "I've heard of haunted houses. That might be a serious drawback, especially with children."

"She might *like* children," the friar pointed out. "And there *are* people who can drive ghosts away."

Madeleine turned to Cristoforo. "Do you believe in ghosts?" She wasn't sure if she did.

"It is possible there are spirits who roam the earth."

"Oh dear," she said, glancing at Jack.

"So it's haunted *and* it's condemned." Jack whistled through his teeth. "Back to the drawing board."

"It's not condemned yet, right?" Madeleine would not lose hope, not yet.

"No, ma'am," the agent replied, somewhat impatiently. "End of the month, I'm told. The good news is there aren't any other offers."

"I can see why," Jack groaned. "Madeleine, aside from ghosts, it would need an entirely new infrastructure, probably double the seven hundred thousand going into it."

"We could make a lower offer," Madeleine said under her breath.

"At least try. It's in a lovely neighborhood, with other houses. Regent's Park is just up the street, with the zoo. I can see this being perfect. It *would* take a little work." It was *Upstairs Downstairs*; it was Oscar Wilde. It was a bit like *Great Expectations* too, but Cristoforo could find someone to get rid of the ghost...if she even appeared.

"We'll think about it," Jack said as they headed for the door. "We'll need authorization at the very least."

Brother Cristoforo had planted himself in the center of the entry. He now raised his arms. "We will sanctify this space of suffering with prayer and work, *ora* and *labora*."

The Benedictine rule, Madeleine thought, as she gazed at the friar's strong jaw line, his outstretched hands, his eyes from another world. *This space of suffering.* He spoke as one who knew. What had he been through, that had given him this air of holiness? She nodded, her heart full. "And with an order of nuns to staff it, just like Rome. And a chapel. Don't forget the chapel."

Joe McGinty authorized Jack to go as high as a million pounds, but that would have to include restoration to bring the property up to code.

Jack offered five-seventy-nine. Dick Barton laughed and suggested six-fifty. Jack countered six, pointing out the cash deal. Madeleine waited, praying, hopeful. All day Friday she paced in front of the mansion, picturing the façade with a new coat of paint. Potted geraniums, or maybe miniature firs, on the porch. There would be a scripted sign, black on white with green and red flourishes, over the front door.

Finally, on Saturday, they met the agent at his office.

"I'm sorry, but something happened, totally unforeseen," Mr. Barton said, after they had taken seats in his narrow cubicle.

"What?" Jack glanced at Madeleine, then Cristoforo.

Dick Barton shifted his eyes about the room. "It seems the property was already under offer. My error. Terribly sorry. Terribly sorry." He spread his hands wide.

"Already what?" Madeleine cried.

"They've taken it off the market," Mr. Barton said with a nervous chuckle. "These things happen. Another offer came in last week for the land alone—at two million, subject to planning permission."

Jack fixed Mr. Barton with a skeptical look. "*Two million* for the land? You've got to be kidding."

"It's a tough market."

Madeleine's heart sank. *What now?*

"Madeleine, don't be discouraged. We still have one more property to look at." It was Sunday morning, and Jack nibbled toast as he glanced at the *Telegraph's* business page.

"Not in London." Madeleine looked out the window to Farm Street Church in an effort to lift her spirits. A headache was forming in her right temple. "Finding a property is more difficult than I'd imagined."

"We may have to give up the idea of a city location, Maddie. You should prepare yourself for that."

"I'm sure something will come along, even if the Oxfordshire one isn't right."

"At any rate, today you can enjoy the Mass at Saint Mary's Bourne Street. You talked about it for days after our last visit. Masses always make you feel better."

She *had* been enthusiastic. It was a stunning Anglo-Catholic church, and she had always wanted to return. With a lighter heart, she turned to her laptop. "I have something on the Anglo-Catholics. I can cite this church perhaps, include it in the chapter."

"Excellent idea."

"I recall a colorful service with great hymns and processions." Fragrant incense swirled about brocaded vestments, as enthusiastic Anglo-Catholics gathered in a nineteenth-century vaulted nave. She found her notes and paused. "Do you think Father Smythe is still there?"

"It would be good to see him. He was a real no-nonsense Scott. But the service may not be so colorful. Aren't we in Lent?"

"Not yet, but almost. It's Pre-Lent, Quinquagesima Sunday. That means Ash Wednesday is this week and *then* we begin Lent."

She skimmed her notes.

Holy Manifestations: The Early Anglo-Catholics
When Henry VIII broke with Rome and became head of the English Church, Anglicanism was born. After his death, his son

Edward ruled as a Protestant. When Edward died at sixteen years of age, Henry's daughter Mary ruled as a Catholic. After Mary's death, his daughter Elizabeth kept the peace in a country divided between Protestants and Catholics. Her reign was long, and England prospered.

Upon Elizabeth's death in 1603, James Stuart VI of Scotland accepted the English crown as James I; his family ruled for forty-six years, insisting on "conformation" to the English Church, supported by their belief in absolute monarchy. By 1649, religious civil war broke out, and Cromwell's Puritans, called "roundheads" for their close-cropped hair, took control with a parliamentary government. They soon executed the king, Charles I.

Jack stacked the dishes. Madeleine checked her watch. She had a few more minutes.

> The Puritan Protestants feared the abuse of pleasure and soon came to fear pleasure itself. Color, music, festival, sensual delight, particularly sexual relations and alcoholic "spirits," were deemed frivolous, not *useful*, and therefore idolatrous. When the Stuart king Charles II was restored to the throne in 1660 the tide changed, but the dour stamp of Puritan prohibitions remained.
>
> Religious life in England would not, for some time, welcome beauty, pleasure, and festival, so these natural aspects of human society found a home outside the Church. The recreation industry was reborn, adopted by the secular.[4] Church life would be serious, bleak, and painful; secular life would be light-hearted, colorful, and pleasure-laden. This false chasm would remove the influence of religious scruples from the secular world. The separation would stigmatize religious belief itself, associate churchgoing with "do-gooders," and isolate the Faith from the economic workweek which was considered "real life." And, to many Protestants, recreation—that necessary re-creating of man's body and spirit, that expression of his longings through art, music, and dance—would be considered sinful.

Jack reached for his tie. Madeleine read quickly, not wanting to lose the thread of her thoughts.

"Ten minutes, Maddie."

"Right."

While the Pelagian-Puritan belief in the perfectibility of man led to the separation of daily life and Sunday worship, the Catholic belief in their union continued to return merriment, color, and festival to religious life. Even so, the gulf would remain. Pleasure would be seen as outside religious experience (except for a few "crazed" mystics), the body would be considered at war with the spirit,[5] and we would enter the twentieth century a people forced to chose between the two. For the most part, the body won.

In the late nineteenth century and into the twentieth, history was re-examined, and many scholars, feeling the yoke of morality to be a heavy one, questioned the dogmas of the Church, even the *existence* of Jesus Christ. Theologians proclaimed loudly, and with some relief, that man was no longer imprisoned by morality, only mortality, for God was and is, after all, dead. The body had won over the soul, aided by the great chasm, the isolation of the church from real life, and the joy of living life in its entirety, its wholeness.

The Anglo-Catholics, those earnest men of the nineteenth-century Oxford Movement, saw that the gulf must be breached if the Church was to be a whole, holy, Body of Christ.[6] Color, song, poetry, image, and the great liturgical dance would unite the bodies and souls of the faithful, as Christ filled them in the Mass.

As Madeleine closed her document, she thought about her words. As a child she had known that separation, that sense that Sundays were in a different world than weekdays. The divorce seemed absolute, and it was only recently that she had felt the Holy Spirit moving her Sunday worship into her weekday life. The action had changed her profoundly, and she awaited each day as though the heavens would open to her, for each flower was brighter and more fragrant, and each suffering more poignant, more meaningful. Life grew intense and real each moment.

She looked forward to their return to Saint Mary's, home of the Anglo-Catholics in London.

Madeleine took Jack's hand as the taxi arrived at 30 Bourne Street, set in a quiet Knightsbridge neighborhood off Sloane Square. The red brick church, built in 1874 as a mission for the poor, stood between neat townhouses, about fifty feet back from the street. To the right of the arched entry, an ivy-covered gate led to a rectory and garden.

They entered through a vaulted cupola and found themselves in the north aisle near a Lady Chapel radiant with flaming candles. The church was not large, with a single nave and two side aisles running under graceful vaults, but it had the quaint air that time lends to beloved spaces, as generations polish and perfect their worship of God. It was a church layered, Madeleine thought, with the lives of men and women, textured with their joys and their sorrows.

They located seats in the back of the packed nave and knelt. Madeleine prayed her customary thanksgivings for the clergy, the people, and the freedom to worship. As the organ sounded the opening chords and the clergy assembled at the foot of the central aisle, she and Jack stood with the congregation, opened their hymnals, and sang,

"Love divine, all loves excelling, Joy of heav'n, to earth come down,
Fix in us thy humble dwelling, All thy faithful mercies crown.
Jesus, thou art all compassion, Pure, unbounded love thou art;
Visit us with thy salvation, Enter ev'ry trembling heart...."

The procession moved toward the altar. A thurifer swung his thurible of burning incense, a crucifer raised his gilded crucifix into the billowing smoke, and two young torchbearers stepped forward, holding their candles steady. Deacons and priests, the celebrant vested in purple, followed.

Through the liturgy, the rhythm of the past led the dance of the present. A deacon read the Ten Commandments, God's rules of right and wrong. A choir sang *Kyrie Eleison, Lord have mercy*, the ancient chant that admitted man's helplessness, his failure to meet those standards on his own. It was the beginning of repentance, a preparation for absolution, forgiveness of these failures, these sins.

The deacons read from Holy Scripture, the people recited the Creed, and the preacher spoke from a carved mahogany pulpit rising over the congregation like a ship's prow. The celebrant, facing the high altar with his back to the people, chanted the ancient Canon of the Mass. As he said the words of Christ that changed the bread into body and the wine into blood, he offered his people, cleansed and redeemed, to God the Father through God the Son.

Madeleine returned from her communion, knowing the Real

Presence of Christ had become one with her flesh. In this moment she was certain Christ would lead them in their search. She was certain he would guide her in the final stages of her manuscript, *Holy Manifestations*. And somehow, she thought as she knelt in thanksgiving, the two were vitally connected, the children's home and the book, for they were both types of incarnations.

Suddenly she had an image of their disheveled friar, and she prayed for Cristoforo. She knew he suffered, yet she did not know how. As she gazed at the Christ crucified over the altar, she thought how secret suffering could be. Saints and sinners, believers and unbelievers, moved through time with hidden souls, often with no outward signs that revealed the inner ordeal, the battle that raged.

Some carried crosses to which they were fused, becoming invisible crucifixes redeemed by Christ. They carried their crosses as banners, high and proud, as they marched to a tune light and colorful, venerable and young. They carried them close, piercing their flesh, as the nails of suffering bound them to the wood. They marched happily, amidst the unhappy and the despairing, in hope that their joy might be shared, might lighten the way, might birth another cross for their neighbor to carry and to fuse. Finally, at the end of time, the trumpet sounded and they looked up. Their crosses reached the heavens, and they climbed them, these bridges of incarnational holiness, these flesh wounds turned into ladders to God.

This, thought Madeleine, was the mystery of the saints' journey through time. She prayed that she could use her minutes, hours, and days so well.

"The Banqueting House is open," Jack said, as he and Madeleine left Father Smythe shaking hands with his people. "Shall we visit Whitehall this afternoon? We've missed some of the official sights. You keep taking me to churches."

"Wasn't that the scene of the execution of King Charles? He is, after all, considered a saint and a martyr."

Jack hailed a taxi. "By some."

Madeleine recalled that the Banqueting House had illustrious beginnings. In the seventeenth century, Inigo Jones designed the Palladian house in the center of Whitehall Palace for James I, and in 1629 Charles I contracted Peter Paul Rubens, then serving in London as a Dutch diplomat, to paint the ceiling. Still used for elegant receptions of foreign dignitaries, its thrones intact, she knew the hall was the only surviving building after Whitehall Palace was destroyed by fire.

Madeleine and Jack climbed stairs to the second-floor room, and Madeleine pointed to the north entrance. "That's where Charles I was beheaded. January 30, 1649."

"Outside the windows?"

"They erected a scaffolding. There must have been a doorway where the windows are."

"So everyone could see from the street."

"Yes."

Jack studied the ornate ceiling of the dining room. "He walked under Rubens' painting of absolute monarchy."

"The one he commissioned." It was England's first regicide, thought Madeleine, as she gazed at the bleak landing where nothing remained of the scene but a plaque. Charles was the second Stuart king and too powerful for the English. Even so, the nation recoiled from their act.

Jack gazed out the window to where the scaffold had once been. "What exactly was his crime?"

"In a word, despotism. Church and State were one, still are for that matter, with a national church. But Charles believed in the divine right of kings, absolute monarchy. He dissolved Parliament and ruled by 'Royal Prerogative' for eleven years. Dissolving Parliament was probably his big mistake."

"Was he an Anglo-Catholic?"

"Before the term was used. But the strict enforcement of belief by his archbishop, William Laud, was doomed to fail. Puritans left for America under James I, and a second wave emigrated under Charles. Catholics were feared for being too Roman and Puritans harassed for being too Protestant. Laud punished those who refused to attend Church of England, Anglican, services."

"Is that what caused the Civil War?"

"It was a major reason. And Charles was executed."

Jack tapped his guidebook. "The Puritan Cromwell ruled much the same way."

"Man doesn't always learn from history."

They sat on a bench, its Queen Anne legs curving onto the marble tiles, and Madeleine feared mankind would never learn from the past, that he would always be condemned to repeat his mistakes, particularly if he failed to teach history's lessons to the next generation. Indeed, it deeply troubled her that Western Civilization had been dropped from the core curricula of many universities. "But it was a time of greatness, too," she said, returning to the seventeenth century.

"Oh?"

"It was the time of the Caroline Divines, saintly men who wrote and preached, seeking a new definition of the Anglican way. Nineteenth-century historians called their solution the Via Media, a middle path between Roman Christianity and Puritan Protestants."

"Sounds sensible."

"Even so, the Divines were actually looking back to the primitive Church of the first Christians."

"Did it work, this Via Media?"

Madeleine shook her head. "Not in their own time. They were ascetics. But the next century built on their ideas. Gradually, a sense of the Church of England emerged." Perhaps what one wrote and said today would have an impact on future generations after all. It was a hopeful thought.

"Emerged into our Anglo-Catholic Church?"

"Yes, our Anglo-Catholic Church."

"Too bad it took a regicide to do it."

"And others lost their lives in the Civil War, brothers fighting brothers. Cromwell's Puritans actually had more in common with the Divines than they realized. They too sought the vision of the early Church, but they feared the power of Rome." *One of those horrible ironies of history,* Madeleine thought.

Jack eyed the thrones at the far end. "This looks like a papal chamber, a room for ceremony as well as a good party."

Madeleine agreed. It was indeed a sumptuous *banqueting* room. Chandeliers lit white columns leading to decorated galleries. "Queen Elizabeth and Prince Phillip celebrated their fiftieth wedding anniversary here. Can't you hear the chatter, the clink of glasses and silver, the harpist playing?"

"And according to this brochure, there's an annual commemoration service for King Charles every January 30."

Madeleine paused, feeling the weight of the king's death. "Less than two weeks ago. Let's get some air."

They descended the stairs to Parliament Street, turned right on Downing, and walked past the famous Number 10, home of the Prime Minister. Downing Street opened onto a glistening Saint James Park. Sun peered through early budding trees and watered lawns sparkled. Pushed by a cold wind, they followed a wide path toward Buckingham Palace to a bridge spanning a long finger lake. The waters shimmered, reflecting the monuments at each end, as birds soared over islet refuges.

Jack took pictures and Madeleine pulled her wool scarf about her. She gazed up and down the lake to its double reflections, Whitehall's offices and the Queen's residence, the two pillars of English rule. A fountain played on a stretch of grass under a darkening cloud. Children skipped along a path, Londoners sat on newspaper-lined benches, all enjoying these golden moments between storms, this Sunday afternoon holding both winter and spring.

Madeleine slipped her arm through Jack's and pointed. "Look at the children."

"Sweet, aren't they?"

"Yes."

"I hope we can make some sort of progress on the children's home. At this point, we're counting on Wednesday's property."

"Do you think it will be the right one?" Madeleine's heart tightened.

"It had better be. Joe isn't going to let us stay on forever."

"This Wednesday is Ash Wednesday."

"So it is. Maybe there's a church in Aylesbury." He kissed her on the forehead.

Chapter Twelve
Hyde Park

*The existence of suffering has its roots in the disordered wills of man,
and the confusion thus created. The remedy is a will
entirely surrendered to God, within this confusion.
But where the two things meet, there is bound to be suffering.*
Raymond Raynes

On the second Saturday in February, Victoria set out for Hyde Park, not far from Brook Street. The weather was dry and the sun promising.

She had read that Hyde Park and Kensington Gardens once belonged to Westminster Abbey, and after that served as Henry VIII's royal hunting ground. Criminals had been hanged from Tyburn gallows in the northeast corner, and she had shivered with the description of their final journey from the Tower of London. Carts carrying the condemned rattled through the narrow streets as bloodthirsty mobs shouted taunts. She had read too that not only criminals were executed there. Others died simply for their beliefs, Protestant *or* Catholic. At least today, she thought, Speakers Corner had taken the place of Tyburn Gallows. Today anyone could make a speech about anything. It was fun to see what was going on there on any particular weekend.

Victoria walked briskly along the Serpentine, the lake calm and gray in its winter slumber, past a statue of Peter Pan. She followed the asphalt path around the lake's tail and through a neoclassical garden, then returned along the opposite shore toward a bandstand with a quaint cupola. She pictured the park in spring with its sweeping lawns and leafy shade trees, where Londoners in striped canvas chairs would take in the sun, well-dressed riders would trot horses along the wide trails, and children would lick ice cream purchased from the boathouse snack bar. She imagined paddleboats with young people laughing and teasing and diving into summery waters.

Families—mothers and children and *fathers*—were enjoying this dry temperate day, and Victoria winced with envy and loss. What kind of a life could she offer her child? Would she have the courage to give him up for adoption? Or the courage to raise him? The question haunted her. But there was still time to figure that out. Her father would help her decide.

She turned left at the bandstand, followed the path to Speaker's Corner and paused to observe the scene before her. A monk or a madman, or perhaps a mad monk, stood on an overturned crate, waving his hands wildly one minute, then folding them quietly the next. A crowd had gathered. This could be interesting. She hadn't seen a monk there before.

The tall friar's brown robes merged into his dark skin, trim beard, and black Afro. "I am Brother Cristoforo, and I tell you, believe in Jesus! He is real. He is alive. I, Cristoforo Francesco, witness to him. Ask Jesus into your heart today!"

Victoria's child weighed heavily, and she gladly took one of the folding chairs a young woman offered. A cold breeze swirled through the bare trees and she pulled her jacket about her.

"You have suffered, no?" The monk tossed the question into the crowd. They squirmed nervously. This was a private matter and best left that way.

"You have suffered. We all suffer, do we not? And why is that?"

"The price of rent, the cost of food...," someone mumbled.

Victoria waited expectantly. How would he answer this one?

"We are fallen. Since Adam disobeyed God, man must work. We work to eat, to provide shelter. There will always be pain, is this not true?"

The crowd grew silent.

He held up a large wooden crucifix, painted with reds and golds, a startling contrast to the gray afternoon. "*He* suffered. He suffered for *us* and he suffers *with* us today. We are not alone."

Victoria couldn't see where he was leading, and she welcomed the next question.

"So what, Brother?" a woman shouted. "So what's your point? Get on with it, man!" She shoved her palms onto her hips defiantly, welcoming war.

Cristoforo turned to the woman. "God gave us free will. We can choose him or not choose him. Adam and Eve chose not. This is why our world suffers." He paused, tracing his finger along the wood of the cross. "Because many do not choose God, but reject God. To reject God is to welcome sin. With sin comes suffering...and death."

His eyes narrowed as his gaze roamed the crowd. "John the Baptist cried, *'Repent ye, for the kingdom of heaven is at hand.'* And I say to you today the same: repent—choose God—follow Jesus! Be one with him in the Mass."

Victoria stared at the brown monk. His sandals were torn and his socks had holes. One long toe protruded. His words held her, and he sounded like one who knew.

"Suffering is the way of this world. We do not admit this. But it is true. When we follow Jesus, we help others who suffer. When we help others, our own suffering is less. Jesus said, *'I am the way, the truth and the life: no man cometh unto the Father, but by me.'* Follow Jesus, come to your Heavenly Father, lighten your burden, and take this gift of life." Tenderly, Cristoforo laid the crucifix against the trunk of a tree, then walked along the front row of his audience. His eyes held Victoria's briefly. In that moment, she felt he knew her.

"Here is one more way to ease suffering, my friends. This way is forgiveness. Jesus taught us how to pray. He said to forgive our enemies. Let go of your grudges. Forgive others. Help others. This is the way of Jesus, my sisters and brothers. Repent! Forgive!"

A woman passed a collection basket, and Victoria pulled a coin from her pocket and dropped it in. She checked her watch. It was 3:30 and time to return. She stood wearily. Soon it would be dark. The Collingwoods expected guests tonight, and dinner would require added preparations. As she glanced back at the monk with his waving arms and flashing eyes, she was impressed with his knowledge, his air of authority. She recalled his words about forgiveness and thought of the man who attacked her.

Could she forgive someone she had never met? Someone who had hurt her so? Who had never expressed sorrow? The thought of him repulsed her. And yet Victoria embraced this child with all her heart, this child created by that violence. How could she feel both? At times her feelings swung wildly, contradictory, impossible to reconcile. She tried not to think of the man who raped her. He was a dark shadow from another time, a ghost. He was not a person she could forgive. She didn't know him. He was outside her life, a force not a person, a catalyst not a human being. She shook her head to erase him from her thoughts.

Forgiveness. Were there others she should forgive? Others who tied her heart in knots of pain? Her mother, surely. Her mother disturbed her with mixed feelings. Victoria would always love her, though her mother's love was a binding, controlling love. She longed to be free, to be *Victoria*. But who was this Victoria?

She had made the right decision to leave Danville. It was a matter of survival, not only of the baby, but of her own survival as well.

She stepped down stairs to a pedestrian tunnel running under busy Park Lane. The walls were defaced with graffiti, and she nervously passed a pile of cardboard that covered a sleeping form.

She emerged on the other side of the busy roadway and walked the few blocks to Brook Street. She opened the green door, hoping her hosts were not yet home. She glanced at the sky. Charcoal gray and threatening, but no rain, yet.

Could she forgive?

Sunday morning, Victoria cooked breakfast for her hosts. She set a platter of scrambled eggs and a steaming teapot on a tray and carried it into the dining room where Fanny and Frederick sipped orange juice from crystal goblets. It seemed that their conversation stopped abruptly as she entered, and an awkward silence filled the air. Frederick eyed Fanny with apparent nervousness as Victoria set down the tray, arranged the serving utensils, and poured his tea.

"Thank you, Victoria dear," Fanny said. "Why don't you start the dishes? I'll finish up later." She flashed her perfect smile, a practiced one, Victoria thought, probably most effective in court, her lids dropping and flickering over green eyes that twinkled fleetingly, teasing an agreement.

Frederick stared silently at the business headlines in the *Times*.

"Of course." Victoria returned to the kitchen, sensing something in the air. She turned the faucet on full force and, with a fierce instinct born of motherhood, listened through the door.

A paper rustled.

"She's arriving on the morning flight from San Francisco." It was Frederick, sounding both relieved and agitated.

"Candice?"

"Right."

"Are you sure you can do that? Rather sinister, isn't it? Sneaking about and all, turning the girl over, as it were."

"My dear," Frederick mumbled, his mouth full, "Candice has powerful friends. I owe Andrew, sure I do, but I can't afford to lose my job. For that matter, *we* can't afford to lose my job."

A fork scraped a plate. "Rubbish. Stand up to her, Freddie. What can Candice do anyway?"

"Her uncle's on the bank's board, my pet. I have no choice."

It didn't take long to pack her things, and in her haste Victoria had no time to listen to her fears. She had thought about what she would do, and today she would do it.

Her hosts left at ten for Sotheby's, for another estate sale with several Pyzinskys, and Victoria calculated she had at least a four-hour head start. A cold wind drove dark clouds across the sky as she locked the green door behind her. With a backward glance at the library window, she walked briskly toward the subway. She carried a duffel bag and a backpack, wore the heavy jacket her father had sent, and slipped her traveler's checks deep into an inner pocket. She emerged at Paddington Station at 11:15 and boarded the Oxford train.

As she gazed through the window at the receding city, she reconsidered her plan. How could she possibly present herself to William in Oxford? And in her condition? All the fears she had tried to ignore now flooded her. *How simple she was, how simple and stupid.* To return to London and her mother was unthinkable. Although she was beginning her eighth month, Victoria knew Candice would find a way to force an abortion.

And where was her father? On his way, he said. Somehow she would contact him. For today, she would distance herself from London, the Collingwoods, and her mother.

But Oxford was all wrong. She didn't want to land on William's doorstep. He would feel obligated, and she humiliated.

As Victoria stepped off the train, a bus heading for Aylesbury pulled into the nearby station. She sat on a bench and thumbed her hostel guide. Aylesbury had a youth hostel. She boarded the coach and slipped her duffle behind the driver, who nodded assent with a pitying glance at her face and then her body. She climbed to the upper level.

Taking a seat in the front, she looked through the wide window as the bus rolled out of Oxford. They passed stone steeples, bookstores, and pubs, and into the countryside of English novels.

On another day she would have lingered in Oxford. She would have located the Eagle and Child, the pub where J.R.R. Tolkien and C.S. Lewis and their fellow Inklings met. She would have found Lewis Carroll's Christ Church College. To pass through the town of these writers and not linger was sad indeed, but the baby was active, pushing and pulling, and a constant reminder of her priorities. She wondered where William lodged and touched the smudged glass with sadness and longing. Another time, Oxford.

By five that evening Victoria Nguyen was safely checked into the Aylesbury youth hostel. Mrs. Huddleston, the elderly manager, had been kind and had given her the only single, close to the bath. In the morning, she would write to William so he didn't worry. Perhaps he could find her father. For now, she was too exhausted to think.

Chapter Thirteen
Hartwell House

*For dust thou art,
and unto dust thou shalt return.*
Genesis 3:19

All day Monday it rained. Madeleine and Jack retreated indoors, reading and writing. Jack read the Scripture passage listed in his book of daily devotions, then opened a legal thriller, his legs stretched out on the bed, the pillows propped up.

Madeleine worked on her manuscript, sitting at the antique desk by the window, concentrating on the English chapters. Hartwell House in Aylesbury, she recalled, had an intriguing history, but probably not pertinent to her work's subject. Her editor had complained her scope was too large. Was it? After all, Hartwell *was* a product of the Enlightenment. What had she written about that "Age of Reason" so at odds with the earlier "Age of Faith"?

> *Holy Manifestations: The Enlightenment*
> The English of the late seventeenth and eighteenth centuries, that age of "enlightenment and reason," scientific advances, and philosophic enquiry, sought to put behind them the age of faith, or at least the age of religious wars so entangled with civil unrest. Strong belief meant bloodshed, therefore sensible people would abolish strong belief. Or, if not abolish it, they would not encourage it, would banish such fervor to the safe confines of Sunday, or, for the reasonable man, Christmas and Easter. Thus, society would be at peace.

Not unlike today's distrust of fundamentalism, Madeleine thought.

This fear of strong emotion was understandable, considering the burnings, disembowelments, and decapitations committed in the name of God in the previous centuries, and was supported by the Puritan influence, the removal of image, color, music, festival, and all passionate enterprises from the realm of the Church. Reasonable men of the Enlightenment would express their moments of vision and joy in coffee houses, pubs, and the emerging theater, safely secular institutions in the growing towns and cities. Philosophers would embrace scientific enquiry rather than theology; belief in God, belief in Christ, was fine if kept in its place. Literature thrived in the measured beat of Alexander Pope, in the careful satires of Henry Fielding, and soon took romantic and Gothic turns, allowing passion free reign in secular subjects.

Man's reasonableness was duly effective in politics and society, even if it did enshroud God, as though preparing him for his twentieth century "burial." John Locke promoted meritocracy, lauding ability over birth, Thomas Paine's polemical *Common Sense* enflamed Americans to seek independence, and the French middle class revolted, using the poor as cannon fodder. But England survived without revolution, easing by degree into a constitutional monarchy, albeit without a *written* constitution.

But in spite of the Age of Enlightenment, man remained a warring creature. In the twentieth century—that century proclaiming the death of God—the holocausts of Hitler, Stalin, and Mao took the lives of over a hundred million, the bloodiest years in man's history. Controlling the religious impulse had made no difference. Was another impulse pushing man to act this way? Was Augustine right and Pelagius wrong? Perhaps man *had* fallen from grace and *was* a sinful creature, needing God more than ever, every day of the week.

Could she pull these threads together? Perhaps Hartwell House, built in this orderly age, would inspire her.

With sufficient grace, she and Jack and the Coronati Foundation would sanctify the neighborhood with faith—faith put to use in a children's home and women's shelter. Was this God's plan? She never knew for sure, and as she waited for the outcome, treading lightly with an open heart, she watched events unfold, hopefully within his will in spite of her wrong turns. As she thought of her wrong turns, she recalled her vow to write the Ash Wednesday chapter that afternoon.

As the rain poured, Madeleine began to write, and by the following evening, she had finished. She reviewed the words that poured like the rain, often too many of them, a flood she could not stop. "At least channel them," her editor said. "The reader doesn't want to be inundated. You need to make choices. All art is about making choices." But to Madeleine, striking through her words was like striking her children. Nevertheless, she scrutinized her latest paragraphs with ruthlessness as Jack finished packing for their drive to Hartwell in the morning.

Holy Manifestations: Ash Wednesday
In many English churchyards lie the bodies of the dead, long ago turned to ash in corroded caskets. Ravaged by time, they remind us of our own bodies' inevitable end.

It was this reminder that the Anglo-Catholics revived in the observance of Ash Wednesday, the first day of the forty days of Lent. Facing death, that is, facing God and eternity, cast a healing light on the sufferings of the present. For indeed, life since the Fall of Adam was one of suffering. Each year on Ash Wednesday and throughout Lent they faced their need for God, their own imperfections, their own sins, as they prepared for Easter joy and the promise of eternal life.

This period of fasting and prayer survived the purges of the Reformation, yet was nearly abandoned by the "enlightened" eighteenth-century Church. The Tractarians,[7] nineteenth-century Oxford Movement scholars seeking to return the Church to the sacramental way, reinstated Lent in recognition of life's wholeness, particularly in terms of the body and soul. For without facing the human condition, the impending disintegration of our bodies, how indeed could we fall on our knees before God? We could not lead full, whole, holy lives, they reasoned, without facing our full, whole, holy destiny.

Madeleine closed her laptop. Tonight was Shrove Tuesday, the day of confessing one's sins and being *shriven*, absolved, before the Lenten fast began. Her list of sins was long, and she knew the first she would confess, the most deadly of all: pride. She could not write this book alone; she and Jack could not build this children's home alone. Tonight she would confess, and she would give both projects to God. Tomorrow they would drive to Aylesbury and see if a miracle would occur before their eyes, and she would trust God to give her the words to finish *Holy Manifestations*.

The following day Jack rented a car, and Madeleine was pleased that he allowed Brother Cristoforo to drive, a relinquishing of control that he had once found difficult. Leaving London behind, they headed for historic Hartwell House, nestled peacefully in the Vale of Aylesbury. A gated entry and gravel drive led to a Tudor manor house, its tall leaded windows, to Madeleine's thinking, both stately and welcoming. A porter carried their bags, leading them to the reception desk off the Great Hall. While Jack checked in, Cristoforo parked the car and Madeleine read the hotel's brochure.

According to the text, William Peverel, son of William the Conqueror, owned the original house in the eleventh century. Over time, the manor was rebuilt; the seventeenth-century façade seen today dated to the Hampden and Lee families, whose descendents immigrated to America. As Hartwell saw the beginning of the nineteenth century, it became a refuge for French royals escaping the guillotine. The market town of Aylesbury, once home to Franciscan friars, became a modern county seat with a Friary Shopping Plaza and a Roald Dahl museum. How nice, Madeleine thought, that a children's author had lived in Aylesbury too.

The friar returned, waving his arms. "The gardener says the monastery next door has a church used by the local parish, Saint Anne's Abbey. There will be Imposition of Ashes at the noon Mass. I will offer my help to Father Dodd, their priest. Will you come?"

Madeleine checked her watch. "That would be perfect."

Jack looked concerned. "We still have the eleven o'clock appointment with the Aylesbury agent to see the monastery property?"

"*Si*. His daughter. Her father is not available."

The Victorian monastery next door to Hartwell House was approached by a half-circle drive. A stone abbey appeared to be adjacent. The façade of the three-story monastery was gray brick, with oriel windows and dormers peeking from a shingled roof. Hefty stone chimneys anchored each end. The entrance, with its gabled porch, was welcoming, and Madeleine could picture jasmine climbing the columns and a broad lawn running out from the drive, filling in the half circle. And, perhaps, rosebushes under the lower windows. How lovely it would be!

As she stepped into the narrow foyer, she had a sense of déjà vu. Had she been here before? The gray walls were bare, the paint peeling. Stairs ascended to the right, and, as she looked up, she could see she was at the base of an open stairwell. Several flights zigzagged above her, and Cristoforo was already lumbering up them. Jack glanced at the agent, waiting for her lead.

Trudy Saunders reminded Madeleine of a student from the sixties, with her baggy pullover, floral skirt, and high boots, but she couldn't have been over thirty-five. Her limp brown hair waved down her back and a fringe of blunt-cut bangs framed an oval face with wire-rim glasses which she pushed up the ridge of her nose with a thin forefinger.

"You can see it's vacant," Trudy said, glancing around the entry. "This building was the dormitory. It once connected to the abbey, but the passage was sealed off after the Second World War. The bedrooms are upstairs."

She led them out the back to an industrial-size kitchen. The basics were there, if old-fashioned: deep sinks, a massive wood-burning stove, a double oven, long yellowing counters, a wooden island in the center of the room. Cupboards lined the walls. Madeleine peeked into a pantry, its shelves thick with dust.

"Needs work," Jack said. "When was it last occupied?"

"Most recently it was a small private school. They moved out about ten years ago."

Madeleine gazed through tall vertical windows to gentle green hills. "The light is good. Peaceful too." One can almost hear the silence, feel it, touch it, she thought. She unlatched a window and a brisk breeze wafted in. "The air's so fresh out here in the country."

Cristoforo appeared in the doorway. "Sixteen rooms. Four baths. *Bene.*"

Trudy Saunders showed them a large dining room off the kitchen. Several other rooms on the main floor had been used as classrooms for the school and before that, meeting rooms for the monks.

"Any ghosts?" Madeleine asked, only partly joking. Any *disclosures*, she thought.

Trudy laughed. "Only in stories made up by the villagers. But the building has been a target for vandals from time to time."

As they ascended the stairs, Jack asked the agent why the property had been on the market so long. Trudy looked at him with an open, honest countenance. "The Trust has a number of stipulations about the property. It's actually owned by the family of one of the monks from the old days. They don't want the house structurally changed. It can't be broken into flats, that sort of thing. It must be kept whole. So that limits its commercial value. Most places this size have been made into condos."

"What are they asking?"

"It depends."

"Oh?"

"The executors will meet with you. If they don't like you, as usually happens, they don't sell at any price. If they like you, like your plans, then you can at least talk about it."

Jack raised his brows. "That's not easy for you as an agency."

She shook her head and flipped a long strand of hair over her back. "My dad gave up on the thing years ago. He says he doesn't have the time. So I show it mostly. I think it's kind of quaint. I like these old places."

"I like old places too," Madeleine said as they paused on the second-floor landing.

Cristoforo turned to Jack. "I must help at the abbey," he said and headed down the stairs.

Madeleine peeked into the bedrooms on each side of the hall and the baths at each end. A third floor followed the same plan, and a fourth floor had attic rooms, with the dormer windows that had charmed Madeleine on their arrival.

"We'll let you know, all right?" Jack said as they returned to the ground floor.

Trudy handed Jack a card. "No rush. I'll be in the office the next few days if you want to set up a meeting with the owners. Then I go on holiday, but my dad can take care of you." She lowered herself into a rusting Morris Minor and drove away, the car lurching forward in fits and starts.

"I like it," Madeleine said as she followed Jack through a lych-gate.

"Me too, but we'll take it one step at a time. We need to meet with these people. They sound eccentric."

"Maybe—or simply careful."

Bells rang noon as Madeleine and Jack walked along a flagstone path through a graveyard and entered Saint Anne's Abbey. The nave was long and vaulted, with columns running to a monks' choir. Beyond the choir a tented tabernacle rested on a stone altar. The lofty space dwarfed the local congregation, and seemed haunted by earlier times, Madeleine thought, when the choir stalls were filled with chanting Benedictines. Today only Cristoforo took a place in the choir; about thirty parishioners knelt in the nave to receive the ashes that would mark the beginning of their Lent. Madeleine and Jack found seats toward the front.

Young Father Dodd, heavyset with a ruddy complexion, censed the altar, swinging his thurible through the air, creating clouds of smoke around and about the stone table.

Madeleine and Jack watched and waited, kneeling in the first pew. The red candle burned alongside the tabernacle, and Madeleine felt the prayers of those who had worshiped there before, those holy men and women who had given themselves to God, then received their lives back a thousand fold.

Father Dodd began the liturgy, moving thoughtfully, reading with marked reverence the prayers in the missal open to his left.

The week before, Madeleine knew, the villagers had given him their palm fronds, carefully saved since last year's Palm Sunday, aged in Bibles and prayer books or behind crucifixes and icons, and Father Dodd had burned them to a fine black ash. Now, standing before the tabernacle, he blessed the ashes and beckoned the faithful forward.

Madeleine and Jack rose and joined the others, kneeling at the altar rail, raising their foreheads to the priest.

"*Remember O man, that dust thou art, and to dust thou shalt return.*" Father Dodd dipped his finger into a bowl of ash and traced a cross on each forehead, linking last year's Easter with the one to come, mirroring the anointing oil of their baptism, and reminding each penitent of their frailty, their eventual death, and their need for God.

"*Kyrie Eleison, Kyrie Eleison, Kyrie Eleison.*" Voices chanted from the choir loft, and the amber tones drifted through the incense as the altar was prepared for the Holy Eucharist.

The Mass was short and the sermon shorter, but the Mass was the same, always the same, whether long or short, Madeleine thought thankfully, and once again she met her Lord.

She had confessed and cleaned out her heart as best she could. She carved her pride into parts: impatience, distrust, and fear that time rolled by too fast. Although only fifty-four, the fact of her inevitable death colored her life with its astounding certainty, and her body, with its sagging skin and creaking joints, reinforced this awareness. Madeleine did not fear death, for she believed in Christ's promise of eternal life, but there was much to do before she died, so many others to carry with her.

She returned to her pew as the ashes flaked upon her lashes, darkening her tears of mourning for the world, and she knew that in the end "all shall be well," as the anchoress Julian of Norwich wrote from her hermit's cell six hundred years ago. Finally, Madeleine let go of her need to save and allowed her Lord to act, for after all, it *was* his job.

The congregation stood, and Madeleine hurried to her feet, joining in the last hymn:

"The glory of these forty days
We celebrate with songs of praise;
For Christ, by whom all things were made,
Himself has fasted and has prayed."

She would fast. She would abstain from meat and sweets for Lent. She would try to say her prayers more often, and possibly the most important, she would trust God.

As the last worshipers left the abbey, Cristoforo began to put away the sacred vessels. Suddenly he turned and walked down the center aisle. Madeleine and Jack followed.

Chapter Fourteen
St. Anne's Abbey

Be ye sure that the Lord he is God;
it is he that hath made us, and not we ourselves.
Psalm 100:3

The morning after she arrived in Aylesbury, Victoria wrote to William in Oxford.

Dear William,
I wanted to let you know I'm staying in the Aylesbury Youth Hostel for a bit of country air. I noticed Oxford isn't far, and would love to come visit, maybe take you up on your invitation.
  Then I could explain why I am here in Aylesbury.
  Your friend,
  Victoria Nguyen

As she waited for his response, she wished again she had his phone number; it wasn't on his card and she hadn't asked for it, the request seeming too forward at the time. Even so, contacting him by mail felt better than using the phone. Letters distanced the message and allowed him to ignore it if he chose to. A phone call would be far more forceful and demanding. And what would she say? Letters were better at this point. Even so, as soon as she gave it to Mrs. Huddleston to post, she wanted to take it back. What was she thinking?

Not sure what to do next but wait for William's response, Victoria explored the town, enjoying the fresh air and exercise.

"Now don't you go too far, lassie," Mrs. Huddleston said at breakfast on Wednesday. She wagged her stubby finger and poured more milk. "And stay away from Saint Anne's and the cemetery, on the other side of town. They say it's haunted for sure, and we don't want anyone scaring you, not at a time like this."

Victoria nodded, enjoying the attention of the kind old woman, who fluttered about like a mother hen. "I'll be careful, Mrs. Huddleston."

She walked up a cobblestone path past half-timbered houses, paused at a gate guarding an overgrown graveyard, and peered through the rusted iron with its forged symbol of cross and chalice. A light rain fell, and as her eye rested on an old stone church, she heard an organ playing and a chorus of mismatched voices. She tried the gate, and it was open. She noticed a sign with faded black script: *Saint Anne's Abbey.*

"Well, Baby, let's go see what there is to see. It doesn't look haunted to *me*."

She wandered the graves, marked by plain wooden crosses, and read their epitaphs, guessing they were clergy; *Dom this and Dom that, monks' titles,* she thought. *Is this a monastery church? William might like to see this.*

People were coming out the doors, walking quietly through the high grass to the gate, and Victoria noticed their smudged foreheads. Was this some kind of cult? It was eerie here amidst the tombstones, with the wet fog, and Mrs. Huddleston had warned her.

But recalling the peace she had known in Faith Chapel, she sneaked through the open door and sat in a back pew. Sweet-smelling smoke swirled in the dark sanctuary, and Victoria could make out candles burning on an altar. A red lamp hung from the ceiling, suspended on a chain. Someone moved around the altar, someone tall in a long brown robe, maybe a monk, straightening things; two others, a man and a woman, knelt in the front, the only ones left from the service, it seemed. The peace of the place did indeed recall Faith Chapel in Westminster Abbey where, for some odd reason, she had begun to cry. She had sensed a great love there, a love that overwhelmed her. In a way, they had been happy tears, good tears. She would rest here at Saint Anne's for a moment.

The monk turned and approached her. *Oh dear,* she thought.

"The Mass is over," he said, "but I can give you ashes and a blessing, my child." He knelt and leaned toward her, a puzzled expression on his face.

Victoria eyed his smudged forehead. "It's Ash Wednesday! I forgot. I was only visiting, but you look familiar. Do I know you?"

"*I* know *you*."

"I remember. You were preaching at Speaker's Corner."

"I was, and you were in my congregation." He smiled and a silver tooth gleamed. "Please, allow me to present myself. I am Brother Cristoforo." He shook her hand as they both rose.

"And I am...Violet Chan."

"Ms. Chan, I am most pleased to meet you." He motioned to the man and woman as they approached. "May I present my friends, the *Signori* Seymours."

"Pleased to meet you," Victoria said, immediately drawn to the woman's friendly face. Kind hazel eyes, crinkling at the corners reassuringly, shone through rimless glasses. Her auburn hair, streaked with silver, was layered in short waves. She was about Victoria's height, of medium build, and she wore a pale pink cardigan with gray flannel slacks. A silk square in pink and gray was tied neatly around her neck and she carried a rain jacket on her arm, the strap of her brown handbag holding it in place.

"Please call me Madeleine," she said, "and we are delighted to meet *you*. This is my husband, Jack."

"Pleased to meet you as well, Mr. Seymour," Victoria said.

The tall man nodded seriously as he shook her hand warmly, smiling. "Call me Jack," he said. His hands were small but his grip firm, and blue eyes peered from a freckled face. He wore a dark jacket, vest, and tie which made him seem English and aristocratic, but his accent was clearly American.

"Are you from the neighborhood?" Madeleine asked tentatively.

"Just visiting," Victoria said, hesitating.

"That's nice."

"I was getting some air, walking around, you know...and saw the church."

Madeleine leaned forward and gently touched Victoria's shoulder. A light dusting of ash fell onto the girl's hair.

"We're staying next door, at Hartwell House." Madeleine's expression held the promise of shared pleasure. "Would you like to join us for tea? It's an intriguing old place."

"I would like that, thanks." The words slipped out. Why did she trust this woman? *She* appeared familiar too, but it wasn't Speaker's Corner. She reminded Victoria of her favorite high school teacher, a woman quietly enthusiastic about some very difficult writers. Mrs. Johnson had made even Chaucer interesting, and they had acted out scenes from Shakespeare. It had been fun, really, not work at all.

Jack turned to the friar, who waited nearby. "Cristoforo, when you finish up, could you meet us at Hartwell?" The friar nodded, bowed, and turned toward the altar.

"Where are you staying, Violet?" Madeleine asked.

"At the youth hostel here in the village."

A few silver strands framed the elder woman's pale face, giving her an aura in the fog. She seemed to be studying Victoria. "A spot of tea would be excellent in this nasty weather. England *is* dreary sometimes, isn't it? And I think you are American. So are we. We shall have such a *lovely* time together."

As they walked into the mist, Madeleine halted abruptly. "Why, I saw you in Hatchard's, and earlier at Westminster Abbey. What a coincidence."

The ashes had settled on Victoria's nose, and she touched the spot without thinking, then looked at the smudge on her finger.

"The children's books," Victoria said, withdrawing. "The children's books—I remember." She had run errands at Fortnum & Mason's and explored Hatchard's next door.

But this woman was American and had been in London. Could she possibly be connected to her mother? Was this really just a coincidence?

Victoria stepped into Hartwell's Great Hall with some nervousness. Having second thoughts, she glanced back at the entry. Why had she agreed to this? She looked about the welcoming room, at the antique furnishings. But what harm could a little tea do?

A dark tapestry covered one wall. A fire crackled in a grate under a white sculpted mantel. Portraits of people from long ago gazed upon overstuffed chairs grouped before the fire. Settees lined a window bay, their faded damasks catching the afternoon light. The Persian carpets, worn thin, reminded Victoria of *Pride and Prejudice*, and in her mind she could see Elizabeth Bennett awaiting her guests as carriages rolled up the drive.

"Wow," she said, unable to find other words.

Jack took their coats, laid them on a chair, and headed for the stairs. "Maddie, entertain Ms Chan for a few minutes. I need to call our broker, unload a few shares, and fax McGinty a report on the property."

"With pleasure." Madeleine turned to Victoria. "This is the Great Hall of Hartwell House. There are three other common rooms that are not so very common, along the west side."

Victoria followed her, tiptoeing in her running shoes, clutching her backpack and resting her hand on her child. She was in a novel.

The next room had a fireplace as well, with another carved mantel under a gilt mirror. The walls were covered in a green and cream paper pattern. The entire ceiling, powder white, was sculpted with flowers and birds.

"In the eighteenth century," Madeleine was saying, "there was no electric heating, so every room had a fireplace, providing function *and* beauty."

They stepped into a library where walls of books were protected by a scrolled iron grill. Guests could recline on silk sofas or pause in alcoves to gaze over broad lawns, early daffodils, and dappled cows. The bookshelves, holding other minds from other times, lives in parchment, as her Aunt Elizabeth had often said, comforted Victoria.

Madeleine sat on a blue silk settee and motioned to Victoria to join her. "This is one of England's great historic houses. In this room the French king, Louis XVIII, signed the papers that restored the monarchy to France." Amazement flickered over her features.

Victoria wondered what the French monarchy was doing in England, not to mention this very room. "Louis XVIII was here?"

"He escaped the Revolution and wandered the courts of Europe for years as an exile, then settled at Hartwell from 1809 to 1814. There were over a hundred family members, courtiers, and servants with him." Madeleine shook her head as though surely it was impossible, but nevertheless it was true.

"I can't imagine it. A hundred people living in this house? It's large, but not *that* large."

"They turned the roof into a garden."

"Seems strange, with all the parkland."

"It does indeed."

"This room is cozy. I like the books."

"I could sit here all day and read. There are trails that circle the park and wide carriage drives, just like in Austen's novels. Have you read Jane Austen, Violet?"

"She was my favorite author at my aunt's when I visited in the summer."

"She's one of my favorites too. You spent summers at your aunt's?"

Victoria happily recalled the time. "Many summers. There was little to do but read, which was fine with me." How good it was to have

121

someone to talk to, but she must not forget this woman was a stranger.

"What do you like best about Jane Austen?"

Victoria slipped easily into the storylines, the tone and mood of the settings, the developing romances of the characters. "I think I like the order of it all. Everything so proper, and everyone has a place they know and understand. And there is a clear sense of right and wrong, of silly and superficial character versus serious and substantial."

"Well said. I agree. Today, it's a bit confusing."

"Mrs. Seymour—Madeleine—I don't think I shall ever understand my place in the world." Victoria gazed at the carpet, embarrassed that she had been so candid.

"I know what you mean."

Victoria looked up. With her fingertip, Madeleine traced a delicate crucifix that rested in the vee of her blouse, and as their eyes met, Victoria sensed the older woman could be trusted. "You know what I mean?" Her eyes were drawn to the miniature Christ hammered in gold.

"I do. But you aren't alone. It takes a lifetime to truly understand one's self. Now, would you like to see the princess' room?"

"The princess?"

"Our bedroom belonged to a French princess, the daughter of Marie Antoinette and Louis XVI, niece of Louis XVIII."

They climbed the grand staircase off the lobby, past massive portraits of royal figures, then entered a corner bedroom with tall bay windows looking out to majestic trees, the bare branches reaching through the mist. A canopied bed faced an antique dressing table and mirror. A portrait of a sad young woman hung on a wall.

"There she is," Madeleine said tenderly, "the Duchesse d'Angouleme, the princess, the daughter of Louis XVI and Marie Antoinette. She was imprisoned with her family in Paris from 1792 to 1794, then freed and sent to Vienna. During her imprisonment her parents and her aunt were executed. No one knows for sure what happened to her little brother, the prince."

"She survived the Revolution? And this was her bedroom?"

Madeleine nodded. "She met up with her uncle, the future Louis XVIII, in Latvia, where he was protected by the Russian tsar. They finally found asylum in England. She was probably about twenty-one when she arrived here."

"Did she ever go back to France?"

"In 1815, after Napoleon's defeat and her uncle's coronation."

Victoria patted her baby, who was kicking again. Perhaps, she thought, she would be safe after all; others had suffered and survived, even exiles.

"Let's find Jack," Madeleine said.

He was seated before a crackling fire in the Great Hall. Victoria lowered herself into an armchair and Madeleine joined Jack on the couch.

"I ordered tea," Jack said. "One pot of Earl Grey and one pot of chamomile."

"Thank you," Victoria said. "The chamomile will be perfect. Do you stay here at Hartwell House often, Madeleine and...Jack?" She attempted conversation, as her mother and Elizabeth Bennett would have done, but she would be careful with her trust. She fixed her gaze on the flames licking the blackened chimney walls.

Madeleine looked about the room with apparent appreciation. "This is our second visit."

"We came here on business once," Jack explained, as the butler laid the tea service on a low table, alongside a plate of sliced nut bread, plump biscuits, tiny bowls of jam and heavy cream, and a plate of what looked to be honeycomb.

Madeleine peeked inside the pots. "Almost ready." She glanced at Victoria. "So what brings you to Aylesbury, Violet? Do you have family in the area?"

"Not exactly." Victoria twisted the napkin on her lap.

"That's okay," Jack said quickly, "you don't have to explain. My wife can be inquisitive."

"But you've been kind, and I *have* been lonely." Was she revealing too much? Her eyes checked the room for her mother, as though she might suddenly appear.

Jack poured Victoria's tea. "We're here on business again this time, a different sort of business. Later we hope to visit Chewton Glen in the New Forest for a few days before returning home."

"Business?" *That's better, talk about them.* She sipped her tea. The chamomile had hints of lemon and vanilla.

Madeleine reached for the pitcher of milk. "We'd like to open a children's home and clinic. It will offer prenatal testing and counseling, adoption services, and a free clinic for the local children. There will be a small orphanage and women's shelter. Brother Cristoforo helps in our Coronati House in Rome. We're hoping he'll find an order of nuns to run this one."

"It's no small task these days," Jack said. "Religious orders have been shrinking."

Victoria leaned forward with interest. *A children's home?*

"Where are you from, Violet?" Jack asked, his voice tentative.

Victoria breathed deeply. "San Francisco, or rather, Danville. It's nearby. To the east of San Francisco."

Madeleine beamed. "We're from San Francisco as well. We know Danville. We have friends there."

Victoria swallowed hard. Perhaps she should leave now, with an appropriate excuse. But something compelled her to stay a bit longer. "You're from San Francisco? *Seymour.* Sounds familiar, but I can't place it." She tucked the name into the back of her mind as she reached for a raisin scone.

Madeleine sipped her tea, then said, "Jack owned Seymour Wines in our other life, before retirement. Maybe that's the connection."

"Really? I know the stores, but I don't think that's it." Victoria rummaged through her past. "There's a store in Danville and my father shops there often."

"We did our best to keep prices reasonable," said Jack.

An answer formed in Victoria's mind. *"I know why you're familiar. My aunt spoke of you."* Why did she say that? She was giving away too much information.

Madeleine's face was open, ingenuous, compelling Victoria to trust her. "Who's your aunt, Violet?"

Aunt Elizabeth's good opinion was enough for now. "Elizabeth Crawford in the Napa Valley. She thought the world of you."

Sadness shadowed Jack's features. "She passed away recently, as I recall. We were sorry to miss her funeral. I believe we were in Rome."

Madeleine fingered the cross about her neck. "Our condolences, Violet. I greatly admired your aunt. She was brave to speak out like she did."

"Thank you." Victoria's heart clutched with the memory, so linked with her child. Would her aunt's death bless that lakeside tragedy and transform it into new life? She lay her hands on her protruding tummy, feeling her son move. Her jeans stretched tight, under her blouse. She was down to two sets of clothes, having grown out of her other things, and there was no point in buying new ones now, even if she *could* afford them. She'd left her smaller sizes at the Collingwood's.

"She was a fine woman," Jack added, looking into the distance and tapping his cup with his finger.

Madeleine leaned forward, her earnest eyes seeking Victoria's.

"Elizabeth Crawford was a supporter of our Coronati Foundation. Jack, didn't you know her even before, when you were in the wine business?"

"I did indeed." Jack looked fondly at his wife, then turned to Victoria as he placed his cup on the table. "Our stores bought Crawford wines. Not great vintages, but good, drinkable-today wines. They made a decent chardonnay at one point. I recall '93 and '94 being exceptional. They did a good pinot noir too, but I've forgotten the years on that one. Once they mixed merlot into their cab, they had an excellent red. I think her stepsons run the operation?"

"They do." Victoria returned her gaze to the fire. The summers on the ranch flickered before her: the paneled library, the bubbling fountain, the dry heat rising from the gentle earth, the vines filling out in their controlled grandeur, straight rows of promise; her frail aunt in the white wicker rocker, reading her prayer book, her feet barely touching the wooden verandah. "Say your prayers each day, and you will be blessed," she would say. But Victoria hadn't tried; it seemed part of her aunt's eccentricity. She would pour her ice tea mixed with lemonade, the flex-straw angled just so, and locate her reading glasses. Then Victoria would curl into the swinging chaise under the oak tree with a book and an apple. The tart sweetness of the fruit filled her mouth as she turned the pages; the crispness of both, the apple and the page, tingled in her memory.

Jack nibbled a slice of nut bread. "I remember Mrs. Crawford well. She knew a friend of ours, Joe McGinty. He escorted her to some of our fundraisers for Coronati House. They seemed like old buddies—and could she dance, considering she must have been in her eighties even then!" He dusted off a crumb from his brown slacks. His jacket looked soft, a fine cashmere checked in blues and browns. "She lived in Saint Helena, right?"

Victoria nodded. "Yes, just outside of town."

Madeleine touched Victoria's arm lightly. "She attended Saint Stephen's, I believe." She lifted the teapot with both hands and carefully refilled Victoria's cup.

"I don't know. I...I'm not exactly religious. She was Episcopalian." In her mind, Victoria heard her aunt start up the old Cadillac and crunch down the gravel drive, heading to town for Sunday Mass, her Welsh Corgi barking in the living room window. Each Saturday evening she had invited Victoria, and Victoria had politely declined. Why? What had she feared? Now it seemed such a loss.

Jack offered Victoria the honeycomb, a golden brick nesting in its own syrup. "Try this. It's really good. They make it here, in the back of the property, would you believe? I never thought England would have enough sun to make honey, but here it is. There's actually an association of beekeepers."

"All they need for honey," Madeleine said, "is bees and flowers, and some brave keepers with strange protective gear." She shook her head with a light laugh and adjusted her glasses.

Victoria laughed, feeling more at ease. Madeleine eyed the honey. "Ah, Lent." She raised her brows and smoothed some clotted cream on the scone. "I gave up sweets for Lent," she explained to Victoria. "Sweets and meats."

Jack looked earnestly at Victoria. "Would you like to stay for supper, Violet?"

"We'd enjoy your company," Madeleine added quickly. "We can compare notes on your aunt."

"I'd love to," Victoria blurted. Why had she said that? Just because they knew Aunt Elizabeth? Tea was fine, but she should keep a low profile and not involve these people any more than she needed to. "Maybe I should call Mrs. Huddleston at the hostel, since she expects me for dinner." That would give her time to make up an excuse to decline. After all, the Seymours really were strangers. Life was so very complicated.

"Of course," Madeleine agreed.

Jack stood, offered his hand to Victoria, and helped her out of the chair. As she crossed the room to the reception counter, she reached for Mrs. Huddleston's card in her pocket. The clerk pointed to an old-fashioned phone in the corner. Victoria scrutinized the number on the card and dialed the shiny black face, a rotary like her aunt's. As the small circles whirred back into position, and her finger searched for the next number, her spine prickled with an unknown dread.

"Ms. Chan?" Mrs. Huddleston sounded relieved.

"Mrs. Huddleston, I called to let you know I wouldn't be back for dinner."

"I'm glad you called, Ms. Chan, 'cause there's been a lady here asking for you, a very smart-lookin' lady, and rather pushy, if you don't mind me sayin' so, yes, a mite pushy, I'd say. She's askin' if I know a Ms. Nguyen, and she described you to a tee, with well, you know—your pretty face and all. She's lookin' for her daughter, she says. She don't look like you, lassie, or anyone called Nguyen for that matter, but it's not me business, so I didn't say you were here."

Victoria held the phone to her ear, paralyzed.

"Are you there, lassie?"

The room grew warm and close, and the walls seemed to be caving in. Her legs wobbled, the handset slipped from her grip, and she crumpled to the floor.

Chapter Fifteen
Chewton Glen

*Faith is that which,
knowing the Lord's will, goes and does it;
or not knowing it, stands and waits,
content in ignorance as in knowledge.*
George MacDonald

Cristoforo removed the sacred vessels from the altar and carried them to Saint Anne's sacristy where he carefully cleaned and dried them. Returning to the altar, he put away the missal, folded the linens, and snuffed the tapers, leaving the red lamp burning. He genuflected slowly, thoughtfully. Making the Sign of the Cross, he padded through the choir, down the nave, and into the damp afternoon. A fine mist drifted, neither rain nor fog, surrounding him with stillness.

The graves in the churchyard were mostly overgrown, but their dark crosses formed neat rows, humbly carved with first names: Dom Anthony, *He loved God*; Dom Peter, *A man of grace*; Dom Vincent, *He dwells with the Community of Our Lord*; Dom Anselm, *He in us and we in Him*. The friar caught his breath: Dom Christopher, *Eternity is now*.

He scratched his beard and touched the scarred ridge of his chin. He traced the crosses, one by one, saying quietly, *Lord have mercy, make me worthy*. Abruptly, he wheeled about and returned to the abbey. He walked down the central aisle, through the choir, and knelt before the high altar. He stared at the tabernacle, praying to the one who gave him life.

Cristoforo had one looming goal: to let God work through him and not to hinder that work on earth. He knew there were times when God used him, usually times of smallness, when his ego had shrunk to nothing and his heart had been scrubbed bare by Christ. And, in these miraculous times God shone a light into his soul and revealed who he,

Cristoforo, really was—his true self, the man he was meant to be.

The ragged friar often thought of Christ's baptism in the Jordan River. As Jesus rose from the waters, the Holy Spirit descended like a dove to meet him. Cristoforo saw himself like that, flying up, out of his ego-jail, and meeting God coming down. And there, at that point of meeting, the friar offered himself, Cristoforo Francesco, to be God's temple. His great dream, the dream that exorcised his past horrors, was that when others saw him, a poor monk with his odd looks, bad teeth, and haggard face, they would still catch a glimpse of Christ. Cristoforo knew that to dream such greatness and not succumb to crushing pride was only possible within the Mass.

The monk's gaze shifted to the red lamp. At times he felt he wrestled with God like Jacob in the Scriptures, dancing with his maker, trying to follow his lead, moving through time with the music, with the heartbeat of creation.

Dom Christopher, his life remembered in this graveyard, knew this—*knows* this—Cristoforo thought, that *eternity is now*, that God is in us perfectly in the Eucharist, filling us, fulfilling us, with himself.

And, the friar thought, when he did not let Christ clean him, fill him, use him, the dark one slithered in, that old serpent of lies, feeding his selfishness and demonizing his nights. No, he must keep the snake away.

Cristoforo genuflected in the aisle and moved toward the door. Halfway down the nave, he turned suddenly and walked back to the altar. There, before the tabernacle, he lay prostrate, face down on the cold floor, his arms outstretched, his body forming a cross.

"Thank you, Lord Jesus, thank you," he bellowed into the stone, his hoarse cry echoing through the chilly air.

Then slowly, he raised himself up, left the abbey, and walked briskly to Hartwell, oblivious to the now pouring rain, his heart on fire. It was nearly four, and he had not broken today's fast. They had invited him for tea, he recalled. Would there be some of the little sandwiches? He would have to watch for those without meat, for it *was* Ash Wednesday and the beginning of Lent, but he was due what his superior called a "light meal." This would be his light meal, and those English sandwiches reminded him of the Italian *tramezzini*.

The first thing Victoria saw when she awoke was Madeleine's worried face. The older woman's brow was pinched and her mouth partly open as though breathless with concern.

What had happened? Victoria felt strange, a little dizzy. Looking around, she realized she was lying on a settee in the Great Hall of Hartwell House, where the Seymours had brought her for tea.

"She's coming around, Jack," Madeleine said. "There's no need for an ambulance, not yet."

Victoria raised her head and felt her tummy. The baby seemed okay.

"You took a bit of a fall, Ms. Chan." Jack appeared alongside Madeleine, his tall frame and curly hair silhouetted against the window. Rain slanted against the glass, and wind wailed in the chimney.

Victoria recalled Mrs. Huddleston and tried to sit up. "I need to leave."

"You need to rest," Madeleine said.

"You don't understand." Victoria pushed herself up on her elbows and looked about the room in panic. She couldn't return to the hostel to retrieve her bag. Thank God, she had her passport and traveler's checks in her backpack.

"Please, let us help." Madeleine put an arm about her shoulders.

"I must go," Victoria said. "There's not enough time—she could take the baby even now. She would, you know; I'm such an embarrassment to her." While Victoria knew her mother wouldn't *physically* force her to abort her child, she also knew that the power of her mother's words and the sheer force of her presence would ensure she got her way. In the end, whether it was her mother's strength or Victoria's weakness, the result would be the same.

"Hold on, young lady," Jack said. "Exactly whom are you talking about? I think more tea is in order and more explanations. Let's stay calm and sit down and figure this thing out."

At that moment, the friar, drenched and dripping, burst into the foyer. The reception clerk screamed, and Jack hurried to the desk to rescue Cristoforo.

Madeleine turned to Victoria. "You're running away, aren't you, Violet?" She peered into her eyes.

"Yes."

"And your name's not Violet, is it?"

"It's Victoria, Victoria Nguyen. I've never been a good liar."

"And why, Victoria Nguyen, are you running?"

Victoria considered what to tell and what not to tell.

"Are you running away from home?"

"Maybe."

"From your parents?"

"Maybe." She twisted her shirt with her index finger and locked her eyes on the faded burgundy carpet, with its green flowers and leaves of sea-blue. Her baby thrust into her side, high, near her waist.

Jack appeared with a barefoot Cristoforo. "Maddie, I'm taking Cristoforo up to the room to dry off and talk him into a hot bath. He's been wandering in the rain. I'll have his tea brought up." He glanced at the friar's worried face. "And sandwiches."

As the two men headed toward the stairs, Madeleine sat beside Victoria. Victoria took a deep breath. It would be good, she thought, to tell someone, to explain it all. "I became pregnant last July."

"Is that why you are running?"

"I want to have the baby, and my mother doesn't want me to."

"Oh dear. And your father?"

"He supported me. But he can't stand up to her."

"I see."

"He arranged for me to stay with friends in London."

"And where is he now? And where are these friends?"

"I don't know where Daddy is. He said he was on his way." She could feel tears were near, and she blinked hard. "And the friends told Mother where I was. I just don't know what to do!" She shook her head and stared out to the rain.

"Is that why you left London? These so-called friends?"

"She can make them do anything. I had to leave."

"And why Aylesbury?"

"It wasn't Aylesbury, it was Oxford because of William, William Collingwood, their son, who was kind, but I realized I couldn't show up on his doorstep, and there was a bus going here...." It all seemed a bit irrational now. What was she thinking? But then, what should she have done?

Madeleine paused, as though putting the pieces together. "Is your mother related to Senator Crawford-Nguyen of California?"

"She *is* Senator Nguyen." Victoria nodded, watching Madeleine's expression carefully. "Do you know her?"

"Our paths crossed once. She's a strong and...powerful woman." Madeleine massaged her temple. "Jack and I aren't really involved in politics. Let's just say we don't share many of her views. I think I understand your situation." Her eyes rested on Victoria's figure.

"Do you?"

"I think I do. But your mother's in Aylesbury now?" Madeleine stood and looked toward the door. "Shouldn't we meet with her?" Her voice trembled slightly.

"No. I'll leave. There's no need for you to get involved."

Madeleine was clearly torn. "If you were *my* daughter, I'd want to see you, Victoria. But if you *must* leave, I'll go with you. The choice is yours."

"Thank you. I'm leaving." She couldn't hold back the tears any longer.

Madeleine pulled her close, rubbing her back as she sobbed quietly. "It's okay. Let it out, let it out. God will protect you, you'll see."

Madeleine thought the drive would never end, the dark and the rain a tunnel of time and space. But while Victoria dozed, Madeleine used the hours to reflect on the sudden change of events.

As Madeleine had packed for the journey, leaving Victoria resting before the fire, Jack had listened to Madeleine's retelling of the girl's story.

"We just need time, a little time," she insisted. "We can't force her to face her mother. She'll run away again. I can't betray her like that, and you know what the senator is like."

"Pretty cutthroat...and two-faced," Jack had said, groaning, and Madeleine could see he remembered her all too well.

In the end, he called ahead to book rooms in Chewton Glen Hotel a few days earlier than planned. The country house was located on the southern coast near Southampton, close to the New Forest. They would help Victoria work things out with her mother. For now, Jack would stay at Hartwell to meet with the trustees of the abbey property and, hopefully, make an offer. He would join them soon.

Now, as the car took them south toward Winchester and west into the Forest, Madeleine recalled their run-in with the junior senator from California. Candice Crawford-Nguyen had appeared at an early fundraiser for Coronati House as a guest of Joe McGinty, who'd hoped to persuade her that the project was a noble one, worthy of her support. But she used the occasion as a self-serving public relations ploy, arranging for photographs that would widen her circle of influence, and upstaging the scheduled speakers. Proof, if any was needed, came the following week when she voted for a bill to deny tax relief for nonprofits receiving support from religious organizations.

Jack and Madeleine had felt used; it was a taste of politics that they, as well as Joe McGinty, would not forget. In fact, Joe's embarrassment fueled his dedication to the Coronati House Foundation. Madeleine often thought his steadfast generosity could be traced to that misguided invitation.

It was late that night when they passed the Swan Pub and continued through dark woods to a lantern-lit gate. They followed a long drive to a red brick manor house, its ivy-covered porch lit by wrought-iron lamps. Madeleine, wearily relieved, was glad to have arrived. She rummaged in her bag for the driver's fare.

A porter opened her door. "Welcome to Chewton Glen Hotel, madam. Not too lovely today, but tomorrow should be. Looking forward to tomorrow, tomorrow should be lovely, just lovely."

"Thank you."

"Now you follow me, right in here, madam, right in here."

Madeleine led the sleepy girl into the lobby and settled her in a damask chair. She spoke quickly to the desk clerk, who took them to adjoining rooms, named as well as numbered: *Tees* and *Ariadne*. An hour later she tucked Victoria into bed in *Tees*, and as her eyes closed, Madeleine said an *Our Father*. She prayed for the three of them, fearing for the baby. She had not asked the due date—soon, she thought. It had happened in July, Victoria had said. That would make her near or, perhaps, already in her eighth month. She made a mental note to locate a doctor.

Madeleine turned out the light and gazed at this girl on the edge of womanhood. Victoria had curled onto her side, her thick black hair falling over her face and birthmark, her thumb oddly close to her mouth. *A child, merely a child having a child.* But both are children of God, and both deserve to live, and God forbid that one child should kill the other. For that matter, he *has* forbidden it.

She tiptoed into *Ariadne*. Green floral draperies hung over white sheers, giving her the sense of sleeping in a garden. She drew them apart and opened French doors to a balcony overlooking a croquet lawn. The night was clearing and a few stars had appeared. An owl hooted, and a light breeze, tailing the storm, rustled the trees in the park. She leaned against the white iron railing and breathed deeply. A full moon rose over the dark forest, bathing the house and grounds in an unearthly light.

Tomorrow would be Valentine's Day, the festival celebrating third-century Saint Valentine, a priest martyred for his faith, whose legend bequeathed a celebration of love. How appropriate, Madeleine thought, that a festival of love, Valentine's Christ-love for others and today's imitation with lacy cards and chocolates, should fall this year on the day after Ash Wednesday. The wholeness of the time appealed to her—to face her death *and* life in the love of God, the heart of Christ. Father Valentine knew that wholeness, that holiness in the union of body and soul. *I believe in...the resurrection of the body, and the life everlasting.* It was a creed she said daily, but did she believe it, really live it? Somehow, through God's love made real in Christ, it was possible, and it all made perfect sense.

That love, she knew, continued in each believer, especially through the Eucharist. That love would bathe the world again and again in the hourly prayers of the faithful. Once again, Madeleine prayed for Victoria and her baby. She prayed that God would guide them through these disturbing and confusing times. She prayed for Jack and Cristoforo, that they would complete the purchase, and that the friar would find nuns for the new home. She prayed for Justin and Lisa Jane, and for little Luke. The list multiplied, each name recommending another, until Madeleine had woven a strong rope to God, pulling those names up with her. She climbed higher and higher, the strands of her love uniting earth and heaven, connecting past, present, and future, infusing time with eternity. Yes, Madeleine thought, finishing up with a last *Glory Be,* these were her ropes of love, all she could offer her creator. Perhaps she would need them to climb one day. She closed the doors and pulled the heavy drapes. Perhaps prayer, sacrifice, and suffering offered to God wove ladders to his glory, his loving glory where time finally stood still.

Within the hour, Madeleine had crawled into bed and angled the light on the nightstand. She opened a hotel pamphlet, neatly printed on glossy paper, giving a short history of the country house and the area. She recalled very little about the New Forest except that it wasn't new and Cistercians had settled in the town of Beaulieu to the east. It was years since she and Jack had visited the Southampton docks looking for a customs agent to explain the intricacies of exporting wine to the States. She opened the brochure and began to read.

> The New Forest is a national preserve encompassing 143,550 acres. On its borders are the great cities of Southampton, Salisbury, Winchester, and Dorchester.
>
> The New Forest was created in the eleventh century when William the Conqueror claimed the land for a hunting preserve. He restricted the rights of local settlers, called the "commoners." Today it is a public preserve and the commoners have restored many of their rights. They farm and raise ponies.

Madeleine recalled that the ponies were the ones Boudicca used for her chariots. Should she work that into her manuscript? Probably not. She read on, looking for bits that would weave into the tapestry of English history.

> Hikers explore the woods, plains, and rivers. Others visit Ringwood's pony and cattle market. Historians search for the Rufus Stone where William the Conqueror's son was murdered. Many literary persons lived here: Alice Liddell, the model for Lewis Carroll's Alice in the Looking Glass, married into a local family. Sir Arthur Conan Doyle lived in Minstead. Henry Lyle, who wrote hymns such as "Abide with Me," lived in Lymington just outside the borders.
>
> Chewton Glen Hotel lies to the south of the New Forest. The hotel has 130 acres of gardens, lawns, parks, and woods. This eighteenth-century manor house is today a luxury retreat with pool, spa, and fitness center.

Madeleine's eyelids flickered, heavy with fatigue. She put the brochure aside and reached for the light switch. She slept deeply that night, dreaming of a sodden path through dark woods to a light far, far, far away.

Chapter Sixteen
The Solent

*The treasure of the Catholic Faith is not ours,
it is not something with which we can barter nor take from its wholeness;
nor is it something with which we can experiment.
It is ours...to give in its fullness to those who see
and to hand on unimpaired to our children.*
Raymond Raynes

The morning was dry, and through the French doors, beyond the croquet lawn, the forest sparkled after the storm. Victoria joined Madeleine in her corner room and was delighted by the "Full English Breakfast" laid out on floral linens: poached eggs with buttery black mushrooms and broiled tomato halves, fluffy croissants in a basket, mini pots of homemade jams. Yesterday, with its dark, rainy fear, receded into the past.

"Shouldn't you call the hostel," Madeleine asked as she poured Victoria more tea, "and let them know where you are, or at least arrange for your luggage to be stored? Jack can bring it with him when he joins us."

Victoria worried that such a call might give her away. "Maybe I should, but I won't tell Mrs. Huddleston where I am. And I'll say Mr. Seymour will be picking up my bag." She rummaged in her pocket for Mrs. Huddleston's card and dialed the phone on the desk.

"Mrs. Huddleston?"

"Ah, it's the sweet dear. After all this time, I've been worried, I have, me lass. There was that lady a-lookin' for you."

"I'm fine, Mrs. Huddleston. I had to leave suddenly. Is she still there?"

"Ah, no, that she isn't. She left in a huff, she did."

"I'm sorry to be such trouble. What do I owe you?"

"You were paid up fine, dearie, but your things are here still."

"Could you pack them for me? Mr. Seymour will pick up the bag."

"Why sure, dearie, I'd be more than happy. But there's another thing here."

"Another thing?"

"A letter, it is, and it looks to be posted from Oxford. Just came this morning."

"Oxford? William Collingwood?"

"Why yes, it is, it surely is. Maybe it's a valentine, it being Valentine's Day and all."

Valentine's Day. Victoria's heart fluttered with the sudden, piercingly sweet memory of her mother bending over the lace cards they cut and glued together. Red construction paper, school glue, doilies. One for each classmate. That seemed so long ago. "I don't think so. Could you open it, Mrs. Huddleston?"

"Oh, that I could now—just a minute." Papers rustled. "Would you like me to read it to you, dearie?"

"Please."

"*'Dear Victoria,'* it begins real nice, *'I'm glad to hear you are so nearby. Do come and see me when you can. We'll have lunch, and I'll show you around.'* Now, isn't that sweet?"

Victoria could feel the woman's curiosity vibrate through the receiver. She breathed deeply. "Is there a number?"

"There surely is." Mrs. Huddleston read it and Victoria wrote it down. "What would you like me to do with the letter, Ms. Chan?"

"Could you keep it with my things?"

"Oh, and dearie, a dark friar is staying here now. Says he knows you."

"Brother Cristoforo?"

"That's his name, for sure, it is. Brother Cristoforo. He's a large man, he is, and with all that brown robe. But gentle, to my way of thinking. A gentle giant."

Victoria recalled the monk stumbling into Hartwell House, dripping with rain. "He's a good man, Mrs. Huddleston. I'm glad he's with you. I'll let Mr. Seymour know about the luggage, and thanks for your help."

"It's my pleasure, young lady, my pleasure indeed, what with your condition and all."

Victoria said good-bye and turned to Madeleine. "Cristoforo has moved into the hostel. And...I have William's number. At last."

"William?"

"A friend in Oxford."

"Good. Yes, the young man you mentioned."

Victoria hung up and dialed. There was no answer, so she left a message and her number on his answering machine. She set the receiver into its cradle. William probably wouldn't call back. Why should he? But then, he wrote, didn't he?

After breakfast, Victoria donned one of Madeleine's thick wool sweaters and followed her out to blue, windswept skies. They headed toward the sea, along a gravel path to the Chewton Bunny stream, over a wooden bridge, and through a creaking gate to a busy highway, which they crossed carefully. Turning down a narrow footpath densely packed with leaves and strewn with pebbles from the storm's toll, they entered a forested ravine. Leaves rustled lightly and a bird called. Soon the path bordered the banks of a tumbling stream. Sunlight, filtered through the foliage, danced on the water.

They stepped in the airy quiet of the damp forest, listening to the soft padding of their feet, climbed over a tree felled by the storm, and entered a clearing, the bright sky opening suddenly before them. The path led to a log-and-sod stairway, and they descended to the river that led to the sea.

As they approached the open shore, the breeze surged into a wind, blowing Victoria's thick hair and slapping her cheeks. They paused and gazed over the broad English Channel. Madeleine wrapped a warm arm about Victoria's shoulders, pointing to the horizon and sweeping her hand through the air as though painting the scene.

Puffy gray clouds hung low, nearly touching the silvery water. A thin band of sunlight separated the cloudbank from the sea, and distant sails flitted over the bay. To the right, the sky opened to searing blues and whites and grays that turned the crashing surf into browns and silvery teals. The shimmering waves reared like stallions, then rolled and pounded the pebbled beach. Victoria longed to fly with the gulls that soared over this watery kingdom of power.

"This is the Solent," Madeleine shouted against the wind, "and across the Solent is the Isle of Wight, and beyond that, across the

Channel, is the French coast. There's been a lot of history in these waters—pirates, shipping, sea battles, the Spanish Armada."

"Didn't Jane Austen's characters visit here too?" Victoria shouted back as she searched her memory for scenes.

"I believe they did, and did you know Austen is buried in Winchester Cathedral? Maybe we can visit."

They followed the wide sea walk running between the shore and steep bluffs, where rows of hefty boulders held the earth in place.

Madeleine pointed to rock walls that formed narrow peninsulas protruding into the sea and yellow signs warning *Beware of the groynes. Danger!* "The *groynes* are those stone seawalls. They slow the erosion."

"California beaches are so different. I've never seen groynes before."

She was a young girl, maybe around five, when she was last on such a rugged coast. She had walked between her mother and father, holding their hands, stepping carefully on the packed sand close to the water's edge. Gulls had cried and a cold wind blew, much like today. Her mother, laughing into the wind, had lifted Victoria high and handed her to her father, who slipped her onto his shoulders. She had watched her mother run down the beach and return to them, her face glowing. They were a family then. What happened?

"I'd never seen them either," Madeleine said thoughtfully. "We have a parish picnic every year near San Francisco's old Cliff House. I don't believe we have erosion like this. Do you get to the beach very often?"

"Not really." Victoria let the memory fade. "But last May I went with a group of friends to Santa Cruz. It was a graduation party. I was only a junior, so I went as a guest of a graduate. The boardwalk was pretty tame compared to here."

Madeleine glanced at her with a worried expression, then looked away. Had she said something hurtful? Victoria asked herself. She hoped not.

They walked west, along the coast and into driving headwinds, watching the sun play on the village of Christchurch on the far side of the bay. Retracing their steps, they followed the sea wall, entered the dappled forest, and arrived at the back of the old manor house. They settled into a deep sofa in front of a roaring fire and ordered lunch.

As the butler set out cups and saucers, pots of tea, pitchers of milk, and plates of sandwiches, Victoria turned to Madeleine. "Thank you, Madeleine. I don't really know how to thank you. My mother won't find me here, will she?"

"Highly unlikely, I would think. And we are more than happy to have your company."

Victoria sipped her tea. The chamomile was brewed from dried flower buds and had a bitter taste to it. "I'm due in April, April tenth." She reached for a ham triangle.

"We'd better find a doctor then, hadn't we? That's only two months away."

"That would be good," Victoria said, relieved to have someone help her with these decisions. "And I'd like to go to Winchester. I enjoyed visiting Westminster Abbey and the little chapel in Poets' Corner."

Madeleine tasted a cucumber sandwich. "Faith Chapel is lovely, mysterious even."

Victoria had been drawn there, and it had been difficult to leave. Now a sudden joy filled her heart as she looked into the pale face of the older woman.

That afternoon as Victoria napped, Madeleine swam in the indoor pool, occasionally glancing up though tall windows to the cypresses bordering the lawn. The tepid water soothed her, caressed her body. She felt weightless. As her arms reached into each stroke, her shoulder muscles loosened and her mind drifted, searching for solutions to Victoria's problems, now her own. But time gripped her still, and she watched the clock carefully, its large face displayed between neoclassic columns. Ten laps, enough. She turned onto her back and floated, gazing at the painted ceiling surrounding a central skylight. White latex clouds swirled against blue sky, as the unreal enclosed the real.

Victoria was in high school. Would the police accuse them of kidnapping this underage girl? Where would they find a doctor? Did they want to make an enemy of Candice Crawford-Nguyen? Would that impact the Coronati Foundation? She *was* a senator, with considerable influence, whereas she and Jack possessed about as much influence as church mice. And *where* was Victoria's father?

She prayed Jack would arrive soon.

Jack took the Saturday evening train down from London.

She helped him with his coat and studied his face. "How did it go? Did you make an offer?"

"I did," he said, setting down his bag and falling into one of the wing chairs. "But we won't know for a few days."

Madeleine ordered supper for him, and when the sandwiches arrived, she turned to Jack. "So tell me all about it."

"Well, I offered them four hundred ninety-nine thousand, a ridiculous offer, but they seemed interested. They liked us, I think, although it was hard to tell. An eccentric bunch, serious and reserved. We met in the local library, where one of the trustees works. There were two others, fellows in sweaters, casual. Trudy came too, and Cristoforo. I called Joe, and he said to be patient, they'll come around." Jack bit into his sandwich. "Who knows?"

Madeleine was pleased. "Sounds promising. At last!" Surely this was it; surely this would be their new children's home! But she shouldn't hope too much; she had no way of knowing the outcome. She reached for a potato chip and again studied Jack's face for clues, but couldn't read any. She and Victoria had eaten earlier, and the young mother was safely tucked in bed. They had spent a lovely three days together, getting to know one another, walking, swimming, having tea.

Jack looked up. "If it works out—but don't get your hopes up, Maddie—we'll need an order to run the place. Did Cristoforo call?"

Madeleine nodded. "Victoria gave him William's number. She thought he might know of an order, being in Oxford."

"Good." Jack's face dropped at the mention of Victoria. "And what do we do about Victoria? Or more to the point, about her mother?"

"I don't know. She's underage, Jack, seventeen at most."

"I was afraid of that. She's a runaway."

"We can't abandon her. And she's not really a runaway. Her father approved, even arranged her trip."

"So we're told. We'll take it one day at a time. Perhaps we can locate him."

"Yes, we'll locate her father," Madeleine said, relieved at the sensible plan.

"Maddie, why not take her out to Osborne House tomorrow? You

141

wanted to see Queen Victoria's summer home, and it would be a welcome diversion."

"Can we go after Mass? It's the first Sunday in Lent."

"Mass? Where would we go to Mass? We're on the edge of the New Forest."

"New Milton must have a church."

"Then we'll go to Osborne in the afternoon."

"Perfect." Madeleine pulled out her laptop. "Queen Victoria...I have something on Osborne. She was one of the digressions my editor complained about, but if I'm discussing the English Church, how could I not talk about Queen Victoria?" She would never be able to compromise enough to please a publisher.

"Read your piece to me," Jack said, "while I finish this. I'll pretend I'm a monk dining in a refectory. Someone reads to the monks while they eat, as I recall."

Madeleine began, grateful to focus on the mysteries of phrasing, the incarnation of ideas.

Holy Manifestations: The Age of Victoria
Princess Victoria was crowned queen in 1837 at the idealistic age of eighteen. She soon chose her royal consort, her dashing cousin Albert, whom she adored, and whom she married in 1840.

"Eighteen," Jack said, "is awfully young to be queen, let alone Queen of England."

"It is."

She reigned a record sixty-three years, giving her name to the era and bequeathing her earnest beliefs, practices, and laws. Our world today is largely a product of her culture in its assumptions and denials. The baby boomers of the postwar generation have grandparents born at the end of that age, a direct and substantial link to the present.

"That's true," Jack said. My mother was born in 1900, an even stronger link."

"And mine in 1920, my grandmother in 1886."

Victoria's uncle, George IV, who reigned from 1820 to 1830 after the senile George III passed on, had by his infamous promiscuity inspired the verse, "Georgie porgie, puddin' and pie, kissed the girls and made them cry." Having secretly married his mistress, he treated his queen, Caroline of Brunswick, with disdain, which led to scandalous but unsuccessful divorce proceedings in the House of Commons. He built a Moorish palace of love at Brighton-by-the-Sea.

When George IV died, his sixty-two-year-old brother, William IV,[8] was crowned. He too produced numerous illegitimate children. In 1837, he left the throne to his niece Victoria, since neither monarch fathered any living heirs, and Victoria's father—Edward, Duke of Kent—had died shortly after her birth.

The tarnished monarchy challenged Victoria. She would be different. She would be good, and good she was.

The queen, with her love match to Albert and her nine children, encouraged family life in England. She imported Christmas traditions from Germany, for both her mother as well as her husband, were from the German duchy of Saxe-Coburg. She set a tone of marital fidelity, lowering skirt hems and raising necklines, encouraging female modesty. Albert bettered society by opening parks and museums; he established welfare programs.

To be sure, they were good.[9]

"My mother was like that," Jack said, "organizing charitable drives and such. She said her mother did the same."

"My grandmother didn't organize things, but I recall she had her standards, her ideals." Madeleine returned to her screen.

Their goodness was built upon the righteous living of Wesley and the subsequent evangelical revivals that had taken root in the middle class and filtered throughout society. The British monarchy and its church lauded the work ethic. Small societies formed around interest rather than class; choral societies, temperance societies, musical instrument societies, and countless groups devoted to the betterment of man proliferated in Victorian England. Scientific advancement and philosophic inquiry, a legacy of the eighteenth century, spurred hope in man's progress, in spite of the horrors of revolution abroad and poverty at home.

Activities once the realm of the upper class filtered to the lower classes, as mass production reduced costs for basic goods. Railways encouraged travel, and public spaces invited increased leisure activity. Novels and newspapers documented and evaluated these changes and reforms. William Morris' Decorative Arts Movement designed affordable and pleasing interiors, and poets found romance in medieval ruins, rejecting sooty cities for old stone set amidst leaves and grass.

"Nice reference to Walt Whitman, Maddie. But he's never been my favorite, I must say," Jack said regretfully. "Actually, I'm not much of a poetry fan."

Madeleine gazed fondly at her husband. "The Romantics tended to idealize nature, which I find troubling, but they have some stunning metaphors and powerful images."

She continued:

> Victoria reigned over these immense changes, influencing moral parameters, and civilizing British culture significantly. Her children and grandchildren married into Continental royalty, influencing all of Europe.
>
> The dark side to this activity was, of course, pride, both personal and civic, as goodness without God became self-righteousness, and moral behavior without humility became priggishness.[10] The individual saw himself as good[11] without the absolution of the confessional, without the bended knee. The nation saw itself as anointed to bless the world, soon to be the Empire, without the binding force of the communion of saints. Man, in an effort to be good on his own, in the true Pelagian tradition, again separated himself from God. The well-meaning queen would one day emerge, in her mind, an unerring empress, shouldering the "white man's burden," the need to recreate the world in England's image.
>
> As Victoria and Albert's family grew, the queen sought a quiet place away from London and Windsor to raise her children. She found an estate on the Isle of Wight, "a place of one's own, quiet and retired."[12] They bought Osborne House and its one thousand acres in 1845 as well as the neighboring Barton Manor for their farm and stables.
>
> "I am delighted with the house," Victoria wrote in her diary in 1844, "all over which we went, and which is so complete and snug. The rooms are small but very nice. With some few alterations and additions for the children it might be made an excellent house."[13]

To be sure, snugness was the goal, and even in Albert's Italianate villa that replaced the original house, the domestic quarters were surprisingly small.[14]

"She sounds like a good person," Jack said.
"She *was* good."
"I'm looking forward to seeing Osborne. The boat ride should be fun. It will take our minds off of our younger Victoria."

Chapter Seventeen
Osborne House

God sent forth his son...
to redeem...that we might receive the adoption of sons.
And because ye are sons, God hath sent forth the spirit of his son into your hearts,
crying, Abba, Father...thou art no more a servant, but a son;
and if a son, then an heir of God through Christ.
Galatians 4:4-7

Late Sunday morning they boarded the hydrofoil to Osborne and Victoria followed Madeleine and Jack into the cabin. Soon the ferry lifted off from the Southampton waters and hummed across the Solent to the Isle of Wight. Victoria had never been on a hydrofoil before, and while she missed being outside and close to the water, the speed and power of the boat made up for the sea-sprayed windows.

Madeleine shook her head. "I still feel bad about missing Mass the first Sunday in Lent," she said quietly, as though to herself.

Victoria sensed that her regret was genuine, and was curious about it.

Jack set down his guidebook. "*You* were the sleepy-head, and you *did* read the Scripture lessons at breakfast."

"That will have to do, I suppose."

Why was Mass was so important to her? Thinking of her Grandma Nguyen, Victoria fingered a long-stemmed rose and turned to Jack. "Thanks again, Jack, for the rose. It's *lovely*, as they say here. I don't think I've ever received flowers before."

"But of course! What else could I do for Valentine's Day—or rather the Sunday after? Such lovely girls deserve much more than a single rose, but that was all I could muster at the New Milton train station, I'm afraid. And those were the last two. Must be hothouse roses, this time of year."

"Let's plant roses at Saint Anne's," Madeleine said. "That is, if our offer is accepted."

"That would be *lovely*." Victoria held the flower to her nose and inhaled the pungent aroma. "Jack, how did the negotiations go?"

"They went well, I think. We're dealing with an estate sale, and the trustees liked our plans. Now we'll see if they like our offer."

Madeleine looked doubtful. "Four hundred ninety-nine thousand? It seems unlikely for such a large house and grounds. I don't want to get my hopes up."

Jack scratched his chin. "But they like us. And Trudy said that was important."

"And we have the power of prayer," Madeleine added.

"I'll hold good thoughts," Victoria said.

Jack moved to the window and focused his camera on the retreating harbor. "I don't think these shots through this dirty glass are going to come out."

Madeleine reached for the guidebook on his chair. "We hope you like Osborne, Victoria. We can take the train to Winchester and Salisbury while we wait to hear from your father."

"That would be great. It would be a nice diversion." Victoria observed Jack, thinking about her father. Where *was* her father? And what about William? He hadn't returned her call, and it had been three days. Would Candice find them down here? The possibility filled her with foreboding—and yet, at the same time, she missed her mother.

Madeleine had found a doctor in New Milton. As Victoria's time drew near, she worried about childbirth. Would it be painful? Women sometimes *died* in childbirth. She would speak to Madeleine. Madeleine had told her about her son Justin and her grandson Luke, and what a joy motherhood was, but what about birth itself?

The ferry docked at West Cowes. A bus to Osborne dropped them off at the foot of a long drive leading to the queen's "palace by the sea." Jack purchased admission tickets in the Visitors Center and they found the entrance in a side wing of the immense four-story house. Touring the floors of the good queen's life, they paused before portraits of her nine children. Victoria followed Madeleine and Jack, resting often on benches that lined the hallways.

The nursery held children's cots, cradles, and miniature chairs. Plaster molds of tiny hands were displayed on an antique table. Victoria admired the chintz curtains and wallpaper, and the neat windows framing the garden outside. "This is how I imagined the Darlings' nursery."

"In *Peter Pan*." Madeleine glanced at Victoria with pleasure. "Peter flew in through the window and out with the children."

"It's a fabulous dream, isn't it?" Madeleine gazed into the distance.

"Never to grow up? I suppose so."

"Or to fly to heaven."

Victoria focused on the room, uncomfortable with the religious reference, then followed Jack down the hall. She hoped Madeleine wasn't trying to convert her. Religion hadn't helped her father. If anything, it made him weak, and *she* needed *strength*. A sudden panic seized her, and she edged toward the door. How had she come to be with these people, strangers really, so far from home?

Madeleine caught up with her. "I used to read *Peter Pan* to Justin when he was little. And my mother read it to my brother and me."

They stepped into another bedroom.

"Maybe," Madeleine added, her voice bright with happiness, "I'll read it to little Luke, my youngest grandchild, like I did with Jack's grandchildren."

"Jack's grandchildren?" This was a new side to Madeleine, an endearing side.

Madeline paused. "Jack has six grandchildren, and I think of them as my own. So with Luke we have seven. Bethany was first and will always be special for that reason. Then came her siblings, Annie and Arthur, twins. Then Todd, Tina, and Stephen."

"Bethany is fifteen now," Jack added, raising his brows as though time was a frightening mystery. "But look here. This is a really historic room. This was Queen Victoria's bedroom. 'The Queen's Room,'" Jack read, "'was kept the same by the queen after Albert died in 1861, age forty-two, of pneumonia.'"

Madeleine nodded. "She wore black the rest of her days, another forty years."

"And," Jack added, "she had a difficult time returning to public life, as I recall, which caused problems with Parliament. They showed that in the movie, *Mrs. Brown*."

Victoria absorbed these facts, envious of the strong bonds of her companions as well as these monarchs. Why couldn't she have a life like that? Would she be punished for doing the right thing? She felt her baby move and placed a protective hand over him, feeling guilty. "I'm sorry, Baby," she whispered, "I didn't mean it."

But she did, and sometimes she felt cheated. After all, she was only seventeen, eighteen in May. She could give the baby up for adoption and make a fresh start, but her heart ached at the thought. Was there no going back? Was she stuck in the present—*this* present? One could never really start over, she thought. One could never lose the past, or change it. It was what it is.

They moved into the Queen's Sitting Room, and Jack pointed to twin writing desks placed side by side. He laughed with a sudden thought. "This is what we need, Maddie, a *his* and a *hers*. Now *that* is sweet."

Madeleine looked satisfied with the arrangement. "He was her personal secretary."

"Don't even think about it. Anyway my spelling is atrocious."

Would she ever find someone like Jack? Madeleine had explained Jack was her second husband, Justin's stepfather. Could Victoria find a Jack who would be a father to another man's child? Could she raise a child alone? The unknowns, the choices, tangled together in her mind.

They rode in a horse-drawn carriage out to the sea to view the royal bathing machine, a carriage used to carry the queen and her children into the shallows and out again. Nearby, the children had played house in a child-size Swiss cottage and tended a vegetable garden. The children were important to this monarchy, little people to be seriously considered.

Victoria followed Jack through the cafeteria line in Osborne's old gatehouse while Madeleine secured a table on the terrace outside.

"So, Victoria," Jack asked as they joined Madeleine, "what do you think about the queen's mansion?" He set the tray down, and they took seats under an early-budding cherry tree. The day was almost temperate, hinting of spring, but they kept their jackets on.

"Are you warm enough out here, Victoria?" Madeleine asked. "February in England can be chilly."

"I'm okay, thanks." Victoria turned to Jack. "And Osborne *is* pretty amazing." She helped set out tuna sandwiches and bowls of vegetable soup, plastic utensils, bottled water, and milk.

Madeleine unwrapped a sandwich. "I liked the story of their life together, but for me the house is a little oppressive."

"Maybe the cement-block walls *are* a bit much," Jack conceded.

149

Madeleine stirred her soup thoughtfully. "Albert was saving money and we can't blame him for that. They used their own funds for the house, rather admirable for monarchs, and they cared about their children."

Jack turned to Madeleine. "*'Suffer little children to come unto me and forbid them not, for of such is the kingdom of God.'* Luke 18:16."

"You've learned another one." Madeleine laughed with admiration.

Victoria turned away, opening an English Heritage brochure and pretending not to hear.

"I thought with nine children," Jack said, "the queen might have liked that one too."

"It *is* appropriate," Madeleine said, "and might be perfect for our Saint Anne's home."

Victoria, amused, listened as she stared at the glossy paper.

"But it might turn some people off," Jack cautioned.

"Perhaps we need a quote from God the Father instead of God the Son?"

"It's the beginning of belief, Maddie. Many people believe in God the Father and not God the Son."

"It's easier, I think."

Victoria glanced up. "Why is that do you think?"

"There are no demands, as there are with the Son," Madeleine said as she spooned her steaming soup. "Or so they think. People often have a sentimental idea of God the Father—the doting Father."

"I see," Victoria said, although not certain she *did* see. She turned to Jack. "Jack, why do *you* believe in God?"

"Common sense, I would say."

"How so?"

"When you look at creation, the ordered universe. Everything points to a grand plan."

"I guess so," Victoria said.

"Take your baby growing from a few cells. That *has* to be God. Even if man figures out the process, he didn't design it, he didn't create life from the dust of the earth. He didn't create the dust itself. There's a great intellect out there, a great organizer, a great creator."

Victoria finished her sandwich, leaving the crusts. She opened her milk carton, inserted the straw, and sipped. It was chocolate, her favorite.

Jack glanced at Madeleine, who was suddenly silent. "And he grows on you."

"He grows on you?" Victoria felt more comfortable talking about this with Jack than Madeleine. He seemed to be a seeker, one who didn't have all the answers, one who was still searching. Clearly he had found some of those answers in Christianity.

"Ever since I've been reading Scripture," Jack continued, "and that's only since last year, I've sort of gotten to know him. And best of all, I rather like him."

Victoria laughed. "You like God? How can you get to know a Supreme Being?"

"I'm engrafting. *Receive with meekness the engrafted word, which is able to save your souls.* James 1:21."

"Was that a Scripture verse?" Victoria studied his face. He wasn't joking. He was serious.

"I'm engrafting. I'm engrafting the Word of God onto my soul. Madeleine now, she says the Mass is everything. I say engraft the Word. It's pretty cool, to use modern lingo." Jack reached for the salt, clearly pleased with himself.

Victoria wasn't convinced. "It sounds like magic, like mumbo jumbo."

Jack moved his soup bowl to the side and started in on his sandwich. "Magic is really only the dark form of religious experience." A bit of mayonnaise had lodged on his upper lip.

Madeleine choked and glanced at Jack as she reached for her water. Then she handed him a napkin and pointed to his mouth.

"Anyway," Jack continued as he wiped the mayonnaise off, "I like having the words in my head. It makes me feel good, secure. Pastor Hayes, whose devotions I'm following, says if you do that, one day you will see—are you ready for this?—you will see the *face* of God. I'm not there yet. I haven't seen his face, at least not that I know of, and I think I would know."

Madeleine excused herself for the restroom.

"So how did you get started?" Victoria leaned forward, amazed she was asking such a personal question, let alone one about religion. There was something sweet about this elderly man gobbling a sandwich and talking about God.

"I simply opened my heart, like Madeleine told me to. I asked Jesus to come in."

"You asked Jesus, not God?"

"You can't get to God except through Jesus."

"Like a tunnel or a bridge?"

"Sort of. Or a pathway. Maybe a road. You see, Jesus says he is 'the

151

way, the truth and the life. No man cometh unto the Father, but by me.' That's John 14:6. That's my all-time favorite. It clears up a host of issues raised by other religions." Jack moved the sandwich plate aside and looked at his cup of tea for confirmation.

"So you simply asked? Then what happened?"

"Well, I was in Notre Dame in Paris—actually I was *on top of* Notre Dame, on the bell tower—"

"Wow, Notre Dame, the famous cathedral?"

"The very same, but you can ask anywhere. Anyway, there I was, and I asked. Nothing happened right away, but, well, with the Scripture thing, God took hold of me and moved right in." Jack leaned forward, his blue eyes locked on hers. "Victoria, I *know* he's there. I simply *know it*. And he's changed my life."

"Wow."

"And now we'd better clear our table, find Madeleine and hightail it to the 3:30 ferry, or we'll miss dinner. And I can't miss dinner at Chewton Glen, even if it *is* Lent."

Victoria didn't say much on the way home. Fatigue settled over her as the baby turned about inside. She thought about what Jack had said. It sounded so simple. But was it really? No one had ever talked to her like that. Her father said to keep her heart open, but what did that mean? Even William hadn't spoken quite like that.

After dinner, Victoria gazed through her bedroom windows to the rain blowing in from the sea. What harm could it do to ask?

"Okay, Jesus. I invite you into my heart, like Jack did. I like these people. I want what they have, and I want my baby to have it too. Amen." There, she said it, and she didn't feel any different.

And what, after all, did they have that she wanted? Victoria pictured Madeleine's face. It was as though Madeleine knew something, a secret that would make everything all right, no matter what happened. A kind of joyful hope, Victoria thought, a happy certainty. And what about Jack? He shared that sense of hope too, but his face also held an eagerness to share, an enthusiasm for these encounters with God he claimed to have, as though he truly experienced transformation. A kind of high. Maybe that's what the evangelicals meant when they spoke of being "born again." A lot of football players talked about it too, even prayed on the field. She'd seen it on TV.

In the adjoining room, Madeleine slipped into bed beside her husband.

"I think Victoria likes you," she said as she turned off the light. "I'm glad. She needs someone she can trust."

"She likes you too, darling. She's just a little nervous with religion."

"I'll try not to push her. For now, we'll protect her as long as we can, if need be until the baby is born. But when I'm around unbelievers, I feel I'm in a mansion and I want to invite them in to enjoy the feast."

"I know you do, sweetie, and I'm starting to sense that too. But we can't force belief, and we can't judge those who believe differently." Jack paused. "Guess what? You missed my sermon."

"I thought I'd give you some space."

"Thanks. I remember what it's like to fear evangelists."

"They often scare people away. No one wants to be told that their life has something missing."

"I suppose so. God has to meet us where we are, as you've said many times, so we can only do the same for others, right? Babies take baby steps, as it were, and eat baby food."

Madeleine gazed at his outline on the pillow, his hands clasped behind his head. "And sometimes," she said, "no matter how grown up we are in the faith, we don't see the whole picture; we see threads of the canvas, or hear a few notes of the music. So, what did you say, exactly?" Madeleine knew Jack would be good at this, figuring out where people were: their mindsets, their weaknesses, their strengths. He had practiced most of his life.

"I told her to ask Jesus into her heart."

How simple, how courageous, how perfectly timed. She had always envied Jack his timing. "That's both profound and pleasing."

"And I told her I was engrafting the Word of God."

"I heard that part."

"After all," he yawned, *"All Scripture is given by inspiration of God. 2 Timothy 3:16."*

"And Scripture *is* the Word, isn't it—God expressing Christ to us, even feeding us with him. God the Father spoke and with his Word created the world, and the Word traveled over the waters....His Word, his Son, enters the host in the Mass, and then enters his body the Church, each of us...Jack? Jack?"

A long gravelly snore escaped into the dark. Madeleine began her prayers, "Lighten our darkness, we beseech thee, O Lord, and by thy great mercy, defend us from all perils and dangers of this night," her soul full, her heart thankful.

In the deep hours of the night, wind rattled the windows. Madeleine woke with a start. As she lay in bed, listening to the storm, she knew sleep would not return easily. She tiptoed to the desk and opened her laptop. Where had she left off before the trip to Osborne? She was somewhere in the English Reformation, the part about Thomas Cranmer, the father of the Anglican *Book of Common Prayer*.

Holy Manifestations: The Reformation in England
Sixteenth-century Henry VIII inherited a kingdom that was both prosperous and stable, but he knew that to ensure such prosperity and peace, he would need a son. His first marriage, to Catherine of Aragon, gave him a useful alliance with Spain, but when the queen failed to give birth to a living son, Henry looked to her lady-in-waiting, Anne Boleyn. He reasoned that Holy Scripture forbade his marriage to Catherine—his brother's widow—so the marriage was invalid in spite of the papal dispensation given at the time. Henry was convinced God was punishing him for living in sin, and that the pope had erred.

Then European politics intervened. The pope at that time was Clement VII and the year 1527, the year the Holy Roman Emperor Charles V sacked Rome and took Clement prisoner. When Henry petitioned Clement for an annulment, the pope was forced to refuse, for he had no choice—Catherine of Aragon was Charles' aunt. Furious, Henry declared himself head of the English Church and married Anne Boleyn.

Anne gave birth to Elizabeth, not the desired son, however Henry's kingdom was now free from Roman meddling, and his Church free from Roman dictate. More absolute in his monarchy than ever, Henry executed Anne and married Jane Seymour, Anne's lady-in-waiting. Jane gave birth to the long-sought prince, Edward VI, but died of childbed fever.

Madeleine glanced at Jack, who slept a troubled sleep, his breathing heavy. Her husband carried "Seymour" into the present, and "Jane" had appeared in every generation since the queen's death. What was our relationship with our ancestors? Was it merely genetic? One day, in heaven, she would know, for she would meet them all.

Henry's Church bore little resemblance to the reformed churches on the Continent. In fact, it was largely the same as before its break with Rome. The new English Church was born out of political protest, not religious, if one can draw the line.[15] To be sure, Protestant rumblings had been heard for years; John Wycliffe claimed man could know God without the Church, and certainly without the pope. And, as on the Continent, the English resented the ten percent tithe exacted by Rome, a burdensome drain of national wealth—and to a foreign power as well. They called it "Peter's Pence," Rome being the seat of the first bishop, Peter.

Thus the Church embarked on a renewed path of self-determination, the country's faith defined by the faith of the reigning monarch. England swung between Protestant and Catholic rule, and as the two sides fought over decoration, vestments, furnishings, and language, they burned, beheaded, hanged, and disemboweled their opponents. Elizabeth finally forged a compromise, Puritans fled to America's new world, and the Church in England began to acquire a character uniquely its own.

But what was that character? Madeleine looked out to the storm, which had lessened to a steady rain, falling straight and heavy. Elizabethan England was not ancient Rome. No one was required to offer incense to a pagan god. No one was asked to denounce Jesus Christ. Politics, fueled by religious belief, was a tinderbox of opinion. It was difficult even for Madeleine to understand the passion that went into defending different ways of worship.

In 1547, at the age of nine, the sickly Edward succeeded his father, Henry VIII. In spite of Henry's claim to *fidei defensor*, "Defender of the Faith," a title granted by the pope for the king's refutation of Luther's heresies, Edward had been educated a Protestant. But it was Edward's uncle, the Protector Somerset (Edward Seymour) ruling as regent, who forced Protestant changes in England. Thomas Cranmer, Edward's archbishop and the architect of Henry's divorce, had been influenced by the Continental Protestants, and also played a key role in laying the foundations for the reformed English, Anglican, Church. Edward VI held the reins of power for a mere seven years; ravaged by tuberculosis, he died at the age of fifteen.

Much that was considered "popish" was jettisoned to please the Reformers. Simplicity was the order of the day; vestments, candles, statues, and incense all smacked of popery. Such an informal style of worship removed reverential distance, and soon, diminished reverence itself.

Church images were banned to discourage superstition, and sermons were lengthened to promote learning. Reverent ritual, now an object of laughter and scorn, no longer framed the transformation of bread and wine into body and blood, and the mystery of the Mass was buried in plain speech, then ridiculed. As word replaced image, the sacramental life of fifteen hundred years slipped beneath the Reformers' whitewash, creating yet another historical irony, for, as liturgical links with God were destroyed, the material link—the Eucharist—was threatened also, so necessary was the foundation of reverence and ritual.

Madeleine recalled her first Episcopal, Anglican, Mass, indeed, her first Mass. When she arrived at Saint Thomas' she knew nothing about the liturgy, its symbols and prayers and rites, but she found herself flooded with beauty—the beauty of sound in the chants, the organ, and the singing; the beauty of vision in the golden tabernacle, the stone altar, and the sunlight streaming onto the crucifix above. There was also the simple beauty of purpose, for everything in the sanctuary pointed to the altar—nothing drew one's attention away—and Madeleine, on that Sunday morning so many years ago, fell in love, in love with beauty. She soon realized that the beauty that entranced her was an expression of God, God himself.

Thinking about that day, happiness filled her heart, and she turned again to her words.

Since Wycliffe,[16] Englishmen had called for a vernacular Bible.

Under Edward, the Miles Coverdale Bible was published. The Cranmer-Coverdale *Book of Common Prayer* followed, with the liturgy translated into English. Cranmer's phrases sang in poetic, reverential language, at odds with the removal of church decoration and rite. He simplified worship, perhaps to its improvement: "Many times there was more business to find out what should be read, than to read it when it was found out,"[17] he said. His vernacular prayer book allowed the congregation to take part in the service.

When Edward died, his Catholic half-sister Mary took the throne. The daughter of Henry by Catherine, Mary was a bitter woman. Exiled with her mother from royal privilege, she witnessed her father marry a young commoner. Her father also denied Mary's Catholic faith. She came to the throne with an agenda.

History has called her "Bloody Mary," and in her efforts to return England to Mother Rome, Thomas Cranmer became a victim. At the age of 63, he was arrested for treason[18] and imprisoned in Oxford, where he recanted his Protestant beliefs six times. But in his last sermon, preached at Saint Mary's on the morning of his death, he surprised the congregation by recanting the recantations.[19] He called the pope the Antichrist, and when he denied transubstantiation, the mob pulled him from the pulpit. He shouted "forasmuch as my hand offended, writing contrary to my heart, my hand shall first be punished there-for."[20] The mob dragged him to the stake in front of Balliol College, where he plunged his right hand into the flames, that hand that had done the heretical signing.

Today, a Martyrs' Memorial recalls the death of Cranmer, as well the deaths of bishops Latimer and Ridley.[21] The three men, strong in their faith, witnessed to the birth pangs of the English Church, as word, image, and sacrament struggled to renew the ancient liturgy uniting man and God.

Behind the memorial stands the church of Saint Mary Magdalene. Originally a part of the eighth-century Saint Frideswide's Priory outside the town walls, the church was taken over by Saint Osney Abbey and returned to the priory under Henry VIII. In 1320 Carmelite friars built the church's south chapel where the Blessed Sacrament is reserved.

Across the busy street, stands a pub called the Eagle and Child, frequented by the Inklings literary group—J.R.R. Tolkien, Charles Williams, and C.S. Lewis.[22] These writers read their words to one another as they searched to express the inexpressible, the sacramental truths of God's manifestations in the world.

Madeleine closed her laptop. She had hoped to visit Oxford from Aylesbury, but now Victoria was her priority. She thought the Inklings would have agreed.

Chapter Eighteen
The Eagle and Child

*Many of the ideas about God which are trotted out as novelties today,
are simply the ones which real Theologians tried centuries ago and rejected.
To believe in the popular religion of modern England is retrogression–
like believing the earth is flat.*
C.S. Lewis

On that same First Sunday in Lent, Brother Cristoforo looked about the Eagle and Child. Students huddled in alcoves under low ceilings, and in the dim light, the friar found a table where a plaque stated that a group of writers called the Inklings had gathered. But Cristoforo was not familiar with their writings, for he could not read English comfortably, nor Italian for that matter. The nuns had tried to teach him, but he had preferred tending his garden.

"May I help you, sir...Brother...?" The server eyed Cristoforo's robes as though she had never seen a monk before.

This is an odd reception, he thought, *since this is Oxford, home of the English friars.* "Please, a cider, thank you." It was Sunday, a feast day, and he need not keep his Lenten rule.

Cristoforo watched the door for William Collingwood. As he watched, he thought of Nadia. He hadn't seen the child since that day in Holloway two weeks earlier. Had she collected enough in the basket to feed herself for a time? She had not returned to the London shelter, and Sister Lucille spoke many harsh words. Was Nadia still wandering in Oxfordshire? Wherever the friar went, he found himself looking for the girl, for the head of dirty hair, the smudged jacket, the crooked shoulders, the impish and defiant eyes.

But even though he had lost Nadia, he had helped Mr. Seymour. Mr. Seymour wanted Cristoforo to stay at his hotel in Aylesbury, but the friar said no, he could not do that. He wanted something more humble.

Mr. Seymour suggested the youth hostel where Miss Victoria had stayed. The room in the basement suited the friar and he helped Mrs. Huddleston plan her spring planting. They consulted her catalogs and they made lists.

On Friday of that week, Cristoforo and Mr. Seymour had met with the trustees of the abbey property, who had approved their plans. The friar did not understand all of the discussion, but Mr. Seymour had been most cordial in speaking to the young Mr. Hicks, the middle-aged Mrs. Peebles, and the elderly Mr. Wilson. The trustees had asked many questions, but Cristoforo guessed they didn't want too many changes.

They would need nuns to run the new home. Mr. Seymour had asked the friar to find a religious order, to call Mrs. Seymour to see if she had any ideas. So Cristoforo had phoned Mrs. Seymour who was smart, he knew, for she taught at a university. But she had no answers, except to suggest that Oxford or nearby Cowley might have sisters. Then Miss Nguyen came on the line. She knew someone at Oxford who was Anglo-Catholic who might know of some nuns. Cristoforo thanked her and said he was staying at the Youth Hostel where she had stayed and thought it very fine. Miss Victoria laughed and said she thought it fine too.

Then he called William. Miss Nguyen described the young man as short and slim, fair-haired, with glasses. But would he recognize him, in this dim pub? There were many students here already. Many had glasses.

Cristoforo hoped he could find the nuns soon. Before returning to Italy, he wanted to preach again. Preaching on the hillsides and in the city parks filled him with life. All those expectant, trusting faces, looked up to *him*, to simple Cristoforo. They needed him, and he could help them. He could give them the Word, the Good News. He could reach them as no other could; he had the gift of the right stories, the right phrases, and, praise God, the humility required to preach, unlike many others, the friar thought. He would be a channel between man and God. He would preach once more, then return to Rome.

The server placed the cider on the table and handed him a smudged piece of paper, folded. The server pointed to the doorway. "A boy left this and ran off, Brother."

The friar opened it slowly, his heart beating.

Brother Cristoforo,
Com to the gravyar acros the street. Bring lotsa food and a shovle. Need yur help.

And then, to Cristoforo's delight, the name. *Nadia.*

Cristoforo grinned and shook his head. Where would he find a shovel? There was a general store down the street. Perhaps they would have one. Would the girl wait? He tapped his large finger on the oak table impatiently. Condensation dripped from the glass, pooling on the varnished planks and dripping through a crack to his knee. Where was William?

He folded the note and slipped it into his pocket, then gulped his sweetly sour brew. He gave thanks to God for Nadia's note. He also gave thanks for Sundays, with no fasting, no abstinence, a feast day in Lent, if he had the chance to eat and drink. He lifted his pint and glanced at the door as a young man entered quickly, scanned the room, smiled sideways, nodded to the friar, and joined him at his table.

"I'm sorry to be late, Brother. You *are* Brother Cristoforo Francesco, aren't you?" The young man extended long delicate fingers, and Cristoforo shook them, surprised by the strong grip.

The friar nodded. "Please, sit down. Would you like a cider?"

"No thanks, I have to study this afternoon. I read Canon Law tomorrow, and Jameson is a stickler."

"You will be ordained, Mr. Collingwood?"

"Please, call me William. God willing, I shall be ordained deacon. After that, I'm assigned to a parish to work the trade, a kind of holy internship." He laughed without parting his lips, then steepled his hands on the table. "You said on the phone that you know Victoria, that she gave you my number?"

"*Si,* I only met her on Wednesday, at the Ash Wednesday Mass."

"How is she?"

"She is okay. She is with the *Signori* Seymours in the New Forest. They care for her. They are good, the *Signori* Seymours."

The waitress approached and William nodded affably. "I'll have a coffee, please, Beth. Strong. Thanks. How's Jeremy?" The young man's blue eyes, set in a pale face of freckles, flashed intensely when he spoke, and he moved jerkily, like a small bird.

"He's better, thanks to you. It's good of you to ask," she replied. "Say, I heard you're getting engaged."

"Word travels fast." Dismay flashed across William's features. "It's not...exactly official, if you know what I mean."

"I won't tell a soul. Well, I'm happy for you." Her voice was edged with disappointment. "But thanks again for helping with Jeremy," she added and hurried off.

"Jeremy's her boy," William explained. "He's nearly two, now. The father took off when the baby was born. Nasty fellow, what? The boy had the chicken pox, and I watched him one shift. It's hard for a single mum, I should say. It's a good thing I had chicken pox as a child." He scratched his arm. "I'll never forget the baking soda baths."

"William, the reason I desired to meet with you—"

"So why did Victoria leave London? And why is she with the Seymours? Who *are* the Seymours?" He leaned forward, his face questioning and concerned. "She wrote me she was in Aylesbury, that was all, and wanted to visit."

Cristoforo gazed at William, who was obviously distraught. What should he say? Mr. Seymour said Victoria was running away from her mother. Should he say that? "She does not want to see her mother," he said, at a loss over how to be clever. "But Mrs. Nguyen found her in Aylesbury. Then Victoria left for the New Forest with Mrs. Seymour."

"Her mother found her because of me." His eyes darted about the room. His coffee arrived and he stared into it, then sipped slowly, his face full of regret.

"You?"

"Senator Nguyen looked me up in Oxford, and I'm afraid she saw Victoria's letter on my desk with the Aylesbury postmark. I had no idea Victoria was avoiding her. Now I know the situation, but it's a little late. Mums and the senator are all in a flap over this." He squinted into the distance, his brow wrinkled, then looked imploringly at the friar.

"And do you know why Miss Victoria avoids her mother?"

"I confess I don't. I should think, what with the baby, she would want her mother nearby."

"Ms. Crawford-Nguyen wants the child aborted."

"Her own grandchild?"

"*Si*. Victoria's father sent her to London, to your parents, until the baby is born. I pray for Miss Victoria and her baby. Her time is soon. But they will be okay."

"Thanks, that explains a good deal. I didn't want to pry. How I wish I could make it up to her."

Cristoforo saw the moment and grabbed it. "You can. I have a way."

"How?" William asked, his eyes serious.

"You can help the Seymours, and maybe Victoria." He told him about the orphanage and clinic in Rome, and the plans to establish one in Aylesbury. "We met with the trustees of the property. They like our plans. They are considering our offer."

"Is it the old monastery property?"

"*Si*, it is good."

"It needs a lot of work, I should think. It's been over fifty years since the monks left. But even so, such a place! The abbey, the conventual buildings, the cloister, the gardens. I'm glad. So where do I come in? What shall be my penance?"

"We need a women's order to run our new Saint Anne's House."

"Of course."

"Do you know of an order that might be interested?"

"As a matter of fact, I do. Try the Sisters of Mary in Cowley, outside Oxford. They sometimes help at Mary Magdalene, across the street." He pointed outside toward the main thoroughfare.

"The Sisters of Mary?"

William nodded. "I heard they were having trouble with their lease, that the owner has a mind to sell. He wants them out."

"And how do I go to Cowley?"

"Here is their address." He wrote quickly in a small spiral notebook and tore the sheet out. "You can catch the bus right outside."

Cristoforo left the pub, satisfied with the deed nearly done, and the sense, once more, of being part of God's plan, a minor part in a major drama. But first he must find a shovel and a graveyard. And food. Soon he emerged from the general store down the block, carrying a garden trowel, three sandwiches, and a quart of milk in a brown paper bag. What was Nadia up to? Would she still be there?

He headed for Mary Magdalene, a stone church occupying an island in the center of the roadway, a curious position, but a church with a graveyard. He entered through wrought-iron gates and stepped between gravestones rising in the green grass like rubble in an earthquake. To the side of the church he spotted Nadia. She was speaking to a gentleman. The man scowled and waved his arm toward the street.

"Get off with you," he said.

"But I've business here," the girl explained. "I'm waiting for someone." She saw the friar. "It's *him* I'm waiting for." She pointed with her finger.

Cristoforo approached the man slowly, walking with as much grace and reserve as he could, fingering his rosary. "May I be of assistance?"

The man straightened his vest and looked up at the monk. "Well, I don't know, Brother, but do you know this girl? She seems to be loitering. I'm the verger here and sacristan as well and keep an eye on the place." He touched his bow tie nervously and straightened his jacket.

"She is my friend, sir. I shall speak for her." The friar shot a serious glance at Nadia.

"Very well then," the verger said, sounding doubtful. "But I shall be waiting inside. Not too long, now, not too long." He eyed the large brown bag.

"We are praying at the gravesite." Cristoforo glanced at his rosary, then at Nadia, who immediately kneeled.

"Aye, we are that." Nadia folded her hands and closed her eyes. "We be praying," she whispered, glancing up at the verger through veiled lids.

As the verger entered the chapel, leaving the door ajar, the friar knelt too. "What are you doing?" he whispered.

"Did ya bring the things?"

"What?"

"The shovel, like I said. And the food?"

Cristoforo opened the bag and she peered in.

"I said shovel. That's a dinky little thing."

"This will do, but why?" Was she going to dig up a grave? In broad daylight?

"Follow me."

The friar followed Nadia to a far corner of the yard, out of sight of the verger, he hoped, and joined her again, kneeling. The girl scooped out some earth, then produced a plastic bag filled with dark ash. "Me mum," she announced, her voice determined. She poured the remains into the shallow grave and covered them with the earth. "Say something, something holy you say when you bury someone."

The friar gazed at the soft mound, a tear forming in his eye. "Nadia. What's your mum's name?"

"Alice Mae. Her name was Alice Mae Kemp."

"Earth to earth, ashes to ashes...we commit Alice Mae to your care, Lord Jesus." He made the Sign of the Cross.

"Amen." She stared at the ground, then made the Sign of the Cross as well. "Bye, Mum, did my best," she said hoarsely, then stood and turned to the friar who rose as well. "Thanks, mate. I wanted her to be in holy ground. Only fitting. Now, where's the food? I'm starving."

"Let us sit on that bench over there. I want to talk to you."

"Give me the food then."

He led Nadia to a stone bench to the side of the graves and handed her a sandwich and the carton of milk. "What happened to your mum?"

Nadia ate ravenously and gulped the milk. "She was sick. When she died, the social worker came to take me and my brothers away. We had lots of pa's, but no one right then to stand up for us." She touched the dark line along her jaw. "Not that they did much in that way, if ya know what I mean."

In a moment, the friar understood Nadia's story: the abusive stepfathers, the single mother, the exhaustion, the illness. Nadia playing the role of parent.

"Did you go to a foster home?"

Nadia's eyes grew wide, and she stared into the distance. She nodded. "We was separated."

"You and your brothers?"

She nodded as a tear slid down her cheek. "They were mean to me."

"The foster parents?"

"Yeah." Nadia had stopped eating.

"Did you run away?" The friar put his arm around the girl, and she hid her face in his sleeve.

"I 'scaped," she said, her words muffled by his robe.

"What happened to your brothers?"

Nadia looked into the friar's face, wiping her cheeks with her fists. "I found 'em." Her eyes held triumph.

"Where are they now?"

"Not *that* far away." Nadia looked through the iron fence and its bordering hedge, and the friar saw movement on the other side, faces suddenly appearing, suddenly disappearing. Nadia returned to her sandwich, finishing it off. "Any more?" she asked.

Cristoforo had planned to mention his stolen offerings in Oxford but couldn't do it. She handed him the trowel, looked in the bag, and darted to her feet. The friar reached for her jacket sleeve. "Wait. How did you get the ashes?"

"That's another story. Too long for now." She pried his hand loose and ran across the graveyard, then turned to wave from the open gate. "Thanks, Cristoforo, thanks a whole lot, but I've gotta go."

The verger appeared when the gate clanged shut. "Finished with your devotions, Brother?"

Full of regret and worry, saddened but not surprised by Nadia's story, Cristoforo said, "Yes, sir, and may I see your good church?"

"With pleasure." The verger's face shone with pride.

Cristoforo followed him in, and the man waited by the door. Brilliant stained glass glimmered behind the altar, but where was the red candle and the Blessed Sacrament? He searched the dim chancel in vain, stepping slowly, inhaling the musty damp, looking around the stone walls. The church was built in a time so far removed from his own time and yet, through the Mass, was so near, he thought. He entered a chapel off the south aisle and found the red flame. He fell on his knees before the tabernacle.

"Lord," he prayed, "watch over thy child Nadia and her brothers, for I cannot seem to do so. May the soul of her mother, Alice Mae, rest in peace with thee, dear Jesus. And let thy will be done in all things. And Lord...let me preach again. Then I will return to Rome."

Ah, to preach again! Maybe, the friar thought, he would ask his superior for permission to preach in Italy as he had preached in England. Yet he knew he was needed at Rome's Coronati House. He also knew he must obey his superior. It was part of being a monk. Normally, he delighted in obedience. He would have it no other way.

The candle flickered, and a wind whistled through the graves outside. A chill swept over him. This was not the answer he sought.

Cristoforo shook his head and pulled himself up. Nodding to the verger, he left the church. He paused outside the gate and glanced back at the chapel. Then he looked up to a tall monument before him, the sculpted images forming a pinnacle intersecting the sky, high above the traffic. As cars rushed by on either side he read slowly the etched plaques, and pieced together the stories of Thomas Cranmer, Hugh Latimer, and Nicholas Ridley. In this place they were burned at the stake by Queen Mary in the sixteenth century.

He scratched his beard, his finger tracing the crevice in his chin. Must we suffer so, he thought, must it be that way? He could see the men. He could smell the burning flesh. They were terrified, no? He heard that Cranmer died at once, like Stephen seeing Jesus in the heavens as he was stoned. But Ridley suffered greatly.

The friar looked beyond the memorial, through the traffic, to the storefronts on each side of the street. Nadia was nowhere to be seen.

The church bell tolled four, and he found the bus to Cowley.

Cowley was not far, and soon Cristoforo was ringing the doorbell of the convent, a single-story building with a neat yard and white porch. A young nun robed in black greeted him, introducing herself as Sister Eileen. Her pockmarked face had once been beautiful, the friar thought, with deep blue eyes and high cheekbones. He guessed she was fair, but her hair was hidden behind a white headscarf. Stepping lightly, she led him down an immaculate hall with bare stucco walls and gleaming wood floors.

She paused before glass doors, and Cristoforo could see into a modern chapel with few furnishings. A plain tabernacle stood on the altar under a crucifix, and a red votive flickered alongside. Two nuns knelt on the floor before the tabernacle, their black robes dropping to the floor like tents.

Eileen looked up at him, her eyes large. "We keep a twenty-four-hour watch before the Blessed Sacrament."

"*Sì*, that is good."

They continued down the hall to the Mother Superior's office.

"Here we are, Brother," Eileen said, "and may God go with you." She closed the door behind him.

This room was also simply furnished. A sculpted Madonna and Child hung on one wall, a chrome crucifix on another, and two folding chairs faced a scuffed oak desk. A window opened on a garden, letting in a cool breeze. An elderly nun sat behind the desk.

She pulled herself up slowly, her habit falling heavily about her, her warm eyes fixed on his. "Welcome. What can we do for you? I fear, my son, that we have little to give you."

"It is I, Mother, who must give to you. I was told that you have no lease next month?"

She nodded sadly and sat down, motioning for the friar to take a chair. "We are here today on borrowed time. The lease expired December thirty-first." She gazed through the window to the garden and then to the opposite wall.

Cristoforo followed her eyes to the crucifix, gleaming in the wintry light. He leaned toward her, his heavy hands folded on his lap, as he composed his face in the most earnest and honest expression he could manage. He told her of their work in Italy and their hopes for England.

"Saint Anne's?" Her voice sounded far away.

"*Si*, Saint Anne's."

"I knew them, you know."

"The monks?"

"During the last war Saint Anne's was a hospital. It was my first assignment after making my vows. They never came back."

"Who, Mother? Who never came back?"

"The brothers. They were sent to the front. Those that survived found another location upon their return, in Kent."

"But they kept the property?"

"Only the abbey. The graves are there, you see, and the abbey still consecrated, used by the village, I believe." She rose, her eyes watery. "It was a long time ago, Brother, but it seems like yesterday." She shook her head, and led him to the door. "I shall take it up with my superior. We *are* Anglican Benedictines, and it would seem a good thing." She laughed softly and tapped her cane. "Maybe you are an angel from God."

"You would be doing a good work. God be with you, Mother."

"And with you, too, my son."

It was late in the evening when Cristoforo returned to the Aylesbury Youth Hostel. Mrs. Huddleston met him in the doorway. She was a woman of ample proportions, in her seventies, he guessed, and she had the air of one who took care of things—the garden, the cooking, the starched sheets and pillowcases, the plumbing, and the guests themselves—as she had once taken care of her large family and Mr. Huddleston, God rest his soul. Her gray hair, pulled into a bun, framed a country face with weathered skin, a wide nose, and dark eyes. Her fingers, thick and calloused, patted the bulging pockets of her flowered pinafore. Cristoforo was grateful she allowed him to stay, for, after all, it *was* a *youth* hostel.

"And where you be all this time, me good father?" she asked, her hands on her hips.

"I am a *brother*, *Signora*, but never mind. I have been working." He paused in the hallway.

Her curious eyes blinked expectantly. "It's late to be out and about."

"*Allora, Signora*, if you would make your delicious tea, I shall tell you all about my day in Oxford."

"And that I will! I've an urge for a spot meself." She chuckled, rubbed her large palms together and tapped her adequate nose mischievously as she shuffled toward the kitchen. "Blow onto the fire, me lad, and we'll have a good talk-to."

Cristoforo entered the homey parlor and breathed deeply, suddenly tired. He placed another log on the fire, shoving it in place with an iron poker. He was fond of the old woman and knew she meant well. He was happy to share his day over tea in front of her hearth. He had managed his evening prayers on the bus. He barely recalled his own mother, and this woman filled him with a surprising affection.

Mrs. Huddleston bustled in and carefully set down a loaded tray on the coffee table. She rummaged in her pocket.

"And this come for you, Father. It...it come opened like that, it really did. Special Delivery too."

Cristoforo unfolded the cream parchment and frowned as he recognized the fine Italian script. He was sorry he had phoned his superior's office to let him know his new location.

1st February, 2002
Order of Friars Minor, Rome
Dear Son,
Return to Rome.

You are cutting yourself off from the community who support you. You are under obedience, and must rely more than ever on the spiritual strength of that community.

You perhaps are responding to demands that are not for you to take on? Do not let pride control your soul. You must give to God what you cannot do.

Are you praying? A wise man once said that a prayer-less priest is a disarmed soldier unable to defend himself, and what is more, unable to defend the Lord's children over whom he watches.

I will send one of the brothers to you soon.
+ Bernardo, O.F.M.

"Are you all right, Father?"

"*Si*, Mrs. Huddleston, *si*, but...no, maybe not. I am not sure. I return to Rome soon. Soon, but not yet. I have greater things to do first."

"Do you, now?" She leaned forward, all ears.

"I must travel, my good woman, I must preach in the countryside. Walk and preach, like the friars of old." Perhaps he would find Nadia.

Mrs. Huddleston clapped her hands. "Indeed, you must. And you will return and tell me all about it."

"I do not know when that will be. But now, about today...."

The friar crumpled the paper tightly in his fist, tossed it in the fire, and turned to his rapt admirer as he reached for his cup of steaming tea.

Chapter Nineteen
Ventan-ceaster

The Christian faith is the most exciting drama...
The plot pivots upon a single character,
and the whole action is the answer to a single central problem:
What think ye of Christ?
Dorothy Sayers

Monday morning, the skies had partially cleared, and Madeleine knocked on Victoria's door. "Jack's left for the train to London, so it's just us. Ready for our walk?"

"Sure am." Victoria stepped into the hall as she slipped on her jacket.

They descended the stairs and passed through the sitting rooms to the back door.

"Guess what?" Victoria said, beaming. "William called back this morning."

"Really?"

"He felt terrible about giving away my location in Aylesbury. He apologized he hadn't called. He said he misplaced my phone number."

"I'm glad. Did he mention the order of nuns?"

They followed the gravel path leading to the sea.

Victoria nodded. "He met with Cristoforo in Oxford yesterday, and William gave him the name of a women's order in Cowley."

"Good." Things were progressing, Madeleine thought, as the fresh breeze slapped her cheeks. She glanced at the sky. "I think we have a break in the weather, but who knows for how long."

All that week Madeleine fussed happily. The ultrasound showed a healthy baby, but Victoria chose not to know the gender. Madeleine wasn't sure why, for *she* would have wanted to know. They took the train to Southampton where they shopped for maternity clothes and a baby layette: tiny one-pieces with snap-pants, flannel receiving blankets, and cotton sleepers with yellow and green bears. They browsed used stores for childcare books, Madeleine finding several titles for Saint Anne's as well.

Madeleine looked forward each evening to Jack's call from London. Monday night she learned that the Coronati Foundation's offer was accepted, and she prayed her thanksgivings. This would be their new children's home. This would be the fulfilling of Jack's vow to build a church.

Jack remained in London to finalize papers. He hired a contractor to see to renovations and reported to Joe McGinty with daily calls and faxes. The elderly millionaire insisted that Jack stay in England until the initial work was complete; Joe hoped to visit soon to see for himself and do a little fund-raising.

"I met with Victoria's father today, Maddie," Jack said on Wednesday evening, "as well as William Collingwood."

"Really? However did you do that? Did you see the senator as well? You didn't let it slip where we're staying, did you?"

"Hold on, my dear, hold on. No, she wasn't there. I played it very cool, I thought. Cristoforo arranged it."

"You saw Cristoforo too? Where is he?"

"No, I didn't actually see him, and who knows where he is at the moment, since he's supposedly preaching in the countryside. Anyway, he told William to call me, and we all agreed to meet in a pub in Oxford. Quite a pub, too! The Eagle and Child where the Inklings met. There's a plaque over their table."

"Really?" Madeleine was envious. Some of her favorite writers. "What happened?"

"Andrew, Victoria's father, seems to be a good man. He actually thanked me for caring for Victoria, for keeping her away from her mother for the time being. Can you imagine that?"

"Then he supports her having the baby."

"He does, or at least he appears supportive. I feel better about the whole situation, but it still makes me nervous. He didn't think it wise for him to visit Victoria or phone her."

"I agree. I'll let Victoria know. It will make her happy to hear you've met not only her father but William. What's William like? Can we trust him?"

"William's a rather nervous sort. But a warm, likable fellow all the same. And as far as trust goes, Cristoforo trusts him. That's enough for me."

"Then I do too." Madeleine wondered how close William and Victoria were, but she wouldn't pry. Victoria still seemed a bit wary of Madeleine, and at times, wary of Jack. One minute she seemed on guard, cautious, and the next moment, off guard, ingenuous. And it's no surprise she vacillates, Madeleine thought, considering what she's been through.

"I should be able to join you this weekend," Jack said.

"Let's go to church in Winchester. We can give thanks for Saint Anne's."

"Yes," Jack agreed, sounding relieved. "My vow is nearly fulfilled."

On Friday Victoria and Madeleine taxied to Ringwood Village in the New Forest. The sky was clearing from the night's rain; low clouds moved across the sky. It was market day, and they meandered about the stalls of clothing and pottery, baked goods and needlework. Fresh fruit was laid out in neat rows; elderly ladies with colorful aprons sold candy and jams. It was half school bazaar and half farmer's market, Victoria thought, delighted with the commotion, the children running about, and the tourists taking pictures.

They bought lunch in a corner pub, and found a table with a view of the square.

"I'm so pleased we found a few more things for the baby," Madeleine said, smiling. "I recall shopping for Justin when I was pregnant. We collected everything secondhand and it was fun to find bargains."

Victoria paused, gathering the courage to ask the question that nagged her. "Madeleine, will it be painful?"

"Will what be painful?"

"Childbirth? Don't women sometimes die in childbirth?"

"Only in the past, or maybe in some countries today. But don't worry, Victoria, you will be fine."

"But the pain?"

"It's painful, but it's a happy pain." The older woman laid her hand on Victoria's, then looked into her eyes. "You will know a love that men will never know, a mother's love for her child, a child that is nurtured by her own body."

Madeleine's words wrapped about her, warming her.

"And, if you decide to keep the baby," Madeleine added, "which is entirely your choice, you will learn how to be a mother. I will help and others will help."

"Thank you," Victoria said gratefully.

Madeleine gazed out the window, touching the silver cross that rested on her navy turtleneck, as though she was seeing inside herself and into the past at the same moment. "Childbirth is the great miracle of life. To be part of such a miracle, why, it's like being part of God."

They lingered in the moment, each in their own thoughts. Then Madeleine turned to Victoria. "So, what's your favorite purchase today?"

"The picture books are great, but my favorite is the wooden pony. Someone carved this with a great deal of love." She pulled the figurine from a bag and ran her finger over the back.

It was no more than six inches long and three inches high, but the grain of the wood had been polished to a soft luster.

"Do you have this kind of thing at home?" Madeleine stirred her coffee.

Victoria recalled her home with pleasure. "I do. My father carves animals and fairytale characters in his studio. I've quite a collection."

"You must miss your father." She held the bowl of her cup in her palm and stared thoughtfully into the creamy foam on top.

"I miss him a lot." A lump rose in Victoria's throat. "He meant well when he sent me to the Collingwoods. I'm sure he didn't expect my mother to find me there."

"Why the Collingwoods?"

"Daddy knew Frederick in Vietnam. Frederick owed him his life."

"Oh my, that's quite a debt. They fought together?"

Victoria paused. It had been painful for her father to speak of it, and she recalled his pain as she told the story. "Frederick was a British correspondent who was taken prisoner in my father's village. He escaped and was sheltered by my father's family. It was just for one night, but when the Viet Cong found out, they shot my grandfather Nguyen. My father, my grandmother, and two uncles escaped on an American airlift."

Madeleine's eyes grew wide. "A life for a life. How horrible for your father and his family."

"Grandma Nguyen is very strong. She lives near us." Victoria could say no more. Tears were near. How she missed her grandma as well. "She is very strong."

Madeleine nodded. "How did your father come to be named Andrew? Isn't that an English name?"

Victoria breathed deeply, grateful for the diversion. "It was actually André, French, named after an uncle in the French occupation of Vietnam. Daddy changed it to Andrew when he immigrated to America. I'm thinking of naming the baby Andrew, if I keep him." How could she not keep him? He was a part of her.

Madeleine looked both happy and sad. "That's sweet. I was hoping to name a child after Jack, but we never had children together."

"I'm sorry."

"It was difficult to accept, but God helped me with it."

"When does Jack return?"

"Saturday, I believe. It's all day-to-day now that Joe McGinty is in town. I hope we can go to Winchester on Sunday. It will be the Second Sunday in Lent already."

The letter was waiting on the carpet, slipped under her door, when Victoria returned. It was the first from her father since his arrival in London, and she recognized the handwriting, the London stamp.

She dropped her bag on the floor, moved to the window, and slit open the envelope with her fingernail.

Tuesday, February 19, 2002
Dear Vicky,
I'm mailing this to you in hopes you get it.
    We arrived in London after you left. William said you are okay.
    I worry about your feelings for your mother. I have not been honest with you. I have not told you everything. I think I should tell you what happened. You may understand why she acts the way she does.
    Your mother had an abortion two years after you were born. The baby was not planned. Vicky, she still grieves over the child, I am sure. And this is

why she will not face what she has done. She cannot admit she was wrong. The horror would be too great. Do you understand?

This is why she wants others to do as she did. She must cover her act in this way.

This is hard and I know it. But you must forgive her. She is trapped in a terrible evil and cannot get out.

I will see you soon.
I love you,
Daddy

Victoria considered his words. Could such a thing be true? That in order to justify an action you whitewashed it to the point of promoting it? Victoria shook her head. The contortion seemed huge. But still, she had seen how one lie could lead to others, could lead to greater and greater blurring of good and evil, right and wrong. For the first time she saw her mother with compassion. Victoria had glimpsed the other side.

The skies were overcast on the Second Sunday in Lent. Jack had returned Saturday night and reported that things were on schedule. He unpacked several small stuffed animals: Winnie-the-Pooh, Peter Rabbit, Paddington Bear. "I couldn't resist a London shop," he said, grinning. "And there's an extra Paddington for Luke."

Now, as Jack finished breakfast, Madeleine opened her laptop to the chapter on Winchester. She had worked on her manuscript during the week, revising here, adding there, checking facts using several reliable Internet sources. She had read portions to Victoria to see if her words made sense, and Victoria had nodded her assent or made suggestions. Today a visit to the ancient royal city would give Madeleine the direct experience needed to make her Winchester chapter credible, and she hoped they could visit Salisbury and Arthur country another day. Her June deadline drew closer each day, but with the Saint Anne's property successfully negotiated, her trust in God's timing was strengthened.

She skimmed the words on her screen.

Holy Manifestations: Winchester

The Romans founded *Venta* (windy) *Belgarium* in 68 AD on the banks of the River Itchen, naming it after the earlier Celtic Belgae tribes from northern Gaul, and built a temple to their gods over a local holy well. By the fourth century, as Christianity took root in southern England, a monastery dedicated to Saint Martin of Tours rose where the temple once stood.

Archeologists have unearthed tiled paths and painted villas, revealing a wealthy and sophisticated Venta. But in 410 AD, when Rome withdrew its protective legions from England, the rural, tribal Celts slowly abandoned the town. By the seventh century little remained of the Roman *ceaster* (town), now known as *Ventan-ceaster*, soon to be called *Winchester*, except the holy wells and the ordered grid of tiled pathways.

During these dark ages, local chiefs fought to retain their Romano-Celtic culture, threatened as it was by invasions of the Germanic Angle and Saxon tribes. One of these chiefs was Arthur, a figure shrouded in time.

Ever since reading Mary Stewart's *The Crystal Cave,* Madeleine had been fascinated by the Arthurian legends. The stories wove together magic and Christian virtues. It was as though Arthur had one foot in the druidic world and the other in the Christian, and his life and legend were the turning point in the transformation and Christianization of the West.

The tale of King Arthur, although romanticized by French chroniclers, rings true. Forming alliances with other kings toward the end of the fifth century, Arthur created a last defense against the Saxons. The Wessex countryside is painted with his memory, and his code of honor became legendary, challenging the cowardly and energizing the lazy. Some believe Arthur's Camelot was Winchester, which was a center of resistance as well as a city of justice and peace.

Eventually, however, Winchester fell to the Saxons, and Saint Martin's monastery became a pagan temple.

When Bishop Birinus arrived from Rome in 634[23] on a missionary journey, he found a heathen people. This "Apostle of Wessex" converted the Saxon king, baptizing him at the ancient well. The king's son built a church over the well and enshrined Birinus' relics.

By the time of ninth-century King Alfred the Great, Winchester was the center of both royal and clerical power. The local Bishop Swithun, a saintly man who cared for the poor, built and repaired churches, walking barefoot to dedicate them; he re-bridged the River Itchen, fortifying the community against threats from the northeast.

But Winchester fell to Danish Vikings.[24] When Swithun died soon after, he was buried in the churchyard, as he requested, for he felt unworthy to be interred with kings inside the church.

God healed through Swithun's bones, and pilgrims journeyed to holy and royal Winchester. Benedictines established Saint Swithun's Priory in the Old Minster and built a shrine to house his relics. On July 15, 971, as the monks processed with Swithun's remains to the shrine, the skies opened and rain poured for forty days and nights. Soon the people chanted:

> *"If it rains on Swithun's Day,*
> *Then forty days shall it rain.*
> *If it be fine on Swithun's Day,*
> *Then forty days shall it be fine."*

Madeleine found such pleasure in the common jingles. They touched her, reaching from the past, carrying the color and temper of the time in a way archaeologists and historians never could. She returned to her screen.

> When William of Normandy introduced French Catholicism in the eleventh century, he replaced English bishops with French ones. He consolidated sees and erected soaring Gothic cathedrals. Over the well of Saint Birinus and the relics of Saint Swithun, he built the immense cathedral of Winchester, soon a popular pilgrimage destination.
>
> But the martyrdom of Thomas Becket diverted pilgrims to Canterbury. Then Winchester lost royal prestige to Westminster's abbey and palace in London. Kings had been crowned and buried in the old capital, but slowly Westminster replaced Winchester.[25]

What would Winchester tell her? The church had witnessed many holy manifestations, many miracles. It had housed much of England's history, the path begun by Joseph of Arimathea, a path continuing to the present day.

As Madeleine closed her laptop, she thought of their children's home. Would God work through them to spread his love?

178

Jack was nearly ready, straightening his tie. She packed her handbag, then phoned Victoria next door. They would try to catch the next train to Winchester.

Winchester's organ thundered through soaring stone vaults, and Madeleine angled her hymnal toward Victoria. The girl stared at the words in awkward silence.

"God himself is with us; Let us all adore him,
And with awe appear before him.
God is here with-in us; Soul, in silence fear him,
Humbly, fervently draw near him.
Now his own, Who have known
God, in worship lowly, Yield their spirits wholly."

Through an opening in the wooden choir screen, Madeleine glimpsed burning candles on the high altar, but today's Mass would be celebrated on the modern altar in front of the screen, closer to the congregation. Sensing Victoria's nervousness, she prayed for wisdom.

She considered Saint Swithun and his devotion to the poor, his practical love, and his humility. Surely, *he* examined his heart and found himself wanting, just as she did. And after penitence and absolution, the good bishop turned to the world to layer God's love onto the canvas of each person, coloring the story of each. Perhaps this was how Christ painted *our* canvases, Madeleine thought.

With each host received, with each word of Scripture heard and each prayer offered, her soul was painted with Christ's love: first the foreground, then land, then sky. Sacrament, scripture, and prayer layered one upon another, reforming, redeeming, healing her.

Would humility and intercessory love make her whole, holy, a complete landscape? Perhaps she might paint a bit of God's love onto Victoria's soul.

The acolytes, deacons, and priests processed out, and Madeleine turned to Victoria. "How about some soup?" she whispered. "I'm starving."

The young mother grinned, nodded, and reached for her jacket.

Chapter Twenty
Winchester

The church is catholic, universal, so are all her actions;
all that she does belongs to all.
When she baptizes a child...that child is thereby connected to that body
which is my head too, and ingrafted into that body whereof I am a member...
All mankind is of one author.
John Donne

Victoria followed Madeleine and Jack into the red brick Visitors Center, where they worked their way through a cafeteria line and found a table in the back. The room bustled with activity. The cathedral was a popular day trip.

Madeleine passed out napkins and utensils, then hung her camel jacket on the back of her chair. "These church cafés serve pretty decent soup and sandwiches."

Jack said grace, making the Sign of the Cross, and Victoria looked away, uncomfortable. "It's not exactly Chewton Glen cuisine," he said, "but timely nevertheless." He opened his paper napkin and spread it over his yellow tie, tucking the sides into his blazer.

Victoria concentrated on her tuna sandwich. She had sat through the service, feeling as if she were a hypocrite. She had asked Jesus into her heart days ago and never told Jack. Now she couldn't even work up the courage to pray in church. She felt no change since she asked. Church still embarrassed her. Her mother said Christianity was a crutch for the weak. Perhaps she was right. Her father had not shared his beliefs with her, such as they were, although he said he prayed. She glanced at her hosts and suddenly wanted to flee. But where?

Jack and Madeleine chatted about the service, particularly the sermon and the "modern rite." They used words Victoria did not recognize: the *Gradual*, the *Propers*, the *Canon*. They seemed upset there was no *General Confession.*

Victoria reached for a bowl of grated parmesan and scooped a bit onto her vegetable soup. Her hosts accepted her silence—at least for now, thought Victoria. But perhaps she did feel different since she invited Jesus into her heart. The preacher today spoke of longing, a word that reflected her feelings perfectly. She *did* long for something greater than herself—something, or someone, she could trust. Was there anyone she could totally trust?

The priest said that all mankind longed for God. Victoria considered that. The longing for God, he said, was the beginning of the search for love, the beginning of moving away from self. He spoke in a hoarse, sliding voice, a frail man with a powerful message.

His merry eyes, hinting that he knew this route from longing to finding, entranced Victoria. He was clearly familiar with the turns and dead-ends, the signposts and ruts of the road, yet still he was merry. Victoria thought he was the kind of person who might invite you home for Christmas Eve. You would sit in an overstuffed chair by the fire, like Lucy with Mr. Tumnus in *The Lion, the Witch, and the Wardrobe*, and he would offer you tea or sherry. Radiating good humor, he might invite you to journey with him, something you longed to do.

During Lent, the preacher claimed, we face our longing for Christ. We air our secrets in his bright light of perfection. We consider which to throw out and which to keep. We clean house, as it were, and make room for him. In this way we turn our poignant, painful longing—yesterday's yearning—into loving, into finding God. Soon our path brings us back to our starting point, for God was there all along, right in our hearts.

Victoria sipped her milk, enjoying the memory. The priest had said something about God being buried by dust and broken furniture, the wants and haves and envies and hatreds, the forgotten accumulations of nothings, the gluttonies and habits of our souls.

"Miss Victoria," Jack said, pulling her into the present, "what *are* you smiling about?"

Madeleine removed their trays and excused herself to visit the restroom.

Jack sipped his tea from a paper cup. "Be sure to finish that milk. It's good for the baby."

Victoria looked into his kind blue eyes. He had a large freckle on his left lid. "I was thinking about something the preacher said." She twisted her napkin and turned her gaze toward the windows where a light rain was beginning to fall.

"It was a pretty good sermon." He glanced at her, then looked into the distance as well.

"Yes."

"I liked the part about the dirty house," Jack said.

"Yes." She glanced at him sideways.

Jack looked as though he was rummaging for the right words, as though lost in a new country. "My house was pretty dirty. I cleaned out a spare room, and God moved in. I think he's in the living room now, and I couldn't be happier with my houseguest."

"Really?" She turned toward him, watching his face, intrigued.

Jack opened his palms. "I knew I longed for something, but I had no idea it was God. And what do you know, it was."

"So how did he get into the living room?"

"One day, I begged him. I was falling back into some bad habits, really beating myself up over it."

"What did you say?" Victoria moved a strand of hair behind her ear and watched him intently.

Jack folded his hands on the table, and leaned toward her. "First, I knelt. I thought kneeling might put me in the right frame of mind. Then I said, 'Where are you, Lord? Do not leave me.' And you know what he said?"

"No."

"'I am in the spare room,' he said. 'Of course,' I said, 'that must be it.' So I considered what to do. I cleaned out all the sofas and paintings cluttering the living room—my sins—you see, and I invited him into the center of my heart. I began to pray each day, to read his Word each day, and slowly I turned my life around, once again."

"You had to do that to find God?" Victoria's baby kicked hard, and she stroked the place, feeling for the moving child.

"It's actually a requirement, and there's more you have to do."

"There's more?" She tipped her carton of milk and sipped the last bit through the straw.

"I went to Mass, for he's there, like Madeleine says, in a special way. Slowly, I climbed out of my ego. I noticed my friends' needs, my spouse's complaints, my own faults. I traveled another path, this one straight and narrow. This path led to...the End of Longing."

"Wow. The End of Longing." Was such a thing really possible?

"Yes, wow," echoed Madeleine, returning. She buttoned her jacket and pulled her sunglasses from her handbag. "Say, what about finding Austen's grave and Arthur's Round Table? Any comers?"

182

"I guess we'd better follow the professor, Victoria. Can't talk theology all day, you know." Jack chuckled and winked at Madeleine.

Madeleine looked pleased, as though their own history had been pulled into the present, their secret, shared history.

Victoria wanted to find someone exactly like Jack.

It was at that moment that she thought of William Carter Collingwood. William playing the piano. William talking about faith in an undercroft café after a concert. William's intensity and devotion. William's sideways sense of humor.

Thinking of William and their ease with one another, Victoria followed Jack and Madeleine down Winchester Cathedral's north aisle in search of Jane Austen's grave.

Jack opened his guidebook. "Look at this." He tapped the shiny pages.

Madeleine shifted her handbag to the other shoulder and glanced at him. "You've been reading up again."

Jack nodded, smiling with satisfaction. "There was a holy well on this spot going back to the Romans, or even earlier, then it became Saint Birinus' Well, and they built the church over it. They replaced that church, and so on. But the well in time has actually produced too much water. This cathedral's been sinking for centuries into the water table."

"You're kidding," Madeleine said, then turned to Victoria. "I didn't know that bit about the sinking cathedral. Rather like Noah's Ark carrying the faithful to dry land." She studied the giant nave. "Amazing."

Jack closed the book. "The Ark's a nice image, Maddie. Didn't you tell me churches are built in the shape of arks? Anyway, the cathedral's been sinking deeper and deeper. A diver had to work twenty feet underwater. He repaired the foundations with bags of cement."

"That's remarkable," Victoria said as she tried to picture the lake beneath them.

Madeleine was searching the floor pavements in earnest. "I found Jane Austen's grave." She pointed to a side bay.

Victoria examined the lettering on the black marble plaque.

> *In Memory of*
> *JANE AUSTEN,*
> *youngest daughter of the late*
> *Rev'd GEORGE AUSTEN,*
> *formerly Rector of Steventon in this County;*
> *she departed this Life on the 18th of July 1817,*
> *aged 41 after a long illness supported with*
> *the patience and the hopes of a Christian.*
>
> *The benevolence of her heart,*
> *the sweetness of her temper, and*
> *the extraordinary endowments of her mind*
> *obtained the regard of all who knew her, and*
> *the warmest love of her intimate connections.*
>
> *Their grief is in proportion to their affection*
> *they know their loss to be irreparable,*
> *but in their deepest affliction they are consoled*
> *by a firm though humble hope that her charity,*
> *devotion, faith and purity, have rendered*
> *her soul acceptable in the sight of her*
> *REDEEMER*

"I like that part about 'charity, devotion, faith and purity,'" said Madeleine, moving toward a brass tablet on the wall nearby. "This plaque was added by her nephew in 1870. It mentions her writings and her 'Christian faith and piety.' Her father was a clergyman, and as I recall, she came to Winchester for medical treatment toward the end of her life and lived in the cathedral close. The location gave her the right to be buried on church grounds, but her family connections allowed her to be buried in the nave, an honor indeed."

"How did she die?" Victoria gazed at the wall memorial. A mixed bouquet sat at the base of the shrine. "Forty-one isn't very old." Younger than her father, Victoria thought.

"Scholars once thought she died of tuberculosis," Madeleine said sadly, "but now some believe it was cancer."

Jack raised his brows. "I wish I'd had time to read famous writers like that."

"Why didn't you?" Victoria asked, then worried she had been too blunt.

But Jack replied with equal candor. "Too busy earning a living."

"What about when you were younger, growing up?"

"I was active with sports and music. We didn't read much in our house. My mother was involved in the PTA and that sort of thing, rounding up clothing for the poorer kids in the community. She was always on the phone, and my sister and I were her go-fers."

Madeleine put her arm around his waist. "Jack, you could say, was more into life than reading about life."

Jack slipped his arm around Madeleine's shoulders. "But someday I just might read something famous, something classic. What's your favorite, Victoria?"

"That's easy. *Pride and Prejudice.*"

"What's it about?"

Victoria paused. She saw in her mind Elizabeth Bennet and her sisters. She pictured Mr. Darcy and Mr. Bingley. "It's about getting to know someone, I think. About not judging a person's character too soon. Elizabeth Bennet misjudges Mr. Darcy and the story is about how wrong she was." How should she judge Madeleine and Jack? Should she trust them, after all this time? And what about William?

Madeleine nodded. "Jane Austen originally titled it *First Impressions.* Trust is a precious thing, that's for sure."

Jack nodded. "It *is* precious. Something one earns."

Madeleine checked her watch. "Let's walk around the church and then find the castle's Great Hall. It's getting late, three already, and we want to catch the 4:50 train back to New Milton."

"But first," said Jack, "let's see the high altar. It has a famous limestone wall."

They walked slowly toward the choir, accommodating Victoria's lumbering gait.

Madeleine grew thoughtful. "Raymond Raynes, the Anglican monk," she said quietly, half to herself, as a dusty stream of light fell upon them, "called the altar a window to heaven, as if Christ entered through it like the sun's rays."

Victoria gazed at the older woman. "That's a beautiful image." Did Christ truly become real upon the altar as they claimed?

"This is the choir," Jack whispered as though stepping on holy ground, "where the monks, called canons in a cathedral, sing the daily services. Have for centuries."

Victoria gazed at the long narrow vaulted space, lined with wooden pews, leading to the pale-gold wall of carvings above the altar.

Madeleine followed her gaze. "And here they said the daily mass. The limestone wall behind is called the *reredos*, Old French for 'rear panel.'"

The stone table was draped in purple; a golden crucifix hung above an ornate tabernacle. Victoria thought the intricate carvings must be figures of saints and martyrs.

"The wall must be fifty feet high," Jack said. "Incredible. Each sculpted figure is perfect, a real character study."

"Much of this," Madeleine added, "was redone by the Victorians, after the Puritans' wave of destruction. It *is* impressive, but I wish they would reserve the Blessed Sacrament here and not in a side chapel. I wonder where the Sacrament *is* reserved."

"Now, Madeleine," Jack said, "don't get carried away." He turned to Victoria. "This is her constant theme."

Victoria smiled, but she wasn't sure what he meant. "No problem." She followed them around to an area behind the limestone wall where four brass torches supported a tented ark that stood several feet above the ground.

"Is this where the pilgrims came?" Madeleine asked Jack. "This must be Saint Swithun's shrine."

Jack angled his guidebook to catch the light from a clerestory window. "'Saint Swithun's remains were displayed on a platform behind the high altar...dating from the 1150s when Bishop Henry of Blois created a unique structure called the Holy Hole.'"

"Wow," Victoria said.

Madeleine shook her head. "A holy hole? I've never heard of *that* before."

Jack smiled at his audience and paused for full effect. "'Pilgrims crawled through a tunnel under the platform to be near the relics and their healing powers.'"

Madeleine frowned. "As I recall no one knows what happened to the relics. The Puritans thought belief in the power of relics to be superstition, and probably destroyed them."

"Do you believe in relics?" Victoria asked Madeleine. Weren't they just bones? How could bones possibly heal anyone?

"Authenticity? Or curative powers? I believe in the authenticity of *some* relics. Others were clearly fakes, and who's to really know? If they have an early history closely associated with the location, I believe they're most likely real."

"But what about the miracles?"

"God probably *did* work miracles through Saint Swithun's bones. It couldn't have been *all* mental imaging, or tall tales, on the part of the pilgrims. Some theologians say that a saint during his lifetime becomes so full of God, the saint's body becomes a channel for God's power, his Holy Spirit, after the saint dies."

Jack looked doubtful. "Let's head for Arthur's Round Table. Are you holding up okay, Victoria?"

"Sure." She felt a little tired but didn't want the tour to end. She had entered another world, one of exploration and discovery. It was like solving a mystery. But the solution would open another door, only to find to another mystery.

She followed her friends through Winchester's medieval streets to William the Conqueror's eleventh-century castle. Puffy clouds scuttled across the skies. Victoria welcomed the brisk breeze.

"The twelfth-century ruins are in the courtyard," Madeleine said, stepping inside the Great Hall. "When a fire destroyed the castle, the court moved to the bishop's palace. But they kept this room for trials."

The long narrow chamber with its dark timbered roof was cold and bare. Victoria shivered, suddenly feeling faint. She lowered herself onto a side bench, her face warm, her breathing heavy. She rested her hands on her protruding abdomen, stroking it gently. *Steady, now,* she thought, *pace yourself, like in jogging.*

Madeleine joined her. "Are you okay? Let's rest here a bit."

"I'm okay," Victoria said breathlessly. "Could you read about the Great Hall, Jack?"

Jack looked concerned but opened his guidebook. "In this hall, Judge Jeffreys, known as 'the hanging judge,' sentenced many Catholics to death. Seems that the most famous of the accused was Alice Lisle, beheaded in 1685."

Victoria cringed. "How awful. What was her crime?"

Jack ran his finger down the entry. "Conspiring against the crown."

"They were terrible times," Madeleine said. "Religious opinion was heated and memories long. Queen Mary's executions were not forgotten. Even so, Judge Jeffreys went way beyond the law."

"Not a fellow to tangle with." Jack glanced at Victoria over his glasses.

Madeleine looked into the distance, as though she had entered that passionate medieval world. She spoke in a quiet voice, describing the scene. "And religious opinion was political opinion. Protestants, in power, worried that the Catholics would revolt. Alice Lisle was convicted of harboring rebels from the Battle of Sedgemoor, a Catholic uprising. She probably *did* harbor her fellow Catholics."

Victoria pointed to a large wheel mounted on the end wall, hoping to pull Jack back into the conversation. "And is that Arthur's Round Table?"

Jack took the bait and skimmed the page. "Let's see...not really. This one was thirteenth century. Arthur was fifth. So it's a replica, I guess, but why?" He looked at Madeleine for help. "I suppose it's hanging on the wall as a display."

Madeleine gazed at the large wheel, as though piecing together a puzzle. "The power of symbol. Kings wanted to claim Arthur's lineage. His name crops up often. Many princes carry his name."

Jack winked at Victoria. "Arthur was a rather romantic fellow and all. I always fancied myself a bit of a knight, chivalry, ladies in distress, that sort of thing."

Madeleine stood and slipped her arm in his. "Indeed you are, and we ladies appreciate a shining knight." Jack kissed her on the forehead gallantly.

Victoria wasn't so sure she wanted to be saved by a knight from the past, or the present, for that matter, and her cheeks burned. "Maybe, maybe not." She looked beyond the Round Table. "What are those silver doors?"

"More romance," Jack said, smiling. "They're in honor of the wedding of Diana and Charles."

Madeleine nodded. "A modern link to royal Winchester and Arthur, maybe even to Joseph of Arimathea, Glastonbury, and Our Lord."

"Joseph of Arimathea?" Victoria searched her memory for the name and found nothing.

"Another story for another time," Madeleine said, looking at Victoria with concern. "Maybe we'll have a chance to visit Glastonbury another day. How are you feeling?"

"Okay."

Jack turned toward Victoria. "Now, as your knight and protector, I must inquire, when do you see the doctor again?" He offered her his hand.

"Next week." Victoria took his hand gratefully and pulled herself up.

They moved toward the exit doors.

"Dr. Murchison seems capable," Madeleine said to Jack. "The baby has a strong heartbeat."

Victoria smiled weakly. "And a ruthless kick. He'll be fine." But would *she* be fine?

"*He?*" Jack asked as they turned toward the train station.

"My father thinks the baby will be a boy."

"Does he? He seems a fine man, your father."

Victoria smiled, recalling the two had met. Her network of trust was growing. "He has these ideas sometimes, intuitions or something. It runs in the family, he says."

Madeleine touched Victoria's arm lightly. "Time will tell. I hope we can meet up with him soon."

"I do too." She hesitated, then said, "Listen, it's time I told you both more of my story. We'll talk on the train. I'm pretty tired."

Victoria composed herself and looked at her friends sitting opposite, as the train rolled through low hills.

"I was running along the lake." She turned toward the window, searching for the right words, as few words as possible. "A man jumped me."

Madeleine breathed in suddenly. "You don't have to tell us."

"Are you saying, my dear, that you were raped?" Jack's voice rose.

"Yes," she whispered, her eyes still fixed on the passing scenery.

"Did they find him?"

"No." She turned to him; his face was flushed.

Madeleine leaned forward and laid her hand, cool and comforting, over Victoria's. "So the baby is a result of this violence."

"Yes," Victoria said.

"My poor girl," Madeleine said.

"Why would anyone...," Jack spluttered, gripping the armrests.

"You're doing the right thing," Madeleine said, "having the baby. We'll help you find a home for him, if that's your choice. You're not alone, my dear." Madeleine's eyes were kind.

Victoria nodded, thankful. "That's what William said and my father too. Daddy is sort of Roman Catholic." With the images of William and her father, the last of Victoria's guard crumbled, and she told them of her previous abortion. She described her mother's beliefs and her aunt's actions.

Madeleine had grown quiet. She wiped her cheek with the back of her hand.

Victoria feared she had caused her friends pain. "What is it? I've upset you both. Please, I can take care of this myself. I don't want to be a burden, and you've been so generous. My credit card is still good, and I have some traveler's checks."

Madeleine raised a palm in protest. "No, no, you're not a burden." She turned to Jack. "I think it's time to tell her about Mollie."

"Maddie," Jack said, "you don't have to bring that up."

Victoria studied them, waiting. Madeleine shook her head. "No, I want to."

Jack watched Madeleine, his eyes full of concern.

"Victoria," Madeleine began, "I didn't want to bring my own tragedy into an already difficult time for you, but you need to know I've been through tough times myself. You need to know that I can sympathize, understand a little." She looked at Jack, then at her own hands, folded tightly, as she composed her thoughts. She turned to Victoria. "Over twenty-six years ago my baby Mollie, only eight months, drowned in a wading pool. It was my fault. I had left her...alone." She raised her eyes to the window and passed her hand over her forehead as though to wipe away the memory.

"How terrible," Victoria said. *And how similar,* she thought. They had each been responsible for the death of a child, their own child.

"Forgive me," Madeleine said, her voice thin, "but this is difficult." She paused, then continued. "Grief and guilt haunted me for a long time. Recently, only five years ago, my old nightmares returned. In the dream, my baby shrinks to nothing and I am helpless. Father Rinaldi, our parish priest, helped heal me of those nightmares."

Jack reached for Madeleine's hand. "We made a pilgrimage to Italy. We visited churches and prayed for healing. Thanks be to God, the pilgrimage helped."

Madeleine leaned forward. "It was a terrible time for both of us. But with God's grace, we made it through. With his grace, you will too."

Victoria winced with her friend's pain. "I had no idea you'd been through so much, and I'm sorry I brought all those memories back." She smoothed her shirt nervously and pulled her sweater about her. What doors to the past had she opened? And the loss of a baby—

"Don't be sorry," Jack said, his eyes earnest. "God made things right in the end. He does that, you know, he redeems suffering. He doesn't cause it, but he brings good out of it."

They paused in mutual silence, as the sway of the car and the throb of the wheels cradled them. It was as if, Victoria thought, their shared pain had created a sudden intimacy.

Jack broke the quiet. "But Victoria, have you decided what you will you do after the baby is born?"

"I don't know. Can I stay at Saint Anne's for a while? I have some big decisions to make."

Madeleine smiled. "Of course. As long as you need, if the house is ready. If not, we'll find a place for you." She moved alongside Victoria and wrapped her arm about the girl's shoulders. "Maybe we should head there soon."

"Aylesbury's too close to London," Jack said. "Let's stay away from Senator Nguyen a bit longer."

Madeleine nodded. "Maybe you're right."

Victoria's lids weighed heavily. "The longer the better. I feel safe with you." Suddenly overcome with fatigue, she lay back on the headrest and closed her eyes. She settled her hands on her child.

"First babies are often late," Victoria heard Madeleine whisper. "Not to worry."

Chapter Twenty-one
Salisbury

*In order to move
forward into the future,
you need to know where you've been.*
Charles Williams

In the days that followed, this second week at Chewton Glen, Victoria fell into a pleasant routine, walking in the woods or by the sea with Madeleine in the mornings, having tea in the afternoon. She swam in the giant pool, finding the weightlessness a relief as she floated on her back and gazed at the pretty skylight high above. She napped after lunch, for she slept poorly at night in spite of the pillows Madeleine propped about her, waking often with thoughts of William and her father, and the new life she carried within her. She was oddly content, as though she and her child were a complete society, as though she was borne on a tide greater than herself, one that removed her from worry and filled her with certainty.

William phoned often, his voice soothing and confident, to see how she was doing. They chatted about his classes, his studies, his exams, the latest Oxford gossip. As she listened to him talk, her heart grew happy with the doings of his world. She soon imagined being a part of it and looked forward to their conversations, just as she had in London.

She was glad Jack had met her father and William in Oxford, and she often saw the three men together in her mind, imagining what they had said to one another. Jack had returned to London to meet with Mr. McGinty and organize dinners for potential donors to Saint Anne's House. Each morning Victoria would ask Madeleine about the previous evening's phone call, but it seemed Jack had not seen or spoken to her father since that one time.

The evening of Sunday, March 3, Victoria joined Madeleine and Jack in the hotel dining room. She had napped for several hours after their return from Salisbury, and now wore the new dress she bought in a boutique near the cathedral. The pink floral rayon gathered toward the top and flowed down in fine pleats. The dress made her feel pretty.

The Marryat Restaurant stretched along an enclosed sun porch tented with billowy white cotton. It was a crisp room with bleached linens and glimmering silver, green ferns and leafy trees in large planters. A candle in a hurricane glass burned in the center of their table, and yellow daisies bunched in a white vase.

Jack eyed Madeleine. *"'Blessed are your eyes, for they see, and your ears, for they hear.'* Matthew 13:16."

Madeleine laughed. "Is that a new one?"

"I've been working on it."

"You've been *engrafting*," Victoria said, pleased she had recalled the word.

"Precisely." He winked.

Madeleine unfolded her napkin. "That's one of my favorites. I think Our Lord meant *understanding* when he said eyes and ears, but I do like sensory things such as hearing, seeing, touching, tasting."

"Amen to that." Jack peered into his menu. "By the way, Joe McGinty was glad to hear you're enjoying yourself, Madeleine."

"He appreciates your work," Madeleine said.

The waiter appeared. "Have you chosen?"

"I'll try the lamb with rosemary," Victoria said, "and a green salad?"

Jack peeked over his glasses. "I recommend the *haricot vert* salad with *foie gras*. You haven't tried that yet."

"That's duck liver, isn't it? No thank you. Just a salad, please, with some tomatoes."

Madeleine looked thoughtful. "Since it's Sunday and a feast day, and I don't need to keep my Lenten rule, I'll have the lamb with Victoria, and the bean and *foie gras* salad to start. I can't pass up *foie gras*, even when it's *pâté*."

"And I," Jack announced, "am having the beef, and I'll begin with the asparagus. And for the wine, Number 134, the Brunello. And Hildon water, and a large glass of milk for the mother-to-be." Jack beamed at

Victoria. Protective pleasure mapped his face.

"So, Victoria," said Madeleine, as the waiter left for the kitchen, "what did you think of the cathedral?"

"Large. White. Dramatic. Outside, the tall spire was as beautiful as that famous painting...was it Constable's? I wish I could have seen it in better weather. Maybe I'll revisit with Baby one day." Was she planning things with her child? Could she even think of planning things? Should she?

The waiter returned and poured the wine.

"We were brave to tackle the storm," Jack said as he swirled the red liquid in his glass.

"The cathedral *is* beautiful," Madeleine said wistfully, "and dating to the 1200s, a real Gothic masterpiece."

Their first courses arrived.

Jack said grace, making the Sign of the Cross. Madeleine made the Sign of the Cross over her head and heart as well.

Victoria watched them, becoming more at ease with the ritual, then asked, "What happened to the old church?"

"The earlier church," Madeleine said, "was called Old Sarum. You can still see the ruins on the road to Avesbury. Old Sarum was also Norman, built by Saint Osmund on a windy hilltop with poor access to water. So when they rebuilt two hundred years later, they moved to the valley and quarried the old church to build the new one."

Jack glanced up from his asparagus. "Do you like the wine?"

"It's excellent," Madeleine said. "It reminds me of Tuscany. Maybe Victoria would like a taste. A little is okay."

Victoria shook her head. "Thanks, but I'll wait until it's totally safe." She paused, then added, "I liked the church service." She mixed her pile of greens with the circling tomatoes. "The children's choir was charming. But I did have a question. Who was Saint Osmund?"

Madeleine swirled the wine in her glass, watching the ruby light dance. "He was Bishop of Old Sarum." She turned to Victoria. "He cared for the poor. He provided a rule for the cathedral called the *Use of Sarum*, which was a precursor to our *Book of Common Prayer*. He also founded a boys' school."

Jack mopped the last bit of olive oil dressing with a chunk of tomato bread. "Today it's a boys *and girls* school. It was great to hear them sing."

Madeleine sat back and gazed happily at Victoria. "I loved the singing, too."

Jack sipped his wine. "I recall seeing *Old Sarum* in our hymnal. Now

I understand the reference." He scanned the room. "This is such a civilized country hotel, isn't it, my ladies? Lovely, as they say, lovely."

"Madeleine," Victoria said, "could I ask you an odd question? I was thinking about the wealth that went into these churches and all the wars over money."

"It's an old problem."

"Why do people always want more?"

Jack's laugh was lined with irony. "You should be asking *me* that question, but you tackle it first, Maddie."

"I'll try. From what I've read, ever since the Fall of Adam, when Adam disobeyed God in the Garden of Eden, we are born with Original Sin, the genetic disposition we inherited from Adam and Eve. We tend to be unhappy with what we have. Our achievements and our blessings quickly become the status quo, our expected rights, our entitlement. Then we search for even greater happiness, the bigger house, the perfect children, the third car. We are forever demanding more."

"It's a natural urge," added Jack, "that's not entirely wrong."

"When directed by God," Madeleine said. "It's a question of idolatry, really, worshiping material goods, rather than seeing them as gifts, as blessings."

Victoria tasted her lamb. "So seeking God is an okay desire?" The meat was sweet and juicy, not too pink, the juice swirling about the plate. She was enjoying the meal and the conversation.

"Exactly, that kind of *more* is the right kind." Jack raised his glass to the light to watch the legs form along the sides. "Nice wine."

"And so," Madeleine added, "we must be wise to God's will."

"He who has eyes to see...," Jack said. He sipped slowly, clearly savoring the taste.

Victoria was determined to follow the line of reasoning through to its end, if there was one. "You're saying that it's the object of the desire, not the desire for more, *per se*."

Madeleine nodded. "Desire for God is always good. What's that quote about loving money, Jack?"

Jack was studying a basket of focaccia. "Right. *The love of money is the root of all evil.* 1 Timothy 6:10. Not money itself, but the love of it. It's all about the ordering of our loves."

Victoria grew thoughtful. "I was also thinking about my mother."

"I thought you might be." Worry flickered across Madeleine's face.

"Mother always needs more things—houses, clothes, cars, and lately, power and control."

"She's probably blinded by habit," Madeleine said, hoping to soften Victoria's judgment. "A little envy leads to greed, which, for some people, leads to theft or murder. Each sin, or wrong choice, creates new habits, a new status quo, inuring us to the sin itself."

That was what happened, Victoria thought, with her mother and her vehement attitude toward abortion. She had become desensitized by her choices, so that she could escape judgment, her own self-judgment.

Jack nodded. "And the opposite is equally true. Good habits, good choices, help us see more clearly."

"Daily confession helps," Madeleine added, seeming to drift into another time.

"We need to clean out those rooms," Jack added, and Victoria recalled their earlier conversation. "And sometimes the cleaning can hurt."

"I suppose so." She wasn't too sure about confession. But it made sense to do a self-examination occasionally, so as not to fall into bad habits, or self-lies. Again, Victoria thought of her mother and her heart ached. How many lies had her mother told herself to come to this place in her life, where she would abort her own grandchild? And for the second time? Did it become easier for her each time?

Madeleine raised open palms. "We simply seek God's will with an open heart."

"And don't forget," Jack said, "we're in this boat, or should I say ark, ha-ha, together. We're a family, God's family by adoption, Paul says. I think I might learn that verse next. We support each other."

Victoria considered Jack's words. "I like that. I don't know if I believe it, but I like it." Could such a thing be true?

Jack motioned for the waiter. "Let's have our tea and dessert in one of the salons."

They sat in front of a blazing fire in overstuffed chairs patterned in burgundy and teal. A waiter appeared with a tray of tea and petit fours which he set on their low mahogany table. A tuxedoed pianist played a shiny baby grand in a corner of the room. Victoria recognized a melody from *Phantom of the Opera* and recalled seeing the show in San Francisco with her father. Her mother had been in Washington.

As she gazed about the cozy room, she longed for home. In spite of Madeleine's careful attention, and in spite of her growing attachment to the child she carried, Victoria at times felt adrift with no anchor, riding a restless sea. How had she come to be here? And so far away? *Lord Jesus, help me,* she prayed.

"It's such a treat," Madeleine was saying, "to be in this charming country house."

"It's not our usual fare," Jack said, rubbing his chin, "that's for sure, but we did improve our lot over the years."

"You pulled yourself up from nothing," Madeleine said, "and I was a single parent—a starving single parent at that." She winced and shook her head. "I *am* sorry, Victoria. I didn't think."

"It's okay."

"No, I'm truly sorry. I *was* alone and poor, living hand to mouth, but I *did* have the Church and I had God and I had prayer. They got me through the tough stretches. And most of all, I had the Mass."

"What about your family? Couldn't they help?" Victoria asked. Had this woman, with her matching sweater sets and pearls, ever been poor? Ever been alone?

"My father was dying and my mother despairing. They couldn't help, nor did I expect them to. Emotionally, I was supporting *them*."

"How old was your child?"

"Justin was born in Canada in '72, and when he was four I left his father, another long story. We came home to San Francisco. We never saw Charlie again, a strange mystery. He remarried, started over, and wished no contact. So Justin and I were on our own, financially *and* emotionally."

"That must have been hard." Victoria watched the older woman closely. How did she ever get through it?

"It was really hard for awhile, but dear Father Rinaldi helped me, helped us. Did you know he founded Cristoforo's convent in Rome? He cared for Cristoforo just like he cared for us. A good man."

Victoria leaned forward. "He was Cristoforo's priest too? In Rome? What a nice connection."

"Yes, it *is* a nice connection," Madeleine agreed. "So Father helped us through that time. When I met Jack at Saint Thomas' and my life changed. I went back to school and ended up teaching at the university."

"Which," Jack said, dropping two sugars in his tea, "brings up the subject of *your* education, Victoria." He stirred thoughtfully, then raised his earnest blue eyes to hers as if negotiating the price of a fine wine.

"You *must* finish high school, and you *must* go on to college, regardless of the child. It's important, and you'll never regret it."

"Isn't it more important to find a father to help me raise my child?"

"That too, if the right man comes along," Madeleine said. "And don't forget you can give the baby up for adoption. You're young. You have your whole life ahead of you."

"But don't sell yourself short," Jack said, arching his brows and sipping his tea, "in the education department."

A waiter approached.

"A call for Ms. Nguyen at the front desk."

Victoria's heart pounded as she slowly made her way to the lobby. *Please let it be William or Daddy.*

"Victoria, is that you?" Her mother's nasal twang seared the line.

"Yes...?" Her mind was numb.

"Are you all right, sweetie? What are you doing?"

"Nothing...Mother."

"We *finally* found you. You've had me worried sick, *and* your father. Freddie's people have been checking everywhere for you."

"Yes...Mother." Tears were near. *Dear Jesus, help me.*

"Your father and I will come down in the morning. Simply stay put and we'll take care of everything. You still intend to have it?"

"Is Daddy there?"

"*Why* would you have it? We'll talk, Vicky dear. I'm not going to pressure you in any way. You hold tight, okay? Of course your father is with me."

"Mother, I want to have the baby." Then it happened. Victoria sensed a bold shift, as though she had caught her balance just before falling. She was filled with an unexpected burst of energy. "Mother, I've decided to have this child, my son, your grandson. We'll call you when he's born."

"*We* will call? Who is *we*?"

"Good-bye, Mother. Give my love to Daddy. I'm doing fine." Victoria Nguyen regarded the receiver as though it might bite and set it on the cradle. What had she done?

She returned to the salon and sat down, leaning purposefully toward Madeleine and Jack, her palms flat on her legs. "I wish to say two things—no, three things."

They waited, and Victoria could feel their concern.

"First, thank you for all you've done. These weeks have been precious. Second, Jack, I never told you I asked Jesus into my heart. I should have told you."

Jack grinned and rubbed his hands. "That's great, Victoria."

"I didn't think anything really happened, until now."

"What happened?" Madeleine asked.

"That brings me to three. That was my mother on the phone. I asked Jesus for help and he gave me strength to say what I needed to say. He may have even given me the words." Victoria studied the room as though Jesus might walk in, sit down, and give her further instructions.

Jack nodded. "When we ask Jesus into our hearts, things happen, sooner or later."

Victoria turned to her hosts. "She's driving down from London tomorrow, with Daddy."

"We'd better move on." Jack folded his napkin neatly. "How about Thornbury Castle near Bath? It's remote enough, and it might be fun for a few days. I read about it recently somewhere. I'll see if we can get a reservation on such short notice. Might be a cancellation." He left for the concierge's desk.

Victoria glanced at Madeleine. In the midst of her near panic, Victoria felt strangely calm. The two women walked up the stairs, pausing before Victoria's door.

"Could you come in for a few minutes, Madeleine? I'd appreciate your company."

Madeleine crossed the room and gazed out the French doors. The rain fell steadily into the dark.

Victoria lowered herself into a wing chair. "What happened, Madeleine? Did God really help me? Or was it all in my mind?"

Madeleine turned, her hazel eyes shining. "I believe God did help you."

"Is it that simple? Merely *asking* for God's help?"

"It is that simple. *'Ask, and it shall be given you; seek, and ye shall find; knock, and it shall be opened unto you.'* Christ's promise, in Saint Matthew's Gospel, I think. God is present in the Mass, in other Christians, in suffering, in love. When we open our hearts, he is able to work miracles. And, of course, if we keep them closed, he has no opportunity."

"Jack said something like that. We need to clean out our rooms."

"We need to make a place for him. The big obstacles are, after all, easy to spot—lying, stealing, killing. Even lust, envy, and pride are pretty easy to recognize." Madeleine turned again to the storm bending the trees against the dark sky. "But the subtle slights, the mean-spirited jabs, or merely the hoarding of one's time and money—these sins are slippery.

They hide in dark corners."

Victoria motioned to the opposite chair. "Please sit with me."

Madeleine joined her and for a moment remained thoughtfully silent, then opened her palms as though releasing doves. "When God's light shines into our hearts we see ourselves, every minute of every day, and we ask the question of each thought, each moment spent, *was he there?*"

Madeleine looked tired, but her face glowed. As the middle-aged woman leaned forward, her hands folded loosely, Victoria inhaled her words like oxygen in a smoked-filled room.

"You see," Madeleine continued, "as *we* grow toward *God*, *he* grows in *us*, and his light illumines our lives, giving us fuller and fuller self-knowledge, whether we like that knowledge or not. His love purifies us."

"I would like that. I would like to know who I am, who I really am."

"Sometimes it hurts."

"But it's better than being a mouse, and that's what I've been."

"You're not a mouse, Victoria. Keep seeking God, and you'll do just fine." Madeleine rose slowly. "We have a big day tomorrow. You'd better go to bed, young lady. You're sleeping for two." She slipped Victoria's thick black hair behind her ears and kissed her on the forehead. "Good night, my sweet girl."

"Good night."

Silently, carefully, Madeleine closed the door behind her.

Victoria readied herself for bed, and as she lay in the crisp sheets, she gazed into the dark, listening to the rhythmic patter of the rain on the roof.

"Thank you, Jesus, thank you," she prayed and fell into a deep, dreamless sleep.

Jack had not returned to the room. Madeleine, a bit concerned, said her evening prayers, crawled into bed, and opened her laptop. Thornbury Castle was near Bath, and not far from Glastonbury. She had researched the medieval shrine of Glastonbury, and now she could visit. And a little work on her manuscript would take her mind off of Jack.

Holy Manifestations: Glastonbury

Legend claims that in 37 AD Joseph of Arimathea[26] sailed to Glastonbury through the misty marshes of Somerset, "Summer Land" of the Celts, and planted his staff on Weary All Hill. When the staff flowered, he knew he must to stay. Locals say he visited this southwestern coast of Britain many years earlier with Jesus, his grandnephew, and Mary, his niece.

Some historians argue that the Glastonbury monks of the Middle Ages promoted the tale of Joseph to draw away pilgrims from other shrines. But some scholars ask, if the tale was invented, why did they choose Joseph rather than an apostle, a far more prestigious claim? Records show Joseph traded for tin in Cornwall. He could easily have brought along Jesus and Mary. In Glastonbury, he may have built with wattle and daub what was to become the first English church.

Legend claims that after Christ's death and resurrection, Joseph of Arimathea journeyed to France with his family as well as Mary Magdalene, Mary Salome, Mary (mother of James), Martha, Lazarus, Maximin, and Zaccheus. Fleeing persecution in Jerusalem, they sailed to the southern coast of France. Lazarus journeyed east to Marseilles, Mary Magdalene further east into the Sainte-Baume mountains, and Martha north to Tarascon, near Avignon. Zaccheus settled in the mountain caves of Rocamadour in central France. Joseph's party continued north, crossed the English Channel to Cornwall, and sailed to Somerset. All of these locales memorialize these saints through tradition and tale.

Madeleine recalled their trip through France. They visited Rocamadour, where Zaccheus was said to have journeyed with Veronica. In the hilltop abbey of Vézeley, they saw Mary Magdalene's relics, thought to have come from Sainte-Baume. In Paris Madeleine prayed before the giant sculpture of Mary Magdalene dancing with angels. Tradition claimed Martha did indeed tame the dragon of Tarascon in Provence. And Madeleine remembered that, every year, the beach town of Les Saintes-Maries-de-la-Mer on the southern coast of France celebrated the arrival of Joseph's ship from Jerusalem.

The village of Glastonbury—the Celtic *Ynis-witrin*, or *Island of Glass*—dates to Britain's Iron Age (700-100 BC). There archeologists have found workshops, storehouses, and kennels in hill-forts characteristic of the times, when the waters of the Atlantic, since receded, lapped its shores. A holy site to the pre-Christian Druids, Celtic legends speak of Avalon, the apple-place, a land of magic.

Little of Joseph's wattle-and-daub chapel remain, but his colorful legacy continues to influence the English Church. Like the shoots of his staff, his story grew and blossomed, telling how he brought from Jerusalem the sacred cup of Christ's last supper, the same chalice that collected the water and blood pouring from Christ's side, the Holy Grail[27] sought by Arthur's Knights of the Round Table. And so the story of first-century Joseph interweaves with the story of fifth-century Arthur, High King of Wessex.

Twelfth-century Geoffrey of Monmouth retold Arthur's tale in his *History of the Kings of England*, drawing on legend and tradition, as well as the histories of Gildas, Bede,[28] and Nennius. Removing Hollywood's portrayal, Merlin's magic, and Arthur's superhuman deeds, a historical hero-king remains. There is strong evidence for the settlement of Camelot in South Cadbury, east of Glastonbury, where traces of a royal family have been found in an Iron Age hill-fort.

Ah, Glastonbury, a mystical place indeed. And mysticism cut both ways, Madeleine knew, opening doors sometimes better left shut. But as a catholic Christian she felt safe. If she visited the ancient ruins and climbed the mountain called the Tor, and if she tasted the healing waters from the Chalice Well, she would think of Joseph of Arimathea and his flowering staff and his wattle church. She would give great thanks for the faith passed on to her through the Church in England.

She returned to her words.

At the end of the twelfth century, a soothsayer claimed that Arthur lay buried in Glastonbury Abbey. The monks searched and finally unearthed his tomb alongside Guinevere's in the crypt.

Finding Arthur's body helped the ruling Normans. Geoffrey of Monmouth had claimed that Arthur had never died, that he had traveled to miraculous Avalon to heal his wounds; such a claim inspired the Welsh to hope for their king's return. After all, the Welsh had fought the Saxons; the promise of Arthur's return gave hope that they would be victorious over the hated Normans. The discovery of Arthur's body destroyed that dream and strengthened Norman rule.

Finding Arthur also helped Glastonbury Abbey, for now pilgrims would be drawn away from Canterbury. The monks traced Arthur to Joseph of Arimathea, four centuries earlier, and thus to Christ, a powerful ancestry.

Arthur's legend permeated English history, supporting royal authority and sculpting western ideals of chivalry: defense of the weak, courage to fight for right, loyalty to the good, courtesy to one's fellows. The Knights of the Round Table embodied the essence of honor and valor, Christian values passed down through the centuries. At first a Celtic hero, Arthur became Everyman, a true Pelagian battling destiny and forging national history.

Madeleine shifted her position in the bed, and glanced at the door. Where was Jack? She returned to her screen.

In addition to Joseph and Arthur, Saint Dunstan made his mark on Glastonbury. Educated at the abbey, he became abbot in 943. In the wake of the Danish invasions, Dunstan rebuilt the abbey and reformed the monastic community; as Archbishop of Canterbury, he helped reform the Church in England with discipline and learning.

Thousands of pilgrims journeyed to Glastonbury Abbey on high holy days, and the libraries and schools instituted by Dunstan flourished until Henry VIII dissolved the monasteries to fatten his treasury. When the abbey fell, and its stone was quarried, an old man foretold that one day "peace and plenty would for a long time abound" in Glastonbury.[29]

Madeleine glanced at the nightstand clock. 11:30. Where *was* her husband? A strange foreboding took hold of her, but she shook it off.

Indeed, today, Glastonbury attracts assorted pilgrims, including pagan New Agers and other diviners of the divine. Here, British Christians search for the origins of their unique island faith: their curious and useful blend of free will and grace, inherited from Pelagius and the two Augustines; their independence and their submission to catholicity in the Roman, Celtic, Saxon, and Norman threads woven into the Anglican communion. Rock concerts, mud wallowers, and Wiccan gatherings compete with Christian liturgies, but still the hallowed waters of the Chalice Well flow, the thorn tree flowers, and the ancient Tor looms above the abbey ruins, lending a sacred presence to the world of matter.

The five-hundred-foot Tor rises from the low Somerset hills, a gently terraced mountain with Saint Michael's Tower at its summit, the Chalice Well at its base. Here, in the well, Joseph hid the grail and Arthur found it, and over the centuries the waters have healed the faithful.[30] Nearby is Weary All Hill, where cuttings of Joseph's thorn tree blossom in winter. The ruins of the great Benedictine abbey lie in the valley beyond, the stark transept piers a last witness to the king's greed and the Puritans' malice. There, between the grass and the broad sky, the remains of the Lady Chapel cradle the site of Joseph's wattle church.

On the second Saturday of July each year, the Glastonbury pilgrimage attracts Anglican, Roman Catholic, and Orthodox Christians. The Anglicans offer the Eucharist in the ruined abbey nave, and the Orthodox celebrate in the Lady Chapel crypt, honoring the icon of Our Lady of Glastonbury. On Sunday, the Roman Catholics sing as they process down the Tor to a Mass in the ancient abbey—

The door opened. It was Jack, looking troubled.

"Honey, where have you been?" Madeleine closed her document.

He sat on the corner of the bed. "I made reservations for Thornbury through the concierge. Then I called a few people at home. I've been doing some thinking downstairs in front of the fire." His voice was heavy and threatening, recalling the old Jack, the one whose temper flared.

Madeleine shut down her laptop as a familiar fear returned. "What kind of thinking, Jack?"

"You're not going to like this."

"Please, tell me. We need to get some sleep."

"We can't keep protecting this girl."

"What?"

"She's underage, Maddie. We could be prosecuted for kidnapping."

"But...you said her father—"

"I don't trust her father to stand up to her mother, to defend us, if push comes to shove. Her mother is the one calling the shots here. You do remember Joe McGinty and that fundraiser?"

Madeleine nodded. She remembered all too well. "But Victoria is afraid of her mother. We would betray her trust."

"I called my attorney, and it's just as I feared. This is a delicate situation."

"Give her a little more time. Give us all a little more time."

Jack breathed deeply and walked to the windows. He pulled aside a drapery panel and gazed into the night. "Okay, we'll take her to Thornbury. Maybe Cristoforo could help after that. He has less to lose."

"How's that?"

Jack turned toward her. "He's clergy, and he's Roman Catholic. The Church gets them out of these things. They have funds."

"That Boston priest isn't doing so well with the molestation charges."

"That's different."

"I hope so."

"We'll take her with us to Thornbury," Jack said, his voice rising, "but that's it. One more week. And if her parents or the police show up, I'm not lying to protect her." He walked to the bathroom and slammed the door behind him.

Madeleine shut down her laptop and turned out the light. As she stared into the dim room, a cold misery seeped through her, contracting her lungs, knotting her insides. Jack soon slipped into bed and rolled over, turning away from her in silence.

She slept little that night and was grateful when the pale gray light of dawn slanted through the draperies. She found her robe and curled up in the chair with a guidebook, turning to *Thornbury Castle*. Glastonbury wasn't that far from Thornbury. Jack's words echoed in her mind, but as she searched for answers, she found none. She tried to concentrate on the words before her, absorbing little, her thoughts returning to the problem of Victoria and the baby, refusing to give up.

She gazed at Jack, who shifted uneasily, wheezing. The night gulf between them, now lit by the day, seemed unbreachable. She breathed deeply and began her morning prayers, including one to Our Lady of Glastonbury. Perhaps Mary could help, intercede in this perplexing situation. *Hail Mary, full of grace, blessed art thou among women, and blessed is the fruit of thy womb, Jesus. Holy Mary, Mother of God, pray for us sinners now and at the hour of our death...*

Finally, Madeleine realized that she had no control, no control at all. *Thy will be done, O Lord.*

Chapter Twenty-two
Glastonbury

And did those feet in ancient time
Walk upon England's mountains green?
And was the holy Lamb of God
On England's pleasant pastures seen?
William Blake

On that third Sunday of Lent, Brother Cristoforo stood on the steep slopes of Glastonbury Tor, looking over the ruins of the abbey far below.

Two weeks earlier he had said good-bye to Mrs. Huddleston and traveled the countryside, preaching to all who would listen. He stood in town parks and churchyards, on lush hillsides and fallow acres, in sun and rain, in swirling mist and biting wind. He worked his way west to Glastonbury, for he heard it was a holy shrine. After Glastonbury, he would return to Rome.

This first Sunday in March, under a dome of gray skies, he preached to his substantial congregation, over fifty souls, he guessed. But there was no sign of Nadia.

"He became like us so we might be like him," Cristoforo shouted to the crowd. He had positioned himself below and to the left of Saint Michael's Tower, a balance he thought effective. His people appeared to be listening.

"Why be a Christian? Why believe in Jesus?" The friar looked into the eyes of each person in the front row. There was a middle-aged woman with a backpack and walking stick, a young couple in black leather, and an old man in a vest and tie, smoking a pipe.

A few tourists came up the trail leading to the abbey. They paused, curious at the gathering. Could he make them stay?

He threw his arms in the air. "There are three reasons to be a

Christian. *First*, Christianity answers an important question: what happens when we die? Jesus Christ promises we will live for all eternity with our loving Father. *Second,* Christianity is true: it depends on a real person, Jesus of Nazareth. It is not only ideas. Jesus is real, my friends, he truly lived on this earth and...he is alive today!" Here the monk stomped his foot on the grass with satisfaction. How he loved that part!

The crowd was listening, and Cristoforo's heart soared.

"The third reason is that Christianity works. God loves all of us. Race and class do not matter." He pointed to himself and stretched out his arms, opening his hands with relief as he looked to the sky with thanksgiving. After all, he was the perfect example. Appreciative laughter rippled through the crowd.

A child cried in the back, and a woman picked her up.

"Christianity works. It helps us to be good. Christ says to love one another. He says to show mercy. He says to sacrifice for others."

"This may be true," said the elderly gentleman as he waved his pipe, "but there are many instances of the very reverse occurring. Consider, if you will, the Crusades or the Inquisition?"

"But sir," the friar said with some condescension, "the Crusaders did much good. They stopped the Turks from invading the West. They tried to save holy Jerusalem. As in all of man's endeavors, there were men who did not act honorably. Some acted only for gain, and that is sin."

"And the Inquisition?" the man asked with an air of satisfied arrogance. "You cannot say that the terrible tortures of the Inquisition did not happen?"

"Which one? There were three. They happened over a span of hundreds of years. They came from the people. Belief was not protected. There was much prejudice toward those who believed differently. But it is better today, when there is freedom of belief."

"Harrumph," the man sneered through a cloud of smoke.

The others, restless, glared at the old man, waiting for the friar to continue. There must be over a hundred now, Cristoforo thought.

"Yes, my friends. Christianity built England, and Europe too. Christianity inspires us to create, to make life better. The Church founded universities, western science. Priests and monks looked through telescopes in church towers and studied the heavens."

A brisk breeze rose, and the heavy air turned cold. The friar pulled his cape about him and paced before his people. "And there is more. Christianity has written down God's great acts in the Bible. In the Old

Testament, Christ is *foretold*. In the New Testament he *is*. He *is*. He *is!*" He threw his right arm into the skies. "Christ is the *Word of God*, God's own Word. That is why we call the Bible *God's Word*. Because it tells of Christ."

Cristoforo pulled a coffee tin from behind a boulder and thought of Nadia. Where was she? He walked into the crowd with his tin, never pausing in his sermon.

"The Bible is important, because it shows us Christ. Jesus Christ is not a book. Jesus Christ is a living person. Like you and me. He came to earth to save us. He came to give us his own life. Jesus says, *'For God so loved the world, that he gave his only begotten Son, that whosoever believeth in him should not perish, but have everlasting life.'* That's John, chapter 3, verse 16, my people."

The friar passed the tin, and it was filling up, the coins clinking. He moved among them, locking eyes with each person, a thrill moving through his body.

A roll of thunder sounded in the distance.

He stopped in front of a boy about ten years old. "You see, Jesus Christ became man and this is called the *Incarnation*. Today, he is in the Eucharist. Incarnate in you and me!"

The boy blinked. "Cool," he said.

How glorious this was! "Now I tell you," Cristoforo continued as he walked (he had perfected the route, heading straight down the center and looping back, making an *S)*, "what happened on the day Christ rose from the dead. He spoke to Mary Magdalene in the garden. He said to tell the apostles to meet him in Galilee. He said he would go before them."

The friar returned to his starting point and placed the full can behind the boulder.

"Then Christ ascended to heaven. He goes before us. He prepares the way." He pointed his finger at the crowd. "It is true. He is alive. He welcomes us into his Church. He gives us strength and sends us back into the stormy world."

The monk had loved and polished that line, but the stormy world was upon him, whipping his robes, the wind rising and wailing. The crowd eyed the dark sky uneasily.

Simply one more challenge, Cristoforo thought, and one more that he would overcome. "Jesus said to leave our old lives, and to take on new lives."

The friar looked into the cynical eyes of the old man. They were like shiny beads, embedded on either side of his bony nose. The man's lips curled as though they might snarl and laugh at the same time.

"He asks each of us," Cristoforo said, "'Who do *you* think I am?' And I tell you now, Jesus *is* the Gospel, the Good News, the Son of God come to save us from death."

Cristoforo turned to the crowd, certain he held them fast with his words, even in these threatening conditions. "Christianity says *yes* to a real person."

Lightning lit the sky and struck the tower. Thunder boomed. The crowd gasped and some ran for cover.

The friar pulled out a basket of bread and handed it to the boy, motioning to distribute the rolls. "*Allora,* you see. Christ gives us real people to pass on the good news. Yes, my friends, I said *real people...*"

The friar placed his hands on his hips. "He trained apostles. But how did they pass on this good news? How do they pass on this news today?"

Another roll of thunder shook the air, and, within five seconds, lightning split the dark sky. Cristoforo ignored it.

"Two ways the news is passed on: *authority* and *sacraments*. Christ's authority passes through *Apostolic Succession,* bishop to bishop. The bishops pass the authority to their priests. *Allora,* this is how they make holy the bread and the wine, the sacraments. This, my friends, is the Church. It is the Body of Christ, you and I. We receive this great Gospel, this new Life, through the sacraments. And we pass it on."

The boy returned with the empty basket, and Cristoforo handed him another full one. The lad passed it to a youth with green eyes, who grabbed it and disappeared into the crowd. The eyes looked familiar. Cristoforo searched the hole in the crowd that swallowed him.

"So you see, my friends. The Church is important. Receive the sacraments! Receive Jesus!"

The friar was nearing the end. He threw his hands in the air and screamed against the wind, as though ordering the heavens to obey him. "This, my people, is our inheritance! Our gift from God our Father! Take it! Pass it on! Meet Christ in the Mass!"

Nadia. It was Nadia, he was sure. The friar looked over the crowd as thunder rolled again, this time closely followed by lightning. He turned and peered at the sky as the wind bit into his cheeks and his cape flew into the air.

Suddenly the heavens opened and the rain poured, slanting down hard. His people headed down the hill to the shelter of the Visitors

Center. Nadia, her cap off and her hair caught by the wind, ran too, with several others alongside. She glanced back at the friar and their eyes locked. She laughed and waved, shoving something into a back pocket. One of the boys held Cristoforo's second basket of bread, trying to cover it with his jacket.

The friar searched for his offering can behind the rock. His robes were soaking, his beard dripping, his vision blurred by streaming water. The can was empty.

"Nadia! Stop!" he screamed as searing pain stabbed his shoulder and he fell into the wet grass.

Cristoforo dreamed he was falling, falling through the dark. Thunder clapped. Lightning grabbed him with hot pincers. He descended, twirling, into a fiery pit, and the heat scorched his soul, piercing him again and again, in his hands, his feet, his side.

"Please, please, please wake up, Brother!" A little voice, a familiar voice, pleaded from far away. A finger poked his ribs, then jabbed his wrist.

He opened his eyes and tried to speak, but no words came.

"Nurse, nurse! He's awake!" It was the little voice again. *Nadia*.

Then another voice, much deeper and softer, full of calm authority. "You've been hit by lightning, friar." A pleasant face peered down, professional and courteous—East Indian he thought. She wore a hospital ID.

From behind the white uniform, another face peeked out. Green eyes and freckles. Red hair spilled from a soiled cap.

"Don't try to talk," the nurse said. "You'll be fine. You're a bit dehydrated, but okay. You need rest and fluids. You're at the Saint Joseph's Clinic in Glastonbury. Your niece, with her friends, brought you in. It's a miracle, for sure. They all saw you go down."

Brother Cristoforo tried to sit up, to reach for the child. "My offerings," he gasped, "my offerings..."

"Delusional, obviously," Nadia said, sounding concerned, "but at least he's woke up."

The friar pulled himself up on his elbow and watched helplessly as the girl ran out the door and high-fived her friends, her *brothers?* Nadia's gang trundled down the hall and into the rain. "Let's get some food." It was the distant voice of one of the boys, merging into the sound of the rain pelting against the ward windows.

Early Monday, in the pouring rain, Madeleine helped Victoria onto the train at New Milton. Silent and withdrawn, Jack loaded their luggage and arranged their dripping umbrellas in a corner of the compartment. By evening they had settled into Thornbury Castle, a sixteenth-century Tudor house with towers, timbered ceilings, stained glass, and deep feather beds.

The following morning Jack left for Aylesbury to meet with the contractor. Madeleine spent the day indoors with Victoria, reading by a dim light in the comfortable library and stoking the fire. There were few guests this weekday in winter; it was as though the castle was theirs. The rain continued, insulating them from the world outside—a comfortable cozy feeling, Madeleine thought.

Wednesday the skies cleared, and the two women boarded a bus to Glastonbury. Entering the abbey grounds through the Visitors Center, they were greeted by an elderly lady behind a counter. She set down an open paperback and regarded them with friendly eyes. "Two pounds," she said in a husky voice. "*Do* tour the exhibits here, my dears." She pointed to a room of artifacts, timelines, photographs, and medieval vestments in glass cases. "We're mighty proud of our abbey here, we are."

Madeleine handed her the fee. "Thank you, but we'd better see the ruins first, in case it rains."

"Right you are, my dears, right you are. You go on through there." She motioned toward a back door.

Madeleine led Victoria into a small courtyard and through a gate out to sweeping lawns. Pausing before a flowering thorn tree, she gazed across the broad field of green to the ruins of the massive medieval abbey, rising against the gray sky.

Victoria pulled her jacket close against the brisk wind. "I wish Jack could have joined us."

"He's seeing to the renovations." Madeleine told a half lie, for his absence was only partially explained by his work in Aylesbury, and she hoped Victoria wouldn't guess the truth. Madeleine understood her husband needed distance from the underage girl, who suddenly seemed to him a stranger. He needed to remove himself physically as well as emotionally. It was his way of dealing with the threat of their association, the appearance of kidnapping. In the meantime, she would find a way to stay with her young friend until the baby was born; she was more determined than ever to see this through. She would take the risk. How could she leave Victoria now?

"That must be the abbey." Victoria pointed to the towering skeleton of stone walls, piers, and arches.

"And we're standing near a shoot of the famous thorn tree." Madeleine studied the pamphlet the woman had given her.

"The famous thorn tree?"

"They say that Joseph of Arimathea came here. He planted his staff, and it blossomed into a thorn tree."

"Who was Joseph of Arimathea? You mentioned him earlier."

"He was a wealthy member of Jesus' family, or so legend says. He provided the tomb for Jesus' burial."

"Really? So he came here?"

"I believe he did. Early Church history is fascinating. Let's look for the Lady Chapel. It's supposed to be in the crypt. It was built over Joseph's wattle-and-daub church, called Saint Mary's." Madeleine led Victoria down smoothly worn stairs.

Roofless, destroyed by the Reformers, even the crypt was exposed to the heavens. Madeleine pointed to the stone altar. "They still celebrate Mass here." Vases holding freshly cut flowers rested in front of the altar, and a dozen benches lined the narrow nave.

Victoria pointed to two large initials, J and M. "Look at this."

Madeleine nodded. "Jesus and Mary. This church has always been dedicated to Mary, centuries before it was customary for churches to take her name, before the rise of the medieval cult. Some think the stone might have been saved from the original Church of Saint Mary."

They climbed up to the grassy field and walked up the path toward the abbey's high altar, open to the sky, surrounded by transept piers and crumbling walls.

"That's where they found Arthur's tomb." Madeleine paused in the center of the field. "This would have been the chancel."

"And here's where the high altar used to be." Victoria moved farther up. "It's so strange. These giant stone walls with no roof, and all this grass. It's like memories growing in a field."

"Well said. It *is* strange. Prayers and sacrifice fill this space, too." Madeleine stared at the empty ruins, her heart still burning from Jack's anger. She would concentrate on the present and appreciate this moment God had given her. She was in Glastonbury, at last, and with Victoria, who had become as dear as any daughter. "This abbey has seen such hate and destruction, and yet has survived. God working in our world continues to astonish me. It gives me hope."

"Then you believe the tales of Joseph?"

Madeleine warmed her hands in her coat pockets. "Yes and no." She glanced at the darkening sky. "Let's walk while we can."

They stepped through the grass, reading the scripted signs: *cloister, choir, transept pillars, kitchen, garden.*

Madeleine searched for the right words. "As a historian, I recognize the scarcity of contemporary evidence. But history is much more than material evidence, and then there are different kinds of evidence. As a Christian, I believe the tales. The place-names reflect the truth of the legends, as do the varying traditions from different locales, as far away as Palestine, which coalesce. These local tales *also* reflect the truth, rather like a mirror."

"But in the end, does it really matter?"

"Some English take great pride that the first Christian church was planted here."

"Like a competition."

"Right. What *does* matter is that we may see Our Lord more clearly as we visit and touch the places he visited. *That* I do care about. To be standing in that Lady Chapel and think how, as a youth, Jesus might have been there and might have helped build the church, why, it fills my heart, Victoria." Madeleine wrapped her arm about the young mother, forgetting Jack for the moment and gazing toward the abbey shell. "Yes, it fills my heart with joy. I suppose it would have been a synagogue at that time, wouldn't it?"

Coming full circle, they neared the thorn tree as the rain hit, the fat drops splattering and forming a torrent. They ran into the Visitors Center for cover.

Victoria wiped the water from her forehead and pushed her hood back. "At least we saw the abbey."

"But I *did* want to see the Chalice Well. The Tor might have been too much of a climb. We're not taking chances with this child."

"The Chalice Well? Doesn't that have something to do with the Holy Grail and King Arthur?"

"Precisely." They moved to one of the chronologies, charts displayed between the glass exhibits. "Christ's last supper could have been in Joseph's house; Joseph would have been at a meeting of the Sanhedrin. The cup Jesus used to institute the Eucharist could have been from Joseph's household. When Joseph buried Jesus in the family tomb, he collected some of the blood and sweat in a *grail*—a cup or chalice—which he brought to Glastonbury with the walking staff, which could have been Our Lord's staff. As most senior kin, Joseph would have inherited Jesus' staff."

"What happened then?"

"Legend says the cup—some accounts say two cruets—was buried in the Chalice Well, causing the waters to have healing properties. And the staff blossomed into a thorn tree."

"It's a good story. I'd like it to be true." Victoria's face was open, unguarded. She appeared genuinely entranced.

"I believe in the heart of legends. People do not make them up, at least not entirely. And after all, that's what's important, the kernel. Something miraculous happened in that first century to keep the story alive for so many generations. I believe Our Lord was here, and after his death and resurrection, Joseph returned with the chalice and staff. It's also probably true that Joseph's descendents intermarried with the local kings, and Arthur descended from this line, as did today's monarchy."

Victoria stared out the window to the rain pouring on the ruins. "It makes me sad, that this is all that's left...it's kind of spooky."

"It *is* sad for such a holy place to be so desolate. Only pilgrims and cultists come, rather like many churches today, where only a few faithful attend. Many visitors are simply spiritual tourists." Madeleine found a bench near the window. "Why don't you rest here, and I'll get some tea from that machine."

"Thanks," Victoria said gratefully and, holding the wrought-iron armrest, lowered herself onto the wooden bench. Madeleine soon joined her, balancing plastic cups of steaming liquid.

"What did you mean by spiritual tourists?" Victoria asked as she reached for a cup.

"Careful, it's hot." Madeleine paused as she stirred sugar into her tea, her heart aching for the modern world. How could she explain this to Victoria? How could she begin to describe today's devastation? How swiftly the drowning waters had flooded the earth with a sea of unbelief, forcing believers into arks tossed among the waves. "The great gift Our Lord gave us, the Eucharist, his Real Presence, his weekly offering of himself to each of us and to his father, has become an embarrassment to many parts of the Church. It is torn from the altars, shoved to the side, abandoned."

Suddenly Madeleine recalled her dream of the night before, and gasped.

"What's wrong?"

"I dreamt about this last night. Maybe it's just *déjà vu*, as they say. I'm never sure about dreams. I've had some strange ones." And some terror-filled ones, she thought.

"What did you dream?"

"It's coming back now," she said as the images formed in her mind. "I was walking down a country lane, in England, I think, toward a medieval chapel surrounded by graves." Madeleine stepped carefully into the scene.

"Go on."

"I walked through a lych-gate, one of those curious gabled gates like the one at Saint Anne's, and down a path between tombstones to the chapel door. Inside, the stained glass over the altar touched me in a powerful way, and I wanted to cry with happiness. The vivid greens and blues and reds danced with such beauty! But the altar was bare, empty. There were no candles or flowers, no tabernacle. Behind me, tourists entered, angling their flashing cameras toward the windows and chattering, breaking the peace. Suddenly I realized the Puritans were right." Madeleine sat stunned, then stood slowly to throw away their empty cups.

"What's upsetting you? What does it mean?" Victoria stared at her, her almond eyes wide.

"I only now realize what I saw."

"What did you see?" Victoria looked up at Madeleine.

"All these empty altars, all these pretty churches, even all this study of history, validate the Puritans' charge that we would worship the image and not the Lord."

"And it's come true?"

"It's a self-fulfilling prophecy. We built beautiful temples to celebrate Christ's presence in the Eucharist and glorified the space with color and image and finery. Then we removed him, his Presence in the Blessed Sacrament. So now, we worship what we created: the art, the image. It's amazing that lightning doesn't strike those empty altars." Madeleine shook her head and sat down.

"And Glastonbury? Are you saying this happened here?"

"Our ancient inheritance, this apostolic gift of the Eucharist brought to England nearly two thousand years ago, is largely abandoned in her churches. And these ruins," she said as she waved her hand toward the abbey, "reflect all those empty altars. Here the faithful mix with spiritual tourists who have no sense of Jesus as the Messiah, the Christ, no sense of God's work in the world or in their own lives. They are faddists hungry for quick and easy fixes."

"But the real pilgrims, the real believers, witness by being here, don't they?"

Touched by her words, as though brushed by angels' wings, Madeleine kissed Victoria on the cheek. How wise this one was, she thought, a true gift from God. "They sure do, my pretty little mother, they sure do. And we praise God for every flame that lights up the dark."

Jack returned Saturday night, having made significant progress with the contractor. He had arranged for early possession of the property, and this small victory softened his anger. Even so, Madeleine was wary, and their relationship remained tense.

In the morning, a stormy Fourth Sunday in Lent, Madeleine surveyed their dim room, *The Duke's Bedchamber*, as Jack made calls to London, San Francisco, Rome. Thick logs burned in a fireplace, and two antique chairs faced a settee. Heavy damask draped a canopy bed. High mullioned windows overlooked a formal garden, admitting little light, and thin Flemish rugs failed to warm the stone floors.

Madeleine had read in a desk brochure that Henry VIII brought Anne Boleyn to Thornbury in 1535, on a "progress" through his realm. As she gazed through leaded panes to pelting rain, she recalled that 1535 was the year the queen gave birth to a stillborn son. It was also the year she watched her husband court Jane Seymour, her lady-in-waiting. Soon the king would behead Anne and marry Jane. What was their visit like? Miserable, Madeleine thought.

Madeleine recalled other Thornbury stories involving Henry and his famous family. In 1521, the king coveted the estate, and soon the owner was charged with treason and executed. The king took possession. In the years to come, Mary, Henry's daughter by Catherine of Aragon, would spend time here as a child. Then came the fateful year of 1535 when Henry executed Thomas More, old Bishop Fisher, and forced the Carthusian monks to die agonizing deaths. And in this year, Henry and Anne stayed in this bedroom. Where did Jane Seymour, Jack's fabled ancestor, stay? She shivered.

Jack replaced the receiver in its cradle. "Should we check on Victoria?"

"Why should you care?" Madeleine asked, and immediately regretted her outburst.

"That's not fair. I do care what happens to her."

She turned toward the window and bit her lip. "I know you do, in your own way, but—"

"Let's not fight over Victoria," he said. "Is she joining us for breakfast?"

"She's sleeping in this morning. I'll check on her later."

"Fine."

They descended spiral stairs to the library where a light breakfast was served and chose an alcove table flanked by more mullioned windows overlooking the rain-drenched garden. A fire burned in the grate, warming the room. A waiter brought scones, nut bread, clotted cream, jam, orange juice, and tea, and they sat in silence, reading the paper. The rain continued to fall, tapping the panes.

A waiter handed Jack a phone. "Telephone, Mr. Seymour."

Madeleine watched Jack's face, which changed from surprise to concern.

"What?...Cristoforo?...Where are you?...Of course...How did you find us?...William, yes...I'll be there in a few hours."

"What is it?"

"Our friar needs rescuing, it appears." Jack raised his brows, his eyes wide.

"What happened?"

"He was struck by lightning."

"Lightning!"

"He's in a clinic in Glastonbury. He seems to be all right, but I'm going to pick him up as soon as I finish breakfast. There's no need for you to come, Maddie. You may as well go on to Mass without me."

"You're sure he's okay?"

"Sounds like he's recovered. I'll bring him back here and you can see for yourself."

"Okay, then." Madeleine, her worries tumbling about, would go to Saint John's in the village. Mass would sort things out.

Chapter Twenty-three
Thornbury Chapel

Thine eyes did see my substance,
yet being imperfect; and in thy book were all my members written;
Which day by day were fashioned, when as yet there was none of them.
Psalm 139:15-16

Victoria breakfasted in her room. She sat next to the window, reading a yellowed copy of *Sense and Sensibility* she had found in the hotel library, glancing occasionally at the sun as it emerged from behind a cloud.

As the skies cleared, she ventured into the castle gardens and was surprised to find Brother Cristoforo sitting thoughtfully on a stone bench. He held his prayer book, his right hand wrapped in a gauze bandage. He asked her to walk with him. They wandered the soggy grounds and chatted, breathing in the fresh rain-washed air and catching the sun's rays sparkling through glistening leaves.

They entered a hothouse at the back of the garden, and Cristoforo paused before some crimson roses beginning to bloom. "Do you like flowers, Miss Victoria?" Cristoforo touched the petals. "Roses remind me of Our Lady, for they are her flower. And they are like life, beautiful but thorny."

Victoria inhaled the sweetness. "I love all kinds of flowers. My father has a garden at home. But Brother, what happened to your hand, and why were you in the Glastonbury clinic? You said you would explain, and you haven't."

"It is true, I have not explained." He smiled, showing his silver tooth. "I blame Nadia, and, *allora*, I thank her."

"Nadia? Who's Nadia?"

"Nadia and her brothers brought me to the clinic. I was struck by lightning, the nurse said. Nadia saved me."

"Wow. Is that the burn on your hand?"

"It runs down from my shoulder. It will remind me of a bad time."

"A bad time?" Victoria was afraid to pry, but she was curious. She welcomed the diversion from Jack's odd distance, from her worries over the baby and William. Then there was her mother. Her mind was full of so many unsettling thoughts, nagging questions about her future, questions with no answers.

"I was preaching in Glastonbury." The friar stared through the rain-spotted panes, his dark craggy face full of regret.

"That's good, isn't it?"

"Friars may preach, but only with permission from their superior."

"And you didn't have permission?"

"*Allora,* I did not."

"Are you in trouble?" They followed a gravel path through a maze of blackthorn bushes bursting with early white blooms.

"I think so." He slipped his prayer book in his pocket and ran his finger along the bandage. "I see clearly now. I have been disobedient. They said I was delirious. I had no identification. Nadia took my wallet and phone, but she returned them to the hospital. The nurse called William, who said *Signore* Seymour was at Thornbury Castle, not far away." He ran his good hand through his frizzy hair. "I spoke with William. He is worried about you."

"Is he? He's sweet to worry, and kind to call like he does."

"He may be...more than kind, *Signorina.*"

Victoria's pulse quickened as she glanced up at the friar. More than kind? Her cheeks grew warm. She changed the subject. "But who is Nadia?"

"A little girl, a tough girl, from the streets. She helped me, but now I am afraid for her." He told Victoria about Nadia in London and Oxford, Nadia's stealing, Nadia's brothers. "They will be in big trouble one day. I must find them."

With his good arm, the friar wiped a bench dry. "Please, sit down. You should rest."

She lowered herself onto the wrought-iron seat. "I wish I could help you, Brother." The baby jabbed hard, finding his home too small, pushing against the stretched skin. Victoria massaged her tummy, thinking it would not be long now.

"You only need to care for your child. For me, I am glad to be alive. I think, too, I am sad. I must make my confession. I must call Rome. It lies heavy on me. *Per favore,* Miss Victoria, will you excuse me?"

"Of course." She was fond of the friar and hoped he could work things out. He looked so tired, his features strained.

"*Grazie.*" Cristoforo lumbered toward the back door.

Bells rang through the moist air. Victoria recalled the hotel clerk saying that Thornbury Castle's old stone chapel was open odd hours for the occasional service. It had been closed all week, but perhaps today, Sunday, it would be open. She crossed the gardens to the edge of the property where the squat tower anchored the ancient church. The door was open. A sign announced that Evening Prayer would soon begin. Maybe she would see what there was to see, hear what there was to hear.

She entered and sat in the back. In the dim light she could make out stone walls and a half-timbered roof. The air smelled of damp wood and incense. About fifteen others, mostly elderly ladies, sat in the front pews as a thin-sounding organ pumped from a choir loft. A red candle flamed on the altar, a wooden crucifix hung above, and a pretty Madonna and Child stood on a pedestal to the left. Victoria thought of the stone abbey in Aylesbury, which was easily twice this size, but perhaps had been built around the same time. As she gazed upon the crucifix, she thought of all the events since that Ash Wednesday. *Were you guiding those events, Jesus?*

It had indeed been remarkable, her time with the Seymours, maybe too remarkable to be mere coincidence, maybe not. The places they had visited had opened new worlds, and this last peaceful week at Thornbury settled over her like the first sunshine of spring. How she loved it here. Her room in the stable wing was small and dark, but there was a good light over the bed, and she had spent hours reading about England and rereading Jane Austen. This was Austen country, after all, and they had visited Bath and seen the salons where Anne Elliot entertained Captain Wentworth in *Persuasion,* the Assembly Rooms where they danced, and the house where Jane Austen stayed.

The time enclosed her like the petals of a flower. Indeed, those roses in the garden opened slowly, imperceptibly—as she felt herself flowering, and the new life within her flowering too. Perhaps here she would learn who she truly was.

A white-haired priest entered through a door to the right of the altar, and the small congregation stood, singing in lilting, wavering voices, the voices of old women carrying gifts from the past into the present.

"Forty days and forty nights
Thou wast fasting in the wild..."

They were now in the middle of Lent, in the middle of the forty days.

Victoria's attention was caught by a glimmer of light on the altar, caused by a fiery ray from the western window hitting the brass door of the tabernacle. The light danced. *Open your heart,* Jack often said. Grandma Nguyen had said the same thing.

Maybe, Victoria thought, God speaks to each of us uniquely, like a burst of love, like this flickering beam. It *was* odd, because sometimes she felt stronger, more confident, and at the same time weaker, more helpless.

The congregation read the Psalms in turn, those on one side of the aisle speaking a verse, then those on the other side saying the next verse. The hum of the chants soothed her, and she pulled a tattered *Book of Common Prayer* from the pew-back in front of her and joined in the reading. The wine-red binding was loose and frayed; she held it carefully in the palm of her hand.

"My delight is in the Lord;
Because he hath heard the voice of my prayer..."

A lady in a tartan skirt—Campbell plaid, Victoria thought, like one Aunt Elizabeth once wore—and a green cardigan approached the lectern, opened a Bible, and read, "A reading from the Prophet Isaiah, Chapter 55..."

Someone slipped into the pew next to Victoria—a nervous, thin young man who immediately knelt. He made the Sign of the Cross with one hand as he set his Bible down with the other. She glanced at him and caught her breath. *William.*

He sat back and turned to her with squinty blue eyes full of worried happiness. "Hi," he whispered. "I'm late."

"Hi." Her blood raced.

"You okay?"

She nodded. "I'm okay." *What is he doing here?*

"Good." He opened his Bible, found the Gospel lesson, and walked to the lectern.

"Here beginneth the forty-first verse of the sixth chapter of the Gospel according to John."

He cleared his throat, caught Victoria's eye, and continued:

"The Jews then murmured at him, because he said, 'I am the bread which came down from heaven.'"

William read in the same way he spoke, as if in serious conversation.

"And they said, 'Is not this Jesus, the son of Joseph, whose father and mother we know? How is it then that he saith, I came down from heaven?'"

Victoria barely detected a smile. He must find this part amusing. She recalled his parents and his absence on Christmas Day.

"'Verily, verily, I say unto you, He that believeth on me hath everlasting life. I am that bread of life.'"

William looked up again and shuffled his feet, moving his eye over the congregation.
Victoria watched, entranced, reaching for each word, for the words sounded real. They sounded important.
William's eye returned to the page.

"'Your fathers did eat manna in the wilderness, and are dead. This is the bread which cometh down from heaven, that a man may eat thereof, and not die.'"

He leaned forward, staging his punch line.

"'I am the living bread which came down from heaven; if any man eat of this bread, he shall live forever: and the bread that I will give is my flesh, which I will give for the life of the world.'"

William's composed features could not hide his satisfaction as he strode back to the pew, swinging his arms with intense energy. He took his seat and beamed at her, apparently delighted to have taken her by surprise. He pointed to the old vicar. "That's my grandpa," he whispered, "and a pretty cool guy too. You'll like him."

At first hesitant, Victoria accepted Father Collingwood's invitation to tea, but as William opened the door and she entered the small vicarage behind the chapel, she was glad she had come.

A plump, middle-aged woman with an air of extreme competence bustled out of the kitchen. She glanced at Victoria and William, beamed a toothy greeting, and turned to the vicar. "Your pie is in the oven and the fire laid, the kettle is on, and the parlor set for tea. I'll be 'round in the mornin' to make your breakfast, Father. Now have a good night, and God bless you!"

Father Collingwood kissed her on each cheek, and held her shoulders in his small hands, looking into her blinking eyes. "Thanks a million and more, me Bessie. God keep you this evenin' and always."

Victoria felt she was home. William hung her jacket on a peg alongside his own, and she looked about the parlor, taking in the cluttered space. Art prints in simple wooden frames tilted on the walls. A wooden crucifix hung over the brick fireplace, a Madonna-and-Child icon resting on the mantel. A worn sofa flanked by two overstuffed chairs faced the grate, forming a welcoming half-circle.

The vicar cleared books off of one of the chairs and offered the seat to Victoria. He tisk-tisked softly through his teeth as he shuffled about in a vain attempt to tidy up. As she watched the elderly man dart about the room, Victoria traced her finger over the intricate pattern of the yellowing doilies on the arm of her chair. William lit the fire, and when the kettle whistled in the kitchen, he left to make the tea. He soon returned with the steaming pot and a bottle of sherry, set them on the coffee table, and took a seat on the sofa. His grandfather joined them, sitting in the other armchair near the fire.

"Grandpa," William said, "tell the story of how you courted Grandma." He reached for the sherry and poured Victoria a drop, just a drop, into a mug, then filled his grandfather's mug halfway, and a splash into his own. He checked the tea. "Not quite ready."

"Aye, that's a story all right, that's a story." The elderly man laughed and patted his chest. His black shirt was stained and his white collar yellowing. "But the lassie don't want to hear all that talk, me lad."

Victoria leaned forward to scratch a russet spaniel that appeared from nowhere, now nuzzling her legs. "But I *do*, Father Collingwood, I *do*. I love stories, especially true ones."

"Well, you're such a pretty lassie, and you're so very beguiling, you've entranced me for sure, just like the true faeries from the old country. So let it be, just let me get com*fort*able now."

He rearranged his posture from comfortable to very comfortable. He smoothed his dark pants with his left hand and took a swig from his mug with his right. He smacked his lips. A few crumbs from the toast and jam lingered on his moustache, and he combed it briefly with his fingers, contemplating the fire, seeing another time.

Victoria wanted to hold the moment forever, sitting in the lumpy chair that smelled of hair oil, dust, and pipe smoke, listening to the vicar's chatter, surrounded by the untidy odds and ends of his life packed into the room. Photographs and a half-empty box of Christmas chocolates sat on a worn spinet against the far wall, and the *Church Times* peeked from piles of mail on a teetering stand near the door. Through the kitchen, she glimpsed a gate-legged dining table covered with a lace cloth and caught the scent of mothballs mingled with lemon oil and charred embers.

"So you see, Miss Victoria—I hope I may call you that, for you've captured me heart—you see she thought I's the *plumber*. Can you believe it? I come 'round to *court* her and *she* thought I'm come to fix the pipes. So I fixed the pipes first, then did me courting. A bit surprised she was, the lassie, but she saw sense eventually." With this he burst out in a deep throaty laugh, then suddenly peered intently from under his raised bushy brows and confided, "I did adore her, you know, lassie...oh, I did indeed..."

"Tell the best part, Grandpa," William said, nodding and laughing at his grandfather's joy.

"But I did, I did, I did!" The vicar chuckled again with the memory.

Victoria laughed too, caught in the contagion of it.

William glanced at Victoria and poured the tea. "Tell about all the repairs you needed to do. You see, her parents disapproved of the match. After all, her father was a town burgher, very important, so Grandma broke things so Grandpa could come to the house and repair them."

"Aye, aye, that was it, that was it!" the vicar cried as his small hands flew into the air.

"First," William continued, "there was a leak here, a toilet plugged there, a sink cracked, then the water turned off completely."

"Her parents," Father Collingwood said, "finally came around, but it was nip and tuck, nip and tuck."

Victoria dabbed her eyes. "Oh my, I wish I could have known her."

"She was a special one, lassie, and I miss her sadly, I do. It's been ten years now, ten lonely years, since she passed on. But God has taken good care of me." He steepled his hands, gazing into the fire, then turned to Victoria, offering her a plate of biscuits. "Now tell me, my dear, when is the fine lad or lassie to be born?"

"My due date is April tenth."

"A month from today."

"Yes, four weeks from Wednesday."

"I shall pray for a safe delivery, my dear."

"Thank you, Father," Victoria said, overwhelmed with gratitude. She appreciated his prayers, and she knew he would do as he promised.

Victoria and William returned to the main house, through the garden, toward the back entrance. The sun was setting, casting a pale light through low clouds. At the door, Victoria turned.

"Thank you, William. I loved meeting your grandfather. What a coincidence he was here at Thornbury."

"I'm so glad you told me you were coming here. I couldn't resist showing up."

"I was totally surprised."

"I thought you might be, although I wasn't sure you'd be at Evensong. My plan was to ask for you later at the hotel."

"I'm glad I decided to go. It was rather spur-of-the-moment."

"Me too. You know, Grandpa taught me about the faith. He made it real, not some namby-pamby Sunday thing. I wish I could explain it to you, show you...."

"I'd like that."

"Are you a believer? I was never sure from our conversations."

"I might be. I wasn't a believer until I met the Seymours. But their faith is real too. I'd like to have that." But she *had* asked Jesus into her heart. Didn't that mean something? Even so, she wavered.

"When I was your age, my grandfather gave me a book that changed my life."

"The Bible?"

William shook his head, chuckling softly. "No, I wasn't ready for that then. It was *Mere Christianity* by C.S. Lewis. It got me on the right road, you might say, helped me make that first leap of faith. I needed to satisfy my mind as well as my heart. I'll get you a copy."

"That would be great." She turned toward the door as the bells rang seven. "It's late. I'd better get ready for dinner. Can you join us? You've met Jack, and you'll love Madeleine."

"I'm sorry, I'm afraid I can't stay. Mr. Seymour is a fine man, and I would love to meet his wife, but I've got to get back to Oxford. It's a bit of a distance on the train."

"I understand."

"Victoria, I..."

"Yes?"

"I...I hope to see you soon. I'm going to be helping at Saint Anne's. The Sisters of Mary are overseeing things and renovations have started. I've agreed to read services there once I'm ordained deacon. Perhaps it shall be my internship, my diaconate."

"That's good." Victoria stood by the door with the sense of words unsaid, and a fragile hope that soon they might be. His wavy hair was parted crooked down the center, the blond strands searching for rest. She wanted to touch the strands, move them to the side of his freckled forehead. His blue eyes searched hers as if he were looking for answers to those unspoken questions. She waited on the edge of the moment, not daring to shift her eyes from his.

With his forefinger, he traced her nose bridge, then followed the dark patch to her cheekbone and down to her chin. "You are so beautiful, Miss Victoria," he whispered and kissed her lightly on the lips. "Until we meet again, may God be with you."

William Collingwood turned swiftly on his heel and walked away, crunching the gravel path with a determined step. At the gate, he looked back and smiled tentatively, his long fingers raised in a nervous wave.

Victoria waved back. *Nobody has ever said that to me.* She touched her lips, sighed with happy surprise at this turn of events, and, using both hands, pulled open the heavy oak door.

Chapter Twenty-four
Thornbury Castle

*Faith is not a refuge from reality.
It is a demand that we face reality,
with all its difficulties, opportunities, and implications.*
Evelyn Underhill

Victoria, excited about sharing her news that William had showed up, joined Madeleine for dinner in the hotel restaurant, an octagonal room at the base of one of the immense towers. A few other guests sat at the damask-covered tables lit by candles in brass holders. A crystal chandelier reflected the flames and cast a soft glow on the ocher walls.

"Where's Jack?" Victoria asked, disappointed.

"He's not feeling well," Madeleine said, "so it's only us tonight. He's having soup in the room. His old esophageal problem has returned. And Cristoforo went to bed early. He's still pretty weak."

"I'm sorry about Jack, and I'm glad Cristoforo is getting some rest."

"I'll say. Struck by lightning in Glastonbury! I'm so glad he's all right. He told me all about preaching on the Tor, said the lightning woke him up. I'm not sure what he meant. Did he tell you?"

"He said he shouldn't be preaching without permission."

Madeleine nodded with understanding. "He's remorseful as well as exhausted." She handed Victoria a small flashlight. "Use this to read the menu. The light is a bit dim, but even so, I like the atmosphere. It's very medieval, don't you think?"

Victoria looked about the charming room. "It's like a fairy tale."

"I imagine romance and chivalry, and try to forget the drudgery and warfare of those times."

The two women studied the menu in silence, and Victoria, thinking of Jack's pressures and Cristoforo's condition, decided to wait to share her news about William. To speak of his arrival seemed so trivial and...lighthearted. She would wait for the right moment. She ran her finger down the list of dishes.

"I've figured it out," Madeleine said, as their waiter appeared. "How about you?"

"The spinach salad and the beef pie."

"Very English. I'm having the vegetable soup and the roast pork."

The waiter nodded.

Victoria studied Madeleine's face. A hopeful reassurance filled her features, in spite of Jack and Cristoforo. Her glasses sat lightly on her nose, and her hazel eyes peered at Victoria like a mother hen, warming her.

"Madeleine," Victoria said as she returned the flashlight. "Why do you seem so content, so happy with life? I hope I'm not being too personal, but I envy your, well, your *cheerfulness*, and it's real, isn't it? Yet I know you've had rough times."

Madeleine paused as though to collect her thoughts. "As Christians, we hope for good, for *the* good, for God, I guess."

"Christians always hope?"

Madeleine's laugh carried an enviable certainty. "Christians are no better or wiser than anyone else, but they *are* different."

"Different?"

"They're hopeful, joyful, happy people. At least they have good reason to be. To my mind anyway, especially catholic Christians."

"But what do you mean by catholic? My grandmother is Roman Catholic and she, I have to admit, is a happy person, and she has had a hard life as well."

"I mean *catholic* with a lowercase *c,* which means those beliefs that have been true throughout time. In essence, it refers to the faith passed on through the Church over the last two thousand years: belief in the Creeds, the authority of both Scripture and Church Councils, the action of the Holy Spirit in sacraments and prayer."

"Traditional Christianity."

Madeleine nodded. "Exactly. Some Christian sects do not accept all the parts of this whole belief. Some say God doesn't work through the Eucharist, doesn't enter the bread and wine. Some say the Church has no authority to interpret Holy Scripture. Some fear images and ceremony. Catholics embrace all of these things, providing, to my mind, a fuller and richer life. God is present at every turn, healing and directing. He's active in our world, in matter."

"Grandma goes to Mass on Sundays, even weekdays sometimes." Victoria recalled her grandmother said the 7:00 morning Mass was her "taste of heaven," and "set her up" for the day.

"She's a catholic Christian. We believe that, compared to God, nothing really matters, and we believe that all things will turn out well for those who love God."

"That must take a lot of faith."

"Yes and no. It does require that first little leap to put you on the path, the earthly road to heaven, as it were."

"But how do you handle all the pain of life?"

"You accept it as part of the sacrifice of love."

"Love?"

"We're called to sacrificial love, to an understanding that to love others means to sacrifice for them, and in such love we find joy. Christ is our example. He showed this kind of sacrificial love when he died so we could live."

"So is all the pain of life a matter of sacrifice?"

"Sacrifice usually means pain, for it means the denial of the self. But, of course, when we are sick or victimized by others, our pain may not be sacrificial pain. This kind of pain is a result of Original Sin, the Fall of Adam, the human condition. God helps us deal with this kind of suffering through the sacraments, through prayer."

They fell into a sweet silence as they tasted their first courses. Madeleine sipped her wine. "It's all a mystery and a journey into the love of God. I recommend it with all my heart."

"William is loaning me a book about Christianity. He said some of the same things you just did." She would move slowly into her news about William. Perhaps this would be an opening.

"Is he now? I like this William already. What's the book?"

"*Mere Christianity*. Do you know it?"

"I read it many years ago. Lewis' arguments converted me, as a matter of fact."

"William said the same thing."

"Sometimes it's a small world." Madeleine's smile held the happiness of a child given a Christmas present.

"And guess what?"

Madeleine looked at Victoria with amusement, as though they were girlfriends sharing a secret. "What?"

"William was here today." Victoria grew warm as she thought about the sudden pleasure he brought her, simply appearing in the chapel like that.

"Really? I'm sorry I didn't get a chance to meet him. I feel like I know him with all the phone calls, and our chats. And Jack likes him."

"His grandfather read Evensong at Thornbury Chapel this evening, and I was watching from the back pew, and William showed up! He sat next to me. I was so surprised."

"What a nice turn of events. His grandfather's a priest?"

Victoria nodded. "He's vicar of several parishes in the area and comes to Thornbury Sunday evenings for Evensong."

"He was probably at Saint John's this morning in the village. I loved the sermon."

"He was. He mentioned it."

"It *is* a small world sometimes."

"I invited William to dinner, but he had to return to Oxford."

"I'm not surprised. Even so, what a sweet thing for him to do."

They ate for a time in silence, each lost in their own thoughts, then Victoria, encouraged by their developing friendship, turned to the older woman. "Madeleine, can I ask you a difficult question?"

Madeleine's face was full of sympathy. "Of course, but I can only try to answer."

Victoria paused, then said, "Am I at fault...for this pregnancy?"

"Not at all."

"What about my first pregnancy? And the abortion?"

Madeleine breathed deeply. She looked into the distance as though listening for a voice. "I don't think so. You were so young. You obeyed your parents, who were influenced by current norms, norms validated by the law of the land. Our culture encourages early promiscuity and prescribes abortion to deal with the consequences."

"Then do catholic Christians think sex is wrong?"

Madeleine paused again and Victoria waited, watching her thoughtful face. "The Church doesn't say sex is wrong," Madeleine began, as though carefully choosing her words, "nor that such pleasure is evil, but rather that today they are...*exaggerated*. After all, God created us *and* our bodies *and* our way of procreating, of loving each other."

"I suppose so. You said exaggerated. So it's a matter of quantity?"

"Right. Christianity recognizes man's total nature, his soul *and* his body. You can't separate them, at least not in this earthly life, and they each have their proper place in God's plan."

"So what about chastity? Don't some people take vows of chastity?"

"Chastity applies to all Christians. Inside marriage, chastity means faithfulness to one's spouse, and outside marriage, abstinence."

"I see."

"Sex is God's way of giving life, so we are entrusted with great power and responsibility. The commitment in marriage encourages us to treat such power seriously. In fact, God shares his own life-giving power with us through sexual re-creation."

"I'd never thought of it that way before. I guess," Victoria said as she caressed her womb, "this child was created by God and me…and the man who…raped…me."

"But by acting violently toward you, he rejected the glory of creation. He rejected God."

"Yes," Victoria said, her eyes wide, "he did, didn't he? He rejected God."

Madeleine shook her head with sorrow and laid her hand on Victoria's arm. "It was a dreadful ordeal you went through. You were the victim of an awful violence."

"But I have this child. And each day I love him more."

"God is with you, my little mother. I can see him all around you. You will be blessed."

"He's turned something terrible into something good."

Madeleine nodded. "That's exactly what I've been trying to say in my own contorted way. God has acted sacramentally through this child to bring a good result."

Victoria nodded and dipped a bit of bread in the beef gravy.

"Maybe we should talk of something else," Madeleine said. "How's the pie? The pork isn't bad, with the homemade applesauce."

"Delicious. But I don't mind talking about it. And I see the importance of sex within marriage. It makes sense. A third person is involved, that new life, and even God himself."

"And you *will* marry, my dear Victoria. God will lead you to the right man. Pray that he does. That's how I found Jack."

"Did you really? You prayed? And you think if I pray it will happen?"

"I know so." Madeleine put her hand on Victoria's. "It will all come out fine. How do you feel about William? I believe you mentioned he's going to be ordained?"

"Yes, he's to become a deacon, around Easter I believe, or shortly after. It was close to my due date. Oh Madeleine, I think I'm falling in love with him. What shall I do? He would never want a girl like me."

"That's not true. Any young man would be lucky to have you. You, my dear Victoria, are the prettiest and brightest thing in this room."

Victoria beamed. Two glorious compliments in one day!

"So what *was* he doing here, anyway?" Madeleine raised her brows. "Exactly what are the young man's intentions? And did you know that *I* proposed to Jack?"

Victoria breakfasted with her hosts in the alcove under the mullioned windows. They had the library salon to themselves this quiet Monday in March, a day brilliantly clear after Sunday's storm, the air swept with spring winds. As she sipped her juice, she watched sunlight fall through the old glass, capture dancing particles of dust, and shower them upon the faded carpet.

Voices came from the lobby.

"We're looking for Victoria Nguyen." *Mother.*

"Is she staying here?" *Daddy.*

Victoria tapped her boiled egg and peeled its cap off gently, forcing herself to remain calm. *Jesus, help me.*

Her mother burst into the room, her father close behind. She carried a beige raincoat over her arm and ran her hand along her fitted tweed jacket. "So we've found you at last."

Victoria stood slowly, eying her parents. "Hello, Mother."

Candice glanced suspiciously at Madeleine and Jack, then gave Victoria a peck on the cheek. Holding her daughter's shoulders firmly, she searched her face and released her. She frowned at her swollen body.

Victoria turned to her father. "Daddy." He wrapped her in his arms. His cashmere jacket was soft, his aftershave familiar, lemony.

"Oh, Vicky," he whispered in her ear, "I'm so glad to see you. You okay?"

"I'm okay. I missed you." Relief surged through her. She stood back and introduced Madeleine and Jack, who rose from the table.

"Have we met before?" Candice said to Jack. "You look familiar."

Jack glanced at Madeleine. "I believe we *have* had the pleasure," he said with marked reserve.

"You attended one of our fundraisers," Madeleine added, "for the Coronati Foundation."

Candice was scrutinizing Jack's face as though searching her memory. "Fundraiser?"

"You came with Joe McGinty, I believe?" Jack looked worried, clearly not wanting to recall the event. "It was at the Hotel Saint Francis in San Francisco."

"I remember," she said, and laughed.

Victoria recognized the laugh, containing both incredulity and arrogance. She had laughed the same way when Victoria said she wanted to keep the baby. Victoria edged toward Madeleine.

Candice continued to study Jack as though he posed a new and pleasing challenge. "I saw the piece in *Wine Spectator*. Was it last month?"

"We saw an early proof," Madeleine said.

"You were in *Wine Spectator?*" Victoria asked.

"They interviewed Jack last year," Madeleine explained, her eyes on Victoria's mother, "about his role with children's charities, since he retired from the wine business."

Candice glanced at Victoria, then turned to Jack. "Jack, if you don't mind my calling you that, could you leave us alone for a few moments?" She flashed a smile, batting her lashes, her eyes narrowed in secret complicity. "Perhaps we could get together for a drink later?"

Victoria recognized the ploy. She looked at Madeleine, who had missed nothing.

Jack nodded, his face flushed. "Sure."

Madeleine glared at Candice and followed Jack to an adjoining room.

Victoria shook her head. Would her mother never change? She looked at her father for a cue. He stood apart, appearing simply relieved to see his daughter.

"Everything's fine, Daddy," Victoria said with hopeful reassurance.

Candice paced. "No, things are not fine, but what's to be done? You'll give it up. To have it at all is absurd, but we may as well go through with it now. You're way too far along, and the press would have a field day. I know a place that's discreet back home, I've got return tickets, and we can catch a flight this week. Why don't you pack your things, sweetie?"

Victoria rested her hands on her child. "Mother, I'm having the baby here, in England."

"You're what?"

"I am, Mother. There's a place near Oxford where I can stay. I think it will be best, and that's the way it is. And William will be there too. He's my friend. I needed a friend."

"William? William Collingwood is no friend to us. Freddie found you in spite of William." Candice resumed her pacing, checking her nails. She paused before a mirror over the mantel to stroke her hair into place.

"Candice, please," Andrew said quietly. "Maybe it would be best if Victoria stayed here. The Seymours seem like good people."

Candice pivoted on her heel and eyed her daughter. "You know, Vicky dear, all Fannie could do was talk about the wedding this summer. Where will sweet William be then?"

"Wedding?" Victoria gasped.

"It's no secret he's engaged." She smoothed a platinum strand behind her ear and pulled out her powder compact. "They've planned a summer wedding, Fanny said. He's making quite a good match. The girl's beautiful, brainy, *and* rich. In fact, I believe she has a title, or some such thing, or will one day." She ran the small pad over her nose and along her chin, then dabbed her forehead.

"Oh." Victoria felt faint. She rested her hands on her child.

"We'll bring you home, and deal with this properly in our own way. It's a family matter."

"Yes," she heard herself say from a great distance. She was falling, falling, falling....

"Vicky, are you all right?" It was her father, far away.

She slipped to the floor with a low moan. "*Jesus,*" she cried.

Madeleine heard Victoria's cry and rushed into the room. Andrew bent over his daughter, touching her cheeks and hair, trying to revive her. Madeleine sensed she shouldn't intrude and waited, numb, seized with fear for Victoria and the baby.

Candice looked about, panic fleeting over her features. "Someone *do* something." She knelt next to Victoria, took her hand, and looked into her eyes. "Call 911."

"I'll get help." Jack hurried toward the lobby.

"She fainted before, and was okay," Madeleine said carefully, eyeing Candice.

Andrew wrapped his fingers around Victoria's wrist. "Her pulse is good, and she seems to be coming out of it."

"Oh...," Victoria groaned as her mother helped her sit up.

"I'm cramping," Victoria whispered to Madeleine, avoiding her mother's eyes. "Am I losing the baby? Oh..."

Candice looked at Madeleine as she rose to her full height. She was a tall woman, with a regal bearing. "Are you a nurse?"

"No."

"Then we had better find a doctor." She, too, headed for the lobby.

As Candice retreated, Madeleine drew near. She knelt and cradled Victoria's head in her lap. "It will be okay, little mother, it will be okay." Madeleine could hear Jack say "five minutes for the paramedics." Then Candice replied something about "getting it born now wouldn't be such a bad thing after all." Madeleine ran her hand down Victoria's hair. "It will be okay. Breathe deeply, slowly, in...that's right...now out...." As she comforted Victoria, she prayed, *Dear Jesus, be with us now, send thy Spirit.*

Andrew remained at Victoria's side. "We'd better not move her. Let the medics do that."

Madeleine glanced at Andrew. "You sound experienced."

"'Nam taught me a few things," he said, never taking his eyes off his daughter.

"Aahh...," Victoria cried, holding her tummy. "Another one."

Dear God, Madeleine prayed, *give the baby a few more weeks. She's still got a month to go.*

The paramedics arrived with a stretcher, carefully rolled Victoria onto it, and carried her out. Madeleine watched them go, her heart tight. She and Jack soon followed.

Madeleine sat in the hospital waiting room, praying, as Jack paced. A door opened and a nurse announced that Victoria was stabilized. *Thank you, Lord.*

Candice stood by the window, making calls, Andrew nearby. With the good news, the senator flipped her phone shut and announced she needed to return to London for a BBC interview. "No point in Victoria's situation hitting the press right now," she said. "Better stay on schedule."

Madeleine and Jack exchanged glances. Andrew's face was masked, unreadable, but Madeleine noticed his shoulders had relaxed with the news of his daughter's stable condition.

"Is there anything," Jack said, looking at Candice, then Andrew, "anything at all, we can do? Shall we call you tonight? Let you know how she's doing?"

Madeleine spoke with hesitation. "Or in the morning?"

"Thank you," Andrew said, nodding and helping his wife into her coat. "I'll wait for your call."

"She seems fine for now," Candice said from the doorway, "and the doctor promised to keep me posted." She tapped her mobile phone, then her eyes narrowed. "But this whole wild goose chase has been totally unnecessary. And what part have you two played, exactly? You *will* keep this...quiet, won't you?"

"We'd better go," Andrew said, taking her arm. "Don't want to get stuck in traffic. London's nearly three hours away."

As the waiting room door closed behind them, Jack turned to Madeleine. "She sounds threatening, Maddie."

"But Andrew is supportive. I could see he wanted to steer his wife out of here as fast as possible. I think he loves his daughter, but he thinks this is the best way to handle things. We should keep in regular contact with him. Poor fellow." Madeleine's heart went out to him. His gentleness surrounded him like a soft cloud. Did he have an inner strength not so apparent from the outside? He seemed like a prisoner trying to do his best from behind bars. But then who could judge a marriage? Marriages were complicated, full of history, laced with both pain and pleasure. "Thank heaven Victoria is okay."

"But I think I'd better follow them to London tomorrow, maybe take them to dinner. Cristoforo can help you with Victoria."

"Where is he? He was here earlier."

"Praying in the hospital chapel."

"A wise man. We need to tell him the good news."

Jack's thoughts had moved on. "Joe McGinty is returning from Rome this week. He's been commuting, it seems. I should meet his plane at Heathrow."

"Has he lined up any donors?"

"We'll see. He has a few Oxford connections. His great-grandmother was an Astor, I believe. He's got interests in hotels too, which may be why he is able to put us up like this."

"That's right, I'd forgotten that."

"You understand I need to go, don't you?"

Madeleine looked into her husband's blue eyes. "Of course, honey. You do what needs doing. Cristoforo and I will be fine. We'll take care of

Victoria. We'll drive to Saint Anne's over the weekend. We can meet you there."

In the next few days Madeleine spent as much time at the hospital as she could, waiting in the sterile hall and sitting beside Victoria, reading to her.

Chapter Twenty-five
Saint Anne's House

The Body of Christ, the Church,
offers itself to become the Sacrificed Body of Christ,
the sacrament, in order that thereby the Church itself may become...
the fullness or fulfillment of Christ; and each of the redeemed may become
what he has been made by baptism and confirmation,
a living member of Christ's body.
Dom Gregory Dix

On Saturday evening, Madeleine pulled aside velvet draperies and peered at the fog enshrouding Thornbury Castle, pressing against the mullioned panes of the bedroom. Victoria had been discharged on Wednesday with orders for bed rest until the baby was born. Now she slept peacefully in an adjoining room. God had sheltered their little mother and child.

The week had been a quiet one, caring for Victoria, bringing her books and meals on a tray. The friar rented a wheelchair and Madeleine pushed her along the garden paths when the weather was dry. It was on one of these walks that she learned the true cause of Victoria's fainting.

"Your mother said William was engaged? Are you sure?"

Victoria spoke quietly as though easing her way through her memory. "She was pretty clear about it."

"There must be some misunderstanding."

"Somehow, I knew it all along. It was so clear, really. I believed he might love me because I wanted to believe it."

"I'm sure there's more to it."

"Madeleine, I don't want to talk about it. I'm accepting the situation as it is."

"I understand."

Madeleine prayed about it and still couldn't believe that Victoria had misread the young man's feelings. But she would *"tarry in the Lord's leisure"* as the Psalmist said, and be patient.

She found a knitting shop in the village and bought yarn and needles and an instruction booklet. It had been twenty-seven years since Madeleine had knitted Mollie's yellow blanket, but it all came back—knit one, purl one—and she taught Victoria what she recalled. Madeleine worked on *Holy Manifestations* while Victoria knitted. They sat in the library, the rain pouring, the yellow yarn taking a shape all its own, Madeleine's book taking a shape all its own.

Madeleine worried about Jack and the senator. Would he be led along by that woman? Candice was not only attractive but powerful, and clearly used to getting her way. Women fell for Jack, a fact Madeleine had faced long ago but never really accepted. But she must trust her husband, and she must trust God. *Easier said than done.*

Jack had called Wednesday evening, and that was reassuring. He had taken the Senator to dinner again, insisting that Victoria was in excellent hands, and Candice had seemed relieved. He was heading back to Aylesbury to oversee renovations.

Victoria reported that Candice had called the clinic daily, or at least an aide had called, to check on her, and Victoria had insisted there was no need for her mother to visit. The aide said that the senator was extremely busy with her London schedule. The BBC interview had caught the attention of Buckingham Palace, and Candice was invited to a royal audience on Thursday. This led to more news coverage, several dinner invitations with Members of Parliament, and a weekend in a country house called Cliveden.

Cliveden. Madeleine recalled its historic and infamous guest list: the Nazi sympathizers of the thirties, the political playboys of the fifties. Today, it was a National Trust Hotel overlooking the Thames, surrounded by Renaissance gardens. It was once owned by Astors. Did Joe McGinty have ties there now?

At any rate, Madeleine was grateful for the time with Victoria. The young woman had indeed become like a daughter, a Mollie she never saw grow up, a Lisa Jane from Colorado. She must call Boulder soon and see how her grandson Luke was doing. Would Luke one day have a baby brother or sister? Perhaps he would have a sister. It would be good to hold a baby girl in her arms once again, as she had held Mollie so long ago.

Madeleine crawled into the canopied bed. She propped herself up with pillows and reached for her laptop. The chill of the March evening seeped through the castle walls, and she wrapped a shawl about her shoulders. Tomorrow they would drive to Aylesbury. In the meantime, Madeleine would seek her usual solace. She would enter her world of words, trying to give material shape to the mysteries of life, to the miracle of God and his acts among men. She was close to completion of this final draft.

Holy Manifestations: The Later Anglo-Catholics
The Anglo-Catholic movement, begun in Oxford in those heady days of the mid-nineteenth century, met setbacks, battles, and wrong turns, as it struggled into the twentieth century, a century of great devastation. Two powerful ideologies promoted this devastation.

Social Darwinism claimed that since only the fit survive, only an elect *should* survive. This idea supported Hitler's policy of extermination; over six million non-Aryans, along with the disabled, the aged, and others targeted for for their beliefs or lifestyle, were murdered.

Moral relativism, a product of Einstein's[31] theory of relativity, denied objective truth and had even farther reaching consequences than social Darwinism. Nietzsche's[32] supermen, the Communists Lenin and Stalin, claimed that no moral authority exists but the self, and therefore might makes right. More than 20 million people were killed in their wake. In China, the Communist regime of Mao Zedong is held responsible for over 70 million deaths.

By the mid-twentieth century, man looked for life amidst the nihilistic rubble. He turned toward God.

In England, the seeds of earlier catholic revivals blossomed during these years, keeping the Anglican way alive with its central belief in the Real Presence. Such flowerings preserved the Church's sacramental life and worship, expressing the inexpressible through action, image, and song. Throughout the twentieth-century holocausts, Anglo-Catholic voices crying in the dark included C.S. Lewis, T.S. Eliot, Charles Williams, Dom Gregory Dix, Evelyn Underhill, and Dorothy Sayers. In fiction, poetry, and essay they wrote of sacramental Christianity, replacing existential despair with historical hope. They carried the torch.

Madeleine's thoughts returned to the senator, to her high cheekbones and creamy skin, her perfect hairdo and manicured nails, her trim figure and close-fitting jacket, her aura of power and confidence. Was Madeleine simply envious of the woman or distrustful of Jack? Probably the former, she decided. She reread her last paragraph.

She recalled reading Lewis' apology for Christianity, compiled from wartime radio broadcasts. She was in her junior year at San Francisco State, deep into Sartre and Camus, deep into existential depression. Why live? If there was no purpose or meaning in life, what difference did it make whether she died now or in fifty years? Then she read Lewis. She had often thought, as she recalled his words, that he saved her life—literally saved her life, for she was a person who needed to have logical reasons to believe, to understand with her mind, not only her heart.

Lewis' apology, his argument for Christianity, was simple: the moral law, or "natural law" (meaning man's innate sense of right and wrong) pointed to a Supreme Being, a loving Creator, an almighty God. Jesus Christ said *he* was God, so he was either a madman or a liar, or indeed he was who he said he was. If you accepted that Christ was indeed God, then his words had absolute authority. The argument had made perfect sense, and she had made that initial leap of faith. In fact, it wasn't much of a leap, but rather, as Jack liked to say, a baby step.

And the senator? Did Lewis' moral law apply to her? Did Candice, somewhere deep, sense she was in the wrong with regards to her grandchild? Grievously wrong? Mortally wrong?

Madeleine scrutinized her words.

> The Anglo-Catholics of the twentieth century also gave new life to the Shrine of Our Lady of Walsingham in Norfolk.

Madeleine had never been to Walsingham, but had heard of it. She hoped one day to visit. Known as "England's Nazareth," it celebrated a unique vision that occurred in the eleventh century, and today the shrine gathers faithful from around the world who pray to Mary for guidance and intercession.

> In 1061, according to tradition, the Virgin Mary appeared to the Saxon noblewoman Richeldis de Faverches. Mary revealed to Richeldis the house in Nazareth where the Angel Gabriel appeared to Mary two thousand years ago, when Gabriel announced that she would bear Jesus, God's son. Mary then asked Richeldis to build a replica of the house.
> The simple wooden structure with its statue of Mary soon

became the center of an Augustinian priory. Pilgrimages began, and ballads were sung throughout Europe in this time of the troubadour. But in 1538, Henry VIII destroyed the Walsingham Priory, as he did so many other holy places in England. It wasn't until 1897, after Roman Catholics restored the wayside Slipper Chapel, that pilgrimages resumed. In 1921 Anglicans renewed the shrine as well. Father Hope Patten, Vicar of Walsingham, erected a new statue of Our Lady, one based on the medieval image, and an Anglican shrine rose around the Parish Church of Saint Mary. Today, Eastern Orthodox come on pilgrimage, joining Anglicans and Roman Catholics in offering prayers for the world.

Madeleine found such hope in these tangible aspects of God's love; a lowly shed and a simple image of the Mother of God had withstood centuries of bloodshed and violence. While it wasn't the same image or the same shed, the shrine prospered. *God's time wins in the end,* she thought.

The twentieth-century renewal in Walsingham continued, in spite of secular cynicism. But after the hardships of two world wars and the Great Depression, the affluence of the 1950s nearly drowned these calls to orthodox belief. Life was good, the economy boomed, and television drugged serious thought. In the sixties the youth of these euphoric times questioned the materialism of their parents' generation, suspecting, often correctly, a hollow shell. Some of those baby boomers read Lewis and Eliot and Sayers and sought to keep Christianity alive. Others burned campuses in their angst, recalling the despair of Jean-Paul Sartre and Albert Camus.[33] Indeed, Sartre was an influential voice in academia in the sixties, with his existential creed insisting that life had no meaning and man must create his own system of belief. Suicide rates rose, crime increased, personal gratification was lauded, and the "me" generation was born, encouraging free love and opening the door to venereal disease, AIDS, and throwaway babies. Moral relativism appeared to have won the day.

And what happened to the Anglican Church? In England, that unique blend of Pelagian independence and Augustinian rule remained fused to government subsidy and power.[34] The Church began to reflect society rather than to inform it, taking the comfortable and profitable road of least resistance.

By the end of the twentieth century, questions of faith and practice, of dogma and ritual, were reevaluated in the light of cultural shifts rather than historic, apostolic, and Scriptural mandates. Individual opinion replaced consensus, leaving truth to be tossed by the slightest breeze. Many "seekers" reinvented their faith, singing to the tune of a local personality or the media's definition of reality. Church attendance dropped, unless a good show was provided, an increasing necessity in an entertainment-oriented, narcissistic society.

Madeleine blamed the rise of television for the phenomenon of decreasing attention spans. TV, in its youth, seemed such a promising technology. Who could complain? Who could have foreseen its addictive qualities and destructive implications? Television was another example of the misuse of a great gift. It really wasn't television and movies themselves, but the ubiquitous misuse of media, leading to the inevitable dumbing down of generations to come, that threatened Western culture.

The catholic stream dwindled in the face of schism and struggled to remain faithful. Issues of faith and practice—the Real Presence, the creeds, the rites and language of the *Book of Common Prayer*—had been decided by historic councils of the Body of Christ. These councils, obedient to the authority of the early Church, upheld a male priesthood, traditional marriage and family life, and the right of the unborn, the handicapped, and the elderly to live. They asserted the truths of Holy Scripture: Jesus Christ, the Son of God, saves us from sin and death, and unites with us in the Mass. But these Anglo-Catholics were only a stream.

The Episcopal Church, the American daughter of the British Church, was not a state institution, and consequently was forced by financial needs to face its diminishing numbers earlier. In 1976, the Episcopal Synod voted to become "relevant," liberalizing belief and practice even more. A few Anglo-Catholic faithful separated, becoming the "Continuing Church" movement, a group of Anglican parishes seeking to practice sacramental life in obedience to historic councils.

The tree of faith planted by Joseph so many years ago flowers today in the New World town of Fond-du-Lac, Wisconsin, where pilgrims visit the shrine of Bishop Charles Grafton, his body incorrupt—undecayed—an Anglo-Catholic saint. The roots of

Joseph's thorn tree reach deep into the earth, its branches climb high into the heavens, and God's manifestations on earth continue to transform our world.

Madeleine slipped out of bed, walked to the window, and stared into the parting fog that shimmered in the lighted garden. She had been at work on *Holy Manifestations* forever, it seemed. She had struggled with the title as she wrote about the churches and shrines of Italy and France, and now England. When she began her research, the relics of saints had been merely words on a page found in some scholarly account. But after visiting these scenes where God's particular presence had been known and witnessed, and after seeing the relics, reading about the miracles, and praying before the Blessed Sacrament, she was certain God had indeed visited his people in these mysterious ways. Such visits encouraged her. Such encounters led to God: in Holy Scripture, in the Eucharist, and in the Church.

Suddenly Madeleine felt blessed, so very blessed that she had glimpsed some of these things that she began to weep for joy.

The following morning was Passion Sunday, two weeks before Easter, a day that promised to be fair. As the car left Thornbury Castle, Cristoforo at the wheel, and headed toward Aylesbury, Madeleine turned in the passenger seat to check on Victoria in the back. She seemed okay. She studied the friar, gripping the steering wheel intently, his injured arm still bandaged. "Your hand and arm must hurt," she said. "Maybe I should drive, Cristoforo."

"*Allora*, no, *Signora*, it is okay."

Cristoforo drove as if on a mission. He sped down the road between high hedgerows, taking shortcuts here and swerving there, hunched over the wheel, eyes fixed on the upcoming road.

Madeleine checked on Victoria again. Her legs were propped up; firmly belted in, she reclined on pillows propped against the side door.

"I'm all right, don't worry," Victoria whispered as her eyes fluttered shut.

"Cristoforo, *please*," Madeleine said under her breath. "We're not in a hurry. We *do* have a mother and child with us, and we're not in Italy, and you're driving on the other side of the road here, and...please slow down!" Her left hand gripped the dashboard as she leaned toward him.

The friar glanced at Madeleine and took his foot off the accelerator. "*Per favore,* forgive me, *Signora*, I forget."

"Think of it as your Lenten penance to drive slowly."

"You are right. I *do* like to drive, *Signora*."

"*Grazie.*" Madeleine sat back and watched the forested hills pass by, grateful the day was dry. "Victoria was discharged with the promise of bed rest."

"*Si, Signora.* Is there a clinic near Saint Anne's?"

"Sister Eileen, from the Sisters of Mary, has her midwife license and phoned in the release."

"*Si,*" Cristoforo said, narrowly missing an oncoming car.

"The hospital wanted an ambulance. I wish I'd followed their advice."

"*Si*, I be more careful. I am sorry."

"Another hour and we should reach Aylesbury."

"And *Signore* Seymour? Will he join us there? From London?"

"Hopefully. He's meeting with possible sponsors of Saint Anne's. One of the newspapers is interviewing him."

"That is good. Many will help."

"He's also keeping an eye on Victoria's parents."

"He spends time with them?"

"He wanted to appease them, so he took them to dinner."

"*Appease*? I do not know this word."

"*Appease* means to calm, to make amends," Madeleine said, dropping her voice to a whisper. "She threatened a lawsuit and criminal charges. Just what Jack feared, and certainly not a challenge he needs."

Sudden understanding flashed across Cristoforo's face and he nodded. "Is *Signore* Seymour okay? Is there more trouble for him?"

"His heartburn has returned. He shouldn't get so upset." The condition called Barrett's Esophagus had led to Jack's cancer two years ago. An old worry was working its way into Madeleine's heart.

She checked her watch. Nearly 10:00. At this rate, they would arrive earlier than expected. It was, after all, Passion Sunday. Maybe there would be a late Mass at the abbey. She prayed that Jack would join them soon.

Before long they passed Hartwell House and turned up the neighboring drive to the three-story convent and attached abbey that would be their new Saint Anne's. As the house came into view,

Madeleine sensed she had come home, that all their work might finally bear fruit. They drove up the gravel drive to the gray brick façade, and Madeleine was thankful. The oriel windows welcomed them, and, since their last visit, new grass had sprouted on the front lawn.

As soon as she settled Victoria, she would walk over to Hartwell. Had Jack made a reservation? She wasn't sure.

Cristoforo could see Saint Anne's needed more work, but a few rooms had been made habitable by the nine nuns from Cowley. The air was tinged with the acrid smell of chlorine.

Sister Eileen met them in the entry. Had it really been four weeks since she had greeted the friar at the convent outside of Oxford? Her fair, scarred face broke into a smile of recognition. "Please, Brother Cristoforo, bring her in here." She led Madeleine, followed by Cristoforo carrying Victoria, his wrapped arm still sending twinges of pain, down a freshly painted hallway to a room overlooking the back garden. "I'll find something in the kitchen for lunch."

The friar laid her gently on a bed, its white sheets folded back neatly. She weighed nothing, he thought, and yet she weighed for two. He looked into her eyes, hoping to ease her worries. Those eyes contained a world of sorrows, a world he wanted to heal. *Si*, he thought, he would like to replace all that sadness with happiness, if he could. He traced the Sign of the Cross on her forehead. "It will be okay, little one. All the saints in heaven pray for you and your new life. You will see it will be good. Trust God, and it will be so."

The bell in the tower rang eleven and the friar turned to Madeleine. "I go now, *Signora*, to the abbey."

"I'll be along soon." Madeleine glanced at Victoria. "No, maybe not. Today my place is here." She sat on the edge of the bed and took Victoria's hand.

As Cristoforo stepped into the doorway, Sister Eileen entered, her long habit dusting the floor. She set a tray of food on a nearby table. The friar paused to watch the three women.

"Thank you, Madeleine," Victoria was saying. Her voice was hoarse and her eyelids drooped. "Tell me...about...Passion Sunday."

Eileen adjusted the covers, shaking a pillow and slipping it behind

Victoria's back. "First some milk and a bite to eat," she said, chatting lightly, her words dancing and disappearing with amazing speed so that Cristoforo had to listen carefully. "We've set up the kitchen, and the medical supplies are laid in the old wine cupboard. Our first patient must be good and follow instructions. Everything will be fine, for you're at Saint Anne's House, my dear." She offered her a sandwich.

"Thank you, Sister."

"The name *Passion Sunday*," Madeleine began, her slower pace easier to follow, "comes from the *passion* of Our Lord—that is, his last days before his death and resurrection. Father Rinaldi, God rest his soul, called the Passion the union of love and suffering. But mainly Passion Sunday focuses our hearts and minds on these last two weeks...."

Cristoforo grew happy with the memory of Father Rinaldi, the Seymours' priest and his priest too, making them family. Perhaps Father watched from heaven, holding them all close to his heart. The monk's spine tingled when he thought how God worked through each of them, saving them with love.

Victoria's room faced the garden, wild now, but that would change, thought Cristoforo, come spring planting. The windows were tall and pleasing, and the cherry tree outside, with its early white flowering, lightly dusted the glass. *God is good,* he thought. *God is good.* He gazed upon the three women leaning toward one another, a kind of sisterly trinity, and shut the door behind him carefully, silently, as though closing the lid of an antique box of precious incense.

The Mass for Passion Sunday was concluding as Brother Cristoforo knelt in a back pew. Standing in front of the altar, young Father Dodd, with William at his side, made the Sign of the Cross over his people. *"And may the Father, the Son, and the Holy Spirit, bless and preserve you this day and always."* He motioned to the organist to begin the recessional hymn.

> "The God of Abraham praise, Who reigns enthroned a-bove;
> Ancient of ev-er-last-ing days, And God of love;
> To him up-lift your voice, At whose su-preme com-mand
> From earth we rise, and seek the joys...At his right hand."

Cristoforo had not confessed, for his superior insisted he must first come home. The friar had not dared take part in the holy mysteries but instead knelt in the back, praying, watching, listening. Now he waited for William to return and snuff out the candles. A woman in the second pew rose and carefully removed the sacred vessels from the altar.

Cristoforo prayed for mercy. He must return soon. But he resisted, often recalling the upturned faces, the crowds thirsty for his saving words. How he yearned to stand again before them. "Give me strength, Lord," he prayed, "for I am sorely tempted."

He repeated to himself the last letter from Bernardo, now written on his heart:

My son,
You are in disobedience. Do you not want to continue the life of God? Do not shut Him out, my son. You do God's will in the little things, not the big. God takes your little things and He makes them big, not you. Each small act of self-consecration to God, each act of doing death to self, these give you the mind of Christ.

God will judge us by how we have tried, not by how we have succeeded. Come home, my son, come home.
+Bernardo, O.F.M.

William joined him in the pew. They nodded to one another, genuflected before the tabernacle, and stepped outside. The sun slanted under a bank of charcoal clouds.

"We walk, my friend?" Cristoforo motioned to the overgrown garden and its hidden paths. *Small acts, yes, a few small acts, and then Rome.*

He cinched his rope belt tighter, for his Lenten fast of one meal a day and his rule of abstinence, giving up meat, had been slimming. He looked at William and waited, covering his bandaged hand with the wide sleeve of his robe. He did not want to explain.

"How is Victoria?" William asked. "I've been worried. She hasn't been returning my calls."

"Victoria is here."

"Here?" William halted abruptly and searched the friar's eyes.

"We brought her to Saint Anne's today. *Signora* Seymour is with her."

They sat on a crumbling stone bench, and Cristoforo described her fainting, false labor, and hospitalization.

"Why did no one reach me?" William ran his hand through his

thinning hair with some distress. He walked toward a wild rosebush climbing a dying elm.

"Miss Victoria did not desire it." The friar stood, staring at William's back, praying for the right words. The boy's anguish filled his heart.

"She didn't desire it?" William turned, his face reddening.

"William, do not be angry. She was shocked by some news...and her pains began."

"News? What news?"

"News of your engagement."

"No!" He raised his palms to the sky in testimony. "I was going to tell her *after* I broke it off."

"And have you broken this engagement?"

"Well, no, not yet." He studied the ground in confusion. "I couldn't find the right time, and I wasn't sure about Victoria's feelings, and we've been concentrating on the baby, and...oh, it's so very complicated. Seventeen is quite young, isn't it? She turns eighteen in May. But that is still too young to marry."

"Some say too young to give birth."

"I see your point." William's eyes narrowed. "Perhaps what some say doesn't count in these matters of life and death."

"And of God. You are to be ordained?"

"Mid-April."

"Do you love Miss Victoria?"

William looked intensely at Cristoforo. "I do. I truly do."

The friar nodded, satisfied. "You must tell her. Then you make plans *together*."

"Together. That's good, isn't it?"

"It is good."

With his hands open as though reaching for the right words, William leaned forward. "She is...everything. She holds my heart in her hands. Her face...pulls me into another world, a fairy-tale world." William's blue eyes begged the friar to understand.

Cristoforo listened to the young man speak of love. His words painted a mystical land, a land where anything was possible, where miracles were common. In Victoria, William was transformed. *That,* the friar thought, *is love.*

"She kissed me, you know," William announced, gazing at the friar with incredulity. "The princess kissed the frog."

"The frog?" Cristoforo tried to follow his meaning but was at a loss.

"I'm not attractive. I know that." William raised his hand to silence the friar's protests. "Nor do I care, one way or another. This...arranged...marriage was a relief, in a way. A vicar needs a wife, don't you know. Mums found me a more than respectable one, too."

"Your mother found you a wife?"

William laughed through his teeth. "She wants me to *be* someone, someone with *expectations*, a man of *substance*. The Church was not my parents' choice. And they *did* provide me with a fine education." Sorrow and regret passed over his features.

"But your vocation must be *your* choice."

William nodded. "So failing to direct my vocation, they hoped to direct my marriage. Mums firmly believes that with this match, I'll be a bishop one day and sit in the House of Lords."

"And now?"

"*Now* there's Victoria. Even if she doesn't want me, she's made me realize the mistake I was making."

"*Si*. But you must not push Miss Victoria. She is very young."

"She *is*, six years younger than I. And then there's the baby."

"She has many decisions before her."

"Do you think she'll keep the baby?"

"I do not know, but others will help her if she chooses to keep the child."

"Maybe she should give up the baby and move on with her life."

"These are *her* choices. You must make *your* choices."

William clapped his hands together with determination. "Brother, could I use your phone? I need to make a call."

Cristoforo pulled out his phone, handed it to William, and returned to the bench. He studied his hand and removed the bandage as he listened to William put his life right in two minutes of conversation. The burn had healed well enough. One more scar would not matter.

"Mother, you heard me. It's off....That's too bad, isn't it.... I never felt right about it anyway.... So, good.... Let Suzanne marry the earl. Sounds perfect.... You'll get over it, Mother."

He punched another number. "Suzanne? Could we meet at Scott's for dinner? Say seven? Good. There's something serious I need to talk to you about.... Seven it is then."

William, looking happy and relieved, returned the phone to the friar. "We'll take it slowly, one day at a time."

"One day at a time. You must walk in faith, my son." Cristoforo often thought of Father Rinaldi's reassuring phrase.

William took a deep breath and steepled his hands. "Yes, a faith walk."

Cristoforo watched the young man leave through the garden gate. *Small acts*, he thought, and offered a silent *Te Deum*.

Chapter Twenty-six
Palm Sunday

Do not argue about it, but believe in it.
Honor our Lord's Presence there by music, lights, flowers, and incense.
He will honor those who love Him. He dwells in His Church.
He veils his Presence, but will unveil it in Glory...
by spiritual but real incorporation into Christ,
the whole body of the faithful rises into the divine fellowship
and progresses in its union with God.
Charles C. Grafton

Wednesday evening Madeleine gazed at a bouquet of flowers in their bedroom at Hartwell House. Yellow tulips, not yet open, clustered amid sprigs of purple rosemary in a crystal vase on the fireplace mantel. Jack had returned from London with the flowers, a gift from Joe McGinty. A nice gesture, Madeleine thought.

Better than flowers, though, was Jack's steady presence, in spite of the recent strain in their marriage. When Jack was beside her, the world seemed once more on track; she felt less off-balance. He was her other half, and his absence made her lopsided. He had not been at Hartwell when she arrived on Passion Sunday but had left a message he would come in a few days, and she had tried not to worry. In the meantime there had been much to do, helping the nuns and spending time with Victoria, heartbroken Victoria.

Madeleine winced with the thought of William. He had tried to see Victoria Sunday afternoon, and Madeleine had met him on the porch with the news Victoria refused to see him. Madeleine liked William immediately, with his honest open face, his friendly and thoughtful manner. William did not mention their quarrel, and Victoria had not brought the subject up again, so Madeleine had respected their wishes.

But the young man had phoned on Monday and again on Tuesday, urging his need to see Victoria, panic lining his voice. Victoria continued to say no, her face determined.

Now Jack had returned, and everything would fall into place. Even so, she was nervous about mentioning Victoria at all, worrying that he would insist they return home.

As they dressed for dinner Jack spoke of London. Joe McGinty had arranged fundraisers and substantial donations had been promised. He had scheduled a press conference. Several dailies were carrying the story about the opening of Saint Anne's House.

"Joe put me up in an adjoining room at Claridges. Did I tell you that? Very nice, very ornate. I did the best I could with the Nguyens. I took them to dinner." Jack straightened his pink tie before a gilt-framed mirror. "The senator's a real piece of work, but I don't think she's pressing charges."

Madeleine studied his face in the mirror. He seemed relieved to be back at Hartwell. "Good. It wouldn't help her with the media. How is Andrew doing, in all of this?"

"He's a patient man. Quiet. We spoke privately at one point. He'll continue to help in any way he can, which is something, I guess. But I'm not sure he has much influence." Jack turned and looked into her eyes. "I'm afraid the wine tore up my esophagus again. I've got to call home for a refill on my prescription."

"A lot of pain?"

"It's under control, but I need to watch my diet."

"I'm sorry, honey. We'll be careful. Is that a new tie?" she said, hoping to lighten his mood.

"I found it at Pym's in the Burlington Arcade. Like it?"

The pink was dotted with silver crests. She touched the fine wool of his lapel. "It goes nicely with the gray herringbone."

"I missed you, Maddie." He leaned down and kissed her tenderly.

She sighed deeply. "I missed you too. I'm so glad you're back."

"Shall we go downstairs for a drink before dinner?"

They descended the grand staircase and sat in a settee before a flickering fire. Outside, a light rain tapped against the leaded glass, texturing the evening darkness. A butler took their order: a martini for the lady and a sparkling water for the gentleman.

"Saint Anne's House is nearly all set up," Madeleine ventured.

"Good, and Cristoforo? Is he still here?"

"I'm not sure where he is—he returned to London to help out at the hostel. But he's talking about going back to Rome. I think his superior wants him home."

"I'm not surprised. How's his arm?"

"He took the bandage off, so it seems to be healing. Sister Eileen's been treating it."

"And the order of nuns? Have they settled in? Do they need anything?"

"They're fine for now. There's much to be done with the building and gardens, and more paperwork, but it's all moving ahead."

"Madeleine, we need to go home."

"Not yet, Jack, please."

"How long do you intend to stay? I'd like to leave England. Those Nguyens make me nervous. She's no one to tangle with, trust me."

"Let's stay through Easter. I want to spend Holy Week here at Saint Anne's, and we promised Father Smythe at Saint Mary's Bourne Street we'd return for Easter, remember?" And Easter was only ten days from Victoria's due date.

He looked resigned, as though he could see through her ploy. "Easter's only a week from Sunday. And Joe McGinty has lined up a few more dinners in London. Okay, we'll stay through Easter. March 31, I believe."

"Thanks, sweetie. Now tell me, did you recognize anyone famous at these fundraisers? Any royals? Let's sign them all up as Friends of Saint Anne's."

She would stay with Victoria as long as she could.

On Palm Sunday Victoria looked about the old abbey. From her wheelchair at the end of the last pew, Saint Anne's appeared two-thirds full. The air was laced with expectancy, as though Lent would soon be over and Lenten rules rewarded. Madeleine had said they would re-enact Christ's entry into Jerusalem, but didn't explain how.

The organ struck the first notes of the opening hymn, and from her chair, Victoria watched the procession form on the porch, both hoping and dreading to catch a glimpse of William. Her heart ached.

Didn't William realize she could not bear mere friendship with a man she loved? She knew he couldn't possibly love her back, in her condition, with her face. There was nothing to love. He was engaged to a far more suitable person, and that was that. She didn't want to hear his explanations or his apologies. After all, it was only one kiss and some conversation. What was there to apologize for? She would move ahead with her life, and if Daddy was right, she would have the funds to do so. But she must keep William Collingwood far away.

The thurifer led the procession, swinging his thurible of billowing incense, followed by the crucifer who raised high the wooden crucifix, then two young acolytes who walked somberly with flaming candles, then William, hands folded, and finally Father Dodd, vested in Lenten purple.

William's eyes moved from side to side and finally rested on Victoria. Their eyes locked and his pale skin flushed. The pain of seeing him was nearly unbearable, and she turned her eyes to the crucifix, for Jesus had known betrayal too. As Victoria's heart throbbed, she placed her hand on her child, strengthened by this life. Madeleine, at her side, squeezed her hand gently, as though aware of her turmoil.

Jack sat in the front row, waiting to read the first lesson. Victoria noticed Cristoforo wasn't in the procession, then located him across the aisle, kneeling, his head in his hands.

Father Dodd blessed a basket of palm fronds and handed them to parishioners at the altar rail. Madeleine brought back an extra palm, and Victoria ran her finger along the smooth flat stem. The congregation then followed the raised crucifix down the center aisle, out the doors, as they waved their palms and sang,

> *"All glory, laud, and hon-or*
> *To thee, Re-deem-er, King!*
> *To whom the lips of chil-dren*
> *Made sweet ho-san-nas ring...."*

Madeleine wheeled Victoria outside to watch. *It's a holy parade,* thought Victoria, as the people circled the graveyard and returned to the porch. Father Dodd knocked three times on the heavy doors, symbolizing Christ's entry into Jerusalem. The doors, representing the gates of the holy city, opened, the procession entered, the people took their seats, and the Mass began.

Victoria absorbed the symbols of the liturgy. They fed her mind and soul with layers of meaning, giving her a wholeness she had not known before. She loved the outer performance of the inner belief; she was transported by the music and the Elizabethan language of the old rite. Rhythm and image wove together in a kind of poetic love song.

Father Dodd climbed to the pulpit and began his sermon. He spoke quietly of the prophecies passed through generations that foretold Christ's coming to earth. He described the Jerusalem crowds who did not understand Christ's mission, who he truly was. It was like today, Father Dodd said, for people do not realize who he truly is.

"And who *are* you, Jesus?" he asked quietly as his eyes rested on each person, touching them. "Jesus Christ is our inheritance through and in time. Do *we* have false expectations too, or do we open our hearts to our redeemer and Lord?"

Victoria looked up to the crucifix, then to William sitting in the chancel in his white robe, and finally to the quiet vicar preaching his sermon. Would William preach like that, or would he be like the wild Brother Cristoforo? He would probably preach like *William*, Victoria thought. Yes, most assuredly, like William. Sadness washed over her, and, as her son tried to turn over, unsuccessfully, she guessed, in his shrinking pool, she feared her future.

Victoria noticed William's eyes seeking hers, discreetly, at every chance.

Over the next few days of Holy Week, Victoria tried not to think about William—William's eyes seeking hers, William in the chancel, William. Her future did not involve his. If only she could trust God like Madeleine did, she would be fine. In the meantime she would practice being thankful.

Each day was a day for thanksgiving, as the child gained weight. Victoria resumed her knitting of the little yellow blanket, finding a curious solace in the rhythm of the needles as they tapped lightly, sliding against one another in a pleasing way. She thought the blanket must be at least three-quarters done. Perhaps she would try a bonnet to match. She arranged the baby's tiny clothes on the other bed in her room, and Madeleine added finds from the village. Sister Eileen taught Victoria breathing exercises to help during labor, and Madeleine coached. Victoria was glad she could make her friend so happy, but was also sad that her own mother was absent. Yet she knew her mother would not have appreciated the role.

The nuns found secondhand chests, tables, and lamps. They hung an icon of the Virgin and Child on the wall at the foot of Victoria's bed to comfort her. Madeleine had produced a complete set of Austen, even some Bronte, Dickens and Trollope. She had found some contemporary authors too: Dorothy Sayers, Evelyn Waugh, P.D. James, Kazuo Ishiguro.

On Thursday afternoon, Victoria was sitting by the window, reading *Persuasion*, propping her legs on a stool as the doctor instructed, when she heard a knock on the door. She looked up and gently closed her book. "Come in," she said and grinned when she saw Brother Cristoforo. "Where have you been? We've missed you."

The friar looked troubled. "I have been helping in London, and helping here. I do what I can. Here. There." He smoothed the fabric of his robe and walked toward her, his shoulders stooped, his forehead creased with worry. "How *are* you, *Signorina* Victoria? You look well."

"Okay, Cristoforo, I think. The baby has a strong heartbeat, strong kick, and the doctor says I'm doing fine, all things considered. I have two weeks to go, so I'm in the safe zone. Do you think I'll make it?"

"*Allora*, for sure you will be fine....*Signorina*, I come with a request."

"A request? I'd do anything for you, Cristoforo. You've been such a help."

"Please, find it in your heart to...see William. He has important news. Will you trust me this is true?"

"It's no use. I'm not right for him, and he's not right for me. End of story." She looked out the window. He had tried to see her again and again, when he wasn't in Oxford, but she had been steadfast in her refusals.

"But it is not end of story. I believe," the friar said, tapping his nose, "that you are right for each other. I know these things."

"You know these things? Forgive me, Brother, but I don't think so."

"Will you trust me? I know *some* things you do not know."

Victoria feared she must face William, if only to say good-bye. "Okay, I'll see him, but only for you."

"*Allora*, he is here. And I must go to the abbey. It is Maundy Thursday, a very important day."

"He's here *now*? Wait..." Victoria smoothed her hair in panic.

The friar opened the door, nodded to William, and disappeared into the hall.

William, his face composed, crossed the room and knelt at

Victoria's feet. He wore a blue pullover and faded jeans, and his shirt collar protruded unevenly. She wanted to straighten it.

She gazed upon the wiry blond hair with its crooked part. He was shaking. He held a small, dark blue velvet box.

"Please," she said, "you don't have to..."

He looked up at her, his blue eyes uncertain. "Forgive me. Victoria, I love you. There is no one else. My engagement is broken."

She heard the words but could not believe them. She searched his eyes. His engagement was broken?

"Will you marry me, Victoria? Will you make me happy, or will you condemn me forever? Will you be my queen, my princess, my life?"

Victoria's tears fell on the shirt stretched over her child.

William stood abruptly, wringing his hands. "I'm too sudden. I should be more considerate. You have many choices. You are young." His voice rose in panic. "I've handled this badly as usual."

"I'll be eighteen soon." Victoria wasn't sure what to say.

William clasped the box in his palm.

"You will be *only* eighteen. You have your whole life ahead of you and these are large choices, Victoria."

"But, William, I love you too."

He drew near and kissed her on the mouth. It was a gentle kiss, a warm kiss of promise, his lips soft and lingering. "I will wait forever. You have many decisions to make, my princess, and we shall work through them, or *you* shall work through them...oh dear, I don't know how to say any of this. And I forgot to give you this." He looked at the velvet box and handed it to her.

"*We* shall work through them."

"Together?" He looked up into her eyes.

"Together." Victoria pulled open the lid. The ring was antique, the gold filigree swirling around a small diamond. "It's exquisite."

"It was my grandma's."

"But you'd better keep it for now."

"Of course. I'll keep it for now." He slipped it in his pocket and kissed her again.

Her heart soared. *William.*

That evening William pushed Victoria in her chair into the abbey for the Maundy Thursday service, settled her with Madeleine and Jack, and excused himself to vest in his acolyte's robe.

Seeing William, Madeleine looked at Victoria questioningly. "Was that William I saw?"

"He asked me to marry him," Victoria whispered. "He was engaged, but not anymore." Her heart fluttered as she said the words.

"I was sure there was more to it. What did you say?"

"We're taking it slowly."

"Good. One thing at a time."

Victoria nodded, and looked about the dim abbey. The evening light was fading quickly.

"Maundy Thursday is the saddest service of the year," Madeleine said quietly.

"And the longest, as I recall," Jack added.

"But no longer than Palm Sunday." Madeleine was looking about the nave.

"But Palm Sunday's more fun."

Victoria gazed at the crucifix above the altar, hidden behind a purple cloth. "But why is it so sad?"

"They strip the church," Madeleine said, her eyes now on the altar.

"They take everything?"

"First the Reserved Sacrament is moved to another location, symbolizing the arrest of Jesus in the Garden of Gethsemane. Then they remove the signs of God's presence on the altar—the candles, the missal stand, the altar linens, sometimes even carpets and chairs in the chancel. I usually cry."

"It sounds dramatic." William, *her* William now, would know all about this.

"It *is* dramatic. And then the Watch begins."

"The Watch?" She had much to learn.

"At least one person is assigned to keep watch before the Blessed Sacrament in its new location. In some parishes, the Watch is kept all night. Those who take part, pray and meditate on a world without Christ, sorting out their own mixed-up lives. The time recalls and re-enacts the watch the apostles kept in the garden while Jesus prayed."

"It lasts all night?" Would William keep the Watch too?

"Usually the young men get the midnight-to-seven duty since today it's unsafe for women and the elderly. Jack and I are taking the first Watch tonight, seven to eight."

The organ began to play, a poignant and triumphant sound, and the people stood. William led the procession, censing the aisle before him with sweet smoke. He glanced at Victoria.

"All-le-lu-ia! sing to Je-sus!
His the scep-ter, his the throne;
Al-le-lu-ia! his the tri-umph,
His the vic-to-ry a-lone;
Hark! the song of peace-ful Si-on
Thun-der like a migh-ty flood;
Je-sus out of ev-'ry na-tion
Hath re-deemed us by his blood!"

As the ancient rite of Maundy Thursday filled the old abbey, recalling Christ's last supper, Victoria was captivated by its beauty and mystery. She wanted to be confirmed, to receive the Eucharist. William would explain everything. For William was once again a possibility, one she had not dared hope for. She couldn't imagine life without him, but she would wait as he said; she needed time. For now, her child was everything.

That evening, William prepared supper trays and brought them to Victoria's bedside.

"It *was* an emotional service," Victoria said.

William set their sandwiches and milk on a side table. "It usually is." He leaned forward. "Maundy Thursday's Mass is especially moving, for it is the night of the Institution of the Holy Eucharist, when Our Lord told us to bring him back, to re-call him, in the Mass."

"But why do they call it *Maundy* when it's Thursday?"

William laughed and handed her a chicken sandwich wrapped in a paper towel. He pulled up a chair. "*Maundy* means commandment. I used to think it referred to the commandment at the Last Supper, *'Do this in remembrance of me.'*" He took a bite from his sandwich.

"But it doesn't?"

He shook his head. "It refers to Our Lord's commandment earlier that evening, *'Love one another.'*"

"I see."

"I have a present for you, Victoria."

William pulled a slim paperback from his satchel.

"*Mere Christianity*," Victoria cried, delighted. "This will tell me all I need to know. Thank you."

"It's a start, that's all. We learn forever, by God's grace. Now, have you chosen a name for this fine lad or lassie, as my grandpa would say?"

"I have a few thoughts."

"It's important, you know, important from a Christian point of view. Christians were the first to give personal names, sealed by God through Baptism."

"Really?"

"They reflect the history of the family, the uniqueness of the child, an individual created by God in his love. Names can be both an inheritance and a new creation."

"How about William Andrew? I think it will be a boy."

William laughed. Victoria, happy in his pleasure, touched his cheek with her finger.

"Most excellent," he said. "After your father, and I think, after me? How fantastic! Thank you, Victoria."

"So tell me more, William. Tell me about the Mass, since it's so important to you."

"It *is* important. It *is*." William's eyes lit up with the excitement of discovery. "For you see, on the one hand we have the mystery of the Trinity, a three-person God who has always been and will always be, who can never be fully comprehended, who is omnipotent over his creation." He opened his palms in awe. "Then all of a sudden, just the opposite happens. God becomes reachable, and one can know him personally. God enters humanity and becomes a child. He becomes poor, humble, and the way to him becomes narrow."

"So when God becomes Jesus we can understand him better."

"Exactly. We can *know* him. In fact, in the Eucharist we can see, touch, taste, smell, and hear him. The total person, body and soul, is involved in this meeting with God, our Creator."

"So you really believe Christ is present in the bread and the wine?"

"I do. And that is why we have such fanfare to recognize him, venerate him. Almighty God is made available to anyone, whether in the humblest village chapel or the grandest cathedral. He knocks on the door of each heart, asking to come in."

"Amazing, if true."

"You'll find it is, my princess. One of my favorite quotes is from C.S. Lewis. He once wrote that 'I believe in Christianity as I believe that the sun has risen, not only because I see it but because, by it, I see everything else.'"

There was a knock on the door, and Madeleine peeked in. "May I come in? I wanted to say good night to our little mother. It's only 8:30, but Jack and I are exhausted. We're turning in early." She moved to Victoria's bedside.

"Did you keep the Watch?" Victoria asked.

"We did, and it always touches me with a deep loneliness. And while I know it helps us experience Easter, it *is* tiring." She looked at William. "It's good to see you, William."

William took her hand. "It's good to see you, Mrs. Seymour. As you can see, I've been allowed a second chance with Miss Victoria."

"I'm sure you'll work it out one way or another."

"William is tutoring me on the faith." Victoria's eyes moved from Madeleine to William.

"Excellent," Madeleine said. "After all, it's our inheritance."

"Well said, Mrs. Seymour, well said. It is indeed." William looked at her gratefully.

Madeleine walked to the window. The wind howled in the dark, and branches scraped the glass. "The earth will be carpeted with blossoms tomorrow."

"You find even a storm good," Victoria said.

Madeleine turned toward her. "We don't deny suffering, but God helps us deal with it." She shook her head as she returned to the bed and took Victoria's hands in her own. "Our Lord said, '*In me ye might have peace. In the world ye shall have tribulation, but be of good cheer, I have overcome the world.*' We must pray that he gives us the grace to forgive those who cause our suffering."

Victoria winced. *Forgiveness.*

"You understand, Mrs. Seymour," William said, "I can see you understand. Somehow, we are both of the world and not of the world. In heaven, yet rooted in earth."

Victoria watched the bond form between the two she loved as she pushed away the thought of forgiveness.

"Just like our Lord," Madeleine added, "and the saints too. After all, as many have said, it's the vocation of Christians to be saints." Madeleine stood and brushed a persistent, wiry strand of hair from her face. "But presently I feel more on earth than in heaven, and I must toddle to bed. Good night, my dears, sleep well. Tomorrow, Victoria, is Good Friday, and if you are up to it, we have Stations, and the Mass of the Presanctified, a big day."

As the door closed behind Madeleine, Victoria looked at William. "Mass of the Presan...?"

"Presanctified." William stacked the tray with their dishes. "I'll explain tomorrow, love."

He kissed her good night, a long, happy kiss. A bundle of energy and purpose, he strode to the door and turned, his face glowing. "Until tomorrow, my Victoria Nguyen, sleep well." He bowed from the waist.

As he left, Sister Eileen bustled in, carrying a robe and towel. "And it's time for you as well, Miss Victoria, to get ready for bed."

Victoria looked out to the pouring rain. Eileen busied herself in the adjoining bath, running the water and humming. The storm had hit hard with no warning, a spring storm of promise.

"Good Friday," Victoria said to her child, with some sadness. "Why do they call it good? Jesus died on Good Friday. It doesn't seem good to me, but we shall see, won't we, Baby. We shall see."

Chapter Twenty-seven
Good Friday

How will the Cross come to us?
Not by seeking after it, not by imposing discomfort on ourselves for the sake of imposing it. It will come simply by facing the whole will of God for us, and seeking to accomplish it.
Raymond Raynes

The tabernacle had been moved to a rough cherry table in the northwest corner of the abbey, a red candle flaming alongside. In front of the makeshift altar, a bed of blue votives burned in an iron stand, and if one died out, Brother Cristoforo lit a new one with a neighboring flame. The friar kept the last of the morning Watch, kneeling on the wooden slat of a prie-dieu, having removed the needlepoint cushion the women had made. As he bowed his head before the Blessed Sacrament in these early hours of Good Friday, he wrestled with his demons, his disobedience, and his penance.

"Lord, what will thou have me do? Tell me and I will obey, for without thee I am nothing."

Cristoforo prayed the Psalms and he prayed the rosary. His loneliness, his sense of isolation from his Lord, his near despair wrapped him in a cold solitude, not unlike the solitude of Jesus on that night long ago. Yet the votives flamed in their blue glass, and he knew God was present, the eternal housed in such a humble place, a carved wooden box with a hammered brass door. Had the monks of Saint Anne's tooled the door themselves? Had they worked their love into the metal, as an icon painter layers prayers into the gilding of a sacred image? The golden crucified Christ glimmered before him.

These many people of God, the friar thought, lit a path for the world. They were the city on the hill, the candle in the candlestick, the leaven in the lump. Even here, especially here, as he shared the loneliness of Christ's human-ness that night two thousand years ago, he knew he was part of Christ's Body, the Body of Christ, the city on the hill.

He also knew something was asked of him, and when he heard the command, he would obey. For it was not enough to merely understand, to believe; he must also act. He had no fear of unknown demands, but only that his heart be too small to act upon them. He would not be thwarted by worldly threats, only spiritual ones.

"Let me share thy cup, oh Lord," he begged.

An early votive flickered out, and the friar rose to light another.

Obedience, he thought, was such a tangled problem in this world. Does a wife obey her abusive husband, or a husband obey his tyrannical wife? Does a daughter obey her mother's demand for an abortion? Must a boy submit to his father's beatings, or to a teacher's unwanted attentions? Can a man be blind to the gas chambers or deaf to the cries of Israel's children in the neighboring village?

Yet the friar knew that the Body of Christ was founded on obedience. There, here, in the garden, Christ obeyed his Father, reversing the disobedience of Adam, becoming the new Adam. And, as the Body of Christ, the Church must obey, for within that Body of Christ, God channeled his will to his people. In the end, Cristoforo knew, he would trust two thousand years of Church councils over one person's claim of direct inspiration. Man was a frail thing, and the entire Body, not a single soul, must convey Christ's commands.

He had been disobedient and wrongly so. As his ego slowly, painfully withdrew, the tremors of his addiction to adoring crowds lessened. It was like *Signore* Seymour said, *open your heart*. It was truly a mystery, the friar thought, as he felt himself drawn into the tabernacle. When his pride swelled, his heart closed down. His pride clutched his soul, grappling for ownership.

"Thy will, O Lord—let thy will be done."

As a rooster crowed in the early dawn, Father Dodd arrived to take Brother Cristoforo's place, and the friar fell exhausted onto a cot in the gardener's shed. Soon the bells tolled nine, and a gentle hand touched his shoulder. He awoke to see Father Rinaldi standing by his bed.

"Father...is that you?" Cristoforo whispered in amazement. His old priest had been dead for years. How could he be here, standing before him? "I must be dreaming."

"No, son, it is really me." Father Rinaldi held Cristoforo's shoulders and looked into his eyes. "You are awake. It is time." He turned and walked outside, through the low door.

As the friar rose from the cot to follow him, he heard the crunch of tires on Hartwell's gravel drive. He ran into the fog, a dense, damp mist nearly obscuring the old manor house. "Father..." he called into the gray whiteness, but Father Rinaldi was gone. Cristoforo stepped through the hedgerow, onto the drive.

A woman emerged from a van in front of the hotel. A police officer joined her, slamming the door behind him, cracking the silence. The friar walked through the fog toward them.

"You seek someone, Officer?" Cristoforo asked. "I am Brother Cristoforo from the abbey next door. Can I help you?"

The woman paused. Her eyes narrowed.

The officer stepped forward. "Can you tell us where we might find a certain Jack Seymour? This lady, Senator Nguyen, is pressing kidnapping charges."

Victoria's mother. She was a tall thin woman with a straight bearing. Her head cocked forward like a crow, and a giant black handbag swung from her shoulder. She moved from foot to foot, as though eager to leave, and nervously adjusted the lapel of her raincoat. Did she not want to see her daughter? the friar asked himself. He knew her daughter did not want to see *her.*

"*Signore* Seymour? No, *Signori*, no," Cristoforo said, seeing his opportunity. "It was *I* who took Victoria. He was not the one."

The officer, clearly puzzled, turned to Senator Nguyen. "Ma'am? Is he the man, or is Seymour the man?"

Candice Nguyen replied with satisfaction as she pointed to the friar. "He's the man."

"Are you sure, now? It *is* Good Friday, not a day to arrest a man of the cloth."

She glowered. "I *said* he's the man." Her voice singed the damp air. "This weather is foul," she said, cursing. She pulled out her phone and stepped into the van. "Arrest him," she shouted through the window.

Cristoforo pointed to the manor house. "Officer, will you allow me to leave a message?"

"Of course." The bobby accompanied the friar inside. "I'm sorry about this. We only need to ask you a few questions at the London station. Just procedure, you understand. We'll get it all sorted out, I'm sure."

"I understand, Officer Judson," Cristoforo said, reading the name on the bobby's jacket, then looking into his blue eyes so full of regret.

He wrote a short message to the Seymours and handed it to the desk clerk. He would not worry these good people. He would obey his call. This was the moment for which he had prayed.

Slipping his hands inside the sleeves of his brown robe, the monk nodded to the bobby. Officer Judson was an honorable man, doing his job.

"Heavy fog, today, Father," the bobby said as they walked to the car. "Don't you worry, now, we'll get this all cleared up soon enough."

Brother, Cristoforo thought, *Brother*. But no matter. "I am happy to help in any way, Officer Judson." He climbed into the van, the doors slammed shut, and the tires rolled over the gravel into the swirling mist.

A fire sputtered in the grate of Hartwell's Great Hall as Madeleine sipped tea and nibbled dry toast. She gazed out to the thick fog, then to her husband returning from the front desk with a note.

"It's from Cristoforo," Jack said, his tone worried. He handed the note to Madeleine and paced before the hearth, rubbing his hands.

Madeleine read the smudged printing.

I do my penance. I obey. Do not look for me. All is grace through Our Lord. I am joy.
   Cristoforo, OFM.

"Where did he go?" Madeleine asked, perplexed.
"Should we look for him?"
"He said not to." What kind of penance? What had he done?
"You'd better check on Victoria. The noon service starts in thirty minutes, and I agreed to ring the bells. Good Friday is tough duty, but I'm more and more convinced a necessary one. How can we experience Easter without Good Friday? I think we have to trust Cristoforo to work out his own spiritual problems. At least for now." He grabbed his coat.

The bells rang twelve as William wheeled Victoria into the nave. How relieved she was that William would be at Saint Anne's all weekend. He'd promised to call his parents on Easter Day and wish them Happy Spring. Madeleine slipped into the pew alongside, and William left to serve as acolyte. Jack soon joined them, and Victoria wondered where Cristoforo was, but the friar had a way of suddenly appearing and just as suddenly disappearing

Victoria gazed at the Reserved Sacrament a few feet away in the side aisle—the north aisle, she had learned, since the high altar faced east. The high altar was bare. She traced the Sign of the Cross over her head and heart.

Two young candle bearers led a silent procession from the sacristy. William followed, gripping the purple-draped crucifix as though the weight of the world rested in its center. Father Dodd followed solemnly, his eyes cast down. There would be no choral procession today, no happy organ-booming. Victoria watched as the ancient liturgy of Good Friday began with Stations of the Cross, the people of God walking the path of their Lord's passion, his way of love and suffering.

The nave was half full today, and the congregation turned toward Father Dodd as he paused before each of the fourteen wooden etchings hanging from the side-aisle columns. This was the Way of the Cross, each station marking Jesus' agonizing path to Calvary, beginning with Pilate's condemnation and ending in Joseph of Arimathea's tomb. At each station, the people and their priest knelt and offered a prayer of adoration, a meditation on the event, and a prayer of contrition, reliving the last moments of Christ's earthly life.

Victoria read from her leaflet and watched the slow progress, intrigued with the graceful movements that transformed the terrible into something sacred, even beautiful.

Next came the Veneration of the Cross. William stood at the head of the central aisle and placed a wooden crucifix on a low stand. The people stepped forward, knelt, and kissed the foot of the cross, as the mournful "Reproaches" were sung: *"O my people, what have I done unto thee, or wherein have I wearied thee? Testify against me...."* Finally, after prayers for the Church and the world, the Mass of the Presanctified was offered, using hosts consecrated from the Maundy Thursday Mass.

Victoria, full of the sorrowful portrayal of Christ's death, read in her leaflet that this was one of the most ancient rites of the Western Church. The present withdrew further and further into this early world, as the choir chanted in minor keys, bearing in their funereal notes these powerful moments of then and now, notes lined with Easter promise.

As the last prayers were said, she turned to Madeleine kneeling beside her. Tears streamed down the older woman's cheeks, and Victoria reached for her hand.

Madeleine turned, her face radiant, and whispered, "Praying for Cristoforo."

Somehow, Victoria knew they were tears of happiness.

A sweet yet sad poignancy lingered as Victoria took William's hand and lowered herself onto a sofa in Hartwell's Great Hall. William sat alongside her, and Jack took a chair facing them. Madeleine seemed far away, standing at the window, lost in thought. The fog outside was still thick, muting the world like a tomb.

A butler appeared. A scowl flickered beneath his features.

"Could we please have some tea?" Jack said. "Two chamomile, two Earl Greys, and sandwiches for four."

The butler raised his brows and lowered his lids as he held his hands behind him, his legs planted firmly. "Sir, if I may be so bold, there's news on the telly about Miss Nguyen." He cocked his head in Victoria's direction.

"Me? On TV?" Victoria's heart pounded. She looked from the butler to William to Madeleine to Jack.

Jack jumped up.

"What news?" Madeleine pivoted on her heel.

William took Victoria's hand.

"I don't know if I should say now, ma'am, what with the young lady in her condition and all." His disapproving gaze rested on Victoria's swelling body.

"Out with it, man," Jack said. "You'd better finish what you've started."

"Sorry, sir, but there's been an arrest in London. At least that's what they announced at Scotland Yard. He looked like the friar I've seen with you, sir. I never liked the looks of that one, no indeed, sir." He shook his head.

Jack gave the butler a piercing look. "Arrest for what?"

"Kidnapping Miss Nguyen, it appears, sir. Kidnapping and maybe worse. They put the chap in jail to protect him from the crowds. The people seem a bit upset, they do, what with him being Catholic and all. Then there's the fuss in America about them boys—"

Jack made a dismissive gesture with his hand. "That's enough. Bring the tea and sandwiches, please."

"Very good, sir. Just thought you ought to know, sir." Shaking his head, he turned toward the kitchen.

"What's happening, William?" Victoria asked. "It's my mother, isn't it?"

"It looks like it."

"The note," Madeleine said to Jack. "That's what Cristoforo was talking about."

"Note?" William asked. "I didn't see see him today, but he's always had an air of mystery about him and a strange authority. What did the note say, exactly?"

Madeleine pulled the paper from her handbag and gave it to William, who angled it for Victoria to read as well.

"William...," Victoria began. Brother Cristoforo was in jail, and because of her.

"He's taking the blame," William said. "That's not right."

Jack eyed Madeleine. "No, it's not right. I was afraid something like this would happen. I'd better call Joe McGinty. He has contacts."

Madeleine massaged her temple with her index fingers. "But he made it clear about not wanting us to interfere. What should we do?"

"That's true," Jack said. "What's going on in that head of his? Maybe we should leave him alone for the weekend. But I'm still calling Joe."

"It's all my fault." Victoria was growing more bewildered with each minute. She rested her hand on her child, quiet now. "What will happen to Cristoforo?"

Cristoforo looked about the crowded room. Officer Judson's desk was one of many, and the room hummed as police and staff moved from cubicle to cubicle. Phones jangled and screens flashed. The bobby led the friar to a window overlooking the square and twisted a long thin rod to partially open the blinds. Protesters milled about, carrying signs.

"Father," Officer Judson said, "we need to keep you here for your own protection. At least until things quiet down."

"No popery!" the crowd shouted. "No idols! No smells and bells!"

"That is okay." Cristoforo peered through the blinds. Placards read: *AWAY WITH PRIESTS, KIDNAPPERS BE HANGED, CHURCH MOLESTERS BE TRIED, CHOICE NOT DOGMA, FREEDOM NOT CHAINS, RIGHTS NOT BONDS.*

"I've seen this kind of thing before. It can get ugly."

"And Senator Nguyen? Is she there too? I fear she does not like the Church."

"She probably organized this. I know these marchers. They can be bought."

"Bought?" How could this be? She could buy people?

Officer Judson shook his head. "Marketing, I'd call it, simply marketing. For the telly. Media marketing." He looked up at the friar. "Something the Church isn't too good at."

Brother Cristoforo noticed several newsroom vans with their video equipment. "Like a movie."

"Exactly. They're making a movie and saying it's the truth."

"That is false witness."

The bobby raised his hands. "Some say so. Others call it freedom of the press. Now, are you sure you want to confess this thing? I can tear up the papers and take another statement. The senator's gone now."

"I will sign."

"You're sure there's no one you want to call? A Church barrister or such?"

"No one."

The officer looked at his palms and dusted them off. "Then let's get on with it. I've got to get home to the missus. This whole thing makes me sick."

Victoria's first contractions hit about midnight, slow and far apart.

"Not to worry, yet, dear," Eileen said. "It's probably a false start. It often happens a week before. I'll take the other bed, if you like."

"Thanks, Sister. Please do, and no, let's not wake anyone yet. It's pretty late."

She lay back and waited for the next searing pain as she stared into the dark, listening to the wind whistle through the trees. At least the fog would be blown away.

Chapter Twenty-eight
Holy Saturday

Lo, children, and the fruit of the womb,
are an heritage and gift that cometh of the Lord.
Psalm 127:4

The abbey bell rang one o'clock in the afternoon as Madeleine sat on the edge of Victoria's bed and wiped her brow. She heard William's footstep, pacing in the hall, a lighter step next to Jack's heavier one. She could hear their voices, too, but not what they said.

Sister Eileen clocked Victoria's contractions with her large wristwatch and checked her blood pressure. "Three minutes apart. Not long now."

"Good," Madeleine said as she glanced up at Eileen, then at Doctor Delaney, a robust figure with white hair, speaking quietly on the phone in a far corner.

"Can William come in for a minute?" Victoria asked. "Just for a minute?"

"Sure." Madeleine walked to the door and partially opened it. "William, are you okay with seeing a little pain?"

William looked up at her with hopeful eyes. "I think so."

"Then, come in, just for a minute." Madeleine gazed at Jack who sat on the hall bench, his hands folded, his head bowed. Once again she was grateful for his steady presence, and now his steady prayers.

William crossed the room to Victoria. Her legs were bent high under the sheet. "William, hold my hand. I'm glad you're here."

"I'm here, love." William's brow pulled together as he gazed upon her red face and damp hair.

"Hold my hand," she said, "another one's coming...*whoo, whoo, whoo.*"

"What's wrong?" William whispered to Madeleine. "She can't breathe...do something!"

"That's normal. It's labor; it's her breathing exercise," Madeleine said, hoping he believed her. She made similar sounds to guide Victoria. "It helps the process."

Victoria crunched his hand as she rode the wave to its crest, then down again. William stared at Madeleine and Sister Eileen. Controlled panic flashed across his face.

Madeleine nodded reassuringly. "It's okay, William, it's okay. It's all normal."

"Are you sure? Can't you give her something?"

"She needs to push the baby out," the doctor called from across the room as she covered her phone with her palm, "not slow him down."

"Oh," William said, sounding unconvinced. "Right."

Victoria's grasp loosened and she exhaled. Eileen blotted her forehead with a towel.

The doctor returned to her call, her voice serious with purpose. "That's right, Harriet, cancel those appointments, please. I'll spend the afternoon here." She clapped the phone shut and approached her patient. Grinning with delight, she touched a silver cross hanging in the vee of her white smock. "It *is* marvelous, Sister Eileen, to finally have the chance to do a little volunteer work and scale back those office hours. Now, how's our patient doing?" Her dark eyes were forceful yet warm, and Madeleine watched her with admiration. Doctor Delaney took control with a natural expertise, and Madeleine was relieved that Father Dodd had suggested her, a member of the local congregation.

"I think she's close," Eileen said. "Let's check the dilation." She nodded to Madeleine.

Madeleine gently touched William's shoulder. "It's time to go."

"Right." William kissed Victoria's damp brow. He backed out the door, staring as though Victoria held the secrets of the universe.

The next moments jumbled together, Madeleine thought later, sliding forward with amazing speed. Sister Eileen and Doctor Delaney hovered over Victoria, checking her pulse and massaging her tummy. Madeleine retreated behind Victoria's head, helping her with her breathing and wiping her brow.

"I can see the crown," the doctor said. "One last push, Victoria."

In the next minute...or two...or three...a baby girl was born, slipping into the world of cool air and strange oxygen, leaving behind the warm safety of the watery womb and nourishing cord, gulping the dry air.

There was a second of silence and the child wailed. Sister Eileen washed her, wrapped her, and placed her in the young mother's arms.

Madeleine kissed Victoria's moist forehead. "A beautiful baby girl." The baby's eyes squinted and her skin was splotched with newborn redness. "Shall I call the men in?"

"Oh yes," Victoria said happily, her eyes on her daughter.

Madeleine opened the door. "You can come in, Jack," Madeleine said, her voice choking, "and William too."

William approached slowly, looking from mother to child, speechless, Jack at his side.

"A girl," Victoria said hoarsely, her eyes full of relieved happiness. "So much for Daddy's intuition."

William sat on the edge of the bed. "A perfect little girl, just like her mum." He gazed at the almond eyes and fine wisps of dark hair, the scrunched face. "Perfect, indeed." He touched the minute fingers, each nail in place. "Oh my."

As Madeleine looked on, Jack wrapped a warm arm around her shoulders. "It's such a miracle," she said, entranced.

"It *is* a miracle," Jack whispered.

Madeleine, her mind full of Victoria and the child, returned to Hartwell with Jack. A group of children on the porch were talking with the butler, whose large frame blocked the doorway. A girl with wild red hair flowing from a baseball cap looked up imploringly.

The butler stood with an air of defiance, his hands squarely on his hips. "Get off and away!" He waved his hands as though swatting flies. "Go on, now, this is no place for the likes of you."

The girl shoved her foot in the doorway. "Please, sir, we've urgent business with the friar, we do. Urgent, it is."

The boys nodded seriously. They clutched their caps in small dirty hands. "We do, for sure," they mumbled to the stoop. "Urgent."

The butler looked up and nodded to Jack and Madeleine. "Good afternoon, sir and madam."

Jack looked at the children, then at the butler. "Can we help?"

"It seems, sir, these ruffians are looking for the friar, him that's been arrested. They're up to no good, is my opinion, sir."

"We can be the judge of that," Jack said.

The butler scowled. "Very well, sir, I'll leave you be, then." He disappeared inside.

Madeleine led the children into the Great Hall.

One of the boys looked about. "We should've slept in the garden of the other house."

"Yeah, and waited 'til we raised someone," another said.

"This place is too *grand* for us," the youngest said, his eyes big.

"Hush," hissed the girl.

Madeleine leaned toward the girl and laid a hand gently on her arm. She looked into the green eyes, so wary like a feral cat's. "I'm Madeleine Seymour, and this is my husband, Jack. You wanted to see Brother Cristoforo?"

"Yes ma'am."

As the girl attempted a curtsey, Madeleine noticed one thin shoulder was higher than the other. She wore a soiled jacket and jeans with holes in the knees.

"He's not in. Could I help you? What are your names?" They appeared hungry, and the boys were scratching their heads. Lice?

"Nadia...West...and these be me little brothers—er, Nelson...er, Nobby...er, Nat...er, Ned. We heard you might have jobs for some hard-working folks like us, maybe in the kitchen or the garden at the house over there." She motioned toward Saint Anne's.

Madeleine's heart soared. *Cristoforo's Nadia.* How glad the friar would be when he learned of their return—if only *he* would return. "When did you last eat, Nadia?"

"It's been two days, ma'am. We *are* a might peckish." She patted her stomach.

Madeleine turned to the butler, who watched with suspicion from the hallway. "Please, could we have tea and sandwiches for five—no, make that milk and sandwiches, and some of that chowder from last night, if there's any left?"

Nadia sighed with relief. The boys looked up, their faces hopeful.

"I think," Madeleine said to Nadia, "we might work something out. We do need some good workers at Saint Anne's, workers we can trust." She led them to the sofa in front of the fire. "Do you think you could wash dishes, or maybe make beds? Do you like babies?"

Nadia fell onto the sofa and stared about the room. Her brothers did the same. "We like babies fine," she said and nudged the youngest to keep his feet off the sofa.

On Saturday evening, Victoria rested as her daughter slept soundly in a basket alongside the bed, the yellow knitted blanket wrapped about her. William stood by the window, watching the sunset. Turning, he walked to Victoria and sat on the edge of the mattress. He kissed her on the cheek.

"I can't believe all this." He shook his head.

Victoria took his hand. "William, dear William. Help me think of a new name." She looked at the baby, whose eyes were tightly shut as though postponing contact with her new world.

"Does that mean...?"

"I'm keeping her. How could I do anything else?"

"Good. I'm relieved, I must say."

"That decision was easy. She's perfect. But she does have my birthmark, only in a better place." She pointed to the right earlobe.

"It's a beauty mark, and look at those dark lashes." He brushed the baby's cheek with his finger.

"But William Andrew won't do."

He laughed. "It certainly will not. Any ideas?"

"What about Elizabeth, my middle name, and my great aunt's name."

William nodded with appreciation. "And a middle name for little Elizabeth?"

Victoria grew pensive. "Madeleine, I think."

"Excellent. After Mrs. Seymour."

"She's been so good to me. I don't know how I can ever repay her. I'm going to ask Madeleine and Jack to be godparents."

William leaned toward the baby. "Perfect. You get to choose a second godmother, you know. A girl gets two godmothers and one godfather."

"I'll have to think about that. Maybe Sister Eileen." Victoria thought she might be perfect. "And guess what? I heard from Daddy."

"Already? It's only been a few hours since Mrs. Seymour called him."

"He sent a letter and a gift. He's coming tomorrow."

"I'm so glad. That means he'll share Easter with us. He seems a good man."

"He is, at heart. William, look at his gift. It's in the box on top of the chest, next to the carved pony. And you'd better get some supper. The Holy Saturday service must be starting soon."

"It's only six. I have another hour." He pulled a maple sculpture out of the box and carried it to Victoria. "It's fantastic. A crèche!"

The stable had been carved out of one piece. It sheltered Mary and Joseph kneeling before the baby Jesus asleep in his maple bed. A cow and a horse had been sculpted out of the back wall. A shepherd, carrying a lamb on his shoulders, stood behind Joseph. Three magi carried gifts, one kneeling, one behind Mary, and one standing nearby. Vines curled up the stable posts, and a star rose from the roof between two angels.

"Isn't it amazing?" Victoria traced her finger along the lines of Mary and Joseph.

"Your father carved this?"

"It's been his hobby ever since I can remember. My room at home is filled with his work, every piece intricate. He paints some of them in pretty colors. He said he would paint this if I wanted him to. I think I like it the way it is." She pulled a folded paper from under her pillow and handed it to William. "Would you read it aloud?" She had missed her father, and now that the baby was born, she missed him even more.

William read:

Dear Vicky,
Please forgive me for not helping you enough. Candice has gone to Washington. We have agreed to a separation.

But I am joyful for my granddaughter. I am sending the gift I made for her. If you would like me to paint it, I will. I guess I was wrong about the baby being a boy.

I spoke to an attorney about your aunt's will, and he thinks you have a case.

I love you, my child–I shall come soon. We have much to talk about. We will make plans.

Love, Daddy

"One day," William said, "I hope to ask your father for your hand."

"He would be honored. And thank you, William, for not rushing me, or us. You and I, we both need time."

"I'm sure of *my* intentions, but I want *you* to be sure. You need to finish school. I will re-propose on the first of every month."

"Didn't Peter Wimsey do that with Harriet Vane?"

"In Dorothy Sayers' novel? I believe he did, or something to that effect." William paused. "I'm sorry about your parents separating."

"It's just as well." Victoria patted the edge of the bed for William to join her. "Mother has been disappointed in us, in Daddy and me, for a long time."

"Do you really think so? Victoria, perhaps you are too harsh."

"Am I? It's difficult to live up to her expectations. She's so successful, so driven. At times she's ruthless, and it makes me uncomfortable. She even imprisoned Cristoforo."

"But one day, you must forgive her, or else you'll carry bitterness with you forever."

"Maybe one day."

"With God's grace, it will happen. You'll see."

"So will you take me to Saint Anne's for Easter tomorrow? If Eileen says it's okay?" She stroked his long fingers.

"If Eileen agrees."

"Good. Now tell me about tonight's rites. I'm afraid I shall miss them."

"Tonight is the Holy Saturday Liturgy of Easter Eve." He turned to little Elizabeth, rocking her basket gently. "It's a mysterious evening for sure. First, the church is totally dark, and we sing the *Exultet*, the Procession of the New Fire, carrying flaming candles down the aisles. All in preparation for the first glorious Mass of Easter..."

Victoria's eyelids grew heavy, and she let them drop, listening to William's soothing voice and seeing the candlelit procession. Slowly, she released his hand. She felt his kiss on her brow and heard the click of the door opening, followed by the light step of Sister Eileen.

"I think she's asleep," William whispered.

"Good," Eileen said. "I came to check and make sure. She needs her rest."

Chapter Twenty-nine
Easter Day

The point of intersection of the timeless
With time, is an occupation for the saint—
No occupation either, but something given
And taken, in a lifetime's death in love,
Ardour and selflessness and self-surrender.
T.S. Eliot

London bells tolled midnight as Brother Cristoforo looked about the small holding cell. A table and chairs stood in the center, a bench ran the length of one wall, and a single light bulb dangled from the ceiling. Two other inmates shared the cold room, filling the space with a sour, acrid stench. The friar moved to a barred window and peered into a dark alley.

"It's Easter, or nearly, Father," one of the men said behind him, "so let's hear a few words from the Good Book." Cristoforo turned. It was the burly one with the three-day beard, straddling a chair backwards.

"Yeah," said the younger one from the bench, leaning forward, his hands on his knees. "Why not, mate? We've got nothing else to pass the time, no broads or booze or pills or nothing. Give us a little, Pops."

How fitting, Cristoforo thought, to preach in such a place and to such a congregation, an appropriate penance. He would preach a sermon to himself, and if they liked, they could listen. The wind howled, rattling the cracked windowpane.

He looked from one man to the other. "I will try, my sons."

The burly man's chin was broad and square, and his thin lips curled when he spoke. He had a scar that ran along his left eye, and his muscular arms were tattooed with snakes. The younger man, a boy aged early, reminded the friar of himself long ago. He had the wary air of a hunted animal, and he could not stop moving, his hands scratching, his feet tapping, his legs crossing and uncrossing, as he sat on the splintered bench.

The friar turned toward the window again and paused, waiting for the words.

"Come on, man," the burly one said to his back. "We ain't got all day."

"Yes we do," the younger one said, "and all night." *Tap, tap, tap.*

"Are you mocking me," the big one said. The chair scraped as he stood. He cursed. "Stop that tapping—"

"How do we serve God?" the friar shouted into the alley, then turned abruptly to face his listeners. The burly one sat down. "We serve God however he chooses. We say *yes* to God no matter the place or the time. We do his bidding at once, without complaining. This is how we save ourselves, our souls. This is how we grow into whole men and become the glorious, *free*, sons of God."

The burly one shook his head. "I don't believe in God, not with what I've seen."

Cristoforo rested his hand tenderly on the man's lice-infested hair as though taming a wild beast. "*Allora*, God believes in *you*."

"Really, now? And how would *you* know?" The man looked up, and the friar saw one eye was glass.

"I've seen a miracle once, Father." The younger man scratched his chin and nodded, then patted his bobbing knee.

Cristoforo turned to the pale face. The youth's head was shaved, his sweatshirt dark with grease and stains. He wore a nose ring. "Did you, my son? And what did you see?" The friar sat cross-legged on the floor between the two men and motioned for them to sit with him. Then he listened closely.

"Aye," the boy said, "I saw me dad take an axe to me mum, but he ran out the door when he seen me come in. Now that's a miracle, don't you say, Father?" He gazed at Cristoforo with vacant eyes.

"*Si*, a true miracle, my son." Cristoforo held the boy's face between his palms with infinite tenderness. "You have suffered too, like many." He made the Sign of the Cross on his forehead. The boy blinked hard and looked away, touching the place. The foot stopped tapping for a moment, then resumed.

"Do you wish to hear my story?" the friar asked quietly, glancing now at the older man. "It's like yours, but different, for I found God. You can too, my sons, you can too."

The two men looked up at him, and Cristoforo began the untellable tale of his early boyhood, a tale he had never shared, not even with

Father Rinaldi.

"I was a young boy. We lived in a village near Alexandria, the great city. They were enemies of my father, who was a good man. I do not know why they hated us. They may have been Algerian cousins who disapproved of my mother's marriage to my father. They came in the day on horses, their swords flashing." The friar ran his finger along his jaw line. "They cut me but I ran and hid. And I saw. There was blood...everywhere...their swords sliced through the air."

The friar paused as his throat tightened, dry. How could he go on? "They cut off their heads—my mother, my father, my baby sister..." His heart thundered as he buried his face in his hands. "Ah..." he keened, wailing with a voice he did not know. He looked up to the ceiling, then to his fellows as though they could erase the horror. The men's eyes were large, as though they sensed there was more, and waited.

Cristoforo grew quiet. He pulled himself together, ready to give them his last ounce of flesh and blood. "That is not all. They cut the child from inside my mother and...*they laughed.*" He wiped his eyes and shook his head, suddenly empty, vacant, numb. "Then they left, galloping." He could hear the pounding of the hooves even then, there in that cell, the horrible and happy thundering of their retreat. And he could smell the blood, acrid and sweet.

The burly one laid his thick hand on Cristoforo's shoulder. The lad tapped the friar's arm. Cristoforo's tears fell onto the cement floor, and as he wept, he sensed he had fallen into a pool of love, a pool that would wash him clean.

Early Easter morning, while it was still dark, Cristoforo awoke. He scratched his eyes and stared. Father Rinaldi approached, his aged walk fragile yet strong from years of penitence and prayer. He raised the host, a flaming circlet of gold. Cristoforo, a simple soul of dust, stood before this wonder, as the fire of heaven penetrated his ashen self. He received the host on his tongue and knew the burning love of Christ. Was he dreaming?

"Father, is that really you?"

"My child, it is not yet your time. You are an Isaac, not a Stephen. Michael's angels will come this night. Go in peace and love him who is the source of all love."

"Father, are you really *here*?"

"Yes, my son, and I leave you a sign of your sanity and your courage, the golden vessel buried with me so long ago, the chalice of our many Eucharists."

And with these words, Cristoforo found that he held in his hands the old cup brought back from Alexandria, the worked metal bowl of his first supper in the room upstairs, the chalice of their many Masses in Rome. He looked up, amazed, but Father Rinaldi was gone.

"Come back, Father, come back...," Cristoforo cried with longing.

An owl hooted in the alley. A brilliant light beamed under the door. The door opened and the light beckoned. Cristoforo followed the light, a sweet glow, onto the street, through the fog, and into the dawn of Easter morning, holding the chalice close to his heart.

Easter morning Madeleine and Jack returned to Saint Mary's Bourne Street. In the afternoon they would host a reception for the new Friends of Saint Anne's.

Jack had reached Joe McGinty, asking him to inquire about Cristoforo, for they worried the friar had taken on too great a penance. There was nothing more to be done at this point, but wait for his report. Madeleine wanted to let the friar know about Nadia. Would that make a difference? She left it up to God: she would know when and how to tell Cristoforo. She trusted in God's timing.

As they entered the old Victorian church through the north aisle, Madeleine inhaled the scent of flowers and burning candles. White tapers flamed on either side of the tabernacle and antique vases held peach roses at each end. The giant paschal candle was alight near the altar, the five wounds of Christ carved into the wax. The candle would burn for fifty days, bearing witness to Eastertide, the days spanning Christ's resurrection and his ascension, the last days he walked the earth. Gone were the purple hangings of separation and mourning; gone was the loneliness of a bare chancel, an empty altar.

The entry doors flung open, and the celebrant cried from the narthex, "He is risen!"

"He is risen indeed!" responded the congregation in unison.

The organ boomed its triumphal opening notes, and the people joined their voices in their first hymn to Easter:

"Jesus Christ is risen to-day, Al-le-lu-ia!
Our tri-umphant ho-ly day, Al-le-lu-ia!
Who did once up-on the cross, Al-le-lu-ia!
Suffer to redeem our loss. Al-le-lu-ia!"

The robed procession moved royally down the uneven aisle: the thurifer, the crucifer, the torchbearers, the acolytes, the deacon, the celebrant. Madeleine and Jack bowed their heads in veneration to the crucifix as it passed.

Madeleine looked about the church, at the many faithful souls present this Easter Day. Today they were one, God's people, Christ's Body, and she gave thanks for this legacy of life. For here, regardless of their petty and great sins of every minute and hour up to this moment, regardless of their ego-bound selves, here and now they loved one another with a divine love, and here and now God wove them together with other faithful through time.

Madeleine was grateful for the careful words chosen through the years of councils and creeds, words that expressed perfectly these truths of creation and her own little heart. And today those words would call her Lord into the elements of bread and wine, making that love, that life, manifest in her and in the members of his Body. Then, through the priest, Christ would offer them to the Father, redeemed, sanctified.

Perhaps in this mystical way they became the Word of God, Madeleine thought, as she gazed at the gleaming tabernacle. God's people, nestled in the ark, the Church, sailed through time, tossed on the waters of the world. Through repeated Eucharists, his people changed, became more God-like, became his own expression, became his own Word made flesh, his own conversation with his creation. And all this while, regenerated by this Eucharistic action, they were protected in the ark of the Church until Christ returned to judge the living and the dead.

Madeleine's eyes rested upon the roses, and she thought how every Mass was a celebration of Easter rebirth, when her butterfly soul emerged from its cocoon of Lenten self. With each new birth, for there were many, her wings grew stronger, and she soared farther. Each time this union of earth and heaven slayed more of the old being, whom Saint Paul called *the old man*, within her.

She thanked God for the birth of Elizabeth Madeleine, her heart skipping a beat as she recalled the middle name. She thanked him for Victoria and William, Justin and Lisa Jane and little Luke. And she did not forget to offer thanksgivings for Jack, who had wrestled his heart and soul into prayer and Scripture once more, accepting the sacrifice of Cristoforo, never saying *I told you so* when the police arrested the friar. Last of all, still in awe that she had finished the manuscript, she offered her thanks for the completion of *Holy Manifestations*. They would return to San Francisco this week, meet with Lois, and see about an assistant who could study her text for errors and pitfalls, clarity and wordiness, and put it to rights.

Madeleine followed her husband up the aisle to receive her Easter communion.

Father Smythe placed the host on her tongue. "*The Body of our Lord Jesus Christ which was given for thee, preserve thy body and soul unto everlasting life.*"

The priest held the chalice to her lips. "*The Blood of our Lord Jesus Christ which was shed for thee, preserve thy body and soul unto everlasting life.*"

God had gifted them greatly, with "*'good measure, pressed down,'*" as Jesus said. Now *they* must greatly give.

The recessional hymn ended on a jubilant note, and they knelt to thank God for another Mass and for the unfathomable gift of life. The organist played a Bach postlude, a happy dance of re-entry into the bustling world outside.

Father Smythe beamed as he pumped Jack's hand and kissed Madeleine on each cheek. "It is so very good of you to come back and see us. You must be almost finished with that fine work. Is the home all set up?"

Jack looked at Madeleine questioningly, then turned to Father Smythe. "You know about Saint Anne's?"

"A tall friar visited early this morning. He gave me a most curious message for you." The rector clearly enjoyed his surprise.

"Cristoforo was here?" Madeleine said.

"How did he–?" Jack began.

"A most curious message, my dears. He said he was an Isaac and not a Stephen and was returning to Rome. He would be in touch. He said something about Paul's escape in Acts."

Jack raised his brows in amazement. "Paul's angel escape—you don't suppose?"

"Why not?" Madeleine asked. "And Stephen was stoned, but Isaac lived on."

Father Smythe's eye was wandering to the line forming behind them. "And he said to let Father Dodd in Aylesbury know too, which I have done. And, my dears, the most interesting thing!" He looked at them quizzically, shaking his head. "He held an old cup close to his chest, seemed to be a chalice, it did, and the friar's eyes were on fire, I should say."

Madeleine considered Father Smythe's words as she and Jack walked toward Sloane Square. "Let's call Rome tonight...he doesn't know about Nadia. And the chalice? What do you suppose that was?"

"I haven't a clue," Jack said. "We'll hear the whole story one day, I'm sure. But I believe the miraculous escape. After all, *To them gave he power to become the sons of God.* John 1:12."

"*At least in the fullness of time.*" Madeleine grabbed his hand, and they ran to catch a taxi.

"Daddy!" Victoria cried from her wheelchair in front of Saint Anne's.

Her father beamed as he approached, looking satisfied, Victoria thought, as though he had turned a corner in his life. But even so a trace of sadness lay underneath. He held her head in his hands and kissed her on the forehead. "Vicky, how I've missed you." He looked into her eyes. "You okay? The baby's okay? Mrs. Seymour said you were both healthy."

"We're fine. You'll come to church with William and me? We were just heading there. Baby Elizabeth is upstairs. Sister Eileen is watching her. You can see her later."

"Elizabeth. Great choice."

Her father shook hands with William and gripped the back of her chair. As they rolled toward the abbey, William walking alongside, chatting, Victoria breathed in the crisp air. In the narthex, William kissed her and left to robe for the Easter Mass. Father and daughter settled next to Nadia and her brothers, now helping at Saint Anne's.

The young mother pulled her shawl about her shoulders, thankful for tiny Elizabeth and Sister Eileen's care, for William and her father, that Cristoforo was all right, the charges dropped. But today Victoria's exhaustion was lined with a new sense of purpose, for the birth had worked in her a profound respect for life, for the miracle of creation. She was humbled, and as her breasts filled to feed her child, she was certain she took part in the greatest drama on earth.

The church was festive with flowers. Petals had been strewn down the aisles and daisies spilled from straw baskets hanging from the pew-ends. Candles flamed on the altar and the tabernacle sparkled. The air smelled of lilies and incense as the procession moved up the nave and William took his place in the chancel. Some of the villagers had formed a choir, their white smocks starched and pressed, their red folders open on their palms. The large nave was nearly full. Where had all these people come from? William had advertised a "High Holy Easter," putting up notices and passing out flyers in the Oxford area, but he hadn't expected this kind of crowd.

Some sang boisterously, some off-key, and some followed along tentatively, one voice joining another, a chorus of joyous song. What were they celebrating? Certainly the resurrection of Christ, but Victoria thought also their own resurrection on this spring day, at least those who kept a good Lent. They suffered his wounds in their fasts and prayers, they lay in his tomb in the silent garden, they repented their sins, and now they rose with him from the dead. They were like seeds planted deep in the ground that today burst from the earth.

The Scripture lessons told how Mary Magdalene came to the tomb to find it empty and ran to tell Peter and John:

> *"They both ran together and the other disciple (John) did outrun Peter, and came first to the sepulchre. And he stooping down, and looking in, saw the linen clothes lying; yet went he not in. Then cometh Simon Peter following him, and went into the sepulchre, and seeth the linen clothes lie, and the napkin, that was about his head, not lying with the linen clothes, but wrapped together in a place by itself. Then went in also that other disciple, which came first to the sepulchre, and he saw, and believed...."*

Victoria pictured the scene, the fear and the hope, the astonishment, how that morning must have changed them forever. They turned down a new path that day, just as she had.

Father Dodd preached about rebirth and new life and unimaginable bliss.

The Canon of the Mass began (she was beginning to understand the parts of the liturgy) with selected prayers leading to the consecration of the bread and wine, words chosen through time to prepare the people to meet their God. She glanced at her father and was pleased to see happy recognition. Some of this must be familiar to him, even after all these years.

Father Dodd, facing the altar, read from the missal, his voice tender and infused with awe. "*For in the night in which he was betrayed, he took bread; and when he had given thanks, he brake it, and gave it to his disciples, saying, Take, eat, this is my Body, which is given for you; Do this in remembrance of me.*"

William, kneeling to his right, rang the Sanctus bells, a loud trilling, a call to attention. Victoria looked up from her pew. Father Dodd raised the host, now holding the Presence of Christ, high for adoration, and William rang the bells again. Victoria made the Sign of the Cross. He rang it a third time, and she bowed her head, then touched Nadia to do the same.

Out of the corner of her eye, Victoria saw the girl nudge her brother, then heard her *psst* to the youngest at the end, tapping the two in the middle on their heads. "Do it right, now, pay attention," Nadia whispered. Victoria could not suppress a smile.

"*Likewise,*" Father Dodd continued, "*after supper, he took the cup; and when he had given thanks, he gave it to them, saying, Drink ye all of this; for this is my Blood of the New Testament, which is shed for you, and for many, for the remission of sins; do this, as oft as ye shall drink it, in remembrance of me.*"

Again William trilled the bells and the people lifted their eyes to the chalice holding the blood of Christ. As they made the Sign of the Cross, Victoria glanced at her father. His eyes pooled with tears as though he had come home from a long journey.

William had spoken about this moment in the Mass. *Remembrance*, he said, really translated to a re-calling, a re-creation of Christ, not merely a memory. At first, she had observed his arguments with some detachment, like a student taking notes, but as the thread of his thoughts wove through hers, she began to believe his words made sense. Maybe, mysteriously, Jesus Christ did offer himself to them in every Mass.

She would begin classes with Father Dodd next week, and once confirmed she could receive the Eucharist. Today she watched as others received and returned to their pews. With Nadia at her side, Victoria stepped slowly to the altar rail to receive a blessing from the priest. With this simple act, she sensed a sudden peace and a beginning certainty.

Returning to her pew, Victoria joined in the great hymn of Easter:

"He is ris-en, he is ris-en!
Tell it out with joy-ful voice:

He has burst his three days' pris-on;
Let the whole wide earth re-joice:
Death is con-quer'd, man is free,
Christ has won the vic-to-ry!"

As the clergy and acolytes recessed down the aisle and into the dappled graveyard, Victoria knew she had glimpsed her true self that morning. She was her mother's daughter and her father's little girl. She was baby Elizabeth's mother. She would always be a devoted niece to her Aunt Elizabeth and a friend to Madeleine and Jack. She was William's friend too, and perhaps one day something more. She could even call herself a follower of the amazing Brother Cristoforo.

But Victoria understood she was something else too, indeed, a great deal more, for she was becoming, changing, transforming with each minute. A window had opened in her soul, and she welcomed the blinding light that revealed her true self. Madeleine said that, once she received the Eucharist with faith and an open heart, this process would begin, but Victoria knew it had begun already. She wasn't sure what she saw, but she saw a new Victoria, a child of God and a woman of power and love. In that moment, she could move mountains. She thought of her mother and felt no rancor, only forgiveness and compassion, a huge weight gone. She thought of the man who attacked her, and prayed for his tortured soul. *Thank you, Lord.*

And thank you for the miracles of my life, my daughter's life, and for William.

She would go back to school. Where, she did not know. Perhaps she and Daddy would settle in England; he might want a new start as well. How he would like Father Collingwood.

"Best you get back, ma'am," Nadia whispered in Victoria's ear as she helped her into her chair and wheeled her around. "Little Elizabeth needs her lunch, and you've got it."

Victoria laughed. "And I need to give it to her, the sooner the better. And here comes William, with Ned in tow."

"Ned wants to be an acolyte and light the candles." William nodded at the eldest boy. "Should we let him play with fire?" He tousled Ned's hair. "He might need a haircut."

William kissed Victoria on each cheek and looked into her eyes as though he could rest there forever, then grabbed the chair handles. Victoria's father walked alongside, smiling with pleasure. The boys crowded about, helping to push the wheels, Nadia leading and whooping with glee. The disorderly procession rolled past the sun-mottled graves toward Saint Anne's House, singing, humming, and la-la-ing:

"He is ris-en, he is ris-en!
He hath opened hea-ven's gate:
We are free from sin's dark pris-on;
Risen to a ho-lier state;
And a bright-er Easter beam
On our longing eyes shall stream...."

Chapter Notes

Chapter Two: Sea Cliff

Epigraph: "The world is trying...." T.S. Eliot, *Thoughts after Lambeth* (1931), quoted in Russell Kirk, *Eliot and His Age, T.S. Eliot's Moral Imagination in the Twentieth Century* (New York: Random House, 1971), 155. Thomas Sterns Eliot (1888-1965), Nobel Prize recipient, American who became a British citizen, is considered by many to be the greatest poet of the twentieth century. He moved from the despairing poem, *The Wasteland*, to *Four Quartets*, celebrating the joy he found in his conversion to orthodox Christianity as an Anglican in the late 1930s.

Saint Aidan: Aidan of Lindisfarne (d. 651), the "Apostle of Northumbria," was a missionary bishop and the founder of the monastery on the island of Lindisfarne, off the English coast. He was proposed as England's patron saint in 2008. Of course, Saint George (275-303) has long held this position. Saint George, an eastern martyr who became popular in the West, was invoked often by English crusaders; his story ("Saint George and the Dragon") was popularized in *The Golden Legend* by medieval chroniclers.

Chapter Three: Danville

Epigraph: "To have a right to do a thing is not at all the same as to be right in doing it." G.K. Chesterton, *A Short History of England, Chapter 10,* quoted in *Chesterton.org.* (American Chesterton Society). G.K. Chesterton (1874-1936), poet and apologist for traditional Christianity, converted from Anglicanism to Roman Catholicism in 1922. He influenced many through his classic work, *Orthodoxy*, and his perceptive use of language.

Chapter Four: Farm Street Church, London

Epigraph: "Glory be to God for dappled things...." Gerald Manley Hopkins (1844-1889), "Pied Beauty," quoted in *A Treasury of Great Poems*, compiled by Louis Untermeyer (New York: Galahad Books, 1992), 978. Gerard Manley Hopkins (1844-1889), influenced by John Henry Newman, converted from Anglicanism to Roman Catholicism in 1866, was for a time at Farm Street Church, London.

His poems celebrate God's glory in the created order.

The Connaught Hotel: Since 2001, the time of this story, this venerable establishment has undergone a major transformation from cozy old-fashioned to state-of-the-art modern. The former American Bar with its paintings and traditional furnishings have been replaced by neoclassic grays and lilacs, mirrors and chromes. A sunroom restaurant sweeps along Mount Street. The menu is country French, not old English townhouse.

Sexagesima and Pre-Lent: The ancient season of Pre-lent refers to the three weeks before Ash Wednesday: Quinquagesima (fifty days before Easter), Sexagesima (sixty days before Easter), and Septuagesima (seventy days before Easter). While Quinquagesima is indeed fifty days before Easter, the latter two names are not accurate, since they actually fall on the fifty-seventh and sixty-fourth days before Easter respectively. The reasoning is unknown, but it is thought these Sundays were linked to Quinquagesima in a general way. See F.L. Cross and E.A. Livingstone, *The Oxford Dictionary of the Christian Church* (New York: Oxford University Press, 1957, 1997).

"*O sacrum convivium....*: "O sacred banquet, in which Christ is received, the memory of his passion renewed, the mind filled with grace and a promise of future glory is given to us."

"*Missa est*": The term "Mass" came from this final greeting, "go forth."

Chapter Five: Westminster Abbey

Epigraph: "And what the dead had no speech for...." T.S. Eliot (1888-1965), "Little Gidding," *Four Quartets* (New York: Harcourt Brace & Company, 1971), 51; Eliot's epitaph in Westminster Abbey, beginning with "The communication...."

Chapter Six: Brook Street

Boxing Day: In the nineteenth century it was customary on the day after Christmas for employers to give bonuses to their workers in a box. It also became customary to box gifts for the poor on this day. It should be recalled as well that the day after Christmas (December 26) is the Feast of Saint Stephen, the first Christian martyr.

Chapter Seven: Westminster Cathedral

Epigraph: "Ten thousand difficulties do not make one doubt." John Henry

Newman (1801-1890), quoted in *The Newman Reader–Apologia, Chapter 5,* (1865). Newman was an Anglican cleric and one of the leaders of the Oxford Movement. He converted to Roman Catholicism in 1845, became a Cardinal, and was proclaimed "Venerable" by the Church in 1991.

Father Southworth's martyrdom: The victim was cut down from the gallows while still alive, his bowels drawn out and burned before him. Finally, he was dismembered.

Chapter Eight: Oxfordshire

Epigraph: "We can believe what we choose...." John Henry Newman, *Letter to Mrs. William Fronde* (1848), in *The Newman Reader–Ward's Life of Cardinal Newman, Chapter 8.*

Chapter Nine: Holloway

Epigraph: "He uses material things like bread and wine...." C.S. Lewis, *Mere Christianity* (New York: HarperSanFrancisco, 2001), 64. Clive Staples Lewis (1898-1963), was an Oxford scholar, known for his Christian apologetic works, particularly through his radio broadcasts during World War II. An Anglican, he was one of the greatest evangelists of the twentieth century.

"To him that ordereth his way aright, will I show the salvation of God." Psalm 50:23.

"The Lord Jesus shall be revealed from heaven with his mighty angels...." 2 Thessalonians 1:7-9.

Chapter Ten: London

Epigraph: "The trivial round, the common task...." John Keble (1792-1866), quoted in *The New Encyclopedia of Christian Quotations* (Grand Rapids, MI: Baker Books, 2000), 1131. Chair of Poetry at Oxford, John Keble wrote *The Christian Year*, extremely popular in Victorian England. He inspired the Oxford Movement with his sermon on "national apostasy" in 1833.

Raymond Raynes: Called "half Jesuit and half Salvation Army," Father Raynes (1903-1958), Anglican Benedictine, Superior of the Community of the Resurrection in Mirfield, Yorkshire, "combined personal holiness with a passionate care for people, intellectual zeal with a life of intense activity." Nicholas Mosley, *The Life of Raymond Raynes* (London: Faith Press, 1961), 24. He continued the mission work in South Africa the Community had begun in 1903.

John Donne: Anglican Dean of Saint Paul's Cathedral, John Donne (1572-1631) is known for his metaphysical poetry and his sermons. He left a legacy of vivid metaphors: "Each man's death diminishes me, for I am involved in mankind. Therefore, send not to know for whom the bell tolls, it tolls for thee," and "No man is an island...."

Chapter Eleven: Saint Mary's

Plasterwork: Used by Roman builders, Islamic architects, and Renaissance/Baroque decorators, this fine art reached its peak in the Victorian/Edwardian eras. In England, the guild called The Worshipful Company of Plaisterers was granted its charter by Henry VII in 1501, and these artisans continue their work today. The neoclassical Nash townhouses bordering Regent's Park used plasterwork and often are restored by today's local firm, Butcher Plasterworks. With the use of rubber molds, fibrous plaster leaves, eggs, medallions, and roses are prefabricated and attached to ceilings, walls, cornices, corbels, and mirrors to give the effect of woodcarvings.

"Love divine, all loves excelling...." Hymn #479.

The Caroline Divines: The seventeenth-century Caroline Divines called for a return to the early church, seeking the "Holy Catholic and Apostolick Faith" as taught by the primitive Church before the Middle Ages. Led by Lancelot Andrewes (1555-1626), the movement included the poet George Herbert (1563-1633), the scholar John Cosin, Bishop of Durham (1594-1672), Jeremy Taylor, Chaplain to the King (1613-67), and businessman Nicholas Ferrar (1593-1637).

The fear of "returning to Rome" was and is as much a political fear as a religious one. In the U.S., this fear has been evident in the rare election of "Catholic" candidates. Voters worry whether any kind of allegiance to a foreign power might be ill-advised in public servants in positions of authority. From time to time, papal directives encourage this fear, as U.S. Congressmen are admonished or penalized for not adhering to "Roman" doctrine and at times these public servants try and distance themselves from such papal directive.

Chapter Twelve: Hyde Park

Epigraph: "The existence of suffering...." Raymond Raynes, quoted in Nicholas Mosley, *The Life of Raymond Raynes* (London: Faith Press, 1961) 97.

"*Repent ye, for, the kingdom of heaven is at hand.*" Matthew 3:2.

"I am the way, the truth and the life: no man cometh unto the Father, but by me." John 14:6.

Chapter Thirteen: Hartwell House

Julian of Norwich (c. 1423): Dame Julian lived as an anchorite in a cell within the wall of the Norwich church. Anchorites live lives of prayer and seclusion, but are able to receive pilgrims asking for spiritual direction. Julian is known for the work, *Revelations of Divine Love*, in which she speaks of her visions of God and his great love for man.

Louis XVIII at Hartwell House: Louis XVIII fled Paris under the name of Michael Foster in 1791 in the wake of the Revolution. He found refuge in Germany, Italy, Latvia, and Poland, and arrived in England in 1807. He eventually rented Hartwell House for five hundred pounds a year. One hundred and fifty courtiers and royal family members lived there with their servants, including the Duchesse d'Angouleme (the daughter of Louis XVI and Marie Antoinette), the Archbishop of Reims (Talleyrand's uncle), and Queen Marie Josephine of Savoy, who died at Hartwell in 1810.

Chapter Fourteen: Saint Anne's Abbey

"The glory of these forty days...." Hymn #61.

Chapter Fifteen: Chewton Glen

Epigraph: "Faith is..." George MacDonald (1824-1905), from his sermon, "The Temptation in the Wilderness," in *Unspoken Sermons* (London: Alexander Strahan, 1867). A Scottish Congregational Minister, MacDonald influenced C.S. Lewis, J.R.R. Tolkien, G.K. Chesterton, and Madeleine L'Engle through his novels, particularly *Phantastes* and *The Princess and the Goblin*.

The Cistercians: Founded in Citeaux, France, by Robert of Molesme in 1098, the Cistercian Order reformed the lax and corrupt Benedictine houses of the time. A life of prayer was followed in remote locations, churches were plain, habits and vestments were simple. Rules of diet and silence were kept. The rule of manual labor supplied Europe with workers who farmed the land and invented agricultural tools and techniques.

The Cistercians in Beaulieu: Beaulieu Abbey was founded by King John as a penance in 1204; the king endowed the monks with large tracts of land and exemption from taxes.

Chapter Sixteen: The Solent

Epigraph: "The treasure of the Catholic Faith is not ours...." Raymond Raynes, quoted in Mosley, Nicholas, *The Life of Raymond Raynes* (London: Faith Press, 1961) 165.

Chapter Eighteen: The Eagle and Child

Epigraph: "Many of the ideas about God...." C.S. Lewis, *Mere Christianity* (New York: HarperSanFrancisco, 2001), 155.

Father Bernardo's letter paraphrases this quote: "A wise man once said that a prayerless priest is a disarmed soldier, unable to defend himself, and what is more awful unable to defend the Lord's children over whom he watches." Raymond Raynes, quoted in Nicholas Mosley, *The Life of Raymond Raynes* (London: Faith Press, 1961), 174.

Chapter Nineteen: Ventan-ceaster

Epigraph: "The Christian faith is the most exciting drama...." Dorothy Sayers (1893-1957), quoted in *The New Encyclopedia of Christian Quotations* (Grand Rapids, MI: Baker Books, 2000), 194. Dorothy L. Sayers, Anglican, Oxford scholar, is known for her mystery series featuring Lord Peter Wimsey, as well as plays, essays, and a translation of Dante's *Divine Comedy*.

"God himself is with us...." Hymn #477.

The "Te Deum laudamus" ("We Praise thee, O God"): The *Te Deum* is a prayer of thanksgiving attributed to Saints Ambrose and Augustine when the latter emerged from the Milan baptismal pool (AD 387). The *Te Deum* is part of the "Order for Daily Morning Prayer," *The Book of Common Prayer*, 10-11.

Chapter Twenty: Winchester

Epigraph: "The church is catholic, universal, so are all her actions...." John Donne (1572-1631), quoted in *The New Encyclopedia of Christian Quotations* (Grand Rapids, MI: Baker Books, 2000), 202. This quote is from his *Meditations Upon Emergent Occasions, Meditation XVIII* (1864).

"I believe in Christianity as I believe that the sun has risen...." C.S. Lewis, quoted in *The New Encyclopedia of Christian Quotations* (Grand Rapids, MI: Baker Books, 2000), 105. This quote has also been attributed to Raymond Raynes.

Chapter Twenty-one: Salisbury

Epigraph: "In order to move forward...." Charles Williams, quoted in *iclebz.com*. Charles Walter Stansby Williams (1886-1945), member of the Inklings, and devout Anglican, was a novelist and poet, and a valued member of the staff of Oxford University Press.

"Ask and it shall be given unto you...." Matthew 7:7.

Chapter Twenty-two: Glastonbury

Epigraph: "And did those feet in ancient time...." William Blake (1757-1827), Anglican poet and painter, in "A New Jerusalem," quoted in *A Treasury of Great Poems* (New York: Galahad Books, 1993) 611.

Cristoforo's Glastonbury sermon: Cristoforo's sermon is based on themes developed by Frank E. Wilson, *Faith and Practice* (Harrisburg, PA: Morehouse Publishing, 1996).

The King's Progress: It was the custom for the king to travel the countryside to control his nobles and receive taxes. He would live off their estates for months at a time, often with the purpose of bankrupting powerful rivals.

Henry VIII's executions: Anne Boleyn encouraged the bloodshed, for those accused challenged her legitimacy. The Carthusians were drawn and quartered at Tyburn and beatified in the nineteenth century. Thomas More, Lord Chancellor of England, and Cardinal John Fisher were canonized by Pope Pius XI in 1935.

Chapter Twenty-three: Thornbury Chapel

"Forty days and forty nights...." Hymn #55.

Chapter Twenty-four: Thornbury Castle

Epigraph: "Faith is not a refuge from reality...." Evelyn Underhill, *The New Encyclopedia of Christian Quotations* (Grand Rapids, MI: Baker Books, 2000), 344. British Anglo-Catholic mystic and author, Evelyn Underhill (1875-1941) wrote of the sacramental nature of Christian faith and practice, the everyday action of God in our lives.

Chapter Twenty-five: Saint Anne's House

Epigraph: "The Body of Christ, the Church, offers itself...." Dom Gregory Dix (1901-1952), *The Shape of the Liturgy* (London: A & C Black, 1988), 247. Monk of Nashdom Abbey, an Anglican Benedictine community, Dom Gregory Dix was known for his scholarly work, *The Shape of the Liturgy*, in which he traces the development of the Eucharist and belief in the Real Presence.

"O tarry thou the Lord's leisure..." Psalm 27:16.
"The God of Abraham praise...." Hymn #285.

Twentieth-century narcissism: For an excellent discussion of this frightening phenomenon in American culture see Diana West, *The Death of the Grown-up* (New York: Saint Martin's Press, 2007). Ms. West makes a good case that many of today's problems are due to arrested adolescence and the resulting scarcity of true adults.

Chapter Twenty-six: Palm Sunday

Epigraph: Do not argue about it, but believe in it...." Charles Grafton, Episcopalian bishop, 1912. Charles Chapman Grafton (1830-1912), Bishop of Fond du Lac, Wisconsin, continued the Anglo-Catholic movement in the United States. His body lies incorrupt and many consider him an Anglican saint.

"All glory, laud and honor...." Hymn #62.

"Alleluia, sing to Jesus...." Hymn #347.

"In me ye might have peace...." John 16:33.

Chapter Twenty-seven, Good Friday

Epigraph: "How will the Cross come to us? Not by seeking after it...." Raymond Raynes, quoted in Nicholas Mosley, *The Life of Raymond Raynes* (London: Faith Press, 1961) 14.

The Reproaches: Twelve verses chanted antiphonally by two choirs are traditionally part of the Good Friday liturgy and consist of Christ's reproaches to his people, "What have I done to thee, testify against me...." Parts date to the seventh century.

Chapter Twenty-eight: Holy Saturday

The Exultet: Known as the "Paschal Proclamation," this chant is sung by the deacon before the Paschal Candle on Holy Saturday, and dates to the seventh century.

Chapter Twenty-nine: Easter Day

Epigraph: "The point of intersection of the timeless...." T.S. Eliot, "The Dry Salvages," *Four Quartets* (New York: Harcourt Brace & Company, 1971), 44.

"Jesus Christ is risen today...." Hymn #85.

"Good measure, pressed down...." Luke 6:38. *"Give, and it shall be given unto you; good measure, pressed down and shaken together, and running over, shall men give unto your bosom."*

"In the fullness of time...." Galatians 4:4.

"They both ran together...." The Gospel for Easter Day, *The Book of Common Prayer*. John 20:1-10.

"He is risen, he is risen..." Hymn #90.

Selected Bibliography

Butler's Lives of the Saints, Eds. Herbert J. Thurston, S.J. and Donald Attwater (Allen, TX: Thomas More Publishing, 1956, 1996).

Chadwick, Owen, *The Spirit of the Oxford Movement* (New York: Cambridge University Press, 1990).

Crook, John, PSA, *Winchester Cathedral* (Andover, Hampshire, England: Pitkin, 1997).

Daniell, Christopher, *A Traveller's History of England*, Series Ed. Denis Judd (Gloucestershire: The Windrush Press, 1991).

Dix, Dom Gregory, *The Shape of the Liturgy* (London: A & C Black Limited, 1945, 1993).

Duffy, Eamon, *The Stripping of the Altars: Traditional Religion in England 1400-1580* (New Haven and London: Yale University Press, 1992).

Duffy, Eamon, *The Voices of Morebath: Reformation and Rebellion in an English Village* (New Haven: Yale University Press, 2001).

Dunning, R.W., *Arthur, the King in the West* (New York: Saint Martin's Press, 1988).

Edwards, David L., *The Cathedrals of Britain* (Wilton, CT: Morehouse Publishing, 1989).

Eliot, T.S., *Four Quartets* (New York: Harcourt Brace & Co., 1971).

Herring, George, *What was the Oxford Movement?* (New York: Continuum, 2002).

Himmelfarb, Gertrude, *The De-Moralization of Society, From Victorian Virtues to Modern Values* (New York: Random House, Inc., 1995).

The History Today Companion to British History, eds. Juliet Gardiner and Neil Wenborn (London: Collins & Brown, 1995).

Johnson, Paul, *The Offshore Islanders: A History of the English People* (London: Orion, 1992).

Kirk, Russell, *Eliot and His Age: T.S. Eliot's Moral Imagination in the Twentieth Century* (New York: Random House, 1971).

Lewis, C. S., *Mere Christianity* (San Francisco: HarperSanFrancisco, 2001).

Lewis, Lionel Smithett (late Vicar of Glastonbury) *St. Joseph of Arimathea at Glastonbury* (Cambridge: James Clarke & Co., Ltd., 1922, 1988).

MacCulloch, Diarmaid, *Thomas Cranmer: A Life* (New Haven: Yale University Press, 1996).

Moorman, John R. H., *A History of the Church in England* (Harrisburg, PA: Morehouse Publishing, 1980).

Mosley, Nicholas, *The Life of Raymond Raynes,* Nicholas Mosley, Faith Press (London: 1961).

Nicholi, Jr., Dr. Armand M., *The Question of God: C.S. Lewis and Sigmund Freud Debate God, Sex, and the Meaning of Life* (New York: The Free Press, Simon & Schuster, Inc., 2002).

Not Angels, but Anglicans: A History of Christianity in the British Isles, Eds. Henry Chadwick and Allison Ward (Norwich, UK: Canterbury Press, 2000).

The Oxford Dictionary of the Christian Church, Eds. F.L. Cross and E.A. Livingstone (New York: Oxford University Press, 1957, 1997).

Palmer, Martin, and Palmer, Nigel, *Sacred Britain: A Guide to the Sacred Sites and Pilgrim Routes of England, Scotland, and Wales* (London: Piatkus, 1999).

Pearce, Joseph, *Literary Converts: Spiritual Inspiration in an Age of Unbelief* (San Francisco: Ignatius Press, 1999).

Russell, Paul S., *Looking Through the World to See What's Really There: One explanation of the first step toward religious belief* (Bloomington, IN: Author House, 2004).

Tames, Richard, *A Traveller's History of London* (Gloucestershire: Windrush Press, 1992).

Underhill, Evelyn, *Worship* (Guildford, Surrey, U.K.: Eagle, 1991).

Visser, Margaret, *The Geometry of Love: Space, Time, Mystery, and Meaning in an Ordinary Church* (New York: North Point Press, 2000).

West, Diana, *The Death of the Grown-Up: How America's Arrested Development Is Bringing Down Western Civilization* (New York: St. Martin's Press, 2007).

Wilson, Frank E., *Faith and Practice* (Harrisburg, PA: Morehouse Publishing, 1996).

Endnotes

Holy Manifestations: God's Presence in Our World

[1] "In stature she was very tall, in appearance most terrifying, in the glance of her eye most fierce, and her voice was harsh; a great mass of the tawniest hair fell to her hips; around her neck was a large golden necklace; and she wore a tunic of divers colours over which a thick mantle was fastened with a brooch...moreover, all this ruin was brought upon the Romans by a woman, a fact which in itself caused them the greatest shame." Second-century historian Dio Cassius, quoted by Neil Jones in "The Warrior Queen," *Realm*, No. 105 (Landisburg, PA: The British Connection, Inc., 2002).

[2] For an intriguing and lively discussion of the Synod and its historical implications see Paul Johnson, *The Offshore Islanders, A History of the English People* (London: Orion, 1992), 35+.

[3] *Livings* were secure positions with set incomes for vicars of parish churches, often controlled or owned by the local lord to give away at his discretion. These positions often went to younger sons (who did not inherit), relations, or friends who paid little attention to their duties, and were sometimes even unschooled. A vestige of the feudal system, this system of livings continued well into the eighteenth century.

[4] Raymond Raynes observes: "Purposeless work leads to passive recreation—recreation which can be bought for money—and this in turn has led to commercializing recreation and turning it into big business—so that it becomes mechanized and profit-making, and a vast industry employs persons to make recreation for others—and we are in a vicious circle. An interesting historical comparison is provided by the Roman Empire...We can moreover see the same tendency for such amusement to become both violent and sensual." Raymond Raynes, quoted by Nicholas Mosley in *The Life of Raymond Raynes* (London: Faith Press, 1961), 189.

[5] The belief that the body is at war with the spirit ironically recalls the Roman belief that infused early Augustinian Christianity and was such an intrinsic part of Catholicism throughout the Middle Ages.

⁶ In this discussion of church life I beg the reader to forgive my over-simplification. Of course Baptists, Lutherans, and many other Protestant denominations have preached the Gospel and worked to serve the needy, outside of Sunday worship. But even the most successful pastor will agree, I believe, that it is a constant struggle to transfer Sunday piety into Monday life and the workweek. There are, of course, in any congregation, those who are exceptions to this rule. Neither do I say that catholic, sacramental Christians have the edge. In theory, however, I believe the action of the Eucharist unites the two—the material and the spiritual worlds—and, therefore holds the greatest promise to create a whole, fully integrated child of God.

⁷ This handful of Oxford scholars wrote tracts elucidating catholic doctrines: John Kebel (1792-1866), a disciple of the Caroline Divines of the century before, Professor of Poetry in Oxford; Richard Hurrell Froude (1803-36), influenced by French thought, died of tuberculosis at age 33; Edward Bouverie Pusey (1800-82), scholarly Regius Professor of Hebrew; John Henry Newman (1801-90), a powerful evangelical figure who became the leader of the movement, and who eventually converted to Roman Catholicism.

⁸ George III had six sons: George IV (1792-1830) married Caroline of Brunswick, no legitimate surviving heirs; Frederick, Duke of York (died 1827); William IV, Duke of Clarence (1765-1837), no legitimate heirs; Edward, Duke of Kent (1767-1820), Victoria's father; Ernest Augustus, King of Hanover (1770-1851), after Victoria in line; Adolphus, Duke of Cambridge (died 1850), after Victoria in line.

⁹ For a thorough and illuminating discussion of Victorian morality and its dangerous erosion in the twentieth century see Gertrude Himmelfarb, *The De-Moralization of Society, From Victorian Virtues to Modern Values* (New York: Random House, Inc., 1995).

¹⁰ Many devout faithful tempered goodness with humility, and many, both Catholic and Protestant, fused sacrificial offering to the Cross, but aside from the Roman minority and the Anglo-Catholics working to give life through the Oxford Movement, church-going was mostly a Sunday affair with little sacramental life to govern it.

¹¹ This idea of goodness was supported, if not created by, the Calvinist belief of the elect. The elect, those selected before time by God to be saved from Hell, that is *predestined*, would be recognized by their good deeds. Ergo, Christians needed to *show* they were saved by their works, an ironic twist to Calvin's creed of faith not works, resulting in pride coated with elitist snobbery. Regretfully, this attitude permeated colonial expansion, feeding a developing racism

supported by Darwin's theory of superior survivors (later used by Hitler). How easily "goodness" without humility before God can be disastrous.

[12] Quoted in *Osborne House* (London: English Heritage, 1996), 26.

[13] Ibid., 26.

[14] Victoria and Albert, both of Germanic descent (Sax-Coburg), sought *Gemutlichkeit*—snugness or coziness—in their domestic life, a sense we try to capture in today's often frightening and fragmented world. To many baby-boomers such snugness represents the safety of tradition and a mannered society, of order, of the simplicities of childhood. Teddy bears are the prime example of this trend, and their rather interesting popularity with adults.

[15] As the Church/State replaced Roman authority, the State would have far greater power over the individual citizen than Rome had exercised, for the State was now spurred with religious fervor and the monarchy's claim of Divine Right strengthened. Today the heritage of an established Church continues, in this writer's opinion, to confuse and distort the Body of Christ in Britain.

[16] John Wycliffe (1328-1384), an Oxford don, was an early opponent of church hierarchy and authority, claiming man is responsible only to God and may reach him directly without the aid of clergy. Wycliffe translated the Bible into English to educate the laity and formed a band of "poor preachers" who traveled the countryside. Of course, there were limited copies of these handwritten Scriptures. Still, he laid the foundation for the sixteenth-century translations produced by the newly invented printing presses.

[17] Quoted in John R.H. Moorman, *A History of the Church in England,* 118+.

[18] The question of Thomas Cranmer's beliefs in the last months of his life has been debated by historians. Some say the recantations and subsequent denials in the University Church pulpit were staged as an embarrassment to Mary and her Catholicism, for the crowd had expected a sermon true to Rome. Others say the truth is perhaps more complicated: Cranmer had not sought the Archbishop's chair and believed in loyalty to one's sovereign. This loyalty spurred him through the years of Henry's machinations and urged him to recant his Protestant beliefs under Mary.

[19] In many ways Cranmer epitomizes the Anglican strengths that were then suffering pains of birth: belief in the creeds and many catholic practices, but denying allegiance to Rome and the rule of clerical celibacy. He claimed in his final statement that the six recantations of his Protestant beliefs were due to his weakened condition and fear of death, and perhaps this was the simple case of

it. Still, to brave the crowd with his last unexpected words showed a man of great integrity and faith. For further discussion, see Diarmaid MacCulloch, *Thomas Cranmer, A Life* (New Haven: Yale University Press, 1996).

[20] Ibid, 603.

[21] Hugh Latimer (c.1485-1555), Bishop of Worcester and court preacher under Edward VI, preached against social injustice and church corruption, and championed the Protestant beliefs of the time. Nicholas Ridley (c.1500-55), Bishop of London and former chaplain to Thomas Cranmer, exerted significant Protestant influence on Cranmer. They were excommunicated under Mary and burned at the stake in Oxford, six months before Cranmer met his death.

[22] J. R. R. Tolkien (1892-1973) wrote *The Lord of the Rings*, heavy with Christian allegory and symbol. Charles Williams (1886-1945) wrote the novels *War in heaven, Descent into Hell, All Hallows Eve*, and other works expressing the Anglo-Catholic view of man and God. C.S. Lewis (1893-1963) wrote apologies for Christianity following his conversion: *The Problem of Pain, The Screwtape Letters, Miracles, Mere Christianity, The Great Divorce*. He also wrote the popular seven-volume *Narnia* series for children and an adult science fiction trilogy: *Out of the Silent Planet, Perelandra*, and *That Hideous Strength*. All of these reflected worlds in which God works actively and purposefully through his creation. Others engaging in a similar conversation with the public at that time were: Dorothy Sayers (1893-1957) who wrote the Lord Peter Wimsey mysteries as well as the more seriously Anglo-Catholic works, *The Man Born to be King* and a translation of Dante's *Divine Comedy*; the critic, poet and playwright T.S. Eliot (1888-1965) who wrote *The Four Quartets, Murder in the Cathedral* and many other brilliant works expressing God's incarnate relationship with man.

[23] Saint Birinus arrived in Wessex a mere forty years after Augustine of Canterbury arrived in Kent, sent by the pope to the far western regions thought to be untouched by Augustine's mission. The many missions to Britain over these years reflect the very real hardships and difficulties of evangelization. The Rev. Percy Dearmer wrote in 1909: "Bit by bit the Gospel spread among the English settlements; but there were many heathen reactions, and we must not think that missionary work won a sudden and universal success, any more than it had done in the days of the apostles or of the early Fathers—any more than it does at the present day. People sometimes imagine that once upon a time missionaries had a magical success and that nowadays they are doing very little. This is not at all true. Those early gospellers to England gave up houses and lands and everything to serve Christ, and lived lives of incredible hardness..." *Everyman's History of the English Church* (Oxford: A.R. Mowbray & Co. Lt., 1909) 19-20.

[24] The kingdom of Alfred the Great was the only English realm to survive the Viking threat, and as the north and east succumbed, Alfred ventured to unite the rest and was the first to call himself "King of England." The battle had only begun, and eventually all of England would be under Danish rule, but this early unification would be considered the birth of the English nation.

[25] For centuries, the real power center was a movable one, following the court and its retinue through the land, albeit royal functions and treasuries were consolidated in one location. In 1290, the royal treasury of silver and records with its attendant guard and staff were still at Winchester, two centuries after Westminster began its pull.

[26] For an intriguing assessment of the Joseph legend and its support by contemporary historical documents and events, see Lionel Smithett Lewis (late Vicar of Glastonbury Abbey), *Saint Joseph of Arimathea at Glastonbury* (Cambridge: James Clarke & Co, Ltd., 1955).

[27] *Grail* comes from the Middle English *graal*, derived from the Latin *graalis*, or flat dish, cup.

[28] The Venerable Bede (672-735), considered the Father of English History and a Doctor of the Church, wrote *The Ecclesiastical History of the English People.* Raised in the Jarrow Monastery in Northumberland (today Sunderland), he became monk, deacon, and priest. His library at Wearmouth-Jarrow is thought to have contained 300-500 books, remarkable for the time, hand copied, including classical writers. His remains are thought to be in Durham Cathedral.

[29] Geoffrey Ashe, *Magical Glastonbury*, www.britannia.com.

[30] In 1750 a local resident was cured by waters from the Chalice Well and within a year ten thousand came to be healed. Martin Palmer and Nigel Palmer, *Sacred Britain* (London: Piatkus, 1999), 208.

[31] Neither Charles Darwin (1809-1882) nor Albert Einstein (1879-1955) intended the far-reaching consequences of their theories, ideas they defined far more narrowly than did their disciples.

[32] The German philosopher Friedrich Nietzsche (1844-1900), like Sigmund Freud and Karl Marx, saw religion as fantasy. He predicted that man would take God's place of influence in the world, filling the vacuum of power. These "Wills to Power" would form and follow secular ideals with no religious restraints, inviting the rise of the gangster dictators of the twentieth century. Paul Johnson, *Modern Times* (New York: HarperPerennial, 1992) 48.

[33] Paul Tillich (1886-1965), American theologian, born in Germany, and Bertrand Russell (3rd Earl Russell, 1872-1970), philosopher, mathematician, and writer, born in Wales, followed in their wake, devaluing truth and creating lesser gods in the subsequent vacuum.

[34] While the Anglican Church remains the Established Church of England, most financial support is from parish tithes and endowments. The State favors the Church in other ways, however, such as the nearly exclusive right to grant marriage licenses and the placement of bishops in the House of Lords.

Don't Miss

PILGRIMAGE

Christine Sunderland

It was a day
when nothing should have gone wrong…
but everything did.

Madeleine Seymour will never forget what happened twenty-two years ago in her own backyard. She's still riddled with guilt. Hoping to banish the nightmares that haunt her and steal her peace, she travels to Italy with her husband, Jack, on a pilgrimage. As a history professor, Madeleine is fascinated by the churches they visit…and what they live about the lives of the martyrs. But can anything bring her the peace that her soul longs for?

For more information:
www.ChristineSunderland.com
MyTravels.ChristineSunderland.com
www.oaktara.com

OFFERINGS

☩

Christine Sunderland

Jack's haunted by fears of the past.
Madeleine holds a powerful secret.
And Rachelle is running away.

For the last seventeen years, her husband, Jack, and son, Justin, have been Madeleine Seymour's world. Then, during Justin's wedding reception, Jack collapses. Jack needs surgery, and he insists it be performed by the doctor who perfected the procedure. But the doctor isn't reachable, and time is running out.

Dr. Rachelle DuPres, plagued by memories of a deadly failure, flees America to search out her roots in her ancestral village in Provence, France. But as she tries to locate the graves of her Catholic uncles and her Jewish parents, will their roles in the Holocaust bring more angst—or the answers she so desperately seeks?

A poignant story about choices made along the way...
and the miracles of the heart.
Set in the breathtaking beauty of France.

For more information:
www.ChristineSunderland.com
MyTravels.ChristineSunderland.com
www.oaktara.com

About the Author

CHRISTINE SUNDERLAND, also the author of *Pilgrimage* and *Offerings* (the first two books in the trilogy), has been interested in matters of belief since she was sixteen and her father, a Protestant minister, lost his faith.

Today she is Church Schools Director for the Anglican Province of Christ the King and Vice-President of the American Church Union (*Anglicanpck.org*). She has edited *The American Church Union Church School Series*, *The Anglican Confirmation Manual*, and *Summer Lessons*. She has authored *Teaching the Church's Children* and seven children's novellas, the Jeanette series, published by the American Church Union.

"In order to write *Inheritance*," Christine says, "I traveled extensively in England to Christian historical sites. It was a fascinating quest."

Christine holds a B.A. in English Literature and is an alumnus of the Squaw Valley Writers Workshop and the Maui Writers Retreat.

For more information:
www.ChristineSunderland.com
MyTravels.ChristineSunderland.com
www.oaktara.com

Breinigsville, PA USA
18 January 2011
253585BV00002B/7/P

3 1901 05261 0179